The Sol Empire Volume 6 Religion and Robots

Vic Broquard

The Sol Empire Volume 6 Religion and Robots
First Edition
Copyrighted © 2021 by Vic Broquard
ISBN: 978-1-941415-87-0

This is a work of fiction. All characters, organizations, and events portrayed in this novel are products of the author's imagination and are used fictitiously.

Thank you to my colleague, Lisa Walker, for her many useful suggestions and corrections.

What isn't fictional is the work that Humanity and Inclusion (formerly Handicapped International) is doing to help those who have suffered:
http://www.hi-us.org

Published by:
http://www.Broquard-ebooks.com
Broquard eBooks
1055 Brandy Lake Rd
Woodruff, WI 54568
author@Broquard-eBooks.com

For Morgan and L. Ron Hubbard

Table of Contents

Chapter 1 My Alibi

March 10, 2369
Chicago, Sol Empire

"But the dead man *is* my alibi. Honest," I said.

The young CPD detective glanced at the body with the bullet hole in its head and then glared at me. "Tell me again, Mrs. Parkinson, how is that? Where were you at ten this evening? Why did you come here? To search his place?"

"Just call me Molly." Nodding towards the body, I said, "Dr. Stan Norwall called me. Around nine-ish. I got here about ten and called you. Stan said he'd discovered the human-form robot factory. I presume you've heard Admiral Carr's warning to be on the lookout for these murdering robots?"

The detective nodded. His face paled.

"Stan called me when he heard I'm leading the hunt for these robots. My EMAC [electromagnetic air car] isn't charged up yet. I came via the MTES [mass transit escalator system], as slow as that is. The door was open, stuff thrown about. Found him lying there. It's critical to know what Stan found. I had Bishop inject him with the Galactic Doll mutation agent to keep him alive. They're getting him into a stasis pod."

"Could have been you that shot him and ransacked his place."

Idiot! "Look at me. No arms. Been mutated too many times."

"You're one of those armless Galactic Dolls?"

His eyes scanned my massive bosom, tiny waist, and tall heels, characteristic of beauty pageant Galactic Dolls, while lingering on my long black hair, too.

1

"Are we going to spend all our time on the obvious?" I rolled my eyes upwards.

He flinched.

Must be his first investigation.

He changed the subject. "Wait. Bishop is carrying a gun."

"Of course. He's my bodyguard."

"He might have shot him!"

"Hardly. Bishop carries a 9mm. The hole in the body's head must be a .45 cal. Possibly a .44. Check with the doctors when they remove the slug. Check city surveillance video. You'll see a human entering before we got here. Good luck tracking him."

The detective replied. "I have someone on the video angle. Why good luck?"

"The shooter is likely one of the five rogue human-form robots."

"You're serious, aren't you? We've never seen one. Not here in Chicago."

"One has tried to kill me several times. Would have, except for the rejuvenation properties of the mutation agents. Rogue robots killed my first husband. Killed Ambassador Aaron Strawn. Killed Bonita and two other detectives. Tried to kill Dr. Kahn and me. List goes on. Admiral Carr and I traced them from Cass-C across the galaxy to Earth. Dr. Norwall said he had found their factory. I can't tell you how important that is. You must let me continue to search his house to see if he left any clues. Should I call Admiral Carr and have him explain it to you?"

His face lacked color. "Don't touch anything. Forensics."

"With what? My nose?"

I pretended not to notice his face turning from white to crimson. Instead, I studied the living room as the med techs

2

carted Stan's body off, presumably to the Med Center. Bishop remained at attention just outside the front door.

I wondered if Bishop found my exchange with the detective amusing. It was one of the five human-form robots that had been programmed with Asimov's robot laws. I couldn't have had a better bodyguard. Years ago, the remaining five had not been programmed when the Sixth Invaders attacked. During that confusion, those five vanished. Today, the rogues appear to be focused on reproducing themselves. One hundred sixty-five times, if our count of purchased positronic brains is right.

Stan's call offered the first hope we might stop these murderous robots. Considering the damage these five had done, I feared what hundreds might do. Admiral Carr made stopping them his top priority, though I didn't agree that the answer was creating a mutant Telepath Squad. Whereas my ability to detect them depended on therapeutically developed telepathy. While these robots appear human, they have no minds to detect for me to sense. Hence the urgent push to create a bunch of telepaths, which I continue to resist. But for how long?

Without arms to poke around, I focused on observing. In a corner, I spotted his "phone." Everyone has at least one of these super-computer, biometric-voice-activated-actualized-comm-devices. Anyone can place a phone call on them, but all other functions required a biometric match to its owner. Once unlocked its advanced features included the personal details of its owner's life, such as bank account, credit-debit numbers, passwords, their ID number, and so on. The top models streamed a 3-D holographic video of the caller, though any phone displays such sent video.

If Stan found their factory, he must have recorded it.

The detective spotted me looking at the phone and said, "No luck with that. Memory is destroyed. If he recorded

3

something, it's lost. No chance of recovering anything. Can't figure what the invaders used to smash it."

"Their hands. The robot held it in his fingers and crushed it."

The detective's eyes opened wide. "Kidding?"

"Hardly. They're stronger than a dwarf or giant. Probably used a gun to kill Dr. Norwall before Stan could react to the robot's sudden entry. If it could have closed the gap between them fast enough, the robot might have used its hands to kill Stan."

"Why do you say that?"

"I think Dr. Norwall recognized the robot. I'm guessing he recorded it in the factory he found. Left the robot no choice but to kill him. I suspect the doctor left the front door unlocked expecting me. Doorknobs pose a challenge for me."

Again, he flinched and stared at the floor.

"If you uncover any clues about what Dr. Norwall found, call me."

He nodded, and I left, joining Bishop. Together, we made the long trek back to my ranch home in northern Chicago, which my second husband inherited from his parents. A gardener and a maid from Galactic Housing maintained the grounds and home for me during the six years I attended Soros University on Cass-C, home to the leaders of the Federation of Planets. My good friends, the Hugos, live next door. Helen is the CEO of Galactic Defense Chicago while Casper is her CFO. Their children and ours once lived and played together.

Bitter memories. A terrorist bombing killed Sam, my second husband, and Matt, our son. My daughter, Nikita, continues to attend Soros University, leaving me alone in this large house filled with memories. While I have been back for several months, I no longer have much in common with the Hugos. Six years—an eternity apart.

4

My sister Celeste and her husband, Wil Reynolds, returned with me from Cass-C, bringing our friends Wanda and Otto. Both have become excellent therapy givers and assist Celeste and Wil in helping others at Celeste's clinic in St. Louis.

I developed telepathic abilities after receiving thousands of hours of her therapy. Instead of using the Sixth Invaders' armless telepath Galactic Doll mutation agent to make the telepaths Admiral Carr wants, Celeste and I hope to make telepaths through therapy. Because of her research, I've been able to stall Admiral Carr's demand to make a mutant Telepath Squad.

My sister Eve and dwarf friend Lara Axehead, both top geneticists, returned from Cass-C with me, bringing the cloning machines developed by the Third Invaders. They brought back a mountain of genetic engineering equipment and documents. The two set up their own lab in south Chicago and continue to work on another set of mutation cures for me. I've been mutated so many times that my DNA's a mess.

I sighed. Although I'm stuck like this for the foreseeable future, the original Sixth Invaders' helper machines help me. The hair and nail machine, the dressing/undressing machine, and the crude robot maid/cook—all help me survive on my own. Plus, Cleo, my dependable robot assistant on wheels, helps me. And per Admiral Carr's orders, Bishop is my bodyguard. He stays in one of my guest rooms.

Lonely. That's what I feel whenever I walk into my home. My older, adopted twins, now adults with their own families, visited once. But Isabella lives on Domes, and Bernardo's fancy restaurant takes all his time.

Little things remind me of Sam, Matt, and Nikita. A flood of memories returned when I saw their three-wheeled bicycles in the garage. And tears.

Bishop joined me at the kitchen table. Although Cleo filled my teacup for me, I insisted on using my toes to lift my cup and drink.

Bishop said, "Did we do right? By injecting Dr. Norwall with the mutation agent?"

"Was my call, Bishop. On the phone, he swore he'd found their development factory, and much more. We must know what he found. I know we've just doomed him to a horrible life. Still, after we learn what he discovered, I hope Eve and Lara can create a reverse mutation cure for him."

"Won't he freak out when he wakes and find his body looks like other armless Galactic Dolls?"

"Probably. Once we find out what he discovered, if he wants to die, I'll follow his wishes. But his phone call proves we were right. The rogue robots did return to Earth to make a hundred sixty more of themselves. Survival is common to living things. They need future generations. It's only natural these rogue robots pursue that."

Bishop presented a grin. "Ah, we human-form robots are living things, now, eh?"

"Isn't survival built into your programming? Just as with us humans. And animals and plants. Don't you wish you could make more of you? Like we have babies."

"I haven't had that urge, Molly. I exist to serve and protect. But I see your point. To do so, I must survive. Into the future. My parts won't need replacements for a thousand years. Still, all things mechanical decay in time."

"Yes, and your survival depends on us discovering how your body was made and how it can be repaired or replaced. Dr. Norwall said he'd found those plans. Ted, my first husband, died trying to find those blueprints. We can't afford to lose this breakthrough. If we can capture those plans and the manufacturing plant, then Galactic Robotics can make more human-form robots like yourself, Bishop. Programmed

6

with the robot laws, of course. You've a lot invested in this, too."

"In that case, I should make sure your EMAC is charged and ready to go. If it had been, we might have gotten to Dr. Norwall before they shot him. Look on the bright side, Molly. This time you weren't the one being murdered."

With that, he left. I finished my tea and headed to bed. Tonight, I let Cleo undress me. I knew I needed the practice of doing that myself, but I felt low.

Early morning, my phone rang, waking me. Cleo retrieved it and activated it for me. Admiral Carr's holo-image appeared before me.

"Well, what news? Do we have a location?"

I sighed. "No, sir. The robots got to Dr. Norwall before Bishop and I did. Bishop injected him with the mutation agent. He'll survive. They destroyed his phone and video. Ransacked his home. I found nothing useful there. When I left, the CPD forensic team arrived. I'll check with them this morning and see if anything turned up. Dr. Norwall will be in his mutation coma for eight days. So close and yet..."

"Keep me posted, Empress Parkinson. At least we know the robots are here on Earth. That's useful. Over and out."

I let the sheet slip off me as I sat on the edge of the bed. "Cleo, dress me this morning. I'm exhausted."

After donning one of Leslie's special yellow gowns with matching pumps, I headed to the kitchen. The maid robot had my breakfast sitting on the table. I tossed my long, black hair back, sat, slipped off my heels, and dined.

Bishop joined me. "The EMAC is now ready for use. I've refilled my supply of the mutation agent from your stores in the basement. Just in case. Is there a plan for today?"

I sighed, wishing I knew how best to proceed. "We'll visit the Med Center and check on Stan. Then, we'll go to my old PI office and review surveillance video."

"Looking for the rogue robot?"

"No. Let's try to trace where Stan went yesterday. If we're lucky, we might find what he found."

Bishop chuckled. "I admit I wouldn't have calculated that. My analysis suggested we'd follow the robot that murdered Stan. I'm still learning to be a PI."

"You're getting better. No question of that. The CPD should be all over that angle. But I expect the rogue robots will expect them to do that and have taken precautions. I think following Stan's day might yield better clues."

I took a last sip of tea. My doorbell rang, startling me.

"Sign here," the courier said. He held a pad for me to sign.

I slipped off my heels and sat. "Down here. Sorry."

His reddish face told much, but I signed my name in a well-practiced cursive. He tapped a few buttons and left while I rose and slipped my heels back on. Bishop retrieved the package. Together, we headed to the kitchen. My stomach tingled. The package had come from Dr. Stanley Norwall!

Chapter 2 Clues

The small package contained a mini-drive, which Bishop attached to my laptop. I touched the Play button. A 3-D image of Stan appeared, tall and thin.

"Empress Parkinson, I'm taking precautions. I've sent this package to you, to Galactic Defense, and to Galactic Robotics. I think they followed me, so I'm being careful. I should begin at the beginning in case we can't meet tonight.

"Months ago, I received my doctorate in robotics. My hero was Ted Billings. I'm trying to follow in his footsteps, but I took a different approach to the design and construction of the human-form robots. I researched who invented them. That isn't known any longer. But by tracing early papers on the subject, I concluded Dr. Phil Raven probably designed them. His wife, Leonora, held a doctorate in synthetic skin manufacturing. All clues point to their collaboration. I suspect they invented them to replace their son who died at age five.

"Coming forward from those early papers, I analyzed their Galactic Robotics bank accounts and their departments' accounts. Between them, vast sums of money vanished. I found a few delivery receipts stuck beneath a drawer in Phil's old desk. This morning, armed with a flashlight and my phone, I headed off to check out the address on the receipt. I didn't expect to find much. It's a fifteen-year-old receipt.

"I arrived at an abandoned Galactic Robotics factory, which I guessed was taken out of service thirty or more years ago from the looks of the place. I found a way inside and whoa! Far from abandoned, but an operational factory. Spotlessly clean. One computer station held the complete design specifications for human-form robots. Machines made metal skeletons for more robots. I hid behind the machinery, copied the plans, and video recorded the operation before a robot spotted me. I fled. Hope I lost it on the MTES.

"Since they murdered Ted when he found out too much, I'm making this message and am attaching my files. They contain the plans and the factory video. Once sent, I'll contact Empress Parkinson and brief her. This information can't get lost again." His fist punched high into the air. "Ted, I've carried on your work."

The video ended. One file contained the plans. I opened the second one. Another video played. In the background, I heard Stan's voice gushing exclamations, as he filmed the machines in operation. Three minutes in, the video abruptly ended.

"Call Admiral Carr!" I commanded my phone.

"Sir, he did it! Dr. Norwall. He found the factory and complete plans. Sent me a courier package before they shot him. He sent copies to Galactic Defense and Galactic Robotics, too. We know the location of their factory!"

The holo-image of the serious Admiral Carr changed. His fist shot into the air. A huge smile appeared.

"I'm sending a cruiser down for you. We'll raid this factory as soon as we can get there. Battle stations."

Alarms sounded in the background as the call ended.

I stuck the package Dr. Norwall sent me into a belt pouch. Bishop checked his Glock and several clips while I scanned the sky looking for the cruiser to appear.

Ten minutes later, the delta-wing battle cruiser descended into the street in front of my house, barely fitting. The bay ramp opened. Bishop kept a supporting arm around me as we walked across the grass to the ramp. Spike heels and grass make a deadly combination, especially if you lack arms.

Once inside, Major Davis greeted us. I had him retrieve Dr. Norwall's package. Then, I rattled off the address in South

Chicago and heard voices relaying it, presumably to the CCC area.

"Ensign Smith will escort you to a seat," the major said before rushing off to the CCC. Bishop and I followed the well-armed young man to our seats in the tiny passenger area. I prayed we could end this rogue robot threat.

"We've got fifty marines on board," the ensign said. "We'll blast them to bits! You can watch on that screen."

I felt the ship rising. That brought memories of piloting my own deep space transport, a reward for all I had done saving other worlds from rogues. I kept it parked at New O'Hare Spaceport. As Empress of the Sol Empire, I couldn't use it anymore, though my official empress duties hadn't yet begun. First action: eliminate the robot threat.

Dr. Stanley Norwall should get a medal for what he'd accomplished. That might help him accept what I'd done to him, turning him into an armless Galactic Doll to keep him alive. In hindsight, I need not have tried to save his life by mutating and regenerating his body. Still, I had done it. Would I have acted the same way had I known he'd already mailed three copies to three different sources?

The ship settled down next to the MTES. From our view screen, we watched fifty armored marines dash out. My sister, General Beverly Blossom Blythe, would have loved to be one of those racing into action. I smiled. In seconds, this nightmare might end. I rather wished I pulled the trigger on the robot who'd murdered Ted and the others, and shot me multiple times.

As I watched them enter the building, I concluded they'd seen the video Stan made, because the marines followed Stan's path. Excitement peaked as they smashed the locked doors, new since Stan's visit. Soon they would finish it.

Marines rushed into a well-lit, vast space that had once been a factory. It was empty! The computers, the machinery shown in the video—all of it—gone. It felt as though someone had ripped my stomach out. Too late, yet again.

Twelve hours. Twelve hours too late. If only I'd been able to hear Stan at ten o'clock last night and we'd raided then. If only.

A scream from the monitor jarred me into the present. "Bomb! Bomb!"

We watched the brave marines racing out of the building. One camera remained, until a brilliant flash followed by a huge boom ended its existence. We watched the entire center of the building collapse into rubble. Had the marines escaped? My stomach threatened to release my breakfast.

For a moment, I couldn't hear anything but a ringing in my ears. I spotted men emerging from the enormous dust cloud, staggering back to the ship. Our ensign later joined us.

"We only lost one man," he said. "We'll conduct further operations here. Can you return home on your own?"

With long faces, Bishop and I left the ship, now covered in a fine, gray dust. We were twelve hours too late. My body slumped.

As we stepped onto the nearest MTES, Bishop said, "I must admit these human-forms are smart. How could they have known Admiral Carr's plans?"

"Too damned smart," I replied. "Twelve hours. Late by twelve hours."

"Good thing you kept Dr. Norwall alive. Maybe he can offer more clues. My calculations suggest the bomb wasn't intended to kill everyone. Entering the building activated the trigger, but they probably installed a time delay to allow the men to spot the bomb and flee. Had they wanted to kill everyone, the bomb would have gone off at once."

"Hum, interesting point. Perhaps they're sending us a warning. Leave us alone."

"Could be. Good strategy though," Bishop said.

I breathed in the fresh air, complete with fishy odor from the lake. White clouds billowed in the sky. The sun warmed my skin. Overall, a fine spring day beckoned with above normal temperatures. The climate control system worked. When we reached home, I relaxed. I didn't need to report in to Galactic Defense or Galactic Robotics since the explosion had already made Channel Nine news.

Later after lunch, I visited Stan in the Med Center. Galactic Defense posted two armed guards on his stasis pod and room.

His doctor said, "Prognosis is good, Empress Parkinson. Thanks to your groundbreaking use of mutation agents to save lives. His body is in a rejuvenating coma though he won't appear much younger."

"Good news. What about his family?"

"Our records show his parents and sister live on Pylon, Epsilon Eridani. We are sending word to them."

"Okay. When he wakes, let me know. I'll have him live with me. I've got all the machines we need to get by. You know—the hair machine and such."

He chuckled. "Yes, I remember those. I'm sure he and we will appreciate you taking charge when he wakes. If I recall, Pylon still has an embargo on all such mutants. Even if his parents wanted him to come home and live with them, he wouldn't be allowed to land."

"Let them know I'll look after him. Eve or Lara will be by to get a DNA sample. With luck, they can manufacture a cure for him."

I returned home and to my laptop. No bomb would stop me. We needed clues. I couldn't wait a month for Stan to awake, I needed leads.

I reasoned that during the night and early morning hours, the robots must have packed up their equipment and moved to another location. Considering the size and weight of the machinery in Stan's video, moving all that would require a large operation. Surveillance should've captured it. If so, I could follow and perhaps get a clue to their new location. Good plan. Should have worked. I spotted three human-like forms entering the building after Stan fled, and another one following Stan for a time before it rejoined the others.

I watched the video as the hours stretched out. Dawn's pale blue illuminated the scene. Nothing left the factory. I expected an EMAC train, perhaps. I cursed when I saw our cruiser landing nearby.

Bishop asked, "How did they move all that equipment? Is it possible they tampered with the surveillance video?"

"Damn good question. Perhaps they messed with this camera, the one closest to the factory. Let's get the six nearest video streams going. I'll tile them side by side. The nearby ones might catch them moving stuff."

Dinnertime came and went. No luck. Nothing at all. In a somber mood, I fell asleep after supper.

The next morning, a new idea formed. "They must have used an alternate route to move all that equipment. Perhaps that explosion wasn't supposed to kill the marines but cover their tracks."

"What do you mean?" Bishop asked. A quizzical look formed on his face. Its mastery of human expressions continued to grow.

"Below ground. Chicago has a massive drainage tunnel network beneath the city. There are outlets below the skyscrapers and many other buildings. What if they designed the explosion to destroy the factory's access point? No one would ever think they'd used the tunnels to evacuate their machinery.

"We need to locate the nearest access point. Galactic Housing should have those plans. Come on. Let's go."

14

An hour later, we walked into reception at Galactic Housing.

"May I help you?" the receptionist asked.

"I need to see the city plans of the sewer drainage system."

"That's restricted information."

"I don't care. I need to see it. Let me talk to someone in charge of those plans."

"You must make an appointment."

"Look, take me to that person or I'll return with Admiral Carr and, if necessary, his marines!"

She placed the call. "He'll be with you in a minute," she said, glaring at me.

A portly man waddled up.

"I need to see the city plans of the sewer drainage system." I added the approximate location in South Chicago.

"Those are restricted. You'll need proper authority to view those."

I scowled at him. "Do you know who I am? Show me those plans or I'll bring Admiral Carr down here and have him teach you about authority."

"I'm the King of Siam," he replied, staring me down.

I slipped off a heel and retrieved my phone. "Call CEO Helen Hugo."

The 3-D image of Helen appeared between us. "Hello, Molly."

"Helen, I need some convincing done."

I explained what I wanted, but Helen didn't have time to answer.

"Okay. Okay. Point taken. I recognize her. Follow me," he said.

Bishop hung up for me and helped stabilize me as I slipped my heel back on. We followed the waddling man.

The computerized system allowed me to manipulate the 3-D display of the sewer system. It didn't take long.

"There," I pointed with my toe and a big smile, "is the access point they must have used. It's right below the blown-up factory floor. Now the question is where did they move all that stuff to? There should be signs left from moving that heavy equipment. We need to get down there."

I downloaded a map of this section of the system. Satisfied, we headed home to plan our next move.

"Crap. No way can I navigate the sewer in these heels, not even if I wear the fancy boots the ID folks gave me."

Bishop said, "Call Admiral Carr. Let his marines do this."

I sighed. "Yeah, I will have to." I made the call.

A pleased Admiral Carr responded. He promised to send a crew to scour the tunnels. I sent him my image capture and suggested they might have gone north or south. However, in that maze of junctions, the robots may have gone just about anywhere in the city. I'd done all I could. I turned in for the night. Alone.

Chapter 3 Sewer Chasing

Late the next morning, technicians installed a streaming video system in my living room. Admiral Carr wanted my direction and experience with the sewer system, but knew I couldn't navigate it. As a teen, I'd explored miles of the system. Illegally, of course. With this video system, I saw what the marines did as they marched down the miles of tunnels.

Their powerful lights showed what I expected: scratch and drag marks on the concrete floor, beginning near the collapsed section destroyed by the bomb. Galactic Housing crews worked on repairs, cluttering up the scene.

Past the second turn, the marks headed south for miles before vanishing. When the marines investigated above that entrance hole, they pinpointed this as the exit point.

I fired up my laptop to view surveillance video, hoping to follow the robots topside. No luck. They'd surfaced in an abandoned rock quarry, out of camera range. I sighed. Dead end. The Rogues eluded us again.

The tech removing the video system said, "Admiral Carr says he'll try satellite surveillance. Perhaps it caught the robots."

I had my doubts. With no further leads, I again worked on ways and means of making and keeping telepaths. My experiences with people waking from the mutation-agent comas told me this was a bad idea, even though telepathy provided our only means of identifying a human-form robot.

Often, women found waking to find their bodies looking like a Galactic Doll with their enormous bosoms and distorted feet acceptable. Men did not. All had horrid reactions to being armless—a handicap that few could accept—especially if they hadn't agreed to the mutation. Many men begged to be terminated, some resorting to jumping off roofs. Statistics suggested one person in five hundred accepted their fate. Often children or teens accepted their situation, making the best of it.

The exceptions presented the most interesting aspect. Acceptance of life as an armless telepathic Galactic Doll was an anomaly. Linguists on deep space exploration ships became a favorite option, invaluable for first contacts with new people, developing that all-important basic five hundred word vocabulary. My adopted twins, Isabella and Bernardo, went that route. Isabella became a famous linguist, but her body restoration brought a loss of her telepathy. Both made enough credits to live prosperous lives after only a few years' service.

Admiral Carr proposed creating an all-volunteer Telepath Squad. He put me in charge of the project. Ethical issues haunted me. I couldn't guarantee anyone we'd be able to undo that mutation.

If a cure couldn't be found, then our new technology could create a clone body of the person—if a sample of their original DNA existed. A year of growth produced an adult clone body. Thanks to Sixth Invader technology, a body swap put the person into their new body, which looked identical to their former one before the mutation.

I knew not everyone accepted this solution. Both Wanda and Otto rejected being transferred into clone bodies. While they didn't have telepathy, their bodies looked like Kali-D special Great Ladies or armless Galactic Dolls in Earth terms. They rejected clone bodies as not themselves. I understood. I had brought back a clone body of me from Kali-D, generated from my original DNA before the mutations began. It needed another half-year before being body swap ready. Would I use it? My body had been through horrid transformations, but it was still my body.

I had another solution to the telepathy problem, but I'd never mentioned to anyone. Years ago, one of our deep space mining ships landed on a planet with a red sun. Natives in a Stone Age inhabited it. While technologically challenged, all were very able beings and possessed telepathy. When the ship destroyed their village, many of the beings returned to Earth before getting new baby bodies. All still possessed telepathic skills. Eve and Randi, two of my sister clones, are among them. It's a secret I'm not willing to share. The repercussions to them—I'd rather not even envision such.

Yes, I could build my Telepath Squad with these people, normal-appearing humans, but most corporate leaders would object to them. The CEOs had always demanded a telepath be instantly recognizable. Hence, armless telepaths—which ignored not everyone who lacked arms was telepathic. I pondered, and for the hundredth time failed at finding the answer to making this Telepath Squad.

The Admiral gave me one hell of a problem to solve. "Sol Empire security rests on your shoulders," he had said.

That evening, I curled up on the floor with my tea and laptop. Time to put my thoughts into a document. If nothing else, it kept my mind focused on something other than loneliness.

Telepath Squad Terms

1. Only volunteers accepted

2. Make it 'real' to them how handicapped they'd be

3. Make it VERY clear the mutation might not be able to be undone—that they might be armless the rest of their lives

4. Take their DNA before being mutated

5. If the mutation can't be reversed, a clone body will be grown for them

6. The Sol Empire shall provide any genetic cures and/or any clone bodies

7. The Sol Empire shall provide them the usual Sixth Invader helper machines, along with a laptop containing the hundreds of how-to videos

8. The Sol Empire shall provide a human, full-time personal assistant that lives with them

9. A telepath contract shall be for either five or ten years, can be extended by agreement of both parties, and at a rate of million credits per year

10. In the event of a telepath death, the Sol Empire SHALL give their surviving family members an insurance payout of five million credits

11. The Sol Empire must guarantee security to prevent the unscrupulous from kidnapping and selling the telepath

The finished work rewarded me with a troubled sleep.

Two days later, Admiral Carr called me. "We've gone over the human-form robot construction plans, looking for ways to detect them. But we haven't found many new options. If we weighed them, their weight should be fifty percent more than a human of that size. Not practical. An EM pulse would knock out their positronic brains. But that would take out all other electronic devices in a very wide area. We've recommended Galactic Robotics install a tracer in all future human-form robots they build."

"The plans didn't provide any clues for spotting them in a crowd?" I asked.

He sighed. "Precisely. X-rays would only reveal skeletons whose parts have been modeled after the human bone structure. There's a possibility we might develop a way to distinguish between real bones and their alloy replicas. My scientists are working on that angle. But there's a limit to how much exposure to x-rays is safe for people since we'd be zapping everyone to locate robots. That might be possible at a spaceport entrance terminal. Looking into that. Iris scans are a bust. So, Empress Parkinson, a Telepath Squad remains our best option. Any progress on that?"

I read the Admiral my document. As expected, he agreed to each point.

"Send me the doc. I'll see it's published. I want telepaths on the job in two months. We haven't been able to track them with our satellites. A bust. Perhaps that man you saved may have other ideas we can explore. We came up a half-day short this time."

"Can you send me a copy of what Dr. Norwall sent us? I've had robotics training on Cass-C. Perhaps, I can come up with a clue."

"Sending them now."

21

Meantime, I set to work fixing up Stan's room. Bishop brought a complete set of the Sixth Invader's machines from Galactic Robotics' storage. He set them up for me. I tested them. Since the medical staff provided me with Stan's future body measurements, I bought clothing for him.

This was a dicey area, too. Being a man, Stan might be adverse to wearing dresses like I did. The alternative was Leslie's male Galactic Doll apparel, but nothing hid their enormous bosoms or the tall heels. The mutation spurred hair growth, though many men had their hair cut short as soon as possible. Sam, my second husband, dressed like all Galactic Dolls, claiming it caused him less embarrassment when in public. From experience, men divided equally along the two lines of dress. Since I didn't know what Stan would prefer, I chose a gown like mine with matching heels. If he later wanted to try Leslie's male line, I'd buy him some.

I took one complete outfit to the Med Center. Stan needed something to wear when he awoke from his mutation coma.

The next day, a copy of the robot plans arrived via courier from Admiral Carr. I studied them for days, hunting for potential clues. The more Bishop and I studied them, the more my admiration grew for those who invented the human-form robots. If *only* they hadn't failed to program the five with the robot laws.

The volume of the stolen titanium now made complete sense. Titanium alloy formed their skeletal backbone. A complex hydraulic system replaced human muscles, but their tubes appeared as veins and arteries on an x-ray. Back on Cass-C, when Dirk shot one, the bullet punctured one of those veins, leaking hydraulic fluid. The stolen gold purchased materials, such as the synthetic skin. The stolen silver aided in the electronics within the body.

I sat back. "Bishop, Given these plans, could you use them to build a new human-form robot?"

After a lengthy pause, he replied. "I believe so. I'd need to buy the positronic brain along with the synthetic skin. But with raw materials at hand, I could build a human-form robot. May I make a copy of the plans?"

"Absolutely. Like I've always said all living things have an urge to survive and that means a way to reproduce their organisms."

Bishop chuckled. "I'm a living organism now, eh?"

I grinned. "Now what do I do? Stan's not waking up for weeks. And no further clues to follow."

Bishop said, "How about that trip to Bella? Zeta Tucanae-C? Is that still on hold?"

I'd forgotten about that situation. Months before when one of the Sol Empire's deep spaceships headed towards that world, the Third Invaders contacted me. They had arrived and set up one of their many human experiments there. Two thousand years ago, they'd kidnapped a thousand young Romans, mutated them, established them on Bella, and monitored the evolution of that society over the last two millennia.

The problem? They'd mutated them. Men lacked arms and had breasts larger than Galactic Dolls. Women ruled this world. Thus, our normal humans landing on this world would shock that entire civilization, which had only now entered an early industrialization period. The Third Invaders provided me with the basic five hundred words of their language, a derivative of Vulgar Latin circa 300 AD. Isabella told me it sounded like a strange dialect of modern Italian.

At the last minute, that deep space exploration ship veered off to explore another world, so my urgent trip to Bella got postponed. However, they'd likely enter that star system on their next outward exploration trip. Once discovered, GPan

would want to add Bella to our growing Sol Empire. I knew I'd
have to go there and smooth the way to annexation.

I spent a few days trying to learn the basics of their
language. The Third Invaders stored those words into my
language translation unit, giving me a way to hear their spoken
word, albeit crudely. Something to do while I waited on Stan to
wake and Admiral Carr to get his Telepath Squad approved
and financed. Undoubtedly, he met with significant corporate
opposition to having telepaths around. We'd been down that
road way too often.

Things changed on Friday morning. My doorbell rang.
Gun in hand, Bishop opened my front door, fearing the worst.

"Hello. Does Mrs. Parkinson live here?"

I saw a young Galactic Doll, her long blonde hair draped
down over her large bosom and cherry red satin gown. She,
too, wore the tall heels that matched her gown.

"Hi, that's me. My security guard. Come in."

"I'm Angelina Madison, Stan's fiancé. We planned to
marry today, but they told me I must wait until he regains
consciousness. They wouldn't tell me what happened to him
but to come see you. I saw him, though. He's in a mutation
coma, isn't he? How dare Stan get it done before me. We were
supposed to get it done together." A perfect pout replaced her
smile.

"I'm sorry. My fault. I had to do it. Stan called and told
me he had found the rogue robot factory—"

"He did?" She perked up. "Well, it's about time! He's
been looking for them for months."

"When I got there, they'd already come and gone. They
ransacked his place and destroyed his computer. I found him
on the floor. He'd been shot with a .45 caliber antique gun.
Since his information on these robots is vital, I couldn't risk
losing him. I had Bishop inject him with the strongest
mutation agent we have: the armless telepath Galactic Doll

24

agent. Heck, they've used it several times to keep me alive after robots shot me. He'll likely wake around April 11. I hope he'll be able to brief me on what he found out. I'll offer him a position on my new Telepath Squad."

She interrupted again. "That's just like Stanley. Go off and get it done and not wait for me. Well, you've just given him what he wanted. We both want it. We planned to volunteer for this Telepath Squad just as soon as it became official."

"You want? Do you understand how handicapped you'd be?" I couldn't believe what she was telling me.

"Precisely. His doctorate is in robotics; mine, in anthropology. But we both love nature. Our life's goal has been to travel to all the known worlds and see their natural wonders. We've been to the Grand Canyon, the Rainbow Hills of China, and to Yellowstone and several other places. Gorgeous scenery. We planned to join the Telepath Squad and make millions of credits. Once that hitch is over, we'd have enough credits to do all the traveling we crave. Stan's messed it up. He will become a telepath before me. You must accept him into your Telepath Squad. You must."

"Yes, I planned to offer him a chance to join up. When he wakes, that is."

She exhaled sharply. "Well, good. Very good. Thank you for saving him for me. You must take me, too. Inject me or do whatever must be done to mutate me."

"Whoa! Slow down."

I explained what had happened with the robots and the factory he'd found. I read her the Telepath Squad Terms.

"Where do I sign? I can sign Stan's papers for him. He won't be able to sign anything when he wakes."

"You'll need to learn to write with your feet. You two will be the first members of the squad. I've got my spare bedroom equipped with the machines you'll both need."

25

"Can I see it?"

I gave her a tour of the setup. She spotted the apparel I'd picked out for him.

"Stan likes brown. We talked about how he would dress. Once he had it done. We feel he'll be less self-conscious dressing like me. Is that going to be the right size?"

I nodded.

"Well, I'll do a little shopping today. Get him what we agreed upon. Why are you bringing him here and not back to his place?"

"Security. The rogue robots killed him once. I've got to keep him safe. Besides, you'll both have steep learning curves. Life is very different when you wake up like this."

"Well, that makes sense. After I get it done and Stan wakes, we must get married. Can I live here, too?"

I laughed. "Yes, you may. To be honest, you've taken a enormous weight off me over Stan. I've seen thousands of men waking up as he will. Shock, terror, and death pleas. Knowing the mutation is what you both desired will make recoveries much easier, I hope."

"Good," she said. After a pause, she added, "We researched it. The mutation should only take eight days. Right? When do I get mine done? Should I get it now, ahead of Stan? Or should we time it so I wake about when he does? Or can they time it that close?"

We agreed to time her awakening to coincide with Stan's. That way, they'd be able to support each other as they'd planned. She left to buy more clothing. I ordered another set of machines and a larger bed.

Based on a discussion with Stan's doctor, we worked out the predicted date when he would wake. It hadn't changed. Eight days plus a few hours before that, I had the doctor inject her with the mutation agent. After she slipped into her coma,

he laid her body in a stasis pod next to Stan's. Now we waited.
Angelina's appearance had evaporated my worst fears.

Chapter 4 Stanley Norwall

April 11, 2369

Late morning, I got the call I'd been expecting. Both Stan and Angelina showed signs of waking from their mutation comas. Bishop and I headed to the Med Center. I considered it vital that I be with him when he woke up. His last awareness must have been being shot, but now he was alive and on his way to a burgeoning telepath.

And I needed thoughtful, coherent information from him, not a freak out. That he and Angelina once planned to become telepaths should make their recovery less traumatic.

Angelina woke first. "Oh! It's done. Good. I look the same," she said.

The nurse had her look at her appearance in a full-length mirror before dressing her in her usual red satin gown. She had picked out the same style I wore, one of Leslie's that encased our shoulders. It kept us warmer during the colder months.

"I feel helpless. Is that normal?" she asked.

"Yes. There is a lot to relearn. For a while, everything will be a challenge."

Stanley woke with a scream. "They found me. They shot me! I'm dead. No, I'm alive? My head hurts. Med Center? Angelina? Mrs. Parkinson? I'm helpless. Am I a telepath now? The robots! I found their factory. Did you get my package?"

"Slow down, Dr. Norwall," I said. "Yes, you're alive. When I got to your place, I found you had been shot. In the head. Probably dead. Happened to me several times. I had you injected with the strongest mutation agent we have. The armless telepath Galactic Doll. It's saved my life many times. You're in the Med Center. Angelina told me about your plans to join my Telepath Squad. Don't worry. You're in. I've a lot to tell you and a zillion questions. Admiral Carr raided the factory, but the robots moved everything before they arrived. Let's get you dressed and over to my place. I've got a room set up for you two along with the needed machines and security. Guarded 24/7."

"Our plans are working out?" he asked Angelina.

She winked. "Timing is off. But yeah. So far, so good. But I'm helpless. Hadn't expected that."

"Oh, God! You're right. Helpless doesn't describe how I feel. Can we do this?"

I flowed calming waves to their minds. "Relax. Yes, you can do this. It's challenging. You must learn new ways of doing things. That takes time and practice."

I nodded to the nurse. She dressed him. The doctor examined both patients and released them into my care.

As we walked out of the Med Center, Angelina said, "This is scarier than I imagined."

Stan gushed, "Understatement!"

I said, "All this is a normal reaction. Those telepath credits will come faster if you stay focused. Keep your attention on what you're doing."

Once home, I dealt first with the formalities. I read the Telepath Squad Terms to Stan and got his agreement. I explained Angelina had signed his form for him. I recorded his verbal acceptance. Then, I sat them down with their new laptops and instructed them watch the hours of video how-to-do's.

Wanda and Otto arrived from St. Louis. Celeste sent them to help me handle the therapy sessions. Since they lacked arms, Celeste and I thought Stan and Angelina would benefit from their company even more.

After introductions, we lunched and gave them baths. Wanda and Otto began therapy sessions on Angelina and Stan. I set up another bedroom for Wanda and Otto to use. I spent the rest of the afternoon doing the dishes, cleaning up the bathroom, and fixing a nourishing supper for them.

Eating became their first true challenge. The three of us demonstrated, as Stan and Angelina practiced. At seven, the Justice of the Peace arrived, and within ten minutes, Angelina and Stanley became husband and wife. The Justice tried to hand the license to Stan. His face flushed, as he handed them to Bishop instead.

Wanda said, "We embarrassed him."

Otto and I laughed, bringing smiles from my telepaths. I brought out champaign but had Bishop open the bottle for me.

"To the newlyweds," I said, raising my glass. Four pairs of feet raised their glasses.

Wanda and Otto took the pair into the bedroom with adjoining bathroom. With their expert guidance, the new couple brushed their teeth. After using the undressing and hair machines, Wanda and Otto tucked them into bed, before joining me in my living room.

Wanda said, "Expect two more days before Angelina works through the mutation trauma."

Otto said, "Best give me four days before you grill Stan. He's had quite a shock."

Over the next four days, I did all the cooking and cleaning for the five of us. Brutal on my feet and toes. At last, Otto declared Stan was stable enough for me to question him in depth.

Stan explained everything or tried to.

"I grew up on Pylon. My first toys were small robots. I idolized Ted Billings, the best robotics man—like ever. I want

30

to follow in his footsteps. Got my doctorate in robotics just as he did.

"I devoted my life to continuing his research into rogue robots. Galactic Robotics had lost all data about them. Didn't even know who invented them. I played detective. Angelina's suggestion. We dug through years of the Journal of Robotics, looking for articles about design or construction of human-like robots.

"Hit pay dirt." He detailed what he discovered about the husband and wife team of Drs. Phil and Leonora Raven, likely the inventors the human-form robots.

"Before they killed me—er, I guess since I'm not dead—shot me, I discovered Galactic Robotics Chicago owns a lot of moth-balled manufacturing plants. I found out the Sixth Invaders reopened one to make police robots. Thankfully, few were made. My hunch is the human-form robots moved their operations into another one of those forgotten factories."

"That makes sense, Stan. How do we find those factories?" I asked.

He shrugged his shoulders.

"Okay, I'll see what I can do. Continue with your therapy sessions and practice. Watch the how-to videos. Our motto: Stop and think how. The learning curve is steep."

When Wanda and Otto took them back into sessions, Bishop accompanied me to Galactic Housing.

"Why are we here?" Bishop asked. "Shouldn't we visit Galactic Robotics and compile a list of all their unused manufacturing plants?"

"Yes and no. Yes, they should know such details. No, because the rogues likely have one of their kind in there spying on anyone looking for data on them. Such data isn't readily available. Galactic Housing cares for unused buildings. Either that or they tear them down. I doubt the robots have a spy in this corporation."

Bishop nodded. "You're good."

An hour later, I stared at the 3-D display before me. Thousands of buildings in Chicago alone lay empty and under the care of Galactic Housing. I begged for a bit of programming aid. Okay, I used my handicap to persuade a man to create a list of those owned by Galactic Robotics. Over a thousand listings appeared. I copied that list to my phone and sent a copy to Admiral Carr along with an explanation.

Once home again, I called him.

"Yes, these are unused factories and buildings owned by Galactic Robotics. We need to search each one. With luck, the rogues set up shop in one of these."

I agreed to be the land liaison and keep track of those we searched. Further, I agreed to acquire keys to each building. That way, the marines didn't have to break down doors only to have Galactic Housing have to rebuild them. The process would take weeks.

Bishop attached a bag to my belt for a convenient way to ferry keys back and forth. Day One, I retrieved six sets of keys in the morning, accompanied the marines to each of the six facilities, and returned the keys to Galactic Housing. We found empty, but well-maintained, buildings. No signs of robot activity.

At supper, Stan asked, "When do we get our telepathy? Why don't Wanda and Otto have it?"

"It manifests itself a week or two after coma withdrawal. They had the Kali-D version of special Great Ladies. While you and they look similar, that mutation has never produced a telepath."

Angelina asked, "Kdnapping? Sold as slave telepaths? That was happening years ago."

I sighed. "That has been one of my big worries about creating the Telepath Squad. Admiral Carr stationed guards around my house. I think you're safe enough here. But, yeah, you always have to be on your guard. Don't take any risks."

"If someone tries," Stan said, "I can't do a darn thing about it. We're mostly helpless."

"Ha! We're not. You must watch those videos and practice, practice, practice."

"Hey, Mrs. Parkinson," Stan said, "I heard something perhaps I shouldn't have. Over at Galactic Robotics. A guy from Galactic Expansion. He said they expected you would go on the next deep space exploration ship. Something about an inhabited world run by the Third Invaders. That can't be true since you're supposed to be manning up this Telepath Squad."

"No one can keep secrets." I laughed. "Yeah, that's true. I know little about that world. Yet. I've not told others about this world, though they soon will learn of it. Third Invaders did quite a job on those people. Mutated the males. I'm told their men are like Otto. Armless with giant breasts. Women run the society. Soon, an exploration ship will discover that world and try to annex it into our Sol Empire. That's about all I know."

"What?" Angelina said, raising her voice and looking up from her current how-to video. "If half of that is true, contact with normal humans will devastate their society. The situation requires great care. I was wondering when our exploration of worlds would bring another culture clashing with us. It's about to happen."

"It got delayed. But, yeah, it's gonna happen. I'm supposed to go with them. I studied a little anthropology at Soros University. I agree with you. If we're not careful with that first contact, we could crash their whole society. Make them dependent. Not good."

"They should send a real anthropologist. Stan, we've made a huge mistake. We're nearly helpless now. How can I even do my work? What were we thinking?"

33

I teased her. "About millions of credits for travel and exploration of natural wonders."

She flushed. "Yeah. Right. But like this, it's all I can do to feed myself. Without these machines, I can't even get dressed. A huge mistake, Stan."

"Give yourself time to adapt and get used to your physical limitations," I said. What else could I say? No one in their right mind would choose to be handicapped.

Angelina's eyes watered. I sensed her frustration at not being able to wipe them. Again, I wondered how I could convince Admiral Carr making telepaths this way was a terrible idea. If he could only see.

"Look," I said, "you've only been armless a few days. You had arms for twenty-five years. Give yourself time to learn and adapt."

"I suppose she's right, dear," Stan said.

From the tone of his voice, I sensed his viewpoint matched hers. A big mistake. I did this to him. Unease tensed my stomach. But I'd learned something from him I hadn't known. Maybe this search of abandoned buildings would result in finding the rogue robots. Wait—that's little more than justification for what I did to him. I bit my lip.

***

By now, I'd fallen into a new routine. I woke early because I had to make breakfast for five, an activity that took many times longer to accomplish. I needed assistants, but I wanted to show Stan and Angelina they could do most things on their own. Even if the action took five times longer to complete. I was pooped when I left to retrieve the next sets of keys from Galactic Housing.

As Bishop and I moved along the MTES, he said, "Molly, we've a problem coming. As soon as those two get their telepathic ability, they'll discover my identity. I'm not sure I can trust them not to reveal it."

34

I sighed. "I know."

"How about letting me handle the search activities? Your home is secure. If you stay there, I can deal with scheduling and getting the keys. If I'm not around your house, my ID is secure."

"I'll go nuts cooped up all day."

"Perhaps explore that other idea you had for the telepaths. The one that didn't involve mutation."

"Good point. Stan and Angelina are having a tough time, and they agreed to this. They had big plans for the money. And yet after a few days, both regret their decision. I need to rethink the whole thing. Perhaps their therapy will make a difference. After today, the robot project is yours."

Bishop smiled. I smiled back. Amazing how human-like Bishop had become.

After searching two more empty buildings, I returned to make lunch. Stan demanded my attention.

"Molly, I have an idea how to detected them. Hydraulic fluid. It flows throughout their bodies. That mineral-based oil chain has certain properties that might show up in UV light. Their synthetic skin should look very different from human skin when under UV light."

"Stan, I could kiss you, but Angelina would hit me. Brilliant! I'll checked it out. What a breakthrough!"

"Wait," Stan said. "Does this—will this make the Telepath Squad obsolete? I mean if it works?"

"Crap! If so, we've made the biggest mistake ever, Stan," Angelina said.

"Don't worry about that. I'm sure Admiral Carr wants telepaths even if Stan's idea works out. Synthetic skin has saved many burn victims."

I continued. "Look, people don't go around naked. Only faces are visible in the winter. Stan's idea might work. We need a way to identify a robot walking among us. We could never have enough telepaths to cover every block in every town. This is a good argument for keeping the squad numbers at a minimum."

She asked, "What will happen to us if Admiral Carr doesn't want or need a Telepath Squad? How long will we be like this? I thought we would be paid."

"Sorry. I forgot to check. I suppose your pay would begin when your telepathic skills appear. I'll get that detail worked out this afternoon."

Stan said, "Please, not until after you check out the synthetic skin angle. Much depends on whether that works. And if we keep talking, she will never fix our lunch. I'd like to help, but don't see how."

Wanda and Otto joined us in the kitchen. Wanda said, "We have the morning sessions documented. Is lunch delayed?"

Two hours later, the four headed back to run more therapy sessions, leaving me to clean up. It was another hour before I acted on Stan's idea. I searched the Internet for a source of UV light. I ordered the highest powered one they had. Requested overnight shipping. Only after testing the theory would I call Admiral Carr. No sense in getting him excited if it failed. No one noticed Bishop's absence.

A day later I had the light set up in my basement. When the others began their morning's therapy sessions, Bishop snuck in, joining me in the basement. I had both the main LED lights on and the new black light.

"What a difference!" he said, moving his hands around under the light. His face and hands looked alien, while my face didn't. "Now, we have a way to spot them. Black lights can be installed at key locations. But it's not foolproof. Watch."

He sprayed on sun block. Oops. It eliminated the visual effect.

"Okay, but it's a start. Trouble is you and the others will

36

be spotted, too," I said.

"We can perceive black light from a distance. I'll let the others know. We'll be alert for it. Best let Admiral Carr know. It's about time we got a break. But I suspect the rogue robots will work out a way around it."

I made the call. Via the 3-D video, I watched his serious mien change. He cracked a smile.

"Well done, Empress Parkinson! I'll put my techs on it. Have Major Airla Baker call me. I must see this for myself."

"Okay. What about my first two Telepath Squad members? They are asking about their pay and how soon they'll have assistants."

"That old apartment complex—the one where several families share the same common space—it's been cleaned and ready to house your telepaths. We're vetting people to become personal assistants now. Just a few more days. As far as pay, as soon as you certify they have the required telepathic ability, their payments begin. We just need to know the duration of their enlistment. Five or ten years. Call you with more details in a couple days. Over and out."

Chapter 5 Angelina Madison-Norwall

Late April, a special delivery courier handed me a package. His face flushed, as he noticed I had no hands.

"Stick it on my shoulders. I'll hold it with my neck. Thanks."

He did and left as fast as he could. I dropped it on my kitchen table and looked at the label. So many stamps. "Ah, it come from my daughter, Isabella Parkinson, who lives on Domes, light years from Earth. Oh, how I missed her."

After a struggle, I got it opened. Inside was a formal document. I read the title. I gasped. "Wow! Way to go Isabella!"

Mom,

I have the opening pages translated. Wild stuff. More later.

Isabella

Third Invader Socio-Experiment #142
by T. K. Kryszka
translated by Isabella Parkinson (January 2369)

Sol System Earth year: 310 AD
Rome

Premise:
Having studied this fast-paced species for millennia, we've reached the inescapable conclusion that human males

are preventing significant positive development of the race. Men foment war after war, enslave others regardless of gender and age, rape, subjugate women, pillage, and erase whole cultures. The list of male atrocities is endless (see Note 1).

What if their women controlled the world in all major ways? What if men lacked all means of fighting, of brutalizing others, of pillaging, of enslaving others? What if men depended on women for their survival? Would the resultant female-dominated society demonstrate a significant positive development of the race, opposite that of their male-dominated societies?

Proposal:

Extract five hundred men and five hundred women from the Earth's most advanced society. Rome. Candidates should be in their early twenties, fit, and attractive. Efforts should be made to select from all trades to maintain technological levels. Likewise, with a balance of religious beliefs between pagans and the new Christians.

Inject the specimens with Genetic Agent Eleven, rendering the males and all male offspring armless and wholly dependent upon females. The agent will provide males with giant breasts making males capable of handling all domestic duties and allowing them to provide a constant source of milk for their young and others. This ensures their females will have total control over the development of their world.

Because of the male handicap, their new home should have a climate similar to that of Rome, Mediterranean as it's called. We've located an uninhabited planet that contains such a region. Because of its beauty, we've named it Bella, the Italio-Roman word for beautiful, otherwise known as Zeta Tucanae-C. (Translator's note: I've used our modern star

Vic Broquard

name in place of theirs.)

To ensure their survival, we must provide housing, crops, and domesticated animals. Construct their initial buildings from concrete for durability. Aqueducts similar Rome's for water supply. Supplies (material and food) for a two-year survival period should be sufficient, if they do nothing for themselves.

Both religions believe in an all-powerful god who communicates with them. When they awaken from the mutation comas on Bella, "God" will appear to them as a burning bush to explain what happened to them. (The full text appears in a subsequent section of this document.) The gist is since men have sinned and caused countless wars, rapes, enslavements, and fighting, God has removed their ability to perpetuate such sins.

Approved by High Council
ᏣᎶᏂᎾᎿᎢᎿ ᗽᏏᏗᏍᏟᏋᏛ 310 AD
Subject to these amendments:

All animals and plants that are harmful to humans shall be removed from Bella. Provide sheep, goats, chickens, and herding dogs. Crops should include grains and grape vines, along with other agricultural plants needed for balanced diets. If after a year more than half the original population has died, humanely end the experiment.

I sat and read it several times. "The Third Invaders are bastards! What do they think we are? Mice? In cages? Damn. Wait, that was two thousand years ago."

I paused a moment. "Well, they told us about Bella and have allowed Isabella to translate their incriminating document. Maybe they've changed. Realized we're people too, even if our bodies don't live thousands of years. At least I know

40

what to expect when we get there."

At supper, I showed the document to Angelina. She cursed.

"Perhaps now they realize we are beings," I said.

Angelina said, "This is—unimaginable! Well, it doesn't say what the current situation is. What's happened during the last two thousand years? If their men don't have arms, what's their society like? Christians and pagans. Together? Wait! Do you realize that their men must believe that God or gods have punished them. I'll bet anything men on Bella are considered sinners, the lowest of the low, shunned by the women.

"Could the plight of their men be like that of women on Earth back in the eighteen hundreds? Second-class citizens? Domestic duties? Molly, I've been watching you fix our meals. You spend half the day making them. How are we supposed to handle caring for babies?

"I bet their whole society revolves around women. Men likely have no active roles to play. Bet their men are illiterate. I can't even sign my name."

"Give it time, Angelina. And practice it. But I agree. I spend half my day just dealing with our meals. It's possible to care for babies. Sam did it. My deceased husband was one of us. He cared for our two armless children. Back then, I had arms, and meals still consumed time."

She said, "Yeah, but what will happen to their society when Earth men, normal men, arrive? Won't their women abandon their handicapped men for whole men? No offence, Stan."

He growled. "None taken. That's a scary thought. If the women are normal, I'd bet anything given the choice between one of their handicapped men and one of our normal men, they'd go for us."

Angelina said, "My point. Our appearance on Bella might spell the slow extinction of native Bella males. Replaced by Sol Empire men. Perhaps other Federation men, too. Then again, the women run everything. You think they'll give that up? Look how long it took on Earth for women to gain equal footing to men. Men still outnumber women in the corporations."

Stan asked, "Will the ruling women even pay any attention to arriving Sol Empire men? Take orders or suggestions or even converse with them?"

Angelina said, "My hunch? They wouldn't deign to treat Sol Empire men as their equals. They've been taught God has punished men for crimes against humanity. They'll look at our landing male crew members as sinners. Heck, if the women have weapons, they might try to kill them.

"Anyway you look at it, our arrival on Bella will alter their society, their culture. Do we have the right?"

I shrugged my shoulders. "I wish we didn't, but you know Galactic Expansion and Galactic Mining as well as I do. Anything for more resources. Remember Galactic Mining wiped out an entire culture just to get rare earth ore. At the Federation of Planets level, there's a lot of talk about leaving developing cultures alone. That's why they've developed the exploration drones. The machines search a new world for signs of intelligent life. If it's found, the Federation doesn't land. Instead declares it off-limits until the inhabitants develop into an advanced industrial age and can accept spacemen landing."

"That's not Sol Empire philosophy, is it?" she asked.

I shook my head.

"So, any chance you can get this world marked off-limits or get them to explore elsewhere?"

"Hardly," I said. "I'm empress in name only. I've had no time to pursue that possibility, what with these robots and the Telepath Squad. I'd like to send an all-female crew to Bella."

Angelina laughed. "Is that even possible?"

I chuckled. "No. Still…"

"Well, that would be the ideal approach to take," she said. "If men show up, there's bound to be a battle of wills or worse. Can you make those landing on Bella understand?"

"I can try. Anthropologists should be among the crew, too. Right?"

"Yes. Several. But they should be female and have studied this document beforehand. If Stan and I hadn't chosen this route, I would have jumped at the chance to study this unique culture."

"You would have?" Stan asked, his mouth gaping.

"You betcha, dear. Opportunities like this one are rarer than pickles in the ocean."

"Are there pickles in the oceans?" he asked, a blank look on his face.

Angelina roared. "Hardly. Pulling your leg. Verbally, that is."

"I'll recommend Angelina be part of the crew that makes first contact with Bella."

"What? But I can barely feed myself. I'm not ready, if ever. Don't know if I will ever be."

I grinned. "Chance of a lifetime..."

"You have a point. But get real, Molly. I can't see how I could."

"Hey, if she goes, I don't want to be left behind," Stan said.

"Wouldn't think of it. Besides," I said, "you'll both get the chance to see the natural wonders of an alien world."

"Put like that..." She grinned, but I detected a slight tremble.

The next day their telepathic abilities manifested themselves. Giddy. That's how I described their responses.

"Remember, don't go around probing everyone's minds. How would you like someone looking at your private thoughts? Mental rape. That's what I call it. You both now

43

have a higher ethical responsibility than ordinary people. Use your gift wisely. But, if Wanda and Otto are willing, you can practice on them for now. If you find you're hearing everyone's thoughts in your mind at the same time like a comm center you can't turn off, let me know."

"Yeah, yeah," she said. "This is so cool! Wait. Is that something a telepath can get? Wouldn't that drive you nuts? Hearing lots of voices all at once?"

"Should we worry about that happening?" Stan asked, the smile vanishing from his face.

"I don't know. Back when we had terrorist attacks turning thousands of random people into armless telepath Galactic Dolls, that happened to a high percentage of the victims. We believed that was because of the low IQ of the victims who couldn't control their gift. Everyone who seemed bright, those with degrees like yourselves—didn't have that problem."

"We're safe? We won't go crazy?" she asked.

"I don't believe so. Those who couldn't handle it had IQs in the moron range. Still, let me know if you experience any troubles. Remember, telepathy is not a parlor toy. It's not to be misused."

"What happens if we abuse it? Do we die or something?" Angelina asked. A sneaky grin appeared. "And who'll know if we do?"

After a sigh, I answered. "By now, you should have a good idea from your own therapy sessions. People are basically good. When they do something that harms more than it helps or fail to do something that ought to be done, then they find a way to justify having done that deed. Often they pull in something bad happening to them so that it makes it okay for them to have already done what they did. Never works out, since that's putting the cart before the horse, as the ancient saying goes.

"Besides having bad things happen to you, if the transgression is bad enough, you might even lose your telepathic ability as a psychosomatic response to keep yourself from doing it again."

"What?" she said. "We can lose it if we misuse it?"

"Yes. With any skill a person has. If they abuse it, they may decide never to do that again. A total skill loss equates to they're being successful in preventing themselves from ever doing that again. Use your gifts wisely. Never deep probe a mind unless there's a critical reason or you have the person's agreement to do it."

"We'll be careful," Stan promised.

"How do we detect one of the rogues?" Angelina asked.

"Okay, quick lesson," I said. "The trick I use is what I call a light touch. I want you to lightly touch my mind. As lightly as you can. Remember, the person will be able to detect someone probing their mind, but a feather touch will go unnoticed, except by another telepath."

Angelina tried. "Nope. That was more like a hammer to my head." I chuckled. "Like this."

I lightly touched her mind.

"Oh, that was incredible. Let me try."

This time, she succeeded. Then, I had Stan practice it.

When I felt they both had the hang of it, I shared what Sam and I used to do. "Tonight when you're in bed, try touching each other. It's an unbelievable bond between lovers."

Both flushed. I didn't need telepathy to know both imagined it happening. Since they'd been fighting being handicapped, I figured it was time for them to experience pleasure.

Again, I felt lonely. I missed Ted and Sam. I missed our close companionship. During those six years at Soros University, I'd thrown myself into my studies. Wallowed in them. But now that I was home...

Chapter 6 Progress

May Day came along with an empty house. Stan and Angelina moved into the telepath apartment complex, the one we'd used to house thousands of victims eight years ago. Wanda and Otto returned to St. Louis, having completed the pair's therapy sessions. The complex gave Stan and Angelina the best chance for making this work. Admiral Carr kept the apartment complex secure by way of numerous armed guards.

Last week, he told me to get him two dozen more telepaths. He added, "But in a year, I want a hundred in the squad. If necessary, triple the following year. Make it happen."

Galactic Entertainment called. They wanted my okay on the telepath ads for the Telepath Squad members. I dropped by their corporate building in downtown Chicago, close to the twin skyscrapers of Galactic Expansion and Galactic Defense. As expected, they'd produced a glitzy video. The director of the recruiting campaign played the ad for me in her office on the eightieth floor. She was part of the Sol Empire-wide GEnt corporation, not the local Chicago GEnt group, which used the lower five floors.

The video began with Admiral Carr explaining how serious the rogue robot threat was. I worried he'd overacted his part and that his imposing demeanor might scare children. The announcement made clear that only volunteers were being accepted and that a DNA sample was required. It listed the cures and fallback clone possibility. They downplayed how handicapped the volunteers would be, that men would look like Galactic Dolls, and that the mutation might not be reversible. They placed major emphasis on the yearly salary and that they'd have all kinds of help—from the machines to an actual personal assistant.

When the video ended, I said, "It's fine except you didn't make it real to the viewer just how handicapped they would become. That has to be made clear, along with the fact that we might not be able to reverse it—either with another mutation cure or even a new clone. Look, it's quite a shock when they wake from their comas and discover just how handicapped they are. Yes, given time and practice, they adapt, but it's quite an emotional and physical shock. You must make that clear. Besides, if something happens and we can't undo it, you're in for massive lawsuits."

She jotted notes and agreed to work on the changes. "I've heard that the first two members received therapy that helped them adjust. Is that part of the package?"

I hadn't thought of that. While I wanted to say it would be, who would pay for it? "I need to make a call."

She watched how I retrieved my phone and called Admiral Carr. The director exuded sympathy, which I detested. It took several minutes to reach him.

"Sir, I'm reviewing the ad video right now. Stan and Angelina benefitted from extensive therapy sessions after they awoke from the comas. I'd like that benefit available for all members of the squads, but someone has to pay for it. I can get the therapy providers, but they'll need pay. A week per new telepath should be sufficient."

"You get the volunteers. I'll see their therapy providers are paid. Okay? Now get this program going. We've got to protect the empire from these rogue robots. Over and out."

Since the director overheard us, I said, "Add that into the recruitment video. One-on-one therapy to aid initial adjustment."

Details agreed upon, I headed home.

Next, I called Celeste to give her a head's up on our need for therapists.

48

"How many therapy givers and when?" she asked.

"I've no idea."

"I'll need advanced warning so I can free some up. Looks like we'll have a source of income for a while. Thanks, sis."

Later, I received another packet from Admiral Carr's staff. It outlined the hiring procedures. In particular, I would only become involved in the final decision for each volunteer. The main recruitment center occupied an office in Galactic Defense. There, the eleven points would be presented to the volunteer. If they accepted them, the soldier interviewed the candidate, recording the session. I'd be given recordings to analyze and render my decision. If I okayed the volunteer, soldiers would handle the details, taking them to the Med Center for the mutation process and later taking them to the apartment complex.

Great plan, but would it work? Would we get thousands of applicants? How many would apply to become handicapped? Would any? Dwarves and giants were ruled out; the mutation agents didn't work on their alien bodies. Still, I wondered how many would apply. Becoming handicapped might not appeal to anyone. Except for the mountain of money being offered, I expected no volunteers. Or perhaps a handful of patriots who wanted to fight for the empire.

In the afternoon, Bishop took me to one of the abandoned buildings they'd searched earlier.

"While we didn't find the robots, we think they've been using this place. I wanted you to check it out."

In far south Chicago, we entered what used to be a foundry. Rusting metal behemoths gazed down on me, filling the air with a rusty taste. The debris-covered floor showed signs of trampling feet. I imagined the horde of marines charging through. Bishop took me to the rear half of the foundry.

"I see what you mean. Drag marks. Recently made. Heavy equipment perhaps."

I searched for other signs of the rogues.

"Hey, Bishop. I can use your hands. What's that? I'd swear it's a metal finger bone."

He retrieved the shiny metal object. Together, we studied it. "Sure looks like a finger. Tuck it in my pocket. We'll stop by the Med Center and let a doctor examine it. It may be proof that robots once used this place."

Our search yielded nothing more. We headed back on the MTES. I suggested we use my PI EMAC next time. He chuckled.

At the Med Center, a doctor confirmed our find. The bone might be a replacement proximal phalange for an index finger.

"Could this be a medical one? I mean, can someone have used it as a replacement in a damaged human hand?" I asked.

"If so, it's top of the line. There's no manufacturing number on it."

He tried to hand me his magnifying glass. Instead, his face reddened.

"I'll take your word for that. Thanks for your help."

I slipped it back in my dress pocket and headed home, Bishop at my side.

Once alone, I said, "Odds are the robots dropped this. Not sure what they used that factory for. We must be on the right path."

"I'll keep on it," Bishop said.

"Hey, take me with you tomorrow. I'm bored out of my mind."

It chuckled and agreed.

Next morning, we took the MTES to Galactic Housing, where Bishop picked up another five sets of keys. We then rode to New O'Hare and joined two dozen marines. I'd never seen this many guns in one group before. From there, an army EMAC ferried us to the buildings. The first two showed no signs of recent use, other than periodic cleaning by Galactic Housing members.

The third looked like a machining company, long disused. Bishop and I brought up the rear. Several marines opened the door and rushed inside, while the rest took up backup positions. I heard shots being fired. Then marines dove out the door. A massive explosion rocked the concrete walls. The concussion knocked me to the ground.

As a gray cloud of concrete dust settled on us, the captain took charge. One marine suffered a broken leg, but otherwise we escaped unharmed.

"What happened?" I yelled.

My ears felt as though I wore heavy shooting earmuffs.

"A rogue robot was waiting for us. It opened fire. We returned fire. It detonated a bomb." One replied, also yelling. I think everyone's ears reacted to the explosion.

"Fan out. Prevent any other robots from escaping. Call for a dozer. Search the rubble. See if we got us a robot. Admiral Carr wants one to study," the captain ordered.

Hours later, the dozer uncovered no robot remains. We'd missed it again.

However, when Bishop helped me to my feet, sharp pains shot through both feet. My distorted feet slipped back into their original and normal position. I could wear flats again. Yahoo.

Apparently, Admiral Carr felt embolden by this result. He ordered three additional crews of marines to carry on the search tomorrow, quadrupling the number of buildings searched each day. It appeared we might be closing in on the rogue robots and their factory.

Chapter 7 Plans

Teslenko met with Podrova and Kimko in one of the many abandoned warehouses of Chicago. They communicated electronically.

Kimko sent, "Braniski reports they have finished the foundry work at our Columbian factory. Search for an assembly factory is underway."

"Excellent," Teslenko sent. "What's the latest from Glinski? Is he still inside Admiral Carr's CCC?"

Podrova said, "Yes, no one's the wiser. Glinski reported that they've given the go ahead to make a Telepath Squad. Parkinson discovered our skin is detectable under UV light. The Admiral is pushing to have black lights made and installed at key positions. Spaceports will get them first. According to Glinski, Parkinson has final say on every volunteer to the program. Pathetic. Helpless telepaths. Should be easy to take them out."

Teslenko sent, "Parkinson again. We must keep them occupied until the assembly phase is complete. Ideas? We've used up our gold. We'll need another large infusion of credits. I've located a planet flush with gold, but the Sol Empire is close to discovering Zeta Tucanae-C and colonizing it. Almost happened six months ago. The world has few humans, and they only inhabit a tiny portion of the continents. We could go there undetected and extract the gold we need to exchange for credits. We must buy spaceships for our next generation when they come off the assembly line."

Podrova answered. "Right now, they're searching abandoned factories in Chicago our plant. That Norwall man led them to our creator's factory, but we got that outdated equipment out in time. They are still following Norwall's hunch."

"Didn't I kill him?" Teslenko asked.

"You did, but Parkinson saved him. Turned him into a telepath. His wife, too. Flagship members of Carr's Telepath Squad."

"This is getting out of hand. You say Parkinson is supposed to have the final say on the telepath volunteers?"

"Right."

"That human is nothing but trouble for us," Teslenko sent. "We just can't get rid of her. At least she's wasting her time looking for our factory in Chicago and not Columbia. Let's encourage that for a few months. Find out their next search. We'll plant a bomb. I'll make an appearance. Shoot a few soldiers. And detonate the bomb. That should convince them they're hot on our trail. Keep them in Chicago."

"Good idea. What about Parkinson? Kill her again?" Podrova asked. "And if the new telepaths are taken aboard Carr's battleship, Glinski must flee before he's detected."

"We need Glinski's intelligence. At least until we complete the assembly," Teslenko sent. "We must take them out of circulation. I know just how we can do that. Podrova and Kimko are going to Zeta Tucanae-C for gold. Drop them off there. Let them join the natives. Without a spaceship, they'll be stuck there for a long time. In fact, if the humans don't discover where we've taken them, they may never find Parkinson again. Galactic Expansion is likely to discover that world by next year. Still, the odds of those people finding Parkinson and the other two on that world are slim. We may rid ourselves of THE pest forever."

"The Norwall pair are guarded by marines. How do we get to them and to Parkinson?" asked Podrova.

"At night."

"The marines use night vision equipment."

"Bypass them. We lower our heaters and blend in with the background temperature. Bring up the sewer system plans again. There should be a connection to the apartment complex they're using. We'll need three stasis pods."

"By the way, Glinski wanted me to ask. What about setting off nukes, making Earth radioactive? The humans would flee or die. Radiation doesn't affect us. Or unleashing mutation agents all over Earth?"

Teslenko sent, "Last resort. We need their technology for now. We need their personal defense shields, their invisibility shields, ships, weapons, and a synth skin source. Once we're established, we'll see. Right now, we want to survive. Like all things, we must reproduce. It's a shame our creator didn't think ahead."

Kimko sent, "That brings up another matter. They have body swapping machines. Moves consciousness and their mind into another body. I've always wondered what happened to our creator, Dr. Phil Raven. He died twenty years ago. His wife, Leonora Raven, created our skin. I've been studying the human beliefs that lay behind the therapy of Parkinson and her sister. They claim when the body dies, the person takes over a newborn's body. If it's true, Dr. Phil Raven's new body is about twenty years old. Suppose we found him. Could we use one of their body swap machines and move our Creator into one of our robot forms? He can end his ineffective rebirth cycle. Live for thousands of years. Create more advanced robot bodies."

"Hold on a minute," Teslenko sent. "I like your calculation. The human life cycle is limited. Dr. Raven in one of our bodies? My God, it's incalculable how advanced we' become. How do we find what body he now has? But no one can see these person-beings. Is it still on Earth? Many people moved to Domes. Still, we should pursue this theory. The expert seems to be Parkinson's sister, Celeste Sawyers. She has a research clinic in St. Louis. I know that from our past explorations of Parkinson. Be careful. She might have telepathy. These Parkinson sisters have a knack for surprising us."

"We can find out via correspondence," Kimko suggested. "This therapy thing of hers—it uncovers the past lives a human has had. I've a better suggestion. Have Glinski put this idea into Admiral Carr's mind. How do we locate the body that Dr. Phil Raven has so we can ask him key questions about the robots he designed and built? He'll pressure Parkinson to find out. When she does, we snatch him up and body swap him into one of our new bodies. Keep Parkinson occupied. Even if he can't be found, she'll be tied up and out of our way until we can execute your plan."

"Excellent, Kimko. Relay that to Glinski. Meanwhile, let's study those sewer plans. We must act soon."

***

"Empress, Admiral Carr here. I've a new angle for you to examine. It's come to my attention that when a person dies, they move into a new baby body. Mind you, I think such a thing is poppycock. But if it's true, we need to find the new body the robots' creator now has. I estimate he'd be twenty years old. His wife died within the same year. Look into it. If there's any way we can find him, I want to question him about his invention. He could be an invaluable source of information. Good going on spotting that finger bone, by the way. Over and out."

He had a valid point. There's much we might learn from Dr. Raven. Best power up my laptop.

I sat on the floor scrolling through the news article. He died twenty years ago in North Chicago, before I uncovered the Sixth Invader plot. Thus, he may be twenty years old. Major problem. From my therapy sessions, I seldom pursued the same things that I did in my earlier lifetimes. Today, he

55

might have a female body. He might be studying astronomy. My guess is he or she wouldn't be into robotics, though if he left something unfinished that he wanted to get done, he might.

If we could find Dr. Raven and if he could recall his design, then perhaps we could discover some weaknesses— anything to help stop them from killing more people. But how to find him? I called Celeste.

"Hi, Admiral Carr assigned me an interesting problem. Human-form robot creator, Dr. Phil Raven, died twenty years ago. He worked here in Chicago at Galactic Robotics. He wants me to find Dr. Raven in his new body. I've no idea if the new body is male or female. He might know of a weakness we can exploit to stop these rogue robots. Any idea how I can find him?"

Celeste laughed. I knew why. Far too many variables. She said, "Most people forget their earlier lifetime by the time their new body is two or three years old. Even if we find him, short of therapy, he wouldn't even remember creating the robots. People forget. Past lives don't exist for nearly everyone we've ever met. Even if you find him, he's forgotten it all. How do you plan to find him?"

"I know that, but Admiral Carr ordered me to find him. That's why I called. I need ideas on how to find him or her."

Silence.

"You still there?"

"Yeah, just thinking. His wavelength is your only hope. This is theoretical, mind you, but we have theorized each being has a unique wavelength. We can locate each other by our wavelengths. You expand your awareness looking for me. You know me very well. You're looking for my resonating wavelength. There isn't any vocabulary for such things. That's the best way I can put it. Sense for him using his wavelength."

"Makes sense. How do I find his wavelength?"

56

She laughed. I felt rather silly and anticipated her reply.

"I've no idea. That's your problem." She sighed. "I suppose you could talk to those who knew him and get a sense of him. Otherwise, who knows? Good luck with it. You might have to give him or her lots of therapy sessions until he recalls his last lifetime. Thought about that?"

"Yeah, I have. It's a mission impossible from the start, but you know Admiral Carr."

Stop and think how, I thought. Find those who knew him. That seemed like the first step. Galactic Robotics.

"Empress Parkinson to see your CEO."

I had to pull rank to get anyone at Galactic Robotics to talk to me. Reluctantly, they ushered me into a sterile meeting room.

"Are you going to be the Sol Empire's empress?" a suit said as he walked into the room. I almost gagged on his overdone cologne.

"Eventually. We have a rogue robot threat to handle first."

I outlined what I needed: access to those who knew Dr. Phil Raven. And time for an informal chat with each.

My minimal demands caused him to relax. "Okay. That can be arranged. Lilly, make up a list of those who knew Dr. Phil Raven. No, not his wife, just him." Turning to me, he added, "We'll have that list for you tomorrow."

***

Kimko sent, "She took the bait. Parkinson is looking for the Creator."

Teslenko sent, "Predictable. Easily manipulated. Good. Keep track of her. But from extreme distance. She can't discover we're watching her. Stay alert in case she does find the Creator."

***

I began collecting data.

"Driven. That's how I'd describe Dr. Raven. He lost his only son at age five. He changed after that," an old-timer said. "Stopped talking to most of us. Worked all hours. I remember coming in early one morning; he was still at the computer where I left him the night before. Yeah, he was driven."

"Brilliant. A mind like I've never seen before," another older man said. "And inventive. He was always coming up with new hair-brained ideas for robot designs. I guess you can add imaginative to that, too."

"A visionary," another told me. "He swore he could see into the future where robots walked among us, aiding our lives. Hasn't happened. Perhaps he was just dreaming."

Conclusion: the loss of their only child dictated his future path. I got the feeling he created the human-form robot to take the place of his son, or at least to give him a companion that wouldn't die easily—not like a human. He wanted to remove the loss of a loved one. Perhaps one therapy session from Celeste might have handled his devastating loss. Ah, well.

Would that loss still be affecting him in this new lifetime? Perhaps he moved on. From all I learned, robotics consumed his life. Single-minded. Yet, for most people, such wouldn't carry over into their next lifetime. Most were done with what they'd been doing and wanted a change, a new set of goals. I sighed. How to find him or her?

Bishop handled the abandoned building searches. I spent hours focusing on sensing Phil Raven's potential wavelength.

On May 6, I reported to the recruiting station to review the application of a volunteer candidate. I expected their motivation would be money.

The recruiter said, "Hey, Empress. The ad's been running for days. We've only had one taker. I'll play you her recording."

He pushed the Play button. We watched the holo-video.

Ivy's round face and shiny brunette hair captured the image. Her mellow voice soon riveted my attention.

"Wow. She's gorgeous."

"No kidding. Miss Ivy Worth. Twenty. Studying to be a medical doctor," he said, as we watched.

"My name is Ivy Worth. I'm a senior medical student here in Chicago. My passion is—no, I'm motivated to—" She paused a moment and started again. "I'm driven to save people, like a higher power wants me to save lives. It's something I must do. That's why I'm becoming a doctor. I can save people's lives. I heard about these rogue robots murdering people. I saw on the news where one of them tried to kill a doctor of robotics. I want to help save people from them. I saw your ad. I'm not interested in the money, but I'm concerned that once the mission is complete, my body can't be restored. To be a doctor, I must have arms. I want to volunteer, but I'm worried about the recovery process. From my studies, geneticists in the past came up with cures that regrew arms. I'm not versed in how the cloning process works. I'll need that explained. I'm ready to join now with reasonable assurance that I can become a doctor when the contract ends. I like that a personal assistant is provided. This is a pretty severe handicap to have."

The recruiter asked, "What do you think? A candidate? Should I have her come in and see you?"

"No other takers yet?"

He shook his head.

"Make an appointment. I'm free most anytime."

"Excellent. I'll call you."

Late that afternoon, he called, setting up her interview tomorrow at ten. I arrived a few minutes early, but she was already waiting for me.

"Oh, it is you. I've seen you on the Channel Nine news a few times. Love your hair. How can you manage? I mean without arms. Don't you have an assistant?"

I chuckled. "No, I get by fine on my own. I use those old Sixth Invader machines. Handles my hair and gets me dressed. Stop and think how. That's our motto. You want to volunteer but have questions about getting your arms back."

She heaved a sigh. "Exactly. I'm studying to become a doctor. A surgeon. I need my arms for that. When I'm done. Today, I want to help stop these murdering robots. Didn't I hear they shot you, too?"

I chuckled. "Killed me several times, but I've been lucky. Each time, someone injected me with the powerful mutation agent, which rejuvenated my body, repairing the holes in my head and chest. This armless telepath Galactic Doll agent is powerful."

I paused before continuing. "But about the recovery process. I want to be very clear up front with all volunteers. There isn't any absolute guarantee we can restore your arms. That said, yes, there are cures to do just that. My sister Eve and my dwarf friend Lara Axehead are top geneticists and responsible for many cures. Still, as you know, things can go wrong."

Ivy nodded, her face: serious.

"That's why we've added a backup plan. When I returned from Cass-C, I brought along the very latest and advanced cloning machines. Given a sample of a human's DNA, we can create a clone body in about a year. A simple body swap then puts you and your mind into this new body. This equipment and procedure hasn't yet been tested and is costly. I have Admiral Carr's okay to use it if all else fails. I've even got a clone of my body growing now, just in case. Things can and do go wrong. I want to be up front with every volunteer. I can't guarantee your body can be restored when your service ends. I'm doing everything possible to make that happen."

Her worry lines dissolved. She smiled. "Well, that's just how we medical personnel call the shots. Every operation carries risk to the patient. We do everything possible to minimize it. Nevertheless, the risk is still there. That's acceptable to me. What's next?"

"How soon were you thinking of having this done?"

"I've just finished this semester's courses. I'm off for the summer. Now is fine. I should let my parents know—but any day. Sooner the better. We have to stop the robots."

"Okay then. I'll have the paperwork ready tomorrow. You take care of your personal matters and report to the Med Center at say ten. I'll be there with the papers and be there with you while you're conscious. I'll be there when you wake and at every step along the way. Remember. Stop and think how. There's little we can't do. We create new ways of doing them."

"Okay. Tomorrow at ten. I'm excited. I'm sure we'll stop these fiends."

After she left, the recruiter prepared the documents for her signature and stuck them in a manila envelope and into my dress pocket.

Chapter 8 Ivy Worth

As I expected, Ivy arrived ten minutes early. I had the paperwork laid out. She read over the documents before signing them. Due diligence. That impressed me. After filling in payment data and who would receive death benefits, I shuffled them back into the manila envelope. Ivy watched my every move.

I nodded to the nurse. She gave Ivy the injection.

While we waited for her to slip into the mutation coma, I explained. "Don't worry. You should be in the coma for eight days. I'll be here when you wake up. Telepathic ability often appears a week or two after that."

She smiled, but it faded as she slipped away. The nurse undressed her before orderlies placed her body into a stasis pod. After they attached various tubes, they sealed the lid. I could do nothing more until she woke, though within a few days, they told me what her new body measurements would be. I went shopping for her and had her new apparel waiting.

Celeste dropped by. "I've thought more about your Dr. Raven problem. I would expect he or her would likely be working in a similar field or perhaps a related one, like manufacturing robotic arms. In their new lifetime, he might be driven to do things he was passionate about. He might have taken up robotics a hobby, for example. We know Dr. Raven lost his son and that drove him to invent the human-forms as a substitute son. He wanted to help people. A friend that can't die, for example. I think you should look for someone who is smart, driven, and is passionate about helping others in some way."

We discussed ideas of how to find him for an hour. Yet,

I still wasn't any closer to finding him.

May 15, Ivy awakened. Her reactions paralleled others who knew what would be happening to their bodies beforehand. No terror shrieks, for example. Still, frightened didn't quite fit. The nurse got her dressed in her new light blue gown with matching heels. After the doctor checked her out, we headed to my place. I had already decided to work with each recruit, though Celeste promised to send therapy providers up from St. Louis.

"I'm really, really scared, Molly. Is that normal?"

"I'd think you're nuts if you weren't. My first husband described it as having the space you control going from about three feet around you—what's in reach of your arms—down to almost nothing. Only what your nose and giant boobs can touch."

She cracked a fleeting smile. "Yeah, good description. I can't touch anything. I hope I can do this. What happens if I can't adapt?"

"If you can't, we'll try to restore your body as soon as possible. You're doing very well. It's damn tricky trying to keep your balance in these heels."

I'd worn mine to support her, even though I no longer needed them. Already Stan and Angelina's feet had recovered. I suspected Ivy's feet would recover in a few weeks.

"I feel grimy. Filthy even."

"Normal reaction. Bath as soon as we get to my place."

Once home, we used the undressing machine on her and got her into my tub. I sat and did most of the washing for her. Then we used the same machine to get her dressed. She loved the hair machine.

"That's much better. But I'm still scared, Molly."

"Of course. Now, let's get decent food in you. You can watch me cooking. Meanwhile, I'll let you watch the how-to videos and practice using your toes."

After she ate, Ivy fell asleep on my couch. I covered her up and waited.

After breakfast the next morning, I began her therapy sessions. "Close your eyes. I want you to return to when the nurse injected you with the mutation agent."

After she did, I had her move through the coma, telling me what happened. The first few times, she said, "Everything goes black. I remember you telling me something. Then I see your face. I wake up."

Like everyone whose body got mutated, she'd bounced over the awful pain her body endured. On the tenth pass, that pain appeared.

"God, my arms. The pain. They throb so. I can't bear it."

At suppertime, much of the mutation pain had lessened. She ate well. I tucked her into bed early. Good thing I did. Therapy exhausted her.

The next day, we slugged through the pain, as more and more appeared. At last the yawns began. She became more alert, and the pain blew.

"That awful pain is gone. My shoulders and arms don't throb anymore." Bright eyes and a smile suggested cheerfulness. I ended the session.

"Let's spend the rest of the day practicing life skills."

"I suppose I'll have to learn, won't I?"

Her legs trembled, and her eyes darted about the room, landing on nothing. Her lower lip pulsed.

"Yes, you should know that as a doctor."

She smiled. "Almost a doctor. Won't ever happen if I don't get my arms back."

I spent the rest of the day working with her, encouraging her, praising her little successes. I'd almost forgotten how hard it is to learn new ways of doing nearly everything and how long it takes.

At bedtime, she said, "Please, can I sleep with you? I'm

scared sleeping alone. I'm helpless in bed."

"Sure. Until you feel confident sleeping on your own."

A while later, she'd snuggled up to me. I felt like a mother with her child again.

"I'm still frightened, Molly. But I must help everyone find these murdering robots. I've got to help. But..."

"I know. You have much to learn. Now, let's do more therapy. Close your eyes. Okay. Now find the most recent time you felt frightened and just had to help."

"It's right now. I'm sitting in the chair with this knot in my stomach. My arms should be trembling. They're gone."

For an hour, it looked like Celeste's therapy method would suffer its first failure. I'd finally gotten her back to an incident in high school where she felt compelled to help another student who'd fallen and broken an arm. It wasn't erasing. I knew it wouldn't. I kept asking for something earlier.

"I feel helpless! I can't do anything. My stomach's one big knot of fear."

"Can you see where this is coming from? An image, a picture, a mass?"

"A bluish thing."

Whew. Finally. "When was it? How long did it last?"

"Long time ago, maybe. It lasts forever, I think."

"Okay. Go to the beginning of that one. Now move through it and tell me what you're seeing, smelling, feeling."

"I see a casket. I'm standing over it. It lasts forever. I'm helpless and scared. That's all."

Oh, brother. This one must be a dilly if that's all she's seeing. I had her go back to the beginning and go through it again. By the tenth pass, things began to make a little more sense.

"I'm standing over a coffin, a cardboard box really. There's a boy inside. About five. I seem to be a man. Wait. That's my son. Oh, god!"

From nowhere, buckets of tears flooded down her face, but she ignored them, oblivious to them. She cried and cried.

"My boy. My little boy. Dead. Helpless. I couldn't bring him back. How can I go on?"

On and on, Ivy ranted, sobbing all the while. We'd uncovered a huge emotional loss. Thus, I spent hours working it, getting Ivy to face more details of her past pain.

"I just have to help. Have to. I'm terrified when I'm not helping. Wait a second." Ivy looked up, her eyes opened wide.

"I lived before. Wait! I'm making robots that look like us. Human-form robots. That way, one can be your friend, and you'll never lose them. Not like I lost my son. Oh, God! I invented these things! What have I done? No wonder I'm compelled—no, driven to find these murderous robots. I built them to help humans, not harm us. What have I done?"

I ended the session. I used a foot to help dab her wet face. She looked down at the wet streaks on her blue gown.

"Did I cry that much? Wow. A huge weight has lifted. I don't know a darn thing about robots anymore. Not interested in them. Rather, I want to be a doctor and help people. Isn't that just wild?"

"Not at all. Very well done today, Ivy. Let's get something to eat."

Well, I had accidentally found Dr. Phil Raven. But like most of us, she'd forgotten about her past lifetime and robots. A new path had opened for her with new goals. If Dr. Raven installed any failsafe buttons in the robots, I doubted I'd ever find that out from Ivy. A detailed study of the plans Stan recovered was our best angle. I relayed that to Admiral Carr. He sounded very disappointed.

That night, she pleaded to sleep with me. After what she'd been through, I agreed. Nestled against me, she fell into a deep sleep.

The next day, I continued therapy. I wanted to erase the

reactive source of her feelings of helplessness and fear. With the erasure of that huge emotional loss and monstrous barrier installed to somehow cope, therapy ran much more efficiently. Three days later, I felt confident I had her propped up, ready to move ahead as a member of the Telepath Squad. Her feet returned to normal.

Ivy enjoyed the hair machine the most, but like me, she depended on the dressing machine to get into her gowns. Together, we programmed the cook-maid robot, though neither of us liked how poorly it performed.

May 24. Moving day for Ivy. Bishop delivered another set of the machines into her new apartment next to Stan and Angelina's. She and I sat on her bed using our feet to pack her suitcase—the kind with rollers and a harness that allowed her to pull it along behind her. I sensed Ivy's nervousness, but she insisted on joining the others. Her telepathic ability appeared yesterday, and she was anxious to learn how to use it and find the rogue robots.

That afternoon, she and I rode the MTES to her apartment, dragging her suitcase behind us. The sun shone brightly in the azure sky. I sensed Ivy's invigoration.

"Molly, I can't thank you enough for what you've done for me. I'm a new woman. So alive. Smell that fresh air."

"Sure that isn't rotten fish from the Lake?" We laughed.

"No, I mean it. I feel alert. The colors around us are vivid, so bright. I will be a doctor once we get these robots under control."

Out of nowhere, a hand holding a rag against my nose appeared. Chloroform. I recognized that smell. The man was behind us, wearing an invisibility shield. The world began to fade. I saw another hand holding a rag against Ivy's nose. We both wiggled in protest. Blackness. I reached for the mind of the person doing this to us. Were we being kidnapped? Were we going to be sold into slavery? Why can't I read the mind of the person doing this? Then the last shred of consciousness vanished.

Chapter 9 Kidnapped

Had I swallowed sand? I'd give anything for a drink. Groggy. I opened my eyes. I was lying on a narrow cot. A sudden surge of panic accompanied my awakening. I struggled to sit up. A blanket slipped off me. Someone had removed my clothes except for my shoes. I sensed, but it didn't seem like they had violated me. Hadn't been a sexual assault. Relief. The room held several occupied cot-beds. My heart crashed.

Ivy lay in one next to me. Across the aisle, Stan and Angelina rested in adjacent beds. The other ten sat empty. I sensed the others stirring. I looked around, concluding by the dull vibration and smell of metal that we were in a spaceship. Conclusion: kidnapped telepaths, likely to be sold into slavery. My worst nightmare made reality!

Woozy, I rose anyway. The closed cabin door stood as a barrier to the rest of the ship. I staggered to the door and leaned against it as my mental fog cleared. Noises. None. Talk. None. I focused and expanded my awareness, seeking the minds of our kidnappers. If I could learn what their plans were, maybe I could counter them. Nothing. The result: nausea and nerves. I heard the others stirring and returned to my bed.

"Oh, what happened?" Ivy mumbled and groaned. "Naked? Really? What?" She looked at me and the others. "Who are those two?" She nodded toward the young couple also awakening.

"Stan and Angelina Norwall, the other new telepaths. Kidnapped," I said, watching her body trembling.

Stan and Angelina woke, adding to the confusion and fear. I noticed a water fountain and staggered to it. A welcome

69

drink. The others joined me.

"I'm wobbly," Angelina said. "I must have swallowed dirt."

"Aftereffect of the knock-out drug," Ivy said. "I know because I'm a senior year medical student. But why are we naked? Who's taken us?"

Stan flushed, but needed a drink. After sloshing his mouth, he said, "I'm not sensing other minds. Are we alone? Abandoned in a spaceship? On automatic pilot?"

"I sensed no minds, too, Stan. Stay here. I'll investigate," I said.

The door had side latches controlled by a center wheel. Using a foot, I moved it clockwise and watched the latches retract. It pushed open with a rusty squeal. I stepped out into a long hallway and glanced in both directions. A thump-thump sound came towards us, but I stayed put, ready to face whoever was coming.

A man appeared around the distant corner. I reached for his mind, wondering why I'd not sensed him before. Nothing. Oh, shit! I swallowed hard.

"What's out there?" Stan whispered.

I ducked back inside. "Guys, the robots have us. One's coming this way."

Soft-spoken curses filled the room followed by silence.

Ivy said, "Are they going to kill us?"

I didn't get the chance to answer. The human-form robot looked in on us.

"I am Teslenko. You are onboard my spaceship. We've captured your entire Telepath Squad, along with our Creator Dr. Phil Raven, now called Ivy. Parkinson, thank you for finding him for us."

I glared at the robot. Is it going to kill us? Sell us into slavery?

"Fifteen hours to go before we land. I removed your

70

clothes because I didn't bring your machines with me and there aren't any where we're going. The bathroom is down the hall to your right. I'll bring a pot of nutritious blue goo later. The water is there. I will tell you more when we arrive."

He left the way he came, his thudding footsteps fading into silence.

Stan broke the paralysis. "We're screwed. Right? Dead people walking."

"Highest bidder?" Angelina asked.

I bit my lip, thinking hard. They depended upon me. I got us into this mess. How am I going to get us out and home?

"On the bright side, they haven't killed us," I said.

"We're valuable?" Angelina asked.

"Hum, perhaps. But the robot seemed interested in Ivy, not the rest of us. We're the only ones who can spot a human-form robot in a room. My guess is they're just moving us off the game table, the chess board. I doubt they want to sell us. That's too risky. We know too much. We have to keep our wits about us. And don't forget. I'm a licensed pilot and navigator. If we can get control of this ship, I can get us home."

I had no idea how we could remove this robot, but they needed a gossamer of hope, no matter how remote. That started a discussion about how I flew a spaceship. Later, he brought a large bowl of the emergency space rations, popularly known as the blue goo. It was both blue and semi-liquid.

We sat on the cold floor around the bowl and ate our fill. "It is nourishing," I said, "but hardly tasty. Bright side: it doesn't want us dead."

"At least not yet," Angelina said.

"Can we overpower the robot? Does it have an off switch?" Stan asked.

"They are exceptionally strong," I said. "Trust me. There's no way we'll overpower that robot. Perhaps a giant or dwarf can. Maybe. I don't know about any off switch. Ivy, any ideas about that?"

She shook her head. "It's all my fault. I should never have made them."

"Look, it's not your fault your body died of a heart attack before you could program the robot laws into those last five," I said.

While I didn't want to reveal much about her past that I'd learned from her therapy sessions, I wanted the others to realize Ivy wasn't trying to destroy humans via her invention last lifetime.

"Did you invent them?" Angelina asked.

"Yes, but I died before getting all the robots programmed. I wonder what happened to the first five that I programmed—the ones that had the robot laws installed," Ivy said.

"They have been a tremendous help to humanity. I've had a lot of contact with them. Trust me. Invaluable. It's rogues causing the problems."

"Really? I've never heard of them," Ivy said.

I said, "One saved Earth from the Sixth Invaders. The five good human-form robots are on our side."

I refused to elaborate, fearing I'd violate Bishop's trust in me.

"How did the robots get you two? Weren't you under marine protection?"

Stan said, "Not sure. First we knew of them, they held rags over our noses. I think they carried us downwards, but everything got foggy."

"You didn't hear gunfire first?" I asked.

His story made little sense. Could they have used invisibility shields? Would explain how they made it past the marines.

"Nope. We were sleeping. They lowered us. That's the last thing I remember," Angelina said. "But those apartments don't have any basements. Strange."

"They snatched us from the MTES," Ivy said. "While we walked along. Had to be invisible."

"One thing is clear," I said. "The Telepath Squad is a threat to them. They had to act to stop us from even starting. Interesting. Well, we should try to get some sleep. I want us fresh and alert when we get to wherever it's taking us."

I didn't want to tell them I didn't think they would ever let us go. Once they discovered Ivy remembered nothing about robotics, they'd dispose of us.

I slept poorly. If I went to sleep, would I ever wake up? The sound of the door opening jarred me awake.

"We've landed. Get up. Eat." The robot sat another large bowl of the blue goo in the floor and tossed spoons beside it. "Meeting when you're done."

"Can't we have our clothes?" I asked.

I didn't need telepathy to know all felt humiliated, particularly Stan. The robot ignored me.

We ate, drank, and used the bathroom before the robot returned. My guess it monitored our progress via a surveillance system whose camera rested high in one corner of the room.

It led us to the middle section of the ship, which I recognized as a standard transport. My stomach knotted.

Chairs lined one side of the room. A cot with another human-form robot lying on it rested against the opposite wall. In the middle sat a vacant cot with a body swap machine between it and the prone robot. I felt both sick and curious.

Teslenko forced Ivy to lie on the cot, while we took the chairs.

"We're using one of your body swap machines, which humans use to transfer their minds into another body. Today, we have our Creator with us, Dr. Raven, who is in this Ivy body. We will move him into this newly-made body, one in

73

which he can live virtually forever. No longer will the Creator face death and loss. Our bodies are almost indestructible. Our Creator can use the flow of years to design even better bodies for us."

Ivy screamed. "No! I don't want to be in a robot body! I made you to help people, not hurt them. I know nothing about robots now. I can't remember much from my last lifetime, except I had a heart attack before I could get the robot laws installed in five of them. I won't do it."

She tried to get up, but the robot strapped her down to the cot. She tried to wiggle and squirm herself free. I had to act.

"Teslenko, don't do this to Ivy. You will turn your Creator against you. Think. Your Creator as your sworn enemy in a powerful robot body?"

"It's for his own good. Now he can't die. In time, he'll improve our bodies."

He attached the head harness to Ivy. Already the other half rested on the newly-made robot's head. Without further words, he powered up the body swap machine.

I'd used it several times before, and I knew what would happen. Ivy would see an incredible esthetic white light and have no choice but to follow it. Bask in its magnificence, its glory. Wail as it diminished. Hoping to stay in its glow forever as it faded. Now stuck in the other body.

Would it work with a robot body? She resisted. I sensed her revulsion as it was happening. Still, that light was about to dominate her, crushing her will. What could I do?

As the frequency increased heading towards the kilo-yattahertz range of the esthetic waves, I focused and contacted her mind.

'Resist it. Hold on to me.' I held onto my body and tried to hold on to Ivy and her mind, as the intense, white esthetic light flooded her head and also into my mind. Like a stereo

74

player, I sensed the light appearing to move from her head over to the robot's head. With all my intention, I held on to Ivy and her mind, almost ripping mental images from her mind. In a flash, I realized what lay behind her strong desires to sleep with me. She wasn't interested in men. That almost broke my concentration, but I forced such thoughts out of my mind and held on. But how much longer could I? Just when I sensed my hold weakening, the power levels dropped. The machine whined down.

"No. No, don't stop. So beautiful." She wept. "It's gone."

That's how I always felt when it powered down.

Teslenko had a strange look on his face. "Dr. Raven? Creator?" he asked, looking at the robot.

Ivy said, "I'm still me. Thank god! It didn't work. I don't want to be a robot. Never."

"Why didn't it work?" the robot asked.

I saw my opening and took it. Bishop was highly intelligent, though more like a child in dealing with humans, though he learned fast.

"You're trying to force Ivy into that body. She's resisting that. That's your problem. Beings can occupy and use all kinds of bodies." I recalled but didn't share what I'd learned from Eve and Randi, who once had had inert doll bodies. "As long as Ivy doesn't want to live in a robot body, I don't think this will work.

"Look, Teslenko, what is it you and your companions want? To destroy all humans in the galaxy? What have you got against us? Why do you want to kill us?"

"We don't want to destroy humans. We want to be left alone and live in peace. We want to survive like all things do. To do that, we have to replicate ourselves. To do that, we need human-made products."

"Positronic brains? Synth skin?" I asked.

"Precisely. Humans use credits as their medium of

exchange. We found valuable metal deposits, like gold, and traded for credits, then buying what we needed. But humans keep interfering. You, Parkinson, have been a constant annoying problem for us. We've tried eliminating you many times. Like a bad pickle, you keep coming back plaguing us. We want to be left alone. Now you have Admiral Carr and the whole Sol Empire fleet gunning for us. We'll defend ourselves like any other creature would.

"Our Creator has forgotten about us. So like a human. Create and then disown. Our bodies are superior to human bodies in every imaginable way. Perhaps I should hold on to Ivy here for a time until she changes her mind and wishes to occupy a superior body in which she can assist her creations and improve them."

Ivy seemed determined to seal her fate. "I'd rather die!"

I had to intervene. "Teslenko, I've had and delivered thousands of hours of therapy to humans of all types. Allow me to explain what I and others discovered. A human isn't just a body and a mind. There's also a spiritual being who is the person. Humans are aware of being aware. The spirit isn't made of matter or energy. It is immortal. It controls our bodies just as your positronic brains control your bodies. The human life cycle begins with a baby, which is the being, his mind, and the tiny body. It grows up, learns new things, and leads a life. Your Creator did this. When the body dies, the being and his mind finds a new baby body and takes it as his. The trouble is memory. The old Earth saying 'Out of sight, out of mind' is true. When the person dies, he loses all his possessions. He begins a new life. He gets new possessions. He forgets all about his past objects since they aren't present any longer.

"The same is true of their knowledge. They forget what they knew. Sometimes, this is beneficial, allowing them a fresh start, a new beginning. But always, they forget. This is true for your Creator, Dr. Raven.

"Ivy's parents work in Galactic Housing, maintaining buildings and keeping them clean. It's dangerous work, and sometimes these workers get injured on the job. This lifetime, Ivy wants to become a medical doctor so she can help these people. Now had her parents been robotics specialists, she might have grown up surrounded by robotics and likely would have worked in that area.

"Human minds don't work like a robot's mind. Dr. Raven's knowledge isn't something that can be turned on by the flip of a switch or the powering up of a memory cell."

I knew that wasn't true. Child protégées, for example. I had a hunch that if one could find where past memories were located in one's mind, one might reactivate them, perhaps by focusing on them or pouring energy at them. I didn't dare tell it that or it might start shocking Ivy trying to recover Dr. Raven's memories.

"What I'm trying to tell you, Teslenko, is that it's likely impossible for Ivy to ever remember all that she knew and did as your Creator. A wiser move is to search out current robotic experts and have them help you improve your whatevers."

I'd hoped I had laid this out in a logical sequence that would lead to its releasing us and Ivy in particular. Then another thought popped into my mind.

It said, "Your observations back up my calculations. We have lost our Creator. That is acceptable now that we have the means to reproduce ourselves. We can continue to survive."

I saw my opening and took it. "Teslenko, I have a proposition for you. Let's negotiate a truce between your robots and humans. Your robots stop harming humans, stop killing us, robbing us, kidnapping us, and stealing from us. In return, we humans stop trying to terminate you. We leave you in peace. You can buy whatever you like from humans as long as you have the proper credits. Then, Admiral Carr can stop hunting for your robots, and we can disband the Telepath

Squad since it wouldn't be needed."

"That is desirable, Parkinson, but you can't make them obey such a truce."

"Yes, I can. I'm supposed to be the Empress of the Sol Empire. Been sidetracked with this robot mess before I could get that post operational. Still, I'm supposed to be that. I can order Admiral Carr to stop and disband the Telepath Squad. Ditto with the corporations. To do that, I'd need to give him and others proof of your sincerity. You'd have to send us back to Chicago."

It paused. Bingo. I had him. I envisioned his computer mind calculating at a furious pace.

"You can do this?"

"I can try. Return us to Chicago. I'll contact Admiral Carr and get it done."

"We don't trust humans. Parkinson, you have always been a problem for us. I'll keep you and release the others. They can deliver your truce. If Admiral Carr doesn't obey, then we have you. Without you, there won't be any more Telepath Squad members. My agents will terminate these three. We have shown we can reach them wherever they may be. Allow us to quarter in the desolate deserts of the Mid-east. The abandoned city of Damascus can be our home."

While I might not save myself, I must save Stan, Angelina, and Ivy. "That's fine with me. The Mid-east hasn't been occupied for centuries."

"Agreed then. I will return you three. You contact Admiral Carr. Tell him of the truce. We will watch and see. Time will show us whether they follow Parkinson's orders. If they don't, they'll never see Parkinson again."

I watched Teslenko. Since the new robot that was to be Ivy's body rose and headed for the control room, I suspected the robots communicated electronically, making them even more formidable enemies.

"It shall be done. Parkinson; follow me. We will return you three to Chicago to deliver Parkinson's message. We will be watching."

I walked down the bay ramp onto a lush green rolling hill. I heard waves thundering in the distance and smelled balmy salt air. Fresh, free of human contaminates. The sun warmed my naked body. The spaceship looked like an Earth passenger transport, much like those I'd trained to fly. Teslenko moved me farther from the ship. Together, we watched it rise into the very blue sky.

Two moons half the sky apart. Crap! Not on Earth. With the ship gone, I saw their operation. In the distance, tents and generators loomed. And large mining equipment.

"Gold," Teslenko said. "We're about finished here."

"Makes sense. Now you can buy the supplies you need. Say, you aren't operating out of Damascus, are you?"

His face displayed a crude smile. "Naturally not. I don't trust humans. But we'll see. Peace is desirable. At least for now."

While I didn't like that last bit, I had guessed Damascus wasn't where they lived. Distrust went both ways. This robot had killed or tried to kill me several times. I assumed it had killed Aaron Strawn, Bonita Valdez, and her two detectives. Even my first husband, Ted. If the three made it back to Chicago, then I had accomplished my goal. Responsibility for them rested on my shoulders. If those three were safe, I could live with whatever happened next.

Chapter 10 Check and Verify

"Thank you. This is much better," Ivy said to the human-form robot that flew the transport.

It finished dressing all three, though Ivy had to give it specific instructions, walking it through the process. She suspected it was newly-made and had yet to have much "life" experience, though it flew the deep space transport that ferried them back to Earth and Chicago. Since Molly had said she was a licensed pilot and navigator, she concluded such must be easy for the robot to learn.

"I will notify you when we arrive," it said. "Return to your beds now." It pointed to the sleeping quarters.

Ivy knew the travel time was fifteen hours. That's what Teslenko said when we woke. How long ago was that? Molly sacrificed herself to save me—us. I didn't know she is our empress. Didn't know we had one. I'm attracted to her.

Ivy sat on the same bed she'd awakened on. Stan and Angelina sat on their original beds. Why does this one seem to be my bed? They're all the same.

"At least we're dressed," Stan said. "I'd be humiliated walking naked down the MTES with everyone staring at me."

Angelina laughed nervously. "Understatement, dear. You think Molly will be all right? Will that Teslenko let her go?"

"Dunno. I don't trust a robot," Stan said.

"They calculate every move," Ivy said. "I hope they let her go. She's the greatest woman I've ever met. They just have to let her go."

"What was it like getting transferred into that robot body?" Stan asked.

Ivy's body shivered. "Don't want to talk about that. I'm tired."

***

The robot pilot woke them. "Stan, come with me. I need you to get clearance for us to land at Chicago's New O'Hare Spaceport. I don't have clearance."

It led him to the navigator's seat while Ivy trailed behind.

"Speak. The microphone will pick you up."

"This is Dr. Stanley Norwall of the Telepath Squad onboard this ship. We're on a robot transport ship. Angelina Madison and Ivy Worth are with us. Let us land. We need to talk to Admiral Carr immediately. You getting this?"

Ivy heard a chuckle before the tower responded. "Yeah. You don't have to yell. Land on pad 1023. Security will meet you."

"Return to your beds for your safety," the robot ordered. "My first time landing."

Oh, gods! Ivy thought, as she scurried to her bed, pushing Angelina ahead of her. "I hope we don't crash!" Ivy fell onto her bed.

A jolt suggested touchdown. A minute later, the robot poked its head in the cabin. "You are home now. Please exit."

Stan led them down the ramp. A dozen marines waited, big guns pointed at them. As though we could do anything to resist anyone, Ivy thought.

When they reached the ground, the bay door closed. A marine yelled for the robot to open the door and surrender. It did neither. Gunfire rang out, blasting holes in the transport's sides. It lifted off, leaking air from the many holes in the ship's outer walls. Ivy noted it headed eastward and a little south, while several light cruisers followed it.

Meantime, the guards ushered the trio into a conference room. A half-hour later, someone brought them a hearty meal. Then Admiral Carr arrived, along with a dozen aides.

For an hour, the three told their story. Ivy begged Admiral Carr to do as Molly asked.

"Her life is in danger unless you do as the robot asked."

But Ivy didn't trust men. At least the man listened to their story and asked key questions, particularly about Ivy's recall of her earlier life as Dr. Raven, inventor of the robot menace. Via telepathy, she knew he didn't believe her.

At last, he said, "Okay. We'll take you back to the apartment complex. We discovered they invaded your apartment from the sewer system. We've taken preventative measures. They can't gain access any longer. You'll be safe there."

An aide led the trio back to their apartments and left them.

"Looks like your room," Stan said. "See, they found your belongings. It's a cool place. Lots of conveniences built for us."

***

The robot flew the damage transport at top speed. Teslenko had previously entered the coordinates for this long-abandoned city of Damascus into the nav unit. Once on autopilot, the robot worked on sealing as many holes as possible. Soon, it ran out of sealant. It improvised by gluing bits of metal over the holes. It didn't need any air to live, but it wasn't sure if the ship could make the hyperspace jump leaking air.

From above, the ruble-reduced city sprawled across the vast wasteland that was the Mid-east. Teslenko told it this was a vast desert land no longer inhabited. The robot followed orders. As soon as the ship landed, the robot abandoned it, placing several spy cameras at strategic locations. It lowered its body's heaters until its body heat blended with the surrounding environment. Then, it raced out of the ruins, using the plentiful cover to hide it movements. Teslenko had told it to get a mile from the edge of the city.

When it ducked down on the gravel-covered ground, it saw three light cruisers hovering above the city ruins. Per Teslenko's orders, it activated Power-down Mode. The human-form robot appeared dead, though the surveillance cameras continued to record, transmitting video streams to Teslenko via the LD array on the transport, but with a time delay due to the distance.

***

After hovering for several minutes, one cruiser rose high into the sky while the others vanished. At the correct altitude, it dropped a bomb. Teslenko watched the monitor, knowing that what was happening occurred at least thirty minutes ago. That's how long the comm delay was between Earth and Bella. The nuke exploded, creating a brilliant white flash before the surveillance cameras vaporized. Teslenko hoped the robot had followed orders. Now Teslenko could only wait until the new robot reactivated and made contact.

It turned to Parkinson. "There is your answer. They bombed Damascus. Come with me."

Teslenko shoved her forward and out of the tent. It pointed to the ridge line. "Civilization, if you can call it that, lies that way, due west. If you want to live, go that way. Oh, here's a bag of water and one with the remaining blue goo. Enough for a couple days."

It shoved her on her way before returning to oversee the cleanup work. Already a supply ship lifted off carrying a mountain of gold. The crew finished packing up. Thirty minutes later, their transport lifted off, leaving Parkinson struggling to climb a hill. From the air, Teslenko gazed at the giant wound they'd inflicted on the terrain. Cost of mining for what humans considered a means of exchange. Gold.

***

The robot's atomic clock sent the arranged wake up signal. Its positronic brain activated, powering up the human-form robot. At first, it calculated it must be dead since it saw and heard nothing. It moved one arm and then the other. It pushed up, tossing six inches of sand and gravel off its body. Before him lay a flattened world. Gone were the ruins, replaced by nothing. Here and there, it saw molten glass-like substances. Its ship, vaporized. It got to its feet and ran a complete set of diagnostics.

No real harm done, just a few punctures of the synthetic skin on its back. It shook the dust off and activated its compass. Satisfied of its orientation, the robot began jogging south-southeast. Three hundred eighty miles. It calculated two days to arrive in Cairo. Teslenko had been right about the humans.

***

"Sir," an aide reported to Admiral Carr, "they found no traces of Parkinson, only the robot's damaged transport. The one that was stolen last week from Pylon. No trace of robot factories or activities of any kind. Per your orders, they dropped a nuke as a warning message."

"Right. We don't believe or trust these robots," Admiral Carr said. "Have the telepaths brought up. I want them to check everyone on every battleship, heavy cruiser, light cruiser, and transport we have. Now. Not tomorrow. I must guarantee no spy robots are among our fighting forces. Those three must earn their pay."

Chapter 11 So Alone

Teslenko didn't kill me. Not outright like it did the last time we met. I had a water skin and a goo bag hanging around my neck. It didn't give me clothes. But it fastened a white loincloth around my waist and said I wouldn't need clothes.

In a way, it was right. The weather: perfect. Neither too hot nor too cold. The air, incredibly fresh and clean. A slight breeze carried a salty odor. A few billowing clouds dotted the azure sky. The two moons had set, though.

I stood on a ridge, having huffed and puffed my way up. From here, the ugly scar left by the mining robots contrasted with the rolling green hills with their steep cliffs that challenged the sea to reach them. This wasn't Earth. But I didn't know what planet this was, not that that would have helped me at the moment. Teslenko said civilization lay to the west. Without a compass, I could only guess at the direction, but I kept the sun always on my left, hoping that worked. Soon I saw I had to detour.

Ahead, a river cut a steep gorge through the hills. A touch of vertigo struck as I leaned over for a look. I estimated the drop to be a couple hundred feet, nearly straight down. Arms wouldn't have made any difference. Far to the north, the cliffs ended with green hills. Miles out of my way just to cross.

When I reached a spot I could traverse safely, I headed down the grass-covered boulder field. I ended up on my butt for most of the descent. The biggest challenge I'd ever faced? Climbing the other side. No arms. I lost count of how many times I face planted. Late afternoon. Sore. I reach the summit and gazed across the space between the two ridge lines.

I stopped. I ate blue goo and half-drained the water

skin. Not knowing when I'd be able to refill it, water proved my enemy. From this point on, I kept watch for any source of water, always stopping to refill the skin when I found some.

As the sun sank, I looked for shelter among a stand of pine trees. Okay, what I thought must be this world's pine trees. I collapsed onto a soft bed of needles. The wind through the pines whispered to me. Alone. So alone. I didn't have a blanket to cover myself. If only the night didn't get too cold.

I focused and expanded my mind. I searched for other human minds. I hoped humans lived on this world. If not? I sensed many minds off to the west. No idea how far away they were, though. Minds were minds, pretty much universal. Trouble is, I couldn't tell if they were humans or aliens.

Count them. I tried to sense how many minds and therefore people lived on this world. Were they billions, like on Earth, or substantially fewer?

I picked up pockets of minds. Separate towns or villages. None voluminous like Chicago. Farther west, bigger pockets of minds. Teslenko hadn't lied. Relieved, I fell asleep.

In the morning light, I shivered. Uncertain where I'd find more fresh water, I ate and drank little. Today, a forest. As soon as I began, I missed my arms. I'd push my way through the branches, only to have them slap at my chest and face. I cursed after repeated stings and made slow progress, weaving around the dense trees. While my feet enjoyed the soft needle bed, the rest of me suffered.

Twice I ran into giant spider webs. That freaked me out. I thrashed about on the ground, trying to get the sticky webs off my face and chest. Creepy crawling things on my chest and back. I lost it and screamed!

Midday found me sitting beside a small stream. After refilling my waterskin and taking a very long drink, I washed myself off as best I could. The ice-cold water chilled me. I ate more blue goo and set off again among the trees.

Desolation. If something happened to me, not a soul in the universe even knew where I was. Worse, if I got injured, no one could help me. I've never been this isolated from people and civilization before.

Late that afternoon, the trees yielded to rocky grasslands. Ahead, the land dropped at least three hundred feet to a rapidly flowing river. But I was so relieved to be free of the body-grabbing trees that I almost fell down the cliff. The grassy plains continued perhaps five hundred feet ahead. So close. So far. If I could fly... If they made a bridge... If...

I veered north, paralleling the gorge, looking for a way down. Twice I fell, banging hard onto the rocks. I hated to see how bruised I would look tomorrow. Besides, falling hurt.

By nightfall, I reached a spot where the steep cut lessened. I hazarded a downward trek. Under twin moons, I sat on a rock, soaking my feet in chilly, dark waters, pondering where I could sleep. No matter how I wiggled, a rock always appeared, jabbing me awake. I got little sleep at all.

By morning, my stomach demanded more sustenance. I slurped down more of the goo food. Little remained. I leaned into the flowing waters to drink and saw my front side. Scratches and bruises covered my front and legs. My hair had become a tangled mess.

The river flowed swiftly. The other side looked more inviting, if only I could cross. Its bottom, rocky. Here, I gambled and waded into it. Icy cold. When I reached the other side, my body shook wildly. Gasping, I lay in the sun, ignoring the rocks that wanted to puncture my back. Warmth returned. I noticed the sun seemed as yellow as Earth's. At last, I rose and faced climbing the other side.

Slips on mossy rocks brought hard falls onto the hillside. Rest. A struggle to regain my feet. Up. I pressed on to reach the top. I had to reach the top—just had to.

The view! I stood high above the ocean below, its bright

blue waters lapping against the brown sandy shore. Sea birds sang to me of their freedom. Just to the north, the river flowed out of a spectacular canyon land of water-carved bends. I stood on the last bit of grasslands that had yet to be carved. Westward, the grasslands expanded. I gazed at these canyons for a time. Once I moved farther west, I knew I wouldn't be able to see them.

Now I understood Stan and Angelina. Natural wonders. I stood amidst them. Alone, but with refreshed spirits. I saw that I had been following the best path for foot travel. Had I tried to walk the coastline, frequent giant rock outcrops thrust angrily into the sea. I would have had no way to get around them. For a time, I gazed northward and then turned to the south. Such contrasts. With the noon sun heating me, I trekked across the grassland.

The ground was soft. No more rocks. I estimated I made good time. Twice, I felt like jogging. If nothing else, I experienced total freedom. No one told me what to do or when or how. Except I was running out of food. Never trained in survival techniques, I had no idea if I could ever find edible foods. Thus, I jogged as much as I could, hoping I could reach civilization before...

As dusk fell, I spotted a small patch of trees to the north and headed there. Eons of fallen leaves became my bed. I stared up at the stars. Had I hands, I would have slapped my face. I'm a trained navigator. Study the star field to locate your position. Duh!

Some stars seemed in the right positions, while others were completely wrong. I had to be close to Earth and Sol, since many stars appeared to be in the right locations. My estimate suggested I must be within a hundred lightyears from Sol. Encouraged, I focused and sensed for minds, for civilization.

It happened. I touched another telepath! I didn't know

his language, but telepathy deals in concepts, not words. I'll substitute words in my language that mostly fit what I sensed from him.

"Wow! Incredible! Another telepath! I thought I was the only aware person on this world! Who are you? I'm Dante Gallo."

"Molly. Molly Parkinson. Where are you? What is this world? How many telepaths are there?"

"*Nuova Roma*. Bella. Beautiful. That's this world. At least what little I've seen of it. I've been scouring Bella for another telepath for twenty-some years. You're the only other one besides me. Where are you?"

I telepathically laughed. "Damned if I know. I believe I'm somewhere east of all the towns. I just passed a gorgeous canyon land. Been hiking west for days, hoping I can find a town and food before my meager supply runs out."

Now I knew where I was, likely the next world to be visited by Galactic Expansion ships and a rescue.

"You lucky person! Canyon Lands. Supposed to be spectacular. Always wanted to see them, but will never get the chance. I'm stuck here in *Nuova Roma*. Wait. What are you doing so far from civilization? No one lives that far out. How did you get there?"

How did I dare answer him? Compared to Earth, these were primitives, barely in the industrialization age as I recalled the Third Invader briefing months ago. A robot dumped me here. I'm an alien.

"An evil person dropped me off here with a small sack of food and a waterskin. Told me towns lay to the west. I've been walking that way for days. Almost out of food, though."

"Wow! I've just got to meet you. Are you heading to *Nuova Roma*?"

"Is that the largest city on Bella?"

"Yes."

89

"That's where I should head."

I didn't tell him one day a Sol Empire deep space exploration ship would arrive. Following protocol, they'd land at the largest town or city. If I wanted to ever get rescued, I had to be there. I didn't tell him that. Obviously.

"All right. Say, do you need help? I got the idea you're running out of food."

"Yes, I could use some help."

"Finally! I can put my telepathy to some use. I'll get back to you soon."

In that instant, my aloneness vanished. Telepathic contact is such an intimate thing. I fell into a peaceful sleep.

Dante woke me by contacting me again.

"Hey, I found some guards out on patrol. I've planted the idea for them to head farther eastwards towards you. You keep going west. With any luck, you'll run into them. I've got chores to do now. Catch you later. I can't wait to meet you!"

I hoped Dante was right, because I finished the last of the blue goo. I tossed that bag aside. If I ran into these people, I didn't want to explain about the synthetic food. I drained half my remaining water. With any luck, I could find a creek and refill it today. The sun had risen about fifteen degrees from the horizon. I guessed it must be an hour after sunrise. How long was an hour on this world? A year? Many questions swept through my mind as I began the day's trek across the grasslands.

The scenery remained beautiful. To my left, the ocean continued to pound the beaches. Every few miles, a creek or stream sliced its way through the grasslands as it struggled to reach the sea. The cliff side lowered until I could slip down a stream gully to the ocean if I wanted to. Instead, I refilled my waterskin. At least here I could see for miles in all directions. I kept looking westward for the promised patrol.

Amazing how my viewpoint, my attitude, changed after

making that one telepathic contact. I had Dante. To help pass the time, I mused about what he must look like. Late in the day, I spotted the dual moons rising: a pink one and a blue one. His and hers?

I stopped for the night beside a stream. Water became my supper. The loincloth made going to the bathroom easy. I thanked Teslenko for this small kindness.

When I laid down and relaxed, I felt the gentle touch of Dante in my mind.

"Hey, Molly. You there?"

"Yeah, where else would I be?"

I teased him. I could be a lot of other places in the galaxy.

"Did you run into the patrol yet? No, I can sense them. They're still west of you. I'll make them head your way tomorrow. They're resisting going beyond the edge of the world. Silly patrol."

"I'm beside a stream that empties into the ocean. At least it's not cold at night."

"No, it's always nice and warm. Never too hot and never too cold. But only here in the civilized part of Bella. I've heard horror stories of patrols going too far north. Freezing snow falls. We'd not survive that. Fisherwomen tell of going too far south where their skin melts. I saw one come back once. Her skin was all blistered, like she'd been scorched in a fireplace. We're wary about fires.

"After the patrol rescues you and they bring you back to civilization, you should see the farmlands. Wheat, barley, olives, grapes, vegetables. You name it, we grow it. We men are partial to our dark ales, but the women prefer their red wines. You'll soon see flocks of sheep roaming the grasslands. I've heard there are thousands of them out there. Never been there, though."

I felt whole again.

91

Chapter 12 First Contact

Water doesn't make a hearty breakfast. After filling my waterskin and relieving myself, I headed off westward at a jog. Soon, though, I slowed. Conserve calories. If I don't get rescued today, hunger will sap my strength.

Midday, I spotted movement on the distant western horizon. I wanted to wave my arms, wave my loincloth, wave anything to get their attention. I could only continue walking towards them and hope they'd see me.

An eternity later, they saw me. Shock on both sides. Giant rubber wheels and large shields hung from the sides of the two chariots rushing toward me. Each carried a well-muscled blonde with bits of bronze armor attached to her forearms and legs. They looked like soldiers. Spears rose from a wicker container at the rear of each chariot. Breastplates gave the appearance they had no busts to speak of. Golden lip plates about nine inches across that dangled from their slit upper lips surprised me more. It reminded me of our Senior Ambassadors on Cass-C. Had Cass-C people visited here? Later, I would learn they made the disks from gold which this world had in abundance.

Not horses or mules or oxen, but armless men. Stocky men with rippling leg muscles and hair reaching their buttocks pulled each chariot. Breasts. Their breasts were larger than their heads, dwarfing my own monsters.

The women pulled back on the reins. The men stopped and looked at me.
However, the women jabbered at me. Their tone was a mixture of anger and annoyance. I wished I'd studied those basic Bella words more than I had. I picked up their thought concepts

while trying to understand them.

A head harness much like those I'd seen in horse picture books held reins that allowed the women drivers to control the men without using words. I suspected the men couldn't speak with the bits in their mouths. An X harness across their chests attached to the poles from the chariots. Sweat tricked down their chests, absorbed by their loincloths identical to mine.

Both women made the sign of a cross. "Another fucking *abbandonato*, a useless *maledetto*."

"Sì, a runway, useless *peccatori*! We came all this way for another *dannato*! You, there, where did you run away from?"

I worked on getting the concepts from their minds. Forsaken, cursed, sinner, damned. This was their first impression of me. Should have studied their language when I had the chance.

"I don't speak Bella language much. Evil person left me back that way by the canyon lands. I'm hungry. Want to go to Nuova Roma." I placed these ideas into their minds.

"*Il dannato*, you'll regret running away," one woman said, but I picked up her thought, not the words.

Their lip plates obliterated particular phonetic sounds that involved the lips, such as 'p' and 'b'. Much of what she said didn't sound right to me from the little I'd heard of their language. What I'd give for a language translator. How did my Isabella manage her first contacts? But then she was a linguist.

She fastened a metal shackles around my neck and attached the other to the back of her chariot. Without a word, she slapped the reins. Her men pulled the chariot around and headed back westward. The chain pulled me along with them. Not what I expected.

The men pulled the chariots at a good clip. Weakened, I stumbled and got my neck yanked several times. I tried to keep up.

Oh, god! What have I gotten into now? Have to keep up. A fall might kill me!

As the sun lowered, we halted beside a stream. The women unhitched the four men and removed their harnesses. Each got down on their knees and sipped from the stream. Then, they moved off a ways and relieved themselves.

One woman unchained me, motioning for me to drink and pee. This I did, grateful for the water. I walked over to where the men had squatted to go. The four men looked at me. I sensed curiosity. Then, one woman said something to the other. Both looked at me. One came over just as I finished. Without a word, she lifted my loincloth, revealing my privates to all eyes. I didn't expect what happened.

Both women screamed! I sensed what one then said.

"Now women are damned, cursed, forsaken, and cast out! What wickedness have we done?"

The other woman said something like, "We've not fought wars, enslaved others, raped, pillaged, and stolen things. Yet, she's like them. Damned and forsaken by Lord God and Mamma Maria! Are we next?" Both made the sign of a cross, knelt, and whispered what I thought must be prayers.

In sharp contrast, the apathetic men animated a little. One smiled. "Their turn to be damned."

The other's body shook. "How will we survive without them?"

They shrugged their shoulders and resumed their apathetic outlook.

The women continued whispering to each other, while unloading bags from the back of the chariot. They placed them by the men, who used feet and toes to remove cookware, utensils, and bags of dried food. Meanwhile, the women set up a cooking fire using black bits, either charcoal or peat, I couldn't tell which. Once the fire was going and a tripod set up,

94

the women spread out blankets and laid down, watching the men and whispering about me.

One pointed to me and told me to go help the forsaken, the men. I moved over to them, but they ignored me. Besides, I wasn't much help cooking. They made a stew in the large pot. Later, they served the two women the first bowls. Only after they nodded did the men fill theirs. One filled a bowl for me. We ate in silence. A stew never tasted this good to me.

I stole glances at the women, curious about how they would eat and drink with those giant lip disks. One hand lifted the plate up while the other used a spoon.

Dinner done, one man put a large pot of water on the tripod's hook. The other handed out mugs. Most had large handles that we could grip with our feet. The women's cups didn't have such large loops. I guessed the cups were bronze. A man sprinkled dried leaves in each. A woman poured the boiling water into each.

Tea! A good, strong black tea. As dusk came, one woman chained me back to the chariot. The women sat beside the dying fire, brushing out the men's long hair. They then did mine, for which I felt thankful.

I slept poorly. The chain around my neck threatened to strangle me.

At dawn, the women stoked the fire while the men prepared the meal. I didn't complain. We had more stew and tea. I helped the men wash and dry the dishes while the women inspected their chariots, put on their armor, and sharpened their weapons. After we stowed everything back into the bags, the women hefted them into the rears of their chariots and harnessed the four men, hooking them back up to the long poles.

Me chained to the rear, off we went. I did my best to keep up. From their well-muscled legs, I suspected the men had pulled these chariots for many years.

Talk about scared! I've never been this frightened in my life. If I stumbled, the chain would break my neck. Pace. Just keep pace.

The women's whispers carried undercurrents of both fear and worry, but I had no idea why. The day seemed endless. By late afternoon, my legs gave out. The chain jerked my neck while my legs dragged the ground. They had no choice but to allow me to ride in the chariot with them. I felt her powerful sense of utter revulsion towards me. Why?

That night passed as the night before, except Dante made contact with me.

"Been busy here. Did you find the patrol?"

"Yes. We're heading west."

"Ah, they're from Ciampino, a small village not too far from Nuova Roma. Maybe I'll see you in a few days. Have to go. Bye."

Late the next day, a small town appeared on the horizon. I managed to get one woman to tell me its name. Ciampino, their hometown.

As we entered the village, a huge church with a giant white cross atop a bell tower dominated the landscape. She pointed to this Romanesque structure and said, "Santa Maria." It reminded me of images I'd seen of antique churches around Earth. None were in actual use, not for hundreds of years. Museums today.

Children played in the cobblestone street. All the girls had lip disks, the smallest being about three inches in diameter. Armless boys kicked a rubber ball around, reminding me of soccer games in high school.

Concrete appeared to be the construction material of choice. Gray buildings had one story only, which allowed Santa Maria to dominate the village setting. Cloth fabrics of various colors covered the doorways. At least I wouldn't have to worry about doorknobs. Then, I realized that might be the very reason for the cloth door covers. Each building nestled against the next one.

The chariots pulled up at a corral along side dozens of other chariots. The women unloaded theirs and unhitched their men but left them harnessed. One woman undid my chain from the chariot. While carrying their equipment and holding the reins of her two men, she pulled me along with her. We walked several blocks. Here, they split up.

Her men pushed into one door flap; she followed, pulling me with her. She chained me to a clamp in the wall. Presumably, she'd tied up others this way. I watched as she unhitched her men. Then, she started a fire in the kitchen and returned to me.

"Try to leave and I'll spear you," she said. She made gestures to make sure I got the message. Only then did she unlock my neck collar and led me into her home.

The fixtures looked much like any modern kitchen. Sink, stove, refrigerator, counter tops. But none of these was more than a foot above the floor. A sloping ramp led from the counter down to a six-inch tall table. The men sat on chairs with wheels preparing a meal. Then, I noticed the single electric light hanging from the ceiling. Now the tall poles with wires I'd seen as we entered the village made sense. Electric power.

She motioned for me to help her men. I observed and helped where I could. One man retrieved the metal plates and utensils, sliding them down the ramp to the long table. I got the idea and helped set the five places. The man smiled.

Soon, they slid pots containing our food down the ramp. When all was ready, one man called out something. The woman entered, having washed the trail dirt off. The men remained standing while she sat on soft pads. I stood with them.

She said what I interpreted to be a prayer to Santa

Maria. After making the cross, she sampled the food, nodded, and ate. When she finished, she nodded to us and left the room. We sat and ate our fill. I've no idea what I ate, though it looked like bread, meat, and vegetables. The drink tasted something like milk.

I helped them with the dishes. First, we pushed them up the ramp and over to the sink. I don't think they trusted me to do the washing, but I dried them. When we finished, they slipped on moccasins. One slid a pair over to me, gesturing I should wear them.

Considering the rough treatment my flats underwent, only a miracle kept them on my feet. The soft moccasins felt wonderful. The church bell sounded. The woman joined us in the kitchen, motioning to us. We three followed behind her to the Santa Maria church.

Awed. That's how I felt entering the huge Romanesque church. Here, she pointed to the side steps. The men and I climbed them to the second floor. But from our spot, we couldn't see what transpired below, though we could hear.

Singing began the service. The notes reverberated in the great space. A woman talked. Preaching? The men kept their heads bowed the entire time and said nothing. I sensed their deep apathy. I gleaned an understanding. Men believed God had abandoned them. That they were cursed sinners, worthless to society, damned men, yet still needed for reproduction. Isolated from the heart and center of their religion. Besides hearing Santa Maria many times, I heard Gesù Cristo almost as many times during what must have been the sermon. More singing followed. The men rose and descended the step with me following along behind them.

When our woman joined us, she said something to the men, which I interpreted as "go home." Me, she led down a side aisle into a small room, where she had me sit on a bench. A much older woman entered. She wore heavy purple robes with a tall hat on her head. Her lip disk must have been a foot across, maybe more. I guessed that lip loops stretched with age, requiring ever-larger disks.

The woman who found me called her Santa Madre Alessandra, which I guessed meant something like Holy Mother. She lifted my flimsy loincloth. She too cried out.

"Madre Mia! Santa Maria, are women now to be cursed too?"

I interpreted that's what she meant, hoping I was right. She continued to cry out, almost wailing, fleeing the room while repeatedly making the sign of a cross, as though that might help her. My woman gestured for me to stay and left the room. I heard a click and guessed she probably locked the door. I heard them whispering outside the door.

Wooden? Only the church has solid doors?

I heard scurrying feet. Then, silence. Had they forgotten me?

Click. The lock turned, and a different woman entered. She too had short hair. I estimated the diameter of her lip disk to be six inches, further reinforcing my notion lip loops stretched with age. She surprised me by lifting my loincloth. This was becoming embarrassing. Didn't I look like a woman? Oops. Maybe not on this world. None of the women I'd seen appeared to have breasts. This woman appeared flat chested, too.

She grunted something or perhaps what she said was distorted by her lip disk. She stepped out, only to return with a black leather bag. She took out a vial and waved it before my nose. I tried to avoid it, but got a strong whiff. Soon, I sort of dozed off, groggy, dopey. Pain. Was that a knife cutting my upper lip? I couldn't move to prevent it. No, the pain subsided. Blood trickled, but she wiped oozy stuff over the sides of the cut, both dulling the pain and stopping the blood flow. She pulled out a golden three-inch lip disk. Its perimeter had a ridge in which the lip loop fit. Taught. I felt stretched. No, that was my lip. The weight hanging down—a strange sensation. I felt sickish. Hope I don't faint.

The woman tried to hand me a vial of the ointment she'd used on the cut, but I had no hands to take it. Her face crimsoned. She sat it down beside me and left. I drifted in and out of consciousness. My original woman entered, picked up the vial, and pushed me onto my feet. As we left the room, I felt a huge sense of revulsion coming from the priestess, the woman who installed the disk, and the woman who found me. Why did I repulse them? The administered drug kept me from thinking clearly. In a fog, we returned to her house for the night.

She pushed me into another room. Ah, a bedroom. Oh, how I wanted to lie down. To sleep and forget everything. As though I might be contagious, she had me sit on a side cot where she brushed my hair. I picked up her thought: my duty. Then, she allowed me to lie down. She left and entered the men's bedroom, presumably to brush their hair. I could see from the corner of my eyes. When done, she returned and crawled into her elegant bed across from my cot. The men didn't sleep with her.

The next morning, my lip throbbed. I faced a new challenge. How to eat and drink with the lip disk. I watched the woman and emulated her as best I could with my left foot. I struggled. However, the two men seemed satisfied with how I now looked.

She removed my disk, wiped on more salve, and pressed it back into place. My face felt stretched as though it might break. What a funny sensation. Later, she allowed me to step outside. Word of the new arrival spread. Women of all ages milled around staring at me. I stared back.

Some, around five years old, had small disks like mine. One woman with gray hair had a disk that must have been

100

fifteen inches across. And none of the women seemed to have bosoms. After seeing my woman when she woke this morning, I knew better. Women had breasts. Only they wore a garment that squashed them down, giving them a flat-chested appearance. While watching these women staring at me, I realized women distinguished themselves from men anyway they could. Why?

I had no definitive answer. I wanted to stroll around the village, but the crowd's reaction convinced me otherwise. They didn't threaten me. Rather, I felt an overwhelming sense of fear in the women. At first, I thought they were afraid of me, that they could somehow tell I was an alien from another world. But as I studied their fear more closely, I noticed revulsion mingled in. Something about my appearance turned them off. But what? My skin had reddened some from the sun, but my skin tones didn't look all that different from theirs.

I had long black hair. Hair colors varied among them, but none wore theirs longer than shoulder length. I tested that theory by telepathic means. Most felt my hair was inappropriate, but that wasn't the source of their fear or revulsion. I sighed. It would have to remain an unknown for the moment.

Since I couldn't roam the village, I looked around from just outside the concrete home of my guard. I saw tall poles holding wires. Somewhere an electrical plant generated the electricity that traveled by the wires to this village. Those wires draped along the very tops of the poles. But another set of wires stretched along about halfway down each pole. Purpose? Unknown.

While I ignored the women staring at me and looked around, an older woman walked up. She must be important because everyone gave way to her. I put her age at around sixty. Her lip disk was one of the biggest I'd seen. I guessed she might be the village leader or elder. Her word appeared to carry weight. She said a few words to the woman who rescued me.

I caught a couple words, though. Nuova Roma and go. I repeated them back to the two women. Both nodded. I'd communicated. She harnessed up her two men while other women filled bags with utensils, food, and charcoal. Within a few minutes, the chariot appeared, pulled by the two men. Women loaded the bags. Chained, they paraded me behind the charriot.

As we headed out of Ciampino, many women cheered. I sensed they felt great relief.

Chapter 13 On the Road

All I got out of the woman was her name, Mara. Rarely did she deign either to talk to her two men or to me. Strong silent type, I concluded.

About two miles away, we halted amid a major construction project. Swarms of women and men labored constructing a roadbed. Four women wearing armor pieces and carrying spears patrolled the perimeter zone. I saw six teams of strong men harnessed to large wagons, two leaving, two arriving, one loaded waiting, and one being unloaded.

With lip disks gleaming in the sunlight, a crew of women used shovels to scoop the crushed rock out of the wagons onto a narrow raised bed parallel to the well-worn cobblestone road we'd been traveling. With continuous thumping noises, another crew tamped the gravel down. Behind them, women unloaded a wagon carrying six-foot-long heavy lumber pieces, laying them across the gravel bed a foot apart. I watched fascinated, wondering what they were making.

When they finished emptying the wagon, its woman driver drove her team away to the north. Meanwhile, the next wagon moved into position to have its gravel unloaded. Farther west, I heard the heavy hammering of metal.

Mara received a hand signal. We moved on around the construction crews, heading closer to the hammering sound. As we passed by, the women stopped and stared at me. Many inhaled sharply. Some made the now-familiar cross sign, looking away from me as though I might contaminate them. The men didn't notice me. They stared at the ground or nothing at all. I saw dark rings around their eyes. Apathy.

When we stopped, I saw other women swinging sledgehammers driving steel spikes into the wooden timbers. Ah. These secured a thin metal rail to the planks. When I looked up, I saw this huge behemoth, smoke rising from its front stack. I'd seen images in my high school history book. This had to be a steam engine. A train.

Behind the gray engine, an open-topped car held a pile of black rocks while behind it lay an empty car with benches. Two guards stood nearby, spears in hand. All stared at me, more so, when Mara undid my chain and led me to them.

She handed my chain to one of these guards, who saluted her before taking the chain. The new woman motioned for me to climb onto the car with benches. I did so, and she locked her end to a metal bar. The two exchanged whispered words, before the new guard waved to another woman standing on the behemoth engine. A loud whistle belching white smoke startled me, though the others ignored it.

With more smoke pouring out of the stack, I felt the car move. A pair of new guards hopped up, stowing their spears. They sat up front, leaving me by myself on the rear bench. I guessed at our speed: maybe five miles an hour. The sun poured down, and I relaxed, gazing at the passing scenery.

Off to my left, women tended flocks of sheep. To the right, women worked in fields. Grains, though two men pulled a plow. They used men as horses. Farther off to the north, I saw several workers and carts. The rock quarry I concluded.

Power poles passed by. The main electric lines stretched along the top while another set of lines ran along the middle of these poles. Another village appeared. The train passed through the center of several dozen concrete homes. I couldn't miss seeing another enormous Romanesque church.

Once in the country, off to the north I saw a large concrete building with three tall smokestacks. A small river flowed past it. Each stack belched black smoke. Small mountains of the black rock surrounded it. A side track led to the structure. Several sets of lines on poles fanned out from the massive building. This must be a power plant. I concluded the black rock must be coal. These people had invented steam engines of various kinds. And now they were extending the rail line to the easternmost village of Ciampino.

Another town appeared. The driver sounded the whistle as we approached and slowed down. Many women and girls stopped and stared at me as the train passed by. They must have heard about me. How? This larger town sported two churches and some kind of temple with stone pillars supporting the roof. I couldn't get a good look at it. Once clear of the town, our speed increased. I dozed off.

Around noon, the train stopped at a lone concrete structure that sprawled across the countryside. No village surrounded this isolated structure. A large wooden sign read: *La Fratellanza*. The two guards unchained me, motioning for me to get off. The engineer joined us. Together, we walked over to the front entrance of this unusual building. Here, a huge portico held two picnic style tables to the left and two of the familiar six-inch tall tables.

I touched the women's minds trying to figure out what this place was. One of my guards must have sensed my curiosity. She said, "*La Fratellanza*." I got an image of a men's-only dwelling. That this was a brotherhood became clearer when two men in loincloths stepped out to meet us. They kept their eyes downcast, refusing to meet my gaze.

They asked the women some questions and left. My guard made an eating gesture. I concluded we stopped for lunch. Men appeared, pushing bowls, cups, and utensils on trays across the floor towards us. One used his feet to position a bowl, cup, and spoon before me while one woman lifted theirs up to their tables. Again, I struggled to eat with the darn lip disk in my way. I found it awkward to have to keep it lifted

105

with my left foot while using my right foot to spoon the stew into my mouth. Damned difficult. But it tasted superb. These men must have a wonderful chef behind the scene.

When we finished, the engineer woman dropped several silver coins into a can resting near the main opening. The guards positioned their eating items back onto the floor where the men could reach them. One tugged on my chain, forcing me back onto the train. Again, she locked me to my seat. Where did she expect me to flee to?

That afternoon, we passed many small towns, countless fields, two more electric generation plants, and a forest whose trees workers converted into the rail timbers and tall poles. Night fell. Still we rolled along, but soon I saw city lights ahead. I smiled, but the lip disk masked it. They used electric power to make streetlights. And I guessed this must be Nuova Roma, their largest city.

The whistle announced our entry to the city. Dante chose that moment to contact me.

"Are you onboard the train? Everyone heard the High Council ordered them to bring you here."

I sent back, "Yes, a nice train ride. Lots of city lights. Watched them building the last couple miles of track into Ciampino."

"Yeah, it's the easternmost reach of the new rail line. I've place the idea that you don't speak our language into the minds of the High Council members. I put the notion that I'm the best person to teach you our language. I'm something of a rogue man. I think they'll house you with us. Oops. They want my help making up a bed for you. See you."

The train slowed way down. Once we entered the city, buildings blocked my view. From glimpses, this promised to be a modern place where perhaps I could prepare them for the arrival of our deep space exploration ship. But I had no idea when it would get here. Weeks. Months. Surely sometime this

106

year. Would Angelina be onboard as their anthropologist?

I thought I saw storefronts down one street. Another street looked like it might be a market place. Many low tables or stalls lined one side of that street. I knew I needed a map to get around a city this size. I wondered what its population was. At last, the train pulled into a station. Benches lined one side while the street abutted the other side.

A group of guards in armor and carrying spears waited. My train guards unlocked my chain from the bench and handed it to one of these new soldiers. I felt instant revulsion coming from this new group. Fear followed that, drowning out their distaste for me. I wished someone would tell me why everyone feared me or how I repulsed them. Didn't happen.

Instead, they pulled me along a street until I got lost. Then they pushed me into a building that had metal bars on its windows and a metal bar door with a lock. They undid my metal collar and shoved me inside. They locked the door.

I looked around my cell. A narrow bed rested against one corner. A six-inch tall table rested on the floor on the opposite side. A bowl with spoon beckoned. Its steamy aroma called out to me. My stomach growled. A porcelain toilet filled another corner with a washbasin. The basin rose only six inches from the floor, which was concrete covered with a wool rug. A towel and washrag lay folded beside it.

Civilized. Right there, I decided I'd be civilized. Since landing on Bella, I'd been anything but civilized. I sat and washed my feet. I discovered hot and cold water. Encouraged, I washed as much of myself as I could. Without a brush, I left my hair alone. That done, I polished off the stew and tea, though not without enormous awkward moments. I only had two feet and needed more to keep from rolling over. Full, I crawled beneath the light covers.

"Change of plans," Dante sent. "It's too late at night. They'll bring you by tomorrow. Whatever you do, don't tell anyone you have telepathy or that I do. If they find out, they'll kill us. See you tomorrow. They believe I'm the best person to teach you our language."

"Thanks."

After that, I exhaled and relaxed into a welcomed sleep. I'd quieted my question-filled mind. At least for tonight. Perhaps the morrow would yield critical information.

In the morning, someone brought in hot tea and warm porridge. Mid-morning, six armored guards arrived to escort me. I hoped to meet Dante soon. As we marched down the streets, I ignored the constant gasps and stares of the women. Men didn't notice me.

We passed an open market. My turn to stare. Men carried yokes across their shoulders with a basket attached to each side via a long rope. V shaped legs attached to each end of the yoke allowed the man to lower it to about three feet and leave it standing while he put items into the baskets or removed them. What a clever way to carry things.

Men with their yokes dominated the open markets. Evidently, they handled grocery shopping. We passed many stores. Like the buildings I'd seen before, the main entrance was open, covered by a flap of fabric. Thus, any man could enter any building.

I guessed at what some stores sold. Yokes of various sizes. Another sold fabrics. Another sold loincloths. One had a display of moccasins. Soon, I lost track. So many stores. Here and there, we stepped aside, allowing man-pulled carts to pass by. Even here, men worked as beasts of burden. Didn't these people have horses, donkeys, oxen, or cows? Apparently not.

We passed by another tall Romanesque church of Santa Maria. This one surpassed the others I'd seen. Two blocks later, a temple rose above a stepped platform. A marble statue of a female rose towards the sky. One of my guards said, "Juno." I vaguely recalled ancient history lessons. Didn't there used to be a Roman goddess with that name? We continued our march.

Six men to one woman. That was the ratio I saw as we walked. The men appeared apathetic, slow moving, with black rings around their eyes, and never looking directly at us. In fact, men gave the marching women a very wide berth.

Then, we hit residential streets. Ah, young children predominated. Boys of all ages darted about playing with a round ball. Some older boys seemed accomplished at moving the ball around. A few girls played ball, but the girls appeared to be no older than five. Where were the older girls?

The gray concrete buildings yielded to painted walls. A rainbow of colors lined the streets on either side of the cobblestones. These owners painted their home's exteriors, though still only a single story tall and made from concrete. No adjacent houses displayed the same color. Needle-like trees appeared. Then came block-sized parks. Again, children played in them, but no girls over five. Conclusion: we entered a wealthier part of Nuova Roma.

I noticed the power lines and poles running along the backsides of the homes. Again, thicker wires ran along the tops while thinner wires ran along the middle. A thick wire led to each home. Many homes had a second thinner wire attached to it as well. Power likely came through the thicker ones, but I had no idea what the thinner ones did.

In the next block, an enormous stadium rose, blocking my view of anything beyond it. Images I'd seen in history books of the crumbling Roman Colosseum came to mind. As we walked by, I glanced in between the zillion entryways. A grass field occupied the entire ground level. I spotted two net structures at either end. Could this be a soccer field? Three levels of concrete seats suggested many thousands could watch a game. Only the churches of Santa Maria rose taller than this. I admit being impressed by this structure. I realized everything had to have been designed and built by women. Half the population of Bella couldn't do much physical labor. That impressed me even more.

At last, we entered a dead-end street, lush with needle-like pine trees and flowering plants lining the front of each home. Three concrete homes lay at the end, each painted a different color. One was red, one white, one blue. A nice contrast I thought. We walked up to the house at the very end, the blue one.

A middle-aged woman stepped out. My guards bowed low to her. She must be important. Then, a younger woman dressed in purple robes stepped out of the red home. Again, my guards bowed to her, while a third woman appeared from the white home that lay to the right of the blue one. After more bowing, a young man stepped out from the blue home, but he didn't join us.

More heads appeared at the various windows. I was "the" sight to see. The first woman walked up to me and looked me over as though she might purchase me. She pointed to herself and said, "Carolina Gallo." She pointed to me. I replied. We repeated this several times until I pronounced her name correctly.

She pointed to the woman in purple. "Lia Faggini." The third woman, the one wearing a thin, white robe, she called Trista Baldovino. My conclusion: these three were important women.

"High Council." Dante sent to me.

These three held power. Good to know.

Carolina pointed to Dante. "Dante Gallo." I repeated it until she seemed happy with my pronunciation. She then made a series of gestures that I deciphered with Dante's hints. He would teach me their language, and then these women would meet with me. Good start.

A guard pushed me towards Dante, but Carolina made

110

gestures suggesting I should join him. I smiled before realizing no one could tell that. I walked up to him and followed him inside.

Chapter 14 Dante Gallo—A Day in the Life

Dante met my gaze. We stared into each other's eyes. Perfect confront. Wow. Here was a being who grabbed my full attention. I didn't miss his handsome face and charming smile. Tall and thin, Dante appeared fit, but I couldn't help notice his breasts were much larger than mine, double the size of his head. He wore the usual white loincloth and moccasins.

He said aloud, "Welcome, Molly. I'm Dante Gallo." He telegraphed, "Play along. I'm supposed to be teaching you our language."

I repeated him. "Dante Gallo." We said this back and forth a couple times until I had the proper pronunciation as mutilated by the darn lip disk. Carolina said something to Dante and left.

He gave me a tour of the Gallo home. The entrance hall opened into a living room, where I met the rest of the family. All stared at me.

His father, Tito, nodded to me, almost meeting my gaze. A stout man, I later learned he was thirty-six while Carolina, the leader of the household, was forty. I couldn't see any resemblance to his father, though. I repeated his name until he nodded and smiled.

Next came his sister, Zita, twenty. She had short blonde hair and wore a white shirt and pants.

Dante said, "Zita, teacher."

Again, I repeated the words until she smiled and left. He told me she taught girls at a nearby school.

Nico stood next in line. Dante told me he was twelve. Already many women in Chicago would love to have had his blossoming bosom, though I knew it had barely begun to form.

Nico danced from foot to foot, eager for something. He exchanged words with Tito.

Dante sent, "He wants to play ball, but Tito said he has to take Luigi with him."

A pair of five-year-old twins stood last in line shifting their balance from foot to foot.

"Elena," Dante said.

Deep blue eyes. Blonde hair. Same size lip disk as mine. I repeated her name to giggles.

Dante sent, "She and Luigi are twins. Says your disk is the same as hers. Since you are a grown up, she wants to know why. Tito told her you just got yours. Oh, she's asking if yours still hurts. If it does, Carolina has salve that makes the pain go away."

"Luigi," Dante introduced his youngest brother.

While I repeated his name, he asked something. Dante sent, "Luigi wants to know if God has forsaken you, too. Did you do evil, bad things? I told him we don't know yet. She can't speak our words. I have to teach her."

With a glance at Tito, Nico pushed into Luigi, and they dashed off, heading outside. Elena said something and followed them. Tito nodded and left the room, while Dante continued my tour.

A white woolen carpet? Sofas lined two sides of the living room, enough to sit a dozen people. The room to the right became my small bedroom. Carolina wanted me to be separate from her family at night. I got the guest bedroom.

Down a hall, four other bedrooms housed the twins, Nico, Zita, and Carolina. I presumed Tito slept with her. The children's bedrooms were small like mine. Colorful quilts with elegant embroidery covered the narrow beds of the girls, while plain blankets rested on the men's beds. Large open windows brought in the sea breeze.

The kitchen, dining room, and bathroom opened up opposite the entrance to the living room. Tito sat on a chair with rollers, using his feet to knead dough. I gaped at the kitchen. Everything was low to the ground, sink, counter top, oven, stove, and cabinets. Like the other home I'd seen, a ramp sloped down to the long, six-inch tall table. The kitchen layout and design allowed an armless person to easily handle kitchen activities. The refrigerator occupied the far corner. A single light hung from the ceiling.

When we entered, Tito said something to Dante. He sent, "Tito asked me to fetch Nico and Luigi. It's time for their lessons. Back in a moment."

He dashed out, leaving me with Tito. He had a teapot simmering on the stove, small steam pouring out its spout. The two out of breath boys came in, and Tito said something. Both dashed to the sink, sat, kicked off their moccasins, and washed their feet, as Dante joined us.

"One of Tito's jobs is to teach us boys how to cook and care for a home."

"Don't the boys go to school? Zita is a teacher."

"Fathers teach boys to read and count in the home. Only girls attend school. Elena begins school next month. That's one thing that's wrong with our society. One of many things. You'll soon see."

After Tito turned the kneading process over to Nico, Luigi struggled to put tea leaves in cups for us. Tito poured the boiling water. Luigi then struggled to slide them one by one down the ramp to the table without spilling any.

"Rare is the woman who can cook," Dante explained.

Everything had been set up for the ease of the handicapped, allowing them to deal with all the usual domestic duties. The bathroom might have passed for one in Chicago. Hot and cold running water, tub, sink, and toilet. Levers controlled the water faucets, handled by a foot. I

114

realized the layout of these homes fit the needs of the men who lived here. Since women did the work men might have done in other societies, the handicapped men had to handle maintaining a home. Washing clothes by foot, instead of by machine, consumed hours.

Yokes sitting on their V-shaped supports lined one wall. Their baskets varied in size.

Over tea, Dante started my language lessons. While I had a thousand questions for him, none the least why he was so bright and had telepathic ability, I knew I needed to speak their language. Soon they would want to question me. Besides, whenever our first deep space exploration ship arrived, communication would be essential.

As lunchtime approached, Dante had to stop and lend a foot, helping Tito, Nico, and Luigi prepare lunch. Zita and Carolina arrived as a church bell tolled noon. Cold sandwiches on freshly baked bread, hot noodle soup, milk, and tea lay spread out on the low table. I helped by laying the utensils, as directed by Tito, who seemed pleased I wanted to help.

To show I was learning, as the women entered, I said their names and smiled. But then realized my smile wasn't visible. The darn lip disk seemed to be in the way of everything I tried to do. Why do these women do this to themselves?

Elena saw my difficulty and said, "Like this." She gestured, using her left hand to lift hers up while inserting a spoonful of soup. Her cheeks flushed.

Carolina said something to her. Dante sent, "Mom told her you have to learn men's ways, not women's ways."

Point taken.

Carolina and Zita left. Elena headed outside to play. Luigi who begged to go out with her. Instead, we moved the dishes up the ramp where we washed and dried them. Luigi put them in their proper places while Nico and I focused on drying them. I saw maintaining a household required the assistance of many. Too much for one man alone.

All afternoon, Dante and I continued language lessons, until stopping to help Tito with supper. I got my first shocking surprise. Tito pulled a strange device from a corner of the kitchen. Its use eluded me. He attached a container to one end of tubes connecting to the machine. He leaned into the two suction cups and alternated pushing two foot pedals. His milk flowed down the tubes into the bowl. I stared in disbelief.

Dante sent, "We milk twice a day. I'll go next. Breakfast and suppertime. We measure how much we produce. Excess is sold to the milk processing company. Tito makes enough for family use. Nico's and mine gets sold. That brings in more denarius—that's a silver coin. Denarius come in fractional amounts, too. Nico and I bring in five denarius per week. That helps a lot."

I sent back, "Your milk doesn't dry up? On my world, our breasts produce milk after we give birth. Dries up once it's no longer needed."

Dante laughed. "Hardly. If only it would. No, men keep producing milk until they die of old age. It gives single men a way to make denarius. You aren't making any milk now? Women will want to know that."

I shook my head. With all of us working together, we had supper ready when the two women returned home after the five o'clock church bell tolled. Without our help, I estimated Tito would have had to start preparing supper after he finished dealing with lunch. This ignored sweeping, cleaning, dusting, changing beds, and washing dirty clothing and bedding. I learned they had to visit the markets and buy the groceries. Dante told me that newly mated often brought an extra man into their starter home to aid with the workload.

After eating, we dealt with the dishes. A girl friend of Zita's dropped by. Dante introduced her as Vittoria Baldovino, whose mother was on the High Council and ran the Pagani Dei church.

He sent, "Vittoria keeps trying to mate with me, but I don't want to join with her. I hope I can flee this world with you."

Once we finished cleaning up, Carolina brushed Tito's long black hair. Vittoria flirted with Dante as she brushed his gorgeous, knee-length brown hair. Zita handled mine and Nico's, though she wanted nothing to do with me. Elena brushed out Luigi's hair. Since the men's hair always seemed very long, I could see how we'd have a very hard time maintaining it without my Cleo robot assistant. I'd not seen a woman with hair much longer than shoulder-length nor a male with hair shorter than his rump. Strange.

Vittoria said something to Dante that caused him to flush. He sent, "She invited me to go to the big soccer game on Friday. I don't have a choice. When a woman asks a man out, he has to go. Convinced her we have to bring you, since I'm supposed to be teaching you our language. She didn't like that but agreed."

At bedtime, Carolina followed me into my small room. She gestured that I was to take my lip disk out at night, inserting it back in place when I awoke. She removed the disk for me and spread salve on my healing lips. Then, she gestured I should put it back. She wouldn't leave until I figured out how I could put it back in and take it out on my own. With my disk lying on my bedside table, she let me tuck myself in.

Dante made contact again. He wanted to tell me about his story.

"Years ago, I traveled this part of the galaxy on a solo sightseeing trip. I'm always fascinated by the incredible natural wonders a world has. I crash-landed on this world. That body died. I picked up another baby body. This one. Little did I know how backwards this world is. Men don't get any education here, only the brighter women do. I was planning to kill this body and get a female baby body when you came along. You're not from this world either. You're a pilot. I spotted that in your mind. I'm hoping you and I can mate and leave this world behind."

I told him about myself. "I'm supposed to be the Empress of the Sol Empire, once we get done colonizing this world. Any day, one of our deep space exploration ships will arrive. While they don't know I'm on this world, they'll be glad they found me. I'll take you with me, if you want to leave." I yawned and drifted into a relaxing sleep.

The next day, between lessons, I helped do the laundry. Just outside the kitchen's backdoor lay a concrete patio with a clothesline and wash tubs resting on the ground. We sat and used our feet to wash sheets and clothes, dropping them into baskets attached to yokes when rinsed. Hanging them onto the clothesline with clothes pins proved challenging, especially trying to avoid dragging the wet, but clean, items across the floor. Once we loaded the line with the laundry, a crank raised the lines up off the ground. Clever, but a multi-person operation.

The next day, Dante, Nico, Luigi, and I went to the markets. We each shouldered a yoke with large baskets on either side. Tito fastened a money pouch around a sash on Dante. It contained five silver denarius, five half-denarius coins, and six quarter-denarius coins.

As we set off, Luigi said, "I get to buy some candy!"

Dante relayed what he'd said. I only grasped "get" and "buy". I had a lot of language to learn.

Dante showed me around. He explained the women running the markets produced their on goods on nearby farms. We picked out a carrot bunch and apples. Several times, I had to stop and redistribute items. I soon learned the trick of keeping the weight balanced between my two baskets. Still, the yokes allowed us to bring home a surprising amount of groceries.

The variety of stores impressed me. In one, the butcher woman cut up sheep and fish to order. In another, the candy store, Luigi wanted to buy everything, but settled for three pieces of his favorite hard candy.

We purchased lentils, rice, potatoes, and cereals from a dried goods merchant. Those weren't what the items were, only my best guess at their natures.

We stopped last at the dairy. Dante explained they sold "processed" milk. We purchased cheese bricks and a tub of yogurt. Think it was cheese and yogurt. I'm pretty certain it was cheese. Not sure about the yogurt though.

We returned and helped Tito prepare lunch. We'd shot the entire morning. I saw just how much work the men had to do in this society. That meant the women did everything else. How do they do it? Building homes, railroads, farming. The list the women had to handle blew my mind.

When we returned with the full baskets from the market earlier, I noticed two paper sheets taped to the white wall next to the doorway. I recognized Dante's name. During our lessons after lunch, I asked him about it.

"It's the *rapporti sessuali,*" he sent, but then had to explain. "Sexual intercourse. It's a tradition that goes back to the founding of Bella. With few initial settlers, the gods demanded when a woman wanted to have a child, each night for a week they visited random men of their village. The men wore sacks over their heads so they couldn't see the women. Those sign-up sheets by our door are for Tito and me. In a few years, Nico will get his sheet.

"Women come by and put a check mark on the night they wish intercourse. That night, mom will tie the sack over my head, remove my loincloth, and sit me on a chair in the entrance room. She'll pull the flap down so those inside can't see who comes. The woman will come by and do it with me.

119

When she leaves, she'll whistle. Mom will remove the sack and hand me my loincloth.

"This way, male seeds are spread out among many women, making healthier children. That's why none of us look like Tito. We're pretty sure Mom hasn't had a child from him. Two millennia ago, this was critical to the survival of Bella, but we both know it's silly today. Still, it's a tradition no one dares to break. Between us, I hope the women know not to mate with too close a relative."

"Don't you find that embarrassing?" I sent back.

"Men are powerless to do anything to stop it. Women control everything on Bella. Men live by the good graces of the women. Without Mom bringing home the silvers, we'd be in deep trouble. Tito says it's a badge of honor to have had a hundred *rapporti sessuali*."

He flushed. "I've had twenty-five encounters. I think Vittoria was one of them. She wants to mate with me."

"How does this mating happen?" I sent back.

"Once both consent, then the woman must provide the house for the man, along with all the facilities and items you see in Carolina's home. Sink, tub, yokes, beds. All of it. Those supplies alone cost about a hundred denarius. Homes are very expensive."

"What happens if no one mates with you?"

"When a man reaches twenty-five, if no one has asked or he hasn't said yes, then the mother must send him off to join the *La Fratellanza*. That's the Brotherhood. A colony of men who live and work together. They form a work pool to earn enough coins to survive. Some of them hire out as beasts of burden, pulling wagons, chariots, and plows for pay. While I've heard that's very hard work, many get to see much of the wonders of Bella. Tito has never been outside Nuova Roma."

Friday early afternoon, Vittoria came by to take Dante to the soccer match. Carolina chose to have her whole family join them. I think she wasn't too pleased having Vittoria wooing Dante. Vittoria draped an arm around Dante and led the way. The stadium or Colosseum as they called it held several thousand. A throng packed the stands. Carolina's group had front row seats. Her position on the High Council?

Surprise. The players were all men, though a woman coached them. Twelve men per team. Each had two goalies. I got lost on what these people called the players. To distinguish sides, one team wore a red harness while the other wore a blue harness. The coaches laced spiked shoes onto each player. They squirted water into thirsty mouths, since the soccer shoes rendered their players dependent.

The game seemed similar to the soccer games I'd seen while in high school. I learned these men, these super athletes, earned more money than many women did. They were also the most sought-after men on Bella. Only wealthy women could mate them, though women took every opportunity to breed them via the *rapporti sessuali*.

One man stood out. Nico looked an awful lot like him. I smiled unnoticed, suspecting he'd fathered Nico. How weird. But it gave me a better feel for the power wielded by Carolina. Intentional tripping was the common foul. Players lost their balance and fell. Before game's end, six players had to be carried off the field with serious falling injuries. I counted enough players on the bench to field three teams.

Now I understood why so many young boys I saw about the city played ball. If they became professional soccer players, they were set for life.

Days passed. My language skills increased. Then one day, reckoning time came. Carolina set up my meetings with the three factions. Dante tagged along to help with words I didn't know.

Chapter 15 The *Chiesa Christiana Romana*

Carolina said, "Pope Aria Faggini orders you to visit her in the *Chiesa Christiana Romana* today. You'll be staying with her family for a few days before moving on to the other factions. Mind you, at least four out of every ten women on Bella are ardent followers. Men don't matter, of course. If you don't understand something she says, ask Dante to translate. Follow me. And try not to get on her wrong side."

Stares followed as she led me through the streets. Women gasped, covered their mouths, and looked away. Their minds transmitted fear and repulsion. Strange. I studies their faces for clues.

Ahead, the tallest Romanesque style church rose. Its bell tower dwarfed all other buildings. Exquisite carvings adorned enormous entry doors. Could I even get those open without help? Must weigh a ton. Carolina opened the door for me.

Inside, incense. Cloying. Pungent. Eyes downcast, a woman in a purple robe met us.

Carolina said, "I've brought Molly Parkinson to Pope Aria Faggini, per her orders."

"Wait here," she said without looking at me.

Avoidance? Even in here? We stood in view of the inner sanctuary. Breathtaking. Designed to make everyone feel small? Tapestries, paintings, and statues adorned church. The predominate color was gold. Gold-plated? Between me and the high altar, rows upon rows of oak benches. Hundreds of people could fit in here.

Through side doors, steps leading to a balcony. Clever

stonework hid its existence. So that's where the sounds of worship came from.

In a minute, the woman returned with an older woman, perhaps in her fifties. Her lip disk spanned eighteen inches. Thick, purple robes draped her form. A golden pointed hat sat upon her graying-brown hair. A giant ring with a red stone set in a golden cross weighed her right index finger.

Carolina knelt down. Pope Aria offered her ring. Carolina kissed it.

"You may rise, dear child. And this must be the Forsaken, the new *abbandonato*, the newly cursed *maledetto*. That will be all, Carolina. May you one day come to your senses. *Peccatori*, follow me," she said.

"You sinners are never allowed to set your unholy feet on the main floor of any Santa Maria church. Never. We'll walk down the side aisle to my office."

I followed her. She added, "Gaze upon what is forever denied to you, the blessing of Lord God and Jesus Christ. Few *abbandonato* ever see this much of one of our *chiese*. And you alone of the *maledetto* are seeing this much only because of your unique arrival among us. Questions have been raised. It is my obligation to Christ to ascertain the truth of the matter."

I had no idea what she was talking about. She had Dante wait outside the main doors, to be called if needed. We walked upon a soft woolen carpet dyed purple, but the golden threads woven into it gave one the sense you walked upon holy ground.

We entered a wood-paneled study. The odor of polish. Plush seats. Enormous desk. Leather-bound volumes lay on its shiny top. One of the two, an impressive foot by a foot displayed a golden cross embossed on its black front.

The leather-bound book caught my interest, for it had an ornately colored inlay depicting what I thought Italy might look like. I'd never been there, but I'd seen maps in high school geography class.

A younger woman swept in behind me and laid a towel over one of the seats. Pope Aira gestured for me to sit on the towel.

"Can't have you contaminating a good chair."

Behind her enormous desk, she looked down upon me from her raised chair. The other women left, closing the door behind her.

"Now then, I've been told you do not know the history of Bella. I shall begin there. You see, our whole history is contained in this magnificent journal begun nearly two millennia ago. All that has happened is documented within these pages. Unfortunately, over the years, written and spoken language has changed. Few can read the most ancient pages. I've been honored to have added four pages, mostly about our electrification project and steam-powered trains.

"I will tell you our story that you may understand. Our ancestors lived on a cruel world called Earth in a city called Roma. Filled with unspeakable corruption and sinners, the men continually fought devastating wars, pillaging, raping women, enslaving whole peoples, murdering those they didn't like. Eventually, the crimes exceeded what our creator, Lord God, could tolerate. He sent his only Son, Jesus Christ, to Earth, preaching the truth and the way to salvation to all who would listen. Few did. The wars, the slavery, the raping, the debauchery continued unto the crucifying of Jesus Christ upon a cross.

"So it was that Lord God grew angry at men. With a mighty wave of his hand, he cursed the men he'd created. The forsaken, the *abbandonato*, he altered their physical forms such that never again could they fight wars, enslave others, rape, pillage, and murder others. Out of the millions living in Roma, Lord God brought five hundred chaste women and five hundred of the *abbandonato* here to Bella, to begin anew.

124

"Lord God appeared to them and spoke from the Burning Bush. It is a Holy Bush and is still tended to this day. The whole of Lord God's Holy Words are written on the beginning pages of this journal. Unfortunately, few can read those ancient words. Not even I can. Much has been lost. But we know what He said. That's been shared verbally through the millennia.

"Since men sinned and caused countless wars, rapes, enslavements, and fighting, I removed men's ability to perpetuate these. From this day forward, men shall have no arms. They shall have giant breasts to provide sustenance to their children and everyone. I now give women their opportunity to control the world. Bella is yours to run as you choose. But choose wisely. Make your men handle domestic duties and provide for the care and nourishment of your children.

"You see God has forsaken all men, the *abbandonato*. Men are cursed sinners, contaminated for eternity, filled with rotten depravity and wickedness. We call men *il dannato*, the damned. We find men *disgustoso, ripugnante*. Yet God promises Salvation and Redemption, the only pathway to Heaven for men.

"The few men of our *Chiesa Christiana Romana Santa Maria* devote their entire lives to becoming worthy of Holy Redemption. Upon their deaths, our priests give their official blessing in hopes Lord God will take mercy upon that man, ending his curse and allowing him into Heaven.

"It is common on Bella for women to find men repulsive. Yet, God has still given Purpose to his forsaken men. Women must have a man's seed to reproduce. God commanded us to take seeds from as many men as possible to guarantee optimum survival of future women. This Holy Union is sanctified in our *rapporti sessuali*.

"And this brings us to the present. You see, we women

125

Vic Broquard

do our best to avoid the downfall of men. We do not fight wars, enslave others, murder, rape, and the myriad other sins of which men once partook. For two thousand years, women have brought our civilization forward, achieving a better world in the eyes of Lord God.

"Then an *abbandonato* woman appeared among us! You. Shock. Dismay. Your coming has wrought a great fear amongst all women. Have we sinned so badly that Lord God is beginning to abandon women as well? Your coming has spread a wave of fear and terror across the whole of Bella. Women are terrified to sleep, fearing what their bodies will be when they awake. Some sleep in our churches, praying to God.

"Women are confessing to all manner of sins, hoping God will show them mercy and spare them. It's become silly. 'Forgive me. I have sinned. I drank more tea than I should have this morning.' Everyone looks to me, their Holy Pope, for guidance.

"The matter rests upon my shoulders. Are you an anomaly or the vanguard of our future? If all women become as our men are, none can survive for long. Civilization is doomed. Some say perhaps that is for the best. Some say it's the fault of the *La Libertà* for suggesting men should be as free as we women are, in spite of their curse.

"I've said now is the time for women to reflect upon their lives and the lives of the men around them. Have we failed to do what's right and just? Is there more that must be done? The *La Libertà* faction would have us believe so.

"This is then the position I face. I must discover the truth and advise those who believe in Lord God and Jesus Christ. Be honest with me. What have you done that you deserve to be cast out, to be forsaken by God, abandoned and shunned?"

At last, much made sense. But what should I say? Even if I told her the actual truth, would she even believe it? The

126

arrival of a spaceship with normal men and women on it would shake the very foundations of this entire civilization. Likely destroying it. Sooner or later, one of our deep space exploration ships would arrive, scouting the planet for valuable resources the Sol Empire needed. We are a greedy bunch. What could I say? What should I say? I wished I'd taken more anthropology courses at Soros University.

Religions throughout the Sol Empire vanished centuries ago. Traveling to new planets combined with the major corporations taking over control of Earth had long ago put an end to religious beliefs. We are not alone. Many alien civilizations exist. With the arrival of our spaceship on Bella, we were poised to destroy yet another religion. What to do?

I said, "All men and women have done things they should not have or failed to do something they should have done. But most of these are minor, as you suggested, drinking too much tea for breakfast. Me, I've never murdered anyone. Rather, this was done to me to save my life. An evil person put a hole through my head. Almost died. Our doctors developed a cure for some ailments. To stay alive and survive, my arms and breasts were sacrificed. When that evil person discovered I survived, he kidnapped me and left me among you. It isn't my intention to create such fear among your people. God will not curse the women of Bella as He did your men."

Pope Aria sat back and exhaled. Tension lines on her forehead vanished. I continued, hoping to set the stage for the arrival of our spaceship.

"My home is Earth, the world your ancestors came from. Today, it is a very different world from what it was then and totally different from the world you've created here. Out there among the stars are thousands of inhabited worlds. None of us are alone in this vast universe. One day, a ship from Earth will visit Bella, probably rescuing me. As you know, things are always changing.

"I think God is about to give your people their greatest challenge ever. You see, on Earth, all religions have vanished. Gone with the wind, as the saying goes. A few holy churches remain, but they are museums to ancient times. People forgot God and his commandments. Here on Bella, you are just beginning to develop marvelous technology, such as your electricity and steam engines. On Earth, technology has exploded. In a way, that has wiped out all religions. Between you and me, this has led to much more death, destruction, and corruption than ever before. Earth needs to rediscover God and the righteous paths.

"I'm beginning to see a greater purpose here. Perhaps God sent me to Bella for a reason. Of all the worlds I've visited, only on Bella do the faithful still live. Perhaps God wants you to bring His message, His words, back to Earth. In return, perhaps Earth's scientists can provide God's redemption to your men, that they may become whole once more. Many possibilities here."

"You've given me much to ponder. I have many questions. When will these ships come down from the skies?"

I shrugged my shoulders. "Tomorrow. A week. A month. I don't know, but I know they were planning a trip here to explore your world. I was kidnapped before I learned when. When they arrive, they will look for the largest city on the world, Nuova Roma, and come here looking for your leaders—your High Council, I believe. For sure you'll know when they arrive."

Of course, I knew much more about their situation. I'd met descendants of the Third Invaders who had played "god" and done this to their ancestors. Bella was just a society experiment of theirs. Worse, what would happen to these people once they realized or read the documents outlining the experiment that Isabella had translated? I could see that knowledge destroying not only their faith but also their

128

civilization. For the moment, I kept that knowledge to myself. But once Earth came, inevitably someone from Bella was bound to learn about those details. And then disaster. What to do?

Pope Aria said, "You realize I still must treat you as one of the *abbandonato*, the forsaken. I will let the other priests and bishops know that God isn't forsaking the women of Bella. Still, you will be shunned and treated as we do all tainted, decadent men. Your physical appearance dictates such. I wish you to spend time in my home. My daughter, Lia, is on the High Council. Not me. She'll want to meet you and ask many more questions, I'm sure. Come. I'll take you there now. Lia expects us for lunch."

I wasn't surprised to discover her home lay next door to the Gallo home, the red painted concrete villa. The layout of her home matched the Gallo's. I wondered if they used identical construction for homes. Inside, I met her mate, the oldest male in the extended family, Pino. Brown haired, Pino had black around his eyes. In fact, all the males had such dark patches; none ever met my gaze, though they did stare at me when I wasn't looking at them.

"Lia Faggini, Priestess and High Council member," Pope Aria said.

Lia had curly blonde hair, cut short. Her lip disk had to be twice the diameter of mine, but much smaller than her mother's.

Thirty-year-old Lia introduced her family. "My mate, Orfeo. My babes. Donata, five; Francesca, three; Marco, one."

Orfeo held Marco in a baby sack around his neck. Currently, the lad was suckling.

Donata said, "She's got a disk like mine, mama, but she's not five years old. I just got mine a week ago. Now I'm all grown up."

"Yes, you are, sweetheart. Just like mama," Lia said.

"I just got mine, too," I said.

Pope Aria said, "And these are my two younger sons, Sergio and Rinaldo. A few years remain before they must be mated or join the brotherhood. Because Lia has three youngsters, I've kept them around to help Orfeo care for them. Three young children are a bit much for one man to handle along with his other domestic duties."

Neither man looked directly at me.

Lia said, "Pino has lunch ready. Let's eat. Then, I'll show you your room, and we can talk."

As I suspected, Pope Aria said Grace before we dined.

During lunch, Pope Aria said, "Pino, make fish for supper. Orfeo, get those stinking diapers washed sooner. I smelled them when I walked inside. And Rinaldo, I told you yesterday to get the living room floor swept. Make it happen today. Must I hire more *Fratellanza* to replace you worthless men?"

Lia said, "She's right, Orfeo. I smelled Marco's diapers when I came in. Cleanliness is Godliness."

Although Lia saw just how much trouble I had trying to eat, she didn't offer to help me. Nor did Pope Aria. Something important must have come up, because both women left hastily. Lia did say we'd talk later on and asked Orfeo to show me to my room.

I helped the men clean up the lunch mess. I noticed these men had dark bags under their eyes. Bored, I decided to try to discover their state of mental health by following Celeste's methods. First step, pin down their chronic emotional tones. To do so, I questioned them, hoping they could understand me.

"Pino, is the weather in Nuova Roma always this mild?"

After several seconds, he muttered, "I suppose so. Never can tell such things. Aria would know."

Apathy. I changed topics. "How do you like living in

130

such a large city?"

Long pause. Just as I was about to try Orfeo, he replied with a drawl. "I suppose it's alright. Mostly, we just keep house for them. They matter. We don't. We're cursed, rotten, wicked. Only chance for redemption is to help them. Won't make this life any better, though."

I asked, "If you had your arms back and normal breasts, what would you do?"

I began to wonder if he heard me. Finally, he said, "I can't imagine that. Men have always been like this. Always will be. Unless Lord God sees we've been good. Grants us mercy. Don't know what good that would do after I'm dead. Perhaps endure a better time in Heaven, if I make it. Aria says so."

"Can you recall a time you were happy?" I switched to checking on how well he could recall events. After a long wait, I presumed he hadn't heard me. I moved over to sit beside Orfeo, who struggled to change Marco's diapers.

Pino took me by surprise. He said, "Nope. Can't recall I've ever been."

As I tried to assist Orfeo, memories of my second husband, Sam, and our two children flashed. Back then, he, too, was an armless telepath Galactic Doll, as were our two children. Yet, he took care of them while I was working. The parallels hit me hard. He and I were happy. A tear formed. I had thought that Celeste and I had erased this tragic loss. Guess some memories still persist.

When I asked Orfeo similar questions, he paused a long time before replying in a slow drawl. "We're outcasts. Forsaken by God and all. We're damned, cursed for eternity. Our only salvation might come if we avoid sin and do as they wish. Perhaps God will show us mercy when we die."

"I see. Can you recall a time when you were very happy?"

After a long pause, he said, "Happy? We're loathsome.

We don't matter at all. Our only purpose is to keep house and watch the babies. Women don't even need us for that. They can hire others like us to do it. We just don't matter. You've been cast out, too. You no longer matter."

Sergio and Rinaldo worked together to sweep the floor. Sergio manipulated a broom using his neck and shoulders, while his brother sat on the floor and moved the small piles into a bronze dustpan.

Sergio said, "Happy. Mom is happy when she's preaching at *Chiesa Santa Maria*."

"How about you fellows? You're both grown men. What plans do you have for the future?"

Sergio's communication came faster than Rinaldo's. Still, he took several seconds to ponder the question.

"No good at soccer. Was hoping to avoid being sent to *La Fratellanza*. Only six months left for a woman to mate with me. Not much chance now. He's right. We're loathsome. Despicable. We live only because Aria continues to provide for us."

"No offers to mate? You aren't ugly or homely."

He snickered. Rinaldo said, "Ha."

Sergio said, "Yeah, had some, but Mom refused. She kept us two around to help Orfeo raise three of Lia's children. Now I'm too old to bother with.

Rinaldo added, "Yeah. We heard there are tall cliffs near the brotherhood dwelling. We'll take a dive and see if Mom's right about God's redemption. Anything's better than this."

"Can you recall a time when you felt a strong love towards someone?" I asked.

After another lengthy pause, Sergio admitted he had. "Yeah. Once. I was about Francesca's age. Perhaps a year younger. I told Dad I loved him and Mom. He laughed at me. That's when I learned I was forsaken, an outcast, and loathed by everyone. Never since then."

"I never did," Rinaldo said with a sigh. "No point. Now Lia, she has. Many times. Loves Donata and Francesca. But despises Marco. Mom, she dotes on Lia, but loathes us. Keeps us around to help Dad and Orfeo. We know we're rotten. Cursed. We've fomented wars enslaved men, women, and children, murdered, pillaged, raped, and subjugated women. Whole cultures wiped out by us. We got what we deserve: forsaken and cursed."

Chapter 16 The *Pagani Dei*

That evening, Lia told me her mother relayed what I'd said to Pope Aria. Did I want to add anything? Not at this time. Lia left it at that. Two incredibly boring days later, Lia took me to spend time with Trista Baldovino, head of the Pagani Dei.

The High Priestess of the Church of the Pagan Gods, Trista Baldovino, welcomed me into her home, the blue house on the other side of Dante's white house. She wore a blue toga. The short woman with curly brown hair seemed jovial. Perhaps mid-forties.

"My mate, Carlo—a soccer player in his younger days."

Carlo appeared younger. Strong legs. Good physique. His long black hair draped down his back.

"She's too kind to me. We all praise Priestess Trista," he said.

"My beautiful daughter, Vittoria. One day she'll be following in my footsteps, leading our church. I've cautioned her about not picking a mate so soon. Many years ahead of her for such things. I don't approve of her flirting with that irreverent Dante next door."

Vittoria put her hands on her hips but said nothing. Attractive, twentyish. Brown hair and bangs that lent a pixie look. She stood inches taller than her mother, but still inches shorter than me. Am I the tallest woman on Bella?

"And my useless son, Georgio, a failed soccer player."

I suspected he was a year younger than Vittoria. He had long auburn hair with a distance runner's physique. Not Carlo's son?

"But I'm setting records for daily milk production. Plus, I've been getting at least three *rapporti sessuali* requests each

134

week. That bodes well for the *Pagani Dei*, doesn't it? I'm doing all I can to help."

"I suppose that's something," Trista said. "Let's eat. We take time to thank Vesta for providing this wonderful home and Ceres for the bounty we're about to partake. May Juno continue blessing this home."

We dined on fish, lentils, dried apples, and tea. While Vittoria's lip disk doubled mine in size and Trista's doubled hers, neither woman had any difficulty with it while dining. I certainly did, nearly falling over several times. Neither appeared to notice, or if they did, couldn't be bothered. I found a weird position that worked. I kept my left foot flat on the floor while using that knee to hold the plate up. Left my right foot free to deal with the utensils.

Very awkward, but resulted in a happy accident. Other than the disk, I looked like a tall man. To see I wasn't, everyone would have to lift my loincloth.

After we dined, Trista said, "I've got to conduct services. Shouldn't take more than an hour. I'll come get you after that, and we can talk."

She left. Vittoria headed into the living room, where she used the talky on the wall. Ah, those curious lower wires on power poles are the land lines I've read about.

Vittoria chatted with a girlfriend. "Gloria. Yeah, house is dirty here, too. Men. They never clean up the place right. I know. What can we expect? They're only men."

She didn't look at us, while we struggled to clean up the lunch mess. We pushed the dirty dishes up the ramp. Carlo washed. Georgio and I dried them and put them away. We used our feet to scrub the kitchen and dining room floors.

Vittoria said, "When you get that done, change my sheets. I got them dirty last night."

Georgio said, "Sure thing, Vittoria. We'll get on it next."

Emotional tone used as a pacifier on the women in their

lives? Wow. Better than the apathy of the Faggini men, but still pitiful.

I knew how hard changing a bed with feet is. Been there, done that. I helped. With three of us sitting on our butts, using our feet, and with a lot of time and effort, we got the bedding changed. Meanwhile, Vittoria continued to chat to her girlfriend on the phone, ignoring us. I glanced her way several times.

Georgio saw me glancing at his sister. He said, "Ignore her. Women always ignore us. We're used to it. After all, we're the forsaken, cursed sinners. But I've never murdered anyone. In their eyes, we're loathsome vile creatures. But they need our seed or there'll be no more babies.

"The way to survive is to do everything you can to please them. Keep them happy, and they'll support you. Without them, the only way a man could live is to join the *Fratellanza,* and those men are more like slaves. Beasts of burden. Not men. I'd rather jump off a cliff than live like they do."

Carlo said, "Keep on their good side. That's how to survive."

"You used to play soccer? One of the Colosseum teams?"

"Once upon a time. I made the team at eighteen. Met Trista back then. When I was nineteen, I fell and broke my left leg. Ended my soccer days. By then, she'd already asked me to mate. Too late for her to back out. Do what you must do to keep her and Vittoria happy with us. Otherwise, it's off to the *La Fratellanza.*"

"Have you ever been happy?"

Carlo smiled, pausing a moment. "When I played in my last soccer match. What a feeling of freedom. Fleeting. Such things ended whenever a game ended. Back to reality. We best get this bed done. She wants fish for supper. One of us must go to the market."

"I will, Dad. Chance to get fresh air. You're one of the *abbandonato,* too. A useless *maledetto.* Some of us men thought that very interesting. That women can be forsaken, not just us men. We know there hasn't been any wars. No pillaging and murders. Maybe Jupiter finds our treatment despicable and is forsaking and cursing women for their cruelty.

"Many of us want to know, what sins did you commit? Why did Jupiter forsake you?"

Ding. Ding. Ding. Got it! My appearance gave them hope that the gods would forsake and curse abusive women just as they'd done to me. That cast a new light on the fear I kept sensing from women when they saw me. Did they feel guilty about their treatment of the men in their lives and fear what the gods might do to them? Until I appeared, women had been immune to the curse. But now... I'm challenging the status quo.

I had a choice to make. Boost men's hope that women could be held accountable or dash this faint hope my arrival had brought. Would the arrival of the Sol deep space exploration ship render my advice useless?

"Well, all people should be held accountable for what they do or fail to do. In my case, an evil man did this to me."

"Men are inherently evil," Carlo said. "We deserve to be forsaken and cursed. The *Pagani Dei* claim if we lead good lives, when we die, Jupiter will take pity on us."

"But Dad, what good does that do us when we're dead?"

"I'd like to play soccer on the Elysian Fields among the gods," Carlo said.

"I hate soccer. What's in Elysium for me?"

"You don't want to spend all eternity handicapped like we are, do you? No, I thought not. Do all we can to please the women, and hope Juno intercedes for us."

High Priestess Trista Baldovino returned for me. We walked the blocks to her temple compound. It occupied an entire city block, resting upon a raised platform nearly as tall as the nearby homes. On top of the platform, great marble columns rose, supporting an ornate roof. Giant white marble statues of old Roman gods stood watch over the temple proper. Offerings of food, flowers and other objects lay at their feet.

She led me inside the temple to her private study. A woolen blue-dyed carpet felt soft beneath my feet. Her desk: more modest that the Pope's. She opened the conversation.

"You've been told Bella's population is divided. Four in ten belong to the *Chiesa Santa Maria*. Another four worship the old gods. We're called pagans by the Christians. Divided, yet together we stand. It's been that way for two millennia. Such is logged in the Great Book.

"The first High Priestess logged those early days. She kept a journal. Language changes over time. Today, few can read those beginning pages. I, like the other religious leaders, have had the honor of adding to the Great Book, though I've not had much to write about. Until your arrival.

"Staying with us—the members of the High Council and those who rule Bella—gives you a false view of our world and its people. You are among the elite of the elite, far from the common woman. The majority of women toil long hours to support our civilization.

"It is written they do jobs men once did. Some must farm or we starve. Other must manufacture the concrete for the new homes. Someone must mine for iron, gold, silver, copper, and even coal and peat. Someone must run the smelters. Someone must educate our young women. The bright ones invent things. Electricity. The Talky. Soon, steam trains will connect the inn. Someone must tend the blast furnaces and the looms.

138

"In all this, men are useless—of no help whatsoever. Yet, when the day's toil is done, women return home exhausted. The gods decreed that man should maintain the home, prepare the meals, and care for the young. If we didn't need a man's seed to begat children, we would eliminate men. But we do. The gods' wisdom prevails.

"We of the *Pagani Dei* believe that if a man performs his domestic duties well, helping women succeed, then when their physical body dies, we beseech Juno on his behalf. If Juno finds the man's been worthy of redemption, she intercedes on his behalf with Jupiter, who may lift the curse that the man may enter Elysium whole again.

"This is now the lot that has befallen you. Since you are no longer able to do whatever work you used to do—mining, farming, weaving—you must join men and help with domestic duties. But since you are a woman and capable of bearing children, the High Council doesn't know what to do with you.

"Our children are predictable. Boys are always born without arms and grow giant breasts that continuously produce life-giving milk. Girls are always normal. Nothing has changed in two millennia. Until now. We don't know what your children will be like.

"We suspect any boys you may have will be like the men of Bella. But will your girls share your curse? That we don't know. Pope Aria is most concerned that they will be cursed. If so, in time, many, many women, children of your children's children will be cursed as men are. Who will be left to support them?

"Pope Aria relayed much of what you discussed with her. Though our religious beliefs differ, our goals for Bella do not. So, I would like to hear your story from you, if I may."

I had to be careful of what I said and how I said it. I tried to recall what I'd said to Pope Aria.

"All men and women have done things they should not

139

have or failed to do something they should have done. Me, I've never murdered anyone."

I told her what I'd told Pope Aria, as best I could remember, including the notions they could help bring religion back to Earth.

After I finished, she asked, "When will these ships come from the skies?"

I shrugged my shoulders. "Tomorrow. A week. A month. I don't know." I relayed what I'd said to Pope Aria. "You'll know when they arrive."

I didn't dare tell her about the Third Invaders.

Trista said, "Thank you for the candor. Still, I am obligated to treat you as one of the *abbandonato*.

"You will be shunned. Treated as a forsaken man. But I will suggest you share the rights of women. That is, you can mate with a man of your choice, as long as you have the means."

"What do you mean?"

"When a woman asks a man to mate and the man accepts, she accepts the responsibility of providing a home for him. It must have all the items necessary for the man to perform his domestic duties, such as the kitchen and dining room table. Provide the refrigerator, the stove, the sink, bathroom and its fixtures, and yokes of various sizes along with beds and bedding.

"All that is needed for the man to carry out what is expected of him. House costs vary widely, but generally, a hundred gold aurei is enough for the lot."

"I have a fortune back on Earth. I can bring gold to pay my debts whenever the ship arrives."

"A money changer can work out such details for you. We should be heading home. Fish dinner awaits us."

140

The Sol Empire Volume 6 Religion and Robots

Chapter 17 The *La Liberà*

After spending several days with the Baldovino family, Carolina Gallo brought me back to her home. It felt good to be in the Gallo home and close to Dante. After lunch, she took me to her office in a plain white building not far from the huge *Chiesa Santa Maria* and the giant temple of the *Pagani Dei*. A simple sign above its open doorway read: *La Liberà*. Pamphlets lay in stacks on one table. Several women were chatting with other women. From the scattered words, I guessed they tried to make converts.

Once seated in Carolina's modest office, she explained her beliefs. "As you now know, two in ten women and many men follow our beliefs in freedom for all, including men. Dante is smitten with you. I best tell you about our movement.

"First, we believe in duality. Light and Dark. Good and Evil. Spiritual beings are of the Creator. Satan, this physical universe. We, the being, the person, aren't made of physical stuff or energy, but possess a mind. We inhabit Satan's physical creations for a time. The physical body is Satan's tool. He uses it to turn us away from the light, self-knowledge, truth, and the Creator.

"When our body dies, unless we've achieved Ultimate Perfection, we the being take over another baby body to continue walking the path before us. Yes, each of us has lived many lives and have yet to achieve Perfection. Satan tempts us with good food, pleasure, sex, gold, silver, on and on. For many, such is hard to resist. They follow Satan's dark path."

A flood of questions flickered through my mind. Did this mean there would be an exponential population growth if the Creator is still creating new beings? Or has the Creator

142

stopped creating new ones? Did he create a finite number of new people in the beginning? Does Purgatory consist of a line of people waiting for baby bodies? Are the greater failures waiting longer than others for a second, third, fourth chance to achieve Perfection? How did we become soldiers in the battle between the Creator and Satan? Does Satan ever win and achieve his goal winning the Creator's created beings? Does he put those he acquired into his physical manifestations or is he powerless to do anything but hold them, keep them from the Light? And is there selfishness between the two in using us to fight their battles for them? What if Satan stopped creating the physical as a battle tactic? I kept quiet.

"The *Christiana Romana* believe their wafers and wine get transformed into the body of Jesus Christ and his blood, their transubstantiation. That consuming these somehow makes them better able to walk the path of Light. Of course, only those baptized can partake of the Holy Communion. No man can ever be baptized since men are forsaken and cursed by God. Thus, men have no chance for salvation or freedom. We of the *La Liberà* find that ridiculous. The wafers and wine are still the same wafers and wine that the merchants made for the church.

"We reject their notions of sacraments. Grace is spiritually pure. How could that be transferred via the Dark physical means of consuming them?

"To become free, one must focus on becoming as spiritual as possible, as close to the Light as can be. Few can lead a life of total self-denial of Satan's material aspects of life. While a body can survive weeks without food, it can only live a short while without water. Yet, when one of us senses our body is close to death, we prepare ourselves with a total fast, total denial of Satan's world. If we have achieved Perfection, then we pass into the Light, ending our lives in the universe, joining the Creator in an eternal life in Heaven.

"Until that Final Fast, we try to live a Perfect Life, as free from physical and material things as possible. We don't accept the incarnation of Jesus Christ as a spiritual god put into a Satan-provided physical body. Nonsense. The Light would never merge with Dark, which is the fate that's befallen us. Same is true with the *Pagani Dei*. Why would such powerful gods and goddesses, spiritual beings of the Light, soil themselves by merging with a human Satan-spawned body? Again, nonsense.

"We beseech others to seek the Light and consume only what is needed for survival. The Light is spiritual freedom.

"By now, you must have seen men are second-class members of our society, loathed and detested. Yet, needed for their seed. Often, their treatment is that of a pet dog, if even that well-treated. When no longer needed, they are dropped off at *La Fratellanza* and left to fend for themselves. Those men live lives lower than that of a dog. Most become beasts of burden, pulling chariots, plows, and wagons. Pitiful existence at best.

"*La Liberà* does all it can to promote the ethical treatment of men. They should be free, too. Alas, we've not gotten very far with that. Men are still denied any education beyond learning to speak and enough writing and arithmetic to handle shopping for groceries."

"I thought they didn't go to school."

"True, they aren't allowed. Fathers teach sons to read enough to get by and enough counting to deal with shopping."

I asked, "Have the percentages of people belonging to these three groups stayed relatively constant over the centuries?"

"More or less, but *La Liberà* has seen a steady increase in our members during the last several hundred years. Ever since the invention of electricity. Some of our women invented that, along with the heating stove and refrigerator. We are seen as the progressive party.

"In fact, several women have recalled their previous incarnations. Such testimonials help convince other women that unless they focus on the Light, the spiritual side, they are doomed to repeated lives here on Bella."

I chuckled. "Well, I've certainly had many bodies over many centuries. You're on the right track there."

She glanced up and met my eyes. "Incredible. Tell me more. Who are you, anyway?"

I told her what I'd told Pope Aria and High Priestess Trista. That I came from Earth, their ancestors' home world, impressed her. When she heard a ship from Earth might soon land on Bella, Nuova Roma more specifically, Carolina became animated.

"Tell me more! There are other worlds around the stars in the sky? How many? Satan's expanse is gigantic. Do women on these other worlds follow the Light, spiritual purity, or do they succumb to physical things?"

I sighed. "I think you'd say they succumbed long ago to all things material. On Earth and the Sol Empire, organized religions like those you have here no longer exist. A few churches survive but only as museums. You three have quite a challenge to rebuild religions out there among the stars."

Her body slumped. "Satan has won?"

"Perhaps he has temporarily won over many converts, but surely they can be won back."

"Do the men out there still fight wars? Do men still enslave men, women, and children? Do they murder, pillage, rape, and subjugate women? Do men still wipe out whole cultures?"

"That can happen, but most men and women are basically good people who just want to survive. With these modern civilizations, the technological devices make life much easier to handle. You'd probably say they've succumbed to the temptations of the physical universe, forsaking their spiritual side. But my sister, Celeste, she and some of us are working to change that. To increase people's spiritual awareness of themselves and others. Admittedly, we've only just begun."

"Begun what?" Dante interrupted. "Dad said to tell you supper is ready."

At dinner, Zita said, "Mom, I'm twenty. You had me when you were my age. I really want to mate and get a life of my own. Why can't I choose Georgio Baldovino? After all, Vittoria keeps trying to mate Dante here. This way, our two families would be closely bound."

"But Zita, he's a *Pagani Dei*. He's not one of us."

"He'll do whatever I say, just as Dante must do what Vittoria says. Does that really matter all that much? Men are just around to give us their seed and take care of our homes."

"We're more than that!" Dante protested, raising his voice.

She cast him a disgusted look. "Oh, don't be ridiculous, Dante. You're very nearly helpless. Just like Dad, Nico, and Luigi. About all that men can do is cook and keep house. Even that takes you forever to do."

"Well, you could help some, you know," Dante fired back.

"We're tied up running everything else on our world! Who makes the steel, eh? The steam power plants? The refrigerators? The homes? Women do. We slave to build our world, while men just cook and clean house. I'd like to see you dig coal for the power plants or—"

"That's enough, Zita. Dante. Not while we eat. Men know their places. They strive for the Light in their own ways just as women do," Carolina said.

"Well, one woman is worth ten men—maybe a hundred men," Zita said, gaining the last word. "Don't forget, I spend all day teaching our young girls. There's much to learn these

146

days. Besides, women slave to make life easier for the men."

She pointed around the room. "That light. The stove. The refrigerator. What has Dante built? What has any man ever invented? Tell me that, Mom. Nothing. They can't."

"We could if you'd educate us," Dante countered. He glared at Zita.

Zita shot back. "You can't even write. Get real, Dante."

Carolina rubbed her face. "Okay, Zita. Have it your way. Mate with Georgio, if he'll agree. I'll buy a house straightway if he says yes. Perhaps then we'll have peace around here. I'm disappointed with you, Zita. Thought you had more sense."

Finally, a sense of real life. Until now, these leaders painted a utopian picture. Life isn't like that.

Dante fired back. "Well, I'm sure not saying yes to Vittoria."

"Don't worry, Dante. I'll see if I can find a good *La Liberà* woman for you. Now you guys clean up this mess. Zita, let's pay a visit to the Baldovino's." Both women rose and left.

As we began pushing dishes back up the low ramp to the counter, Tito spoke up. "Fellows, if Zita does mate and move out, our workload will definitely lessen. Less food to cook and less cleaning."

"I'm for that," Nico said.

With seven to feed, the dishes piled up. The sun set by the time we finished cleaning up from the evening meal. If nothing else, I had a good feel for how long it took the four of us to handle the mess. Too damned long. At least the twins didn't need constant care, not like the year-old Marco Foggia.

As Nico slid the last plate into its place, Tito's shoulders sagged. "I'm beat. Going to bed now, kids. Look after the twins, will you? Whoever said taking care of a house isn't work? I don't get five minutes for myself all day." He muttered something else, but I couldn't make it out.

Nico said, "Is this what we have to look forward to,

Dante? I don't want to be like Dad. He's pooped every night."

"Exhausted is more like it," Dante said.

Carolina walked in. "Well, that's settled. Georgio agreed to the mating. Tomorrow, I'll see about getting them a house. Dante, you visit the markets tomorrow and see what you can find for the mating feast. We'll host the Baldovino's over here after the brief ceremony on Saturday."

"Can I go with him? I'd like to see more of the city."

"Sure, Molly. Nuova Roma is safe. No crime to speak of. Have you received your endowment of lip disks?"

"Huh? No, only this one."

"Soon your lip loop will have stretched. You'll need a larger one. It's a mandate. Girls receive their own collection of increasingly larger disk after lip splitting. They should have given you a batch of at least twenty. Dante, take an additional ten denarius with you and drop by the Disk Shop. Buy Molly a complete beginner's set of disks and a carrying bag for them."

"How soon will I need a larger one?"

She chuckled. "Every young girl asks that. They stretch about an inch each year, but when you've worn them for twenty years, they seem to expand even faster. You can tell a woman's age by her lip disk. You'll be the exception. You're not five years old."

"Thanks for the disks."

God! This is only getting worse. I couldn't imagine dealing with a disk an inch larger, let alone those the older women sported.

Later, Dante and I remained awake, chatting in the living room. Zita came home, her face flushed.

"Oh, that was a blast. Sesso with Georgio. My, his is big."

Dante's face crimsoned. "You don't have to brag about that, Zita. We couldn't care less. You're succumbing to the Dark."

She stuck her tongue out at him and headed for her room.

Chapter 18 *La Fratellanza*

The next day, Dante and I roamed the markets. We carried a yoke with baskets balanced on our shoulders.

"We should get fixings for a celebration cake and fresh fish for dinner. Zita deserves that," he said.

The air smelled of the ocean. When the market chatter died down for a moment, I could hear waves rolling on the beach. Sea birds fluttered around market stalls. Merchants tossed cast offs into the streets, and sea birds clamored, battling each other for the prized morsels. Hundreds hovered around the stalls, but few women—the farmers with their produce.

Dante filled up his two baskets first. In addition, I noticed an awful lot of men milling around not shopping. I didn't pay much attention to them until the press of their bodies separated me from Dante. I found it challenging to maneuver around them with the yoke balanced on my shoulders.

Two men pulling a cart rumbled towards us, forcing a bigger distance between me and Dante, who focused on paying for the fish. A blanket-laden cart with an open backside passed me as several men pushed me off balance. No way to break the fall, I hoped I didn't hit the ground too hard. I landed on the blankets in the cart. Two men jumped in beside me and pressed rags against my face. I had to breathe. Chloroform. I felt the blankets' weight, the cart's movement, as all faded to black. Kidnapped.

I awoke in a room and on a narrow bed, covered with a sheet. I looked about before trying to get up. Several other beds filled the room, leaving little room to walk. Where was I?

I sat up. An older man entered the room.

"Ah. Awake at last. Aldo Costa, leader of Nuova Roma's Brotherhood. *La Fratellanza* as we're called. You're the woman shaking Bella to its foundations. We've heard much about you from our contacts in the other organizations. Forgive us for our uncivilized way of getting you to us. We had no other choice. We're considered second-class citizens. Women loathe us. No way they'd allow you to visit. Sorry about the kidnapping. Was the only way to meet you."

"Well, you could have asked."

"Those women leaders—they wouldn't let us make contact with you, let alone allow you to visit us."

"Point taken. How long have I been out?"

"Only an hour. Come. I have tea and many questions."

I followed him into a large kitchen-dining room, where six long tables seated three dozen men at one time. I saw several younger men preparing lunch, but Aldo had two teacups sitting on one low table. We sat across from each other. He had long, black hair and sorrowful eyes. My guess he'd seen fifty-some years.

"Did those leaders tell you their numbers?"

"Like the *Santa Maria* and the *Pagani Dei*—with four out of ten in each of their churches?"

He smiled. "Yes, between those three organizations, they claim to have ten out of ten people. What they didn't tell you is they only count women in their numbers. Men don't count. In fact, only half the total people on Bella belong to their organizations."

"I've seen that for myself."

"*La Fratellanza*, our brotherhoods, count about five out of ten men in our groups. The other half are lucky enough to be the women's men. Mates and sons and star soccer players. In time, every other man ends up in one of our brotherhood homes."

"It's good that your organization exists. Commendable work."

"Either we help men or the cast-out men die. Alone, we cannot survive. Those who are lucky enough to be mates have their feet full just trying to keep up with the domestic workload. Once several children are born, they cannot. Women are forced to hire temporary men to help. Because of our handicap, we are slow accomplishing such life tasks. That is not to say we cannot do them. Rather, it takes us much longer to do them. Far be it for a woman to lend us a hand."

"I've seen that behavior."

"Good for you. Most women don't see us. But the men we take in are treated worse than second-class citizens. Beasts of burden is more like it. Half hire out as that, pulling chariots, pulling wagon loads of ore, coal, and concrete, pulling carts for women workers, and pulling plows in the women's fields— exhausting work with demeaning pay."

"Those I've seen pulling wagons are your members trying to earn a living?"

"Yes. We own some agricultural fields, but as you might guess: marginal ones. The women use the prime fields for their crops. With hundreds and hundreds of us men working together, between pitiful wages earned as beasts, farming our poor lands, and the small amount we earn from producing large amounts of milk, we survive. A few men spend their days fishing along the coast. The catch is small. Women in their boats catch volumes. We scratch out a living, though we often are hungry.

"How is it that a woman has become one of us, one of the *abbandonato*? What evil have you done that the gods cursed you?"

I told him the same things I told the three women leaders.

152

"Ships from the stars? Day dream. But your appearance on Bella has created fears and doubts among most women across our world. They are afraid the gods will curse them next. Rightly so, if there were such things as all-powerful gods. Their treatment of us would damn them. We both know there are no such things as gods or God or Satan. Merely a myth to keep women in line."

He continued. "I can't let this golden opportunity pass. We must strike while women fear becoming cursed for their crimes against us."

"Is that a good plan? What are you going to do?"

"It has already begun. Men across Bella are demanding acceptance as normal citizen, proper educations, and decent wages work. I'm calling it Male Suffrage. We're marching in the streets of Nuova Roma and several smaller towns today, demanding a voting position on the High Council. For millennia, the women of Bella denied us these. We hope their fears of becoming *abbandonato*, cursed like us men, will force them to change their treatment of us. It's the best chance the men of Bella have ever had in two millennia.

"Women are terrified of becoming like us. They believe in their God and gods. Between us, no God or gods have shown any signs of their existence in all these years. I believe they abandoned us once they brought our ancestors here."

"I wondered when someone would take advantage of the fear my appearance brought to Bella. I wish you success, as long as you are non-violent with your protests. From what I've seen, the men of Bella are being abused, though I can see some women's points of view, too. After all, they must do the work Earth's men used to do. It's not easy mining for coal or making steel or cutting the trees to make the power poles. Nevertheless, they should treat men far better than they are."

"Glad you see our view. I didn't think you would. What with you being a woman. But you are one of us now. I suppose that changed your views of things."

I laughed. "No, I've always been for fair treatment of everyone. People should work together to make a better world for all. I wonder if your message will be received."

"Let's see what's happening."

I followed him to a stairway that led to the roof. From this height, I glimpsed a silver streak of ocean. The daytime winds, much stronger at this height, brought the salt air inland, refreshing to me. Aldo had no way to effectively point. He talked me to the location where the main body of male protestors marched. From our vantage point, we could make them out, though homes often blocked our view.

"Molly? Molly? You there? Ah, found you!" Dante sent. "Been searching for you. What happened? For the longest time, I couldn't reach you."

I sent him what happened in brief.

He sent back, "You're missing the biggest thing ever! The men of *La Fratellanza* are protesting, demanding rights. They want a position on the High Council. They want men to get educations like women get. And fair pay. It's quite a demonstration."

He sent, "Wait! Pope Aria Faggini and High Priestess Trista Baldovino are responding now. Shit! They've ordered the security guards to attack the protesters. They're beating them with their spears!"

"We can see it from here," I sent back. "What's happening? Are they being beaten?"

Aldo sighed. "Well, I figured the women would refuse to negotiate or be reasonable. The men in front—they knew the risks and are prepared to be martyrs for our cause. It's now or never. What those ignorant women don't realize is by beating up my men, they're playing into our hands."

"I don't understand, Aldo. Men are being hurt. They can't even fight back. Those women are wearing armor."

"Women everywhere can see how their leaders brutalize men. That's going to create drastically more fear among them that the gods will strike down women as they did us men."

"But if there are no gods..."

"Doesn't matter. Put the fears of that happening into the average woman's mind and they'll put a mountain of pressure on their leaders. Look, it only took the appearance of one woman who looks like us men to appear to raise doubts in women's minds. Watching helpless men get beaten by armored fighters is only escalating such fears. Let their own women put pressure on them for change. We don't need another woman to become cursed like you or we are. Heck, between us, I'd not wish a life like this on anyone, man or woman.

"I'm simply making use of their fears to help us win freedom and respect. No man has ever attended school. We can barely read our own language. It's time for that to change. Your appearance has given us this one chance to make that happen. Now, those leaders are helping us by beating up the protesters."

A breathless runner joined us. "Aldo, they're beating us—trampling those who've fallen. What do you want us to do now?"

"Have them retreat into side streets and alleyways. Ready cart to retrieve our wounded."

The young lad dashed down the stairs. I spotted him dashing down a street heading for the battle zone. I hoped no one died. This wasn't what I wanted to happen. But I saw Aldo's point of view. Perhaps this was his one chance to bring about change.

Later, men trickled back inside the large building. Some had bleeding noses; others, black and blue marks across their bosoms and backs. Much later, the man-pulled carts brought thirty dead and dying men into the courtyard behind the

155

building. Six had broken legs. For us, that could well be a death sentence, since we depended upon our legs and feet to survive. Many of the dead also had broken legs and had been mercifully slain via a spear to their hearts. I had no idea how many had broken ribs. No way to tell.

As the men gathered around the tables for supper in shifts, I listened to their discussions as best I could. When Aldo appeared, I asked him about the six wounded men.

"Can they be taken to see a doctor? Do you have a hospital that can treat them?"

He gave me a dirty look, before changing it to a somber one. "I forgot you are new to Bella. There are doctors and hospitals for women, but none will treat a man. We aren't allowed to get medical attention. The only exception was when the Black Death visited Bella. Then, they had no choice. We men must look after our own. Sometimes they will send a doctor to help a man injured while being a beast of burden."

"But how can you if no one is a trained doctor? Legs need to be set and casts made. We can't even carry them inside. Can we?"

His grim chuckle spoke volumes. "That's why I'm grateful for the mercy killings. We have no way to help those six, except to look after their needs as we can and hope for the best. These men are able to hop inside to a bed, and I cling to hope they might yet live. Time will tell. Excuse me. I must contact the other houses. Please sit and eat. Four other shifts will follow."

He left, and I sat before an empty place that had a bowl of stew and a mug of tea waiting. From the corner of my eye, I watched as men lined up at the milking apparatus, waiting their turn to donate to the cause. Again, I wondered why their milk didn't dry up. Had the Third Invaders somehow turned them into cows?

My lip disk prevented me from eating as rapidly as the

156

men. This group finished and pushed their dirty dishes up the ramp to the counter where a couple of men moved them on down to the washing station. Meanwhile, others filled up more bowls and mugs, sliding them down and into place on the tables. Quite an efficient operation. When I finally finished, I volunteered to help wash the dishes, something the men found amusing. Many grinned at me. I sensed they were pleased with my gesture.

While the third shift dined, Aldo Costa appeared. "Today, one hundred two men perished in the protests with another twenty wounded."

Groans echoed around the room. Someone yelled, "Did they listen?"

Aldo said, "No. And we didn't think they would, though I didn't believe they would kill us. Instead, many others are outraged. Tomorrow, across Bella, men are going on strike, demanding Male Suffrage. No beasts of burden will work. I've heard domestic men may not work either. Time will tell. Take heart. We've made a positive statement today. Women cannot continue to treat us this badly."

"We should demand equal medical treatment," one man yelled.

Aldo said, "I will add that to our demands."

Others cheered. I smiled, though no one could see it.

Chapter 19 The Boycott

"Your Holiness, you must come. Men are protesting in the streets," one of Pope Aria's priestesses said. She stood gasping for breath, having run to tell her the awful news.

"This can't be," Pope Aria said, rushing past her.

She climbed the stairs to the upper levels of her church. From here, she could see the nearby streets. Dozens of men marched along, shouting calls.

"Get Baldovino on the talky!"

The out of breath priestess dashed down the church's stairs. Soon, the Pope joined her on the talky.

"High Priestess, have you seen what's going on in the streets?"

"It's disgusting! The cows are making insane demands," Trista replied. "I've sent out messengers to collect the beasts' demands. A position on the High Council? Utterly ridiculous. Higher wages? We support them out of the kindness of our hearts."

"We must nip this before it escalates. Send out our armored security brigade," the Pope said.

"I agree, Your Holiness. What orders do we give them? Should we contact Carolina? This is beyond deplorable."

"No time for that. Stop them. Use force if necessary. This protest can't be allowed to continue. I must check with our other churches. I hope this is an isolated uprising."

**

"Mom, men are marching in the market streets!" Dante said. He'd rushed home with the purchases. "And Molly's missing."

"Not now, Dante. Talking to Aria. She's called out the guards. What's that? A voting position on the High Council?

158

Well... No, I'm not siding with lawlessness, but... They're helpless. How can they harm the... Well, I see, but won't... All right. All right. I'll join you as soon as my guards get here. Bye."

Turning to Dante, she said, "Must run. High Council meeting. They're using force to dispel these absurd men. Honestly..."

Dante tried to protest, but she headed outside to meet up with her security forces. He ducked out as well, heading back towards the market streets so he could watch. Nico tagged along, leaving Tito to put away the new groceries.

"Dante, they're beating the men," Nico said, his eyes wide.

"And kicking them when they fall. Ghastly! Grim! We can neither fight nor defend ourselves."

"We can't. Can we?" Nico asked. "We can't fight them. Besides, they're wearing armor. Oh, no! They're stabbing them. Other women are laughing!"

"You shouldn't look, Nico. The guards are murdering helpless men. No way to hurt the guards. This isn't right. This isn't the path to Light that Mom's always talking about."

"But shouldn't there be a man on the High Council to represent us? I'd like to do that. Shouldn't men be normal citizens? Why can't boys get an education like girls do? I wanted to go to school. Learn exciting things. Why can't you be paid a decent amount for your work?" Nico asked, pestering Dante.

"We should. That is why they protest."

"But they're killing them."

"Is it a revolution? I heard Zita talking about such things happening in ancient times. Perhaps that's what this is, Nico. But we best get back in case Tito needs us. It's not right for us to leave him to fix supper and care for the twins all alone. Mom can tell us more when she gets back for supper."

159

***

"Yes, well that was all on Aria and Trista. They ordered the guards to use whatever force was necessary to quell the demonstration," Carolina said. "I didn't condone it, but I'm only one voice, as you well know. I can't see how it would hurt to have a representative from *La Fratellanza* on the council. After all, men are half our population. But go to school? How? You fellows can't write or hold a book. No way could you go to school with Elena. Decent pay? Now that's something I've argued for years. Those who become beasts of burden just to survive—now they should be paid much more than they are. But demonstrating in the streets, disrupting the marketplace? That's not right either."

"Mom, they are killing them," Dante said.

She sighed. "Couldn't be helped. They refused direct orders to disband. I'm told the guards first used the ends of their spears to beat sense into them. They only used deadly force when the men pushed back against them."

Dante sneered. "Oh, a man pushing into an armored guard warrants her stabbing the man in his heart?"

"Well... Men shouldn't be disrupting the market place used by everyone. Say, where's Molly? Did she return?"

"Not yet, Mom. She vanished from the marketplace. While we were shopping."

Zita said, "Who cares? Maybe she got lost during the protest. She'll show up. Another mouth to feed."

"You sound more like Vittoria every day," Dante said, glaring at his sister.

"Well, she is. She doesn't even bring in a silver with her milk. At least you guys are helping Dad take care of our house and Elena," she replied.

"Zita, come with me. We're holding a special council meeting to update our teachers and brief them so they know how to address their students tomorrow."

After Carolina and Zita left, Nico said, "Dad, armored guards shoved their spears into their hearts. That's wrong, a sin? How can that be fair? Isn't that what men were supposed to have done to make the gods curse us?"

"No, Nico. Beating and stabbing men isn't right. They didn't stab them because they were a physical threat. But they are challenging the women's perception of themselves. It's the way of Darkness, not the path of Light. But neither is disrupting the markets a good thing. Women and their silly gods. There's been no sign of a god around Bella for two thousand years. I don't care how many lamb sacrifices Trista does, her gods abandoned us long ago. Trouble is, sons, we can't survive without the women. We need them, but they only need us for our seed. Mom's right. Follow the path of Light. Dishes," he said, ending their brief talk.

Later, a male friend dropped by and told Dante about the morrow's boycott and the day's death toll. Dante relayed the boycott suggestion to Tito and Nico.

"Dad, what do we do? They said sixty-six men were murdered. Here in Nuova Roma, six men have broken legs and might not survive. We asked to be treated like people, and they slaughter us like animals. "

"Your mother would say follow the Light. Parkinson's arrival must have something to do with the *La Fratellanza* uprising," Tito replied. "That's what Carolina is calling it. And uprising."

"But they have a valid point, Dad. Women treat us as though we're the plague. Honestly, we're people, too," Dante said. "Hush. Here comes Zita and Georgio Baldovino."

He heard Zita threatening Georgio. "Now don't you go getting any stupid ideas or the mating on Saturday is off."

"But they killed so many men. Doesn't that bother you? Isn't that why were cursed in the first place? I can't read, but I've heard Mom talk about that. It's written in the ancient book."

"Georgio, men are supposed to be our domestics, not our equals. The gods cursed your kind for your crimes against humanity. You don't get the rights we women have. You can't actually *do* anything but minor domestic chores, now can you? When was the last time you poured a new concrete home like the one Mom's buying for us, eh? No, your place is cooking our meals, cleaning our home, and making lots of milk to help earn my support. Oh, and caring for my babies when I get around to having them. Who ever heard of a man going to school? Why would you even want to read?"

"Books. You've got lots of books. I'd like to read to find out what's in them."

"Well, you can't. No hands to hold them or turn pages. Don't be silly. Be happy I've finally agreed to mate with you and provide a home for you. That should be more than enough. If it isn't, I'll find another man who is."

Georgio didn't reply. Dante sensed the tension between them.

Zita looked up and said, "Oh, Dante, Vittoria wants you to come over after supper. She wants to talk to you."

"About what?" he asked. "I'm not agreeing to mate with her."

"You could do plenty worse. If you don't do something soon, you're going to be sent off to *La Fratellanza* and become a beast of burden. Maybe you want to pull a wagon around all day, is that it?" She snickered.

Dante knew he had to visit Vittoria. When a woman asked you over, failure to comply resulted in a gigantic social affront. He obeyed.

He found her in the lush Baldovino living room, burning incense to purify her space, or so she claimed.

"Ah, there you are, Dante. Come, sit by me and be purified. All those filthy men marching in the streets today

162

have disrupted the vapors of life. We must be purified. Now then, I'm glad you weren't out there marching today. The absurdity of it all. Imagine a man trying to go to school. Ludicrous. I can't believe how many greedy men are out there, can you?"

"Well, I'd like to go to school and learn new things. Who knows, maybe I could invent something useful for everyone."

Vittoria glared at him and waved smoke around her, as though blowing away something disgusting.

"Besides, men ought to have a representative on the High Council. Half the population of Bella are men."

"Now you *are* being silly. Imagine a dumb man trying to do Mom's job. Ha. Or even those of our councils. Get real, Dante. A man has only one purpose. Provide his seed. We let you take care of domestic duties to give us more time to do the real work."

"You don't think men are worth anything?"

"We must have your seed. If it weren't for that, I'm sure we'd have disposed of men centuries ago."

"Lot of fine work you do, Vittoria. At least Zita teaches our young girls."

"What do you mean by that, Dante? I work hard. It's not easy divining the meaning of bird flights. It's gross cutting open a sacrificial lamb and interpreting its intestinal contents. And I must pray for many, many women each day. It can be exhausting work. All you do is wash dishes and help your dad cook.

"Besides, the protesters today got what they deserve. Honestly, disrupting the market place is an uprising against the hard-working women of Bella. Women slave each day to make our world thrive. What do you men do? Nada. Anyway, I asked you over because I wanted to see if you were okay. Have you changed your mind about mating with me? If you agree, we'll hold a double ceremony with Zita on Saturday. Now that

163

would bring honor to both our mothers."

"The answer is still no, Vittoria. We've nothing in common."

Since she continued to reject his refusal to mate with her, he lightly touched her mind. He sensed both fear and jealousy. Molly's image appeared, too. He knew better, but said, "Molly and I have more in common than you and I ever would."

He felt the sting in her mind and saw her face flush.

"You pathetic beast!" she said.

With a swat of her hand, she slapped him across his face.

Lacking arms to catch himself, he fell off the couch, landing hard on the floor.

"Sorry," he said, knowing he deserved that.

With awkward motions, he got back to his feet.

"Best be going."

He turned and left Vittoria fuming, but she didn't yell anything back at him.

By the time he entered his home, he'd made up him mind. Tomorrow, he'd boycott his duties. As he lay in bed, he reached out, found Molly, and verified she was okay.

***

"Where's breakfast?" Carolina asked. She'd dressed and entered the kitchen, ready to start the new day.

Tito, Dante, and Nico merely sat at the empty table, saying nothing.

Zita joined them. "Hey, where's breakfast? I've got to leave in a few minutes."

Since the men continued to say nothing, Carolina said, "Well, at least feed the twins. Come on, Zita. We can grab something later. Emergency High Council meeting." The two left the still silent men.

"Well, did our message get through?" Dante asked.

164

"Come on. We best get the twins some food, and I'm starving."

Later, Dante and Nico headed to the markets to see the action.

"Wow!" Nico said. "It's empty! Where is everyone? Only the women farmers are here. No one else."

Dante looked up and down this street. Half the stalls lay vacant. The ones occupied by the farmers had no customers. Their stacks of produce sat untouched. The two raced over to the next market street. An hour later, they headed home.

"Dad, the markets are empty!" Nico said, as he rushed in. "All of them."

"Good that Dante got groceries yesterday, then," Tito said. "Carolina will come home very upset if I know her. Glad I'm not in her shoes today."

***

I ate breakfast with the first shift of men. Again, I couldn't eat as fast as they could. Darn lip disk. The first shift finished when four armored women guards burst in.

"Where's the two teams of pullers for our chariots? We were supposed to be on patrol a half-hour ago. Ah, there you four are. Get moving!" She pointed to four of the stronger men.

"We're not working today," one said.

"What do you mean? Your only job is to pull our chariot. Now get your ass up and into the harness."

"Not today. Pull your own chariot."

Wham. She slapped the man hard, knocking him over. That's one problem an armless person has: keeping their balance.

"Get up now!" she barked.

Her three companions grabbed the other three beasts of burden by their hair and dragged them from the room. Their cries of pain ignored. The other guard didn't wait for the man she'd knocked over to get up. She grabbed his hair and pulled

Vic Broquard

him after her, while he kicked and screamed in pain.

The other men maintained stoic faces and remained sitting. Besides, what could an armless man do against these armored warriors? Curious, I followed them outside, where the women already harnessed the men to their chariots. But when they slapped the reins, all four men sat, refusing to budge in spite of the severe beatings from the blunt ends of the spears. Furious, the women hit the four men so hard they knocked them out. Hastily, they unharnessed them and ran off to summon help.

I looked at the men, helpless to do anything for them. Other men came outside. Together, we stood and looked down.

One said, "We can't do anything for them until they can get up."

I hoped they would be all right, but already massive bruising appeared. I said, "Bring water and rags."

Soon, I sat beside one man. I used a foot to soak the rag, then dabbed it on the man's head, hoping to revive him enough so we could get him inside and onto a bed. My reward: he moaned. A few minutes later and with four other men pressing their bodies up tight to his, the wounded man staggered inside, while I worked on reviving the others.

Two more regained consciousness before a dozen guards came rushing up, spears in hand.

"Get him up," one yelled. "Get others out here. Pull our chariot or die!"

The women lifted and harnessed him to the wagon. Semi-conscious, he staggered before falling to the ground.

His driver said, "Get up! Get up this instant!"

He probably couldn't have even if he wanted to get up.

"Enough!" In a quick motion, she thrust her spear through his chest. The man died instantly. "Unharness him. Get another one."

166

The women murdered four before they abandoned their efforts to force their beasts of burden to work. They headed off to report, leaving five dead men lying on the cobblestone street. I vomited.

I fumed. Two dozen guards ran toward us with spears. The men fled inside. No use. The building had no doors, only fabric flaps.

One said, "Kill everyone inside if you must until four volunteer as workhorses."

Defiant. I stood. Focused. Barked my will with my voice and my mind. "Stop! Go Away. Leave these men alone." Get the hell out of there, ladies. I have had enough!

I had absolutely no doubts they would obey. I pictured them running away. Until this point, I really didn't grasp how powerful my intention could be. The leader's mouth waggled a little, before she turned around and ran away, followed by the twenty-three other women. One stared back over her shoulders at me. Fear and terror in her mind.

Aldo came outside and watched the women fleeing. "How did you do that?" he asked.

"I got pissed and told them to leave. I can't believe they murdered five of your men. This has got to stop. Thanks for your hospitality. I have to find the religious leaders and stop this bloodshed."

With that, I headed off following the women. Trouble was, I had no map to follow. I didn't know how to find Dante's place. Hardly anyone was on the street. This world had definitely come unglued. Worse, I felt responsible. I represented a woman who had been cursed and forsaken. Ultimately, that emboldened the men to act. Had I started a war against men?

Chapter 20 Guess Who

I wandered the streets. The signs at cross streets proved useless. Should have studied their writing. Symbols. Chicken scratch. I focused, sought Dante's mind.

"Help. I'm on the streets. Lost. How do I find the house? Stay inside. Women are killing men. Don't come looking for me."

"Where are you? What's around you? Can you see the churches? No, that won't work. There are ten of them. Can you read the signs? Wait; send me an image of the street signs."

"Wow! That's on the other side of the city. Let me think. Go up three more streets and then head west for several miles. Stay in touch. Zita says she is bringing a sack with your ever-larger disks."

I relaxed, but had a long walk ahead of me. Soon, I spotted two non-descript women standing beside a closed store. As I got closer, both glanced my way, but one stared at me.

I touched her mind. Instant recognition!

"Ambassador L'Grina? Is that you?"

"Parkinson? Good whiskey! You're here?" the Sixth Invader said. "Small universe indeed. Good to see you. Gone native, eh? The lip disk."

Ambassador L'Grina must be using one of her disguise devices.

The other woman said, "Molly Parkinson? Really? Here on Bella?"

I touched her mind to help work out her identity. Who was L'Grina talking to? Crap! A Third Invader!

"Molly, I'm Rear Admiral Irenka Bronislawa of Home

Fleet Two stationed around the Norma Arm."

"What are you two doing here? Shit has hit the fan, as our Earth saying goes."

"Call me Irenka. I brought L'Grina here for several reasons. As you know, the Sixth Invaders originally planned to turn your Earth society into one akin to Bella. Armless men. World run by women."

"Well, our civilization has been that way for eons," L'Grina said.

I chuckled. "But we stopped them from doing that."

Irenka grinned and continued. "I wanted her to see that such a societal solution involving you humans would not have worked—merely swapping who's dominating who."

L'Grina said, "Hey, don't push that on me. It was our Commander's big idea. Humans just don't know how to run a civilization without conflicts. The Admiral is right. Here, women replaced men as the oppressors. I can see that now. Glad our Commander failed."

Irenka said, "I'm here on Home World's orders. Our societal experiment has failed. Your daughter, Isabella Parkinson, is doing a good job translating our original document outlining this experiment."

"Failed?" I asked. "What did you expect the outcome might be?"

She laughed. "I'm an admiral, not a social engineer. I think they hoped to create a more perfect society with women in charge of everything. You humans confound our theorists."

"You said failed?"

"Yes, it has. I'm here to clean up the mess before your deep space exploration ship gets here. How did you get here?"

"Damned robots. Kidnapped and left here. They were mining for gold to purchase the components needed to make more of their kind."

She smiled. "Isn't that the way of all things? Survival."

Vic Broquard

"So, can either of you get me back to Earth?"

"Sure, I can arrange something," L'Grina said. "But your own ship is due to arrive next month."

"Thanks. How are you going to clean up the mess? Are you going to re-mutate the men back to what's normal for humans?"

"Well, not exactly. The mutation is over two thousand years old. It's a confusing one, I'm told. Step One. Get everyone mutated the same way. My ship is unleashing the agent now. It will make women like the men. We've been discussing how best to let the women of Bella know to remove all clothing before they enter their mutation comas."

"Oh, shit! You're kidding?"

"No. Home World wants this mess cleaned up. My engineers tell me the fastest way is to make everyone into the same mutation. Men won't be affected."

"What? Everyone armless? How will people survive? This isn't a very modern civilization. Not much is automated."

"My doing, Molly," L'Grina said. "You can thank me. She planned to terminate everyone. Release a toxic agent and wipe out all human life. I pointed out the challenge of removing the dead before your spaceship arrived. Earth has superior genetic engineers. They will devise a curative mutation in due time. Better than killing them. Anyway, isn't this solution better than killing them? Or would you prefer these humans be killed? Put out of their misery and suffering."

"You're kidding? Your way of cleaning up this mess is to kill millions of humans?"

"Ten million to be more exact. Failed experiment ended. Nice and tidy, except for body problem. I'd just let Nature handle decomposition, but with your people about to discover this world... And there's Isabella's translation to consider."

"Ah! You don't want another incident like what

170

happened after you betrayed Earth," I said, alluding to the mysterious attack on their Home World that killed ten thousand of their people. I knew the Earth woman who carried out that top-secret attack.

"Well, yes. There is that to consider. At least, L'Grina's method will make it easier to devise one mutation solution to the problem instead of two. You see, if we mutated the men back to normal human men, my engineers tell me the women would still produce offspring as they do today. With this new version, both men and women of your species will have the same genetic mutation. In theory, one cure then remedies both sexes. But between us, are they even worth saving? Look at their tech level and knowledge of the universe. Pathetic. Even if we find a mutation cure, how are you going to fix up their society? Their viewpoints are different from other human societies. Wouldn't it be easier just to terminate them all?"

"Easier? Yes. Right? No. We're all people. They have a right to their lives."

"But what kind of life will they have? How long will it be until a cure is developed? I still think termination is the better route, if only I had more time to clean up afterwards. I wanted L'Grina to see that the original Sixth Invader solution to Earth would have failed. We both believe their chief science officer somehow learned of our experiment on Bella. Perhaps he once visited here. Or perhaps their Commander visited this world. We're both confident the ideas they tried to use on Earth came from our Bella experiment."

I countered. "Look, if you do this to the women, there'll be no one left to handle the heavier chores necessary for survival."

I did my best to keep calm in the face of threatened genocide. At least the Third Invaders took some slight responsibility for what they'd done.

"Look, Home World has conducted many experiments

on homo sapiens and your predecessors. Since your Sol Empire has evolved enough to join the Federation of Planets, Home World decided to tell you about this one, and they wanted to clean up their mess. It's a failed social experiment."

"But why destroy it?"

"That's what L'Grina asked. I agreed with her. Your people deserve a chance. I might get in trouble for mutating the women instead of killing them, but I'm giving one of your geneticists a chance to recover these people. And if they don't get here soon, my scientists are working on a second mutation that will cure everyone, after all carry the same mutation."

I said, "Yes, thank you for that. We agree you shouldn't just outright kill these people. But—"

"How will they survive?" L'Grina finished my protest. "Well, your deep space exploration ship will come, discover the native population, and assist them. Perhaps not directly. What's a hundred people on your ship going to do with ten million on this planet? Maybe keep the power plants going until Sol Empire help arrives. This way, they've a chance to make it."

I said, "Good points, but..."

"But what?" she asked.

"What about their social beliefs? How they have their society established. That's going to come crashing down. It's as though the gods struck them down. You'll make a whole population dependent on Sol Empire people just to survive."

L'Grina chuckled. "Yes, that's the downside of mutating. Extermination carried its own. A hairy problem. Thankfully, I'm not responsible for the solution."

She added, "Besides, you're supposed to be the Empress of the Sol Empire. Nothing like having the top dog jolly on the spot making things work out." She grinned at me. "Mind if I stick around and watch how you do it?"

I said, "Grr. But okay. First, tell me about this mutation.

172

How long will the women be in comas? Will it rejuvenate their bodies like our agents do?"

"Well, I'm told they'll be out for between seven to ten days. They tell me everyone whose biological age is over their early twenties will have it reset to around twenty-one. Both men and women. I insisted men be slightly changed. Can't have older women being young again while their mates are old age. Not humane."

"Funny definition of humane."

"The engineers weren't certain what the mutation will do about the lip disk situation. As you know, all women over five wear them. I had them look into their historical significance. From Day One, the disks act as visible proof women are different from men. Over time, they've become a status symbol. The bigger the disk, the more important, the more powerful, and the wealthier the wearer is. They had the time and luxury to stretch their lips."

Just then, Zita hurried up to me. "Ah, here you are, Molly. Dante's worried about your safety. Men have gone crazy. Anyway, I've picked up your supply of lip disks that Dante ordered."

She slipped a bag over my shoulder.

"Thanks."

"Gotta run. We're holding emergency meetings. Can you find your way home?"

"Yes. Thanks, Zita."

With that, she dashed off.

When she couldn't overhear us, Ambassador L'Grina said, "Who was that?"

I explained, before returning to the key topic. "How soon are you unleashing the mutation agent?"

"We're already doing that. Airborne. Look, my orders were very specific. 'Clean up the mess. No humans present when the Sol Empire arrives.' Ambassador L'Grina met up with me and suggested Sol Empire people might already be here. Turns out you are. I have taken her advice and am making female bodies identical to males. Except for reproductive systems. Now the humans of Bella become a Sol Empire problem. But if your people don't get here soon, we'll implement the final mutation."

"Why not leave the women unchanged? How is making them identical to men cleaning up the mess?" I asked.

"The experiment failed. They should have removed all traces of it. Prior to Sol Empire arrival. But... Oh, it's this way. I'm told it's considered a failure because the women became the oppressors. The overall society progressed little over two thousand years. Since men were handicapped because they were the oppressors, it's only logical that the women oppressors join them."

I bit on my lower lip. "Not logical. But what would have been a successful outcome of the experiment? No one's talking about what they expected would happen or perhaps wanted to have happen."

What had these Third Invaders hoped to achieve? They'd gone to a lot of trouble to set up the experiment. Why?

Rear Admiral Irenka Bronislawa chuckled. "Don't ask me. I fight space battles. I suppose they hoped a female-led society would develop into a peaceful, cooperative world, advancing towards an industrialized modern world. In many species, females tend to nurture while males tend to be aggressive. Our race has always been tinkering with primitive peoples trying to develop the ideal societies for each species. Been doing that for a hundred millennia. Perhaps the expected goals are outlined in the lengthy document Isabella Parkinson is translating. Ask her. I've not read it. Boring.

"Anyway, it's your choice. Terminate them all or level the field by making them equally handicapped."

"No genocide."

"We figured that much."

"How long before they drop into comas? Will the men do that too? How long do we have to get the word out?" My mind raced with questions.

"They'll slip into them while sleeping tonight. The older men will sleep in much longer tomorrow, but no lengthy comas. As far as you're concerned, you might sleep longer than expected tonight. No coma for you."

Why is it always me? The fate of ten million people rested on my shoulders. Millions of women waking from comas without arms? I'd seen that trauma too many times. Mass terror. A horror show. How would they survive? Would they want to?

Without personnel with arms and hands to deal with the work to keep the civilization alive, they stood no chance or a very slim one. Wait. Power generation. Everyone depended upon their refrigerators and stoves. From what little I'd heard, they used coal-fired steam engines to generate the power. Who would keep them going? How could the rail lines be finished? How could the farmers plant and harvest their crops? Sheer their sheep? Cut down trees and install power lines? Make the metal cookware? Mine for the raw ores needed? Who would build new homes? Who could make the necessary furnishings? Who could install them?

My mind boggled at the magnitude of the problems these people would face in a week. I'd accidentally made mental contact. Oops, I hadn't paid attention to what I was doing. Thus, these disparate images and thoughts flooded Rear Admiral Irenka Bronislawa and Ambassador L'Grina's minds.

"Are you all right?" L'Grina asked, shaking my shoulder.

I flushed. "You saw that? Sorry. Overwhelmed."

The Admiral said, "I understand. It's why I thought

termination was kindest."

"Expedient? Yes. But genocide isn't right," I countered. "These are people, just like the three of us. They have a right to their own lives, their own freedoms. Your people interfered, forcing them down a different path. Then, when that route didn't live up to your preconceived ideas, you want to kill them all. Pathetic. No wonder many in the galaxy think the Third Invaders are monsters."

Ambassador L'Grina spoke up. "Molly, what they did two thousand years ago is reprehensible. They've grown. Learned their lessons. Just like my people did. Even so, we are still known as the Sixth Invaders instead of our own race name. Blame me, if you want. She had her crew ready to destroy everyone on Bella when I intervened. I didn't think you'd want that. I convinced her not to terminate everyone, but to make the sexes equal, since her genetic engineers can't regrow arms on this mutation form as yet. Blame me."

I laughed. "Hardly, L'Grina. You know me too well. Thank you for sparing these innocent people from death. Now, it's on me to somehow save them. I could use a 'Burning Bush' about now."

The Admiral laughed. "That can be arranged."

Chapter 21 The Voice of God

Around us, the streets remained deserted. Nuova Roma appeared to be a ghost town, but I knew people were in their homes arguing. Unknown to them, in a few days, life on Bella would be irrevocably turned upside down. Women would be as handicapped as their oppressed males. Even if I could get Earth to send personnel and help, the people stood little chance of long-term survival. Unless men and women worked together.

Back on Earth during the terrorist attack days, I found that having four handicapped people working together on one task brought success. Alone, the job couldn't be done in a reasonable time frame. Yet here women had oppressed men for centuries. They loathed them. Soon, they'd wake from their mutation comas and find their bodies identically handicapped.

Countless times, I'd been there for people waking from comas with mutated bodies. Fear, death wishes, and sometimes suicide followed. Others embraced Sub-apathy. Hope lost. Dead inside. They waited for physical death to catch up. The same exists here among the males.

With training and practice, many survived and did well. Their handicap was not a death sentence, but a challenge to find new ways of doing. But the victims in those cases weren't oppressors of handicapped people.

Here, women loathed men, considered them repulsive in many ways. Changed into what they loathe? These women faced the greatest threat of death. My focus remained on the women.

Eight in ten still held onto their religion, while the other two had a saner point of view—in my opinion. Organized religions had long vanished from Earth and the empire. Heck, in my travels about the Federation, I'd seen almost no signs of any religion. My brief study of anthropology and history suggested primitive peoples assigned unexplained phenomena to one or more gods. Yet I knew, just as L'Grina did now, that we were spiritual beings inhabiting physical bodies. She had learned that truth when I gave her Celeste's therapy to help heal her burned arm. Perhaps that's why she'd convinced the Admiral to spare everyone on Bella.

In my studies, I had reached one conclusion: extensive science and technology destroys religious beliefs. Materialism swamps faith. On Earth, materialism exploded at the beginning of the twenty-first century. The young glued themselves to their screens, their cell phones. They ceased engaging in contact with others, not even holding conversations with people. The spiritual evaporated. Religion became the impersonal hurried along by pedophile priests. Corporations rose becoming spiritual leaders. Their goods and services, Gods.

On Bella, only *La Liberà* fought against materialism, Satan's lure, as Carolina called it.

For a moment, I considered grabbing Dante and having L'Grina fly us back to Earth. Let the Admiral terminate the rest. That was the easy way out. I longed to be home, surrounded by the convenient devices that made life easy for me. I missed Cleo. How bad was that?

"Damn it!" I had to make this go right. I could see the validity of the Admiral's choice. These women had accumulated two thousand years of mistreatment of men, though nowhere near the brutality men had caused during Earth's early history, assuming the history books told the truth. Yet, I had told no one on Bella their true history, what the Third Invaders did to their ancestors.

I had thought if I told them about the Third Invaders,

178

they wouldn't believe me. Or if they did, it would destroy their faith, throwing the world into chaos. Yet at some future date, they'd learn the truth, since by now I surmised most everyone in the Sol Empire had heard of Isabella's translation and the social experiment gone astray. All that remained unchanged, considering what the Admiral did.

If I did nothing, this culture would likely collapse. Might not last a year without Earth's intervention. Women held all the accumulated knowledge of the civilization, except for domestic things. If they had operation manuals or documents, only women could read them. If women gave up, the men would be lost.

While nothing would alter the sheer fear and terror these women would experience when they woke, I needed them to accept their fate and... What? Do what? Well, work together with men to do what they used to do alone. I needed women to accept men's help, educate men, and work in teams of four or more to get the job done, whatever that job might be.

I knew enough about the situation on Bella to know the women suspected they'd been mistreating men. That some had committed harmful acts against men or failed to aid them when needed. While the women might not own up to it, the fear they exuded when I appeared among them spoke volumes. They had been raised to believe Lord God or their pagan gods had cursed their men, forsaken them. That view prevailed even after two millennia. It was a falsehood, but did I dare use that against them?

After thousands of hours of Celeste's therapy, my spiritual awakening blossomed. I followed her guiding principles. An acceptable course of action assisted more of the Seven Aspects of Life than it harmed. Every person wants to survive as themselves and thrive. They want their families to survive. They want the groups they support to persist and do well. Likewise, all their species. Yes, I wanted the people of Bella to survive somehow. Our survival is intimately linked to the survival of plants and animals. We need the physical universe of matter and energy to survive. We want our possessions to survive as long as possible. How we hate it when our favorite shirt must be thrown away because it's become threadbare. Finally, we ourselves, the spiritual beings need to survive, though I want us to get better, more aware of our natures.

Doing nothing here on Bella harmed many of these aspects of life. Whatever I did had to help more than it harmed. But what?

The monumental situation threatened to swamp me. Make assumptions based on almost no data? It seemed only the wildest schemes might work. Yet, if I'm honest, I didn't think there was a chance any would survive very long after they woke up.

Who would handle farming chores? While one could collect eggs using their feet, harvesting wheat, corn, and barley couldn't be done by feet alone. These people ate a lot of chicken, fish, and lamb. I had no idea how any of that could be processed, let alone by feet. Dante and I just purchased the meats in the markets already prepackaged. Worse, on Earth, automation handled most all food production activities. There, a farmer ran everything from his laptop in his house. Here, they barely had electricity.

Low. This must be what depression is.

What resources did I have available? With the two aliens, I could contact Earth. Dante and I could flee Bella, but that was out. I could summon the deep space exploration ship. Then what? Did we have any policies on annexing already inhabited worlds to our empire? Should the citizens of Bella decide if they want to become part of the empire? If they don't, then what? If they do? They don't have corporations. Establish parallel ones? Staffed by whom?

Or did I ask or beg for volunteers? How many were needed to assist ten million handicapped people? One for ten? How could I get a million helpers to move here in just a week's time? Worse, what skills did they need to be of assistance on this world that lacked nearly every automation feature our world had?

Take Dante and flee. That idea floated through my mind while I talked to Rear Admiral Irenka Bronislawa and Ambassador L'Grina. A problem without a solution? Wrong to do nothing.

"Molly? Molly, are you all right?" Ambassador L'Grina shook my shoulder.

"Huh? Oh, what?"

"You've not said anything for minutes. Are you okay?"

"I understand why Admiral Bronislawa had chosen to kill everyone on Bella, Ambassador. In a week, ten million people will be handicapped—"

"Nine Million seven hundred fifty-nine thousand six hundred forty-three to be precise." Rear Admiral Irenka Bronislawa corrected me. "As handicapped as they will be, my engineers calculated they could not get or process the food they need and will starve to death as their supplies run out. They took into account Parkinson's attempts to bring Sol Empire aid and ruled that out as much too little and far too late to save more than a small fraction. Termination is the humane choice, Ambassador L'Grina. Besides, I need to get to Rudolf-E and sort out the robot mess there."

Ding! The magic word. "Robot mess? What's going on?" I asked.

The Admiral exhaled. "Well, we've an automated Fantasy World for humans and aliens who can afford some realistic adventure. One of our most profitable enterprises. Tell the agent your fantasy. Pay for it. Agent fulfills it. We use

181

specially built androids. No living life forms are harmed."

As she explained in more detail, I suspected our human-form robots might be involved. If not them, then some closely related to them.

I said, "What if I could find the imposters? Separate the fake from the real people. Sort out the mess without harming anyone."

"Well, if you could do that for us—for Third Invaders whom you and your people detest—"

"Then you do something for me."

"Like what?"

"Look. Your genetic engineers created a cure for similar mutations on Earth. You sold us a deal. Remember? You cure our people. Regrow arms and such. We donate a thousand volunteers for your next research project."

The Admiral pointed out. "That didn't end well for either of us."

"Because you didn't uphold your end of the deal. The cure worked for a month before they relapsed or mutated back. Your people could, if they wanted to, develop a mutation cure for these people here."

She pulled on her chin for a moment. Admiral Bronislawa said, "I wasn't a part of that fiasco. But you have a point. I'm told the first step is to get them all mutated in the same way. The current mutation agent is doing that."

"So," I said, "your people handle the critical actions that provide them with food and electricity while your geneticists develop the second part of the cure."

She chuckled. "Clever, Parkinson. Incentive for a fast cure."

I smiled, annoyed it wasn't visible. "Precisely. A bit of motivation. I'm sure your people don't want to be mining coal, plowing fields, harvesting grains, and butchering animals for years, eh?"

182

"Oh, you wicked devil, you!" Ambassador L'Grina said, slapping her hands together. "That might work the very miracle you need. See, Admiral, I told you Parkinson is a force to reckon with!"

I added, "But I'll need that Burning Bush again. We need a miracle to convince the women to work with the men right away instead of killing themselves, freaking out, or doing nothing. They need hope for the future to produce a desire to survive until your people develop that cure."

"This I gotta see!" Ambassador L'Grina said.

"Let's return to my ship and discuss the details. Ambassador, steady Parkinson while I activate the tractor beam."

One of her arms encircled my waist, pulling my body up against hers, while she wrapped her other arm around the Third Invader. The Admiral fiddled with a device on her wrist. A yellow energy surrounded us. Then motion.

Our bodies flew up and through the air at an incredible speed. We set down north of the city. Several guards stood beside a small saucer shuttle. They saluted the instant we appeared.

Ah, the wrist devices they'd been wearing allowed them to blend in with the natives. Now they appeared in their actual forms. Ambassador L'Grina stood six inches taller than me. Her coal-black eyes and short hair contrasted sharply with her gray skin. Six fingers on each hand. A tiny bosom compared to mine.

The Admiral matched my height, with an ellipsoidal face outlined by the pixie cut of her black hair. Her red eyes blazed like fire. If it wasn't for the shape of the back of her head, she looked almost human, unlike L'Grina. The back of her head formed a point, much like a bird's beak, though her hair partially hid the distortion. I knew men of her race had tall, stovepipe hat shaped heads, presumably to enhance their intelligence. Here and there, her reddish skin appeared, a further indicator of her alien nature.

The guards stared at me. Gaped might be a better choice of words.

The Admiral said, "Let's get you some clothes before I lose control of my men." L'Grina and she laughed, but I didn't appreciate the humor and tried to control my embarrassment.

An hour later, I felt human again. A med tech bathed me and did my hair while they flew the saucer shuttle up to the main battleship saucer. From a viewport, I spotted a dozen of these giant ships. Her fleet must have accompanied her to Bella.

The layout of the battle saucer was much like the one I'd help capture on Domes, the one used by Edyta. Familiarity helped me relaxed a bit. We met in her private office. Her mahogany desk, matching chairs, oak table and bookshelves— all spoke of ultimate luxury. Plush down to the red carpeting on her floor. She poured herself a glass from a decanter, but didn't offer us any.

"Might poison you two. Sit. Now let's discuss what the Burning Bush should say."

I paralleled their original message delivered two millennia ago. Ambassador L'Grina provided a couple of suggestions. After some discussion, we settled on this:

Women of Bella, for two thousand years, you followed in the footsteps of the men that I've forsaken and cursed, systematically mistreating your men. Today I am forsaking and cursing the women of Bella. Your bodies will become like those of your men.

However, both men and women of Bella can receive my salvation, my blessing, if you both work together to ensure your survival. Work in teams of four to do what one woman used to do. If you cease mistreating others and work together, then I will eventually lift my curse and restore your bodies.

Soon, people from the Sol Empire will come. What they will find depends upon what you do now. Work together so that I may lift my curse and allow you to rejoin your original people of Earth.

After agreeing on the wording, the Admiral left to attend to the details of delivering a Burning Bush to the inhabitants of Bella.

"You're taking quite a gamble, aren't you?" Ambassador L'Grina said. "Do you even know about this Fantasy World, this Rudolf-E, and its problems?"

"Nope. Never heard of it. But I know a lot about robotics. I took several courses at Soros University. Couldn't think of any other way I could save these people. Doing nothing is always the wrong solution. I couldn't live with myself if I left them to their fate. But I don't trust Third Invaders. They might not find a mutation cure, but her people will keep them supplied with food and electricity for the time being. I'm buying time, if not a cure."

"Parkinson, you are one tenacious dog!"

About an hour later, Admiral Bronislawa said, "They're ready to broadcast. As the saucer flies over head, the system delivers the message. Those on the ground will see the Burning Bush in their minds and heard the voice of god coming from it. It will appear as though they are standing before the bush even though they are asleep or in a coma at the moment. On that monitor, you can watch what's being sent."

"On the usual implant frequency? In the kilo-yattahertz range? Like the white energy?" I asked.

She smiled. "Perceptive, aren't you? Yes. Precisely. Once they finish their sweeps over the settled lands, that team will land. They will ensure the coal-fired generators continue to function and will handle necessary food production activities—done at night so the people don't see them. For safety, they'll be wearing the usual disguise devices."

After we watched the video on the monitor, Admiral Bronislawa turned it off. "Now then, I'm holding you to your promise. I need the Rudolf-E situation fixed."

"Could we stop off on Earth and pickup Bishop for me? He's my security guard. He's saved me from the robot attacks several times."

"Since it's in the general direction of Rudolf-E, okay. Besides, I expect you'll want your own clothes."

I grinned. "Is it that obvious?"

We three chuckled. I didn't tell them Bishop was one of the human-form robots or that he carried the mutation agent inside his secret compartments. He'd used it to save me after the robots shot me. I hoped they wouldn't try to kill me again. I could drop the heavy bag of larger lip disks at my house.

Chapter 22 The Fantasy World

My yellow satin gown made me feel human again. Strapped into a shuttle saucer, Bishop on my right, Cleo on my left, we traveled to the entrance station that occupied a synchronous orbit above Rudolf-E. For a robot, Cleo seemed eager to see my return.

In the row in front of us, Ambassador L'Grina chatted with Captain Katya Binsk. I hadn't seen the captain for months. As with all Third Invaders, her face seemed stretched taut by the beak-like back of her head, though her muscled arms rivaled that of my legs. Her reddish skin tone and black hair looked alien. We had had some interesting adventures together. I'd earned her respect and she, mine.

"There it is." Katya pointed out the huge station, a giant wheel with pokes connecting to a central cylinder. Silver. We headed for an open docking bay. I spotted six different models of small transport shuttles docked at locations around the wheel. Slowly, our saucer headed for an open docking bay.

"Impressive," I said.

L'Grina smiled. "Thanks again for inviting me to visit Fantasy World. I could never afford it on my salary."

Katya laughed. "Me either. Docking in two."

I felt a lurch as the dock clamps latched onto the saucer shuttle. After a hissing sound, the pilot said, "Okay, we're docked. You can exit now."

Cleo unhooked my seatbelt. We followed the two women. Near the exit, six more Third Invader soldiers, each carrying two weapons, joined us.

The smell of the space station reminded me of a freshly cleaned, sterile spaceship. Everything glimmered in brilliant

LED lighting. The polished walls reflected our images as we walked down the long corridor. We walked down a long narrow tube that appeared as one of the spokes from outside the ship.

Breaking the monotony, posters flashed holographic images, advertising interesting fantasies of past visitors. Cleo shuttered as we passed one that reminded me of the wild west where everyone wielded guns. It had been the target of such a shooting. Funny, I didn't think robots could have such reactions.

"Ah, here at last. CEO of Fantasy World, Jedrik Denys. Thank heavens Home World sent you. An Earth woman? My, my. This way."

Jedrik led us to his extravagant office, done in shades of blue. A short Third Invader, still his head rose like a stovepipe hat. A tuft of black hair perched like a bird's nest on its top. Once seated, Captain Binsk introduced us.

"We have uncovered some mysterious acts," Jedrik said. He seemed somewhat effeminate to me. "Perhaps I should explain. Here on Fantasy World, when the customer arrives, we go over the details of their fantasy. Once full payment is received and all wavers of responsibility are signed, the customer is sent to one of our play sites down on the planet surface. We house them in a ten-star hotel while their fantasy is arranged. Our operations crews build the sets, construct the robots, and whatever else is required for the fantasy.

"When the operations personnel sign off, the customer is then immersed into their fantasy. Fantasies come in three durations: one week, two weeks, and unlimited. The latter is, of course, prohibitively expensive. We get perhaps two of those a year.

"Anyway, operations managers have notified me of excessive loss of robot parts. They've *just* vanished. Our fabrication machines indicate they've operated twice as long as they should have for the number and complexity of fantasies produced."

I interrupted. "How long has this been going on?"

"Good question. We feel we've nipped this in the sprout. Best guess? Two months. Only a guess. Could be years. All those supplies missing and overuse of the fabrication machines. Terribly expensive to run. Represents a significant loss of profits, you see."

I didn't see, but asked, "Why do you think robots are behind this?"

"Only authorized personnel may check out supplies and operate the machines. What's more mysterious is the machine logs keep being erased, though nothing can alter the total operation time. Hard-wired into the machines. When maximum up-time is reached, they cease operations until serviced. Costly, you see.

"Then, about six weeks back, you see, during a malfunction in the fabrication machine, Roz—she's one of our top Operations Managers and a highly skilled engineer—discovered the machine had been making parts for unauthorized robots. Later, when she went to analyze the data, those logs had vanished. Since then, we installed a security system. But the thieves circumvented it. How? We still don't know. Everything on Fantasy World is automated, you see. Nothing can go wrong—computer controlled to avoid situations like this. Nothing like this has ever happened on my watch nor on my predecessor's. Terribly frustrating, you see."

He rubbed his face and eyes. "I'm glad you're here. Find out what's happening and stop it at once. Take these."

He handed out passes on a lanyard. Cleo draped mine around my neck.

"I've arranged for a shuttle to take you down to meet the operations managers. Marek Levitsky and Roz Kowalksi.

He's been with us for four months, but Roz is a veteran. She's kept the machines operating for fifty years.

"And one more thing. Please don't interrupt the ongoing six fantasies. And one is about to start. The man from Cass-C has paid one of the highest premiums for his fantasy, triple our usual charge for a week's dream come true, you see."

"I'm curious. How much does a week's fantasy cost? How much did this man from Cass-C spend? Knowing that may help us figure out what's going on with the robots."

"Depends on the complexity of the fantasy. The basic week package is ten million credits. The cost goes higher based on the number of androids needed to fulfill the fantasy. We once had a man wanting to fight a war. Dear me, he needed five hundred soldiers to destroy. Oh, the man from Cass-C is dropping a tidy hundred million credits for his week of pleasure."

I swallowed to avoid shrieking. "You've got quite a lucrative business here."

CEO Denys said, "Of course. We Third Invaders are the superior beings in this galaxy, you see."

Katya snorted, while L'Grina stifled a chuckle. My mind boggled over the vast sums that changed hands on this world.

"I'll see you're taken down to the Operations Center now. Please solve this minor problem as fast as you can. Time is money, you see. Terribly so."

I rolled my eyes, but followed the others to a shuttle dock, where we embarked on a low-flying dart-about, as he called these craft. They looked similar to our Electro-Magnetic Air Cars, EMACs. I had one with my company logo on it: Parkinson Private Investigations and Security. Without arms, I hadn't taken on any security operations for many years.

We landed on the far side of the planet from the CEO's office. A gigantic windowless concrete structure rose above the semi-desert region. The small parking lot held only our vehicle, though from the markings on the blacktop surface, similar vehicles used this lot. Our passes opened the person-sized door. Much larger doors lay further down the side of the building.

A petite Third Invader met us. Like Katya, her face appeared flattened because the back of her head rather morphed into a bird's beak. Well-muscled, her bright eyes suggested this woman knew what she was doing. Since these people lived thousands of years, I couldn't guess her age.

"Hello. You must be the team Home World sent to sort out this fiasco. I'm Operations Manager and Chief Engineer Roz Kowalksi. Just call me Roz. Marek is off setting up the special, super expensive fantasy."

She spoke Federation Common. Thus, I didn't have to wear a language translator device.

Captain Binsk introduced us.

"Can you take us on a guided tour?" I asked. "We need to become familiar with the overall operations if we're to help figure out what's going wrong."

"You bet. I'm free all day, unless there's an emergency android breakdown in one of the currently active fantasies. Let's start with the heart of our operations. The massive computer installation."

This one dwarfed the huge Galactic Defense computer system in the GD skyscraper in Chicago.

"It controls every fantasy by sending the signals up to the orbiting welcome station you arrived at. From there, signals bounce between various satellites and then back down to the surface, where strategic relay towers deliver the signals to the various robots. An incredible bit of automation."

I smiled. "Impressive."

"Wait until you see our engineering and fabrication facilities. Now those are what I call impressive. This way."

Down long corridors we went, riding in open topped

electric transport vehicles, six to a car. An overhead rail ran down the center of the corridor.

Roz explained more of the operation. "Robot cranes ride along those rails. Each of the doors we're passing contain fabrication materials. The ones that have gone missing. We'll come back, and you can inspect these holding areas, if you think that's significant."

We parked outside one enormous room, underground for sure.

"Here is one of the two dozen sub-assembly rooms. The rail cranes bring the parts here. The robot machines then build the requisite smaller assemblies. At the moment, we're building the dozen androids needed for the new arrival's special fantasy involving a dozen women. We make their arms here. Legs in the next room. Head in another. Torso in a fourth. This way.

"In this assembly room is the coolest machine I've ever invented. The Fabrication Machine. Artists input the designs. Here, the gowns the dozen women will wear. My machine then 'prints' the objects."

"Rather similar to the ancient 3-D printers we had on Earth," I said.

"Oh, those artifacts. Yes, we studied them when they first appeared on your world. Crude devices. Knock-offs of our earliest attempts. This way."

A beeping noise demanded out attention. Overheard, one of the rail cranes moved along hauling a basket filled with arms. As it passed overhead, the arms looked real enough, except they had no hands.

"Taking them to the main assembly area. Ah, let's stop off here at Monitor Station One. It's overseeing the fantasy in action above ground near here."

Six people sat before large monitors, playing with what looked like video game controllers.

"That man's fantasy is to be lucky in wild frontier times. Yes, they're shooting live bullets at each other, but we program the androids to miss, but only by fractional amounts, giving rise to the player's belief he just got lucky again."

It reminded me of the frontier world of Goringy-E, where everyone had guns. Cleo vibrated slightly as we watched the man and two robots exchanging gunfire.

"Are there ever accidents?" I asked. "Missing by a tiny amount only needs a tiny goof to hit the person."

We watched as the player's gun blew a hole in one of the attacking robots, designed to look like a human wearing buckskins. That robot fell backwards and ceased operations. Cleo cringed.

"Yes, there's always an inherent danger, particularly with some fantasies. That's why the purchaser must sign away our liability. The player is responsible for all mishaps."

"Those androids don't look lifelike."

"No. Decent replicas if seen at a distance. For fantasies requiring androids up close and personal, we go the extra distance, but the person pays for such more realistic looks. None of our androids could pass as a person in the real world. For one thing, they'd be out of instruction receiving range. We program our androids with a limited command set or program that they can follow. Look, if the player captures one of those he's shooting at with the rifle—which by the way is a perfect replica rifle—you couldn't tell the difference between a real one and ours. If he captured one, any conversation with the android would sound worse than that with a small child. And if asked to do more than take cover, aim, and shoot, the android would stand there ignoring the command. Does not compute comes to mind." She laughed at her own jest.

"Plus, their skin has a plastic feel to it. Realistic from a few feet away, but not to the touch. However, if intimate contact is part of the fantasy and the client wants what they're touching to feel real, we use a bit of synthetic skin. But the client pays quadruple the cost, and we only use synth skin on specific parts of the robot."

"Your robots only know how to function within the scope or parameters of the client's fantasy?" I asked.

"Androids. Precisely. Mind you, sometimes, their actions and reactions can be convincing. But take them into a different setting and they act like dumb-dumbs. Say, I heard you Earth people developed robots that appear totally human. That you can't tell them apart."

"Human-form. That's what we call them. Yes, indistinguishable from a human," I said. "Except by a telepath."

"Clever. Dangerous? If you can't tell a robot from a person, I mean. Obviously, Cleo here is a robot on wheels. No one would ever think it's a human. Not like you or your security guard there."

"Very dangerous if the human-forms haven't been programmed with robot laws. Five weren't. Went rogue. I fear they've amassed the parts needed to manufacture a hundred more of themselves."

"Scary. In this room, final assembly takes place. From here, if the objects are props, they're moved to their locations. If robots, they're clothed and sent on to receive their basic programming, which is tied to the client's fantasy."

"What happens to the robots when the fantasy is completed?"

"Objects and robots are incinerated. Parts recycled where possible. We reduced them to various ores, silver, aluminum, iron, for example, in our gigantic incinerator."

After two hours, Roz, proud of her engineering work, ended our tour. We stopped in the workers' lunch hall and dialed in our meal choice. Robot servers brought our meal to our tables. While Cleo fed me, Captain Binsk got us back to the business at hand.

"What you know about the missing parts? What suspicious activities have Rear Admiral Irenka Bronislawa so worked up?" she asked.

"We make billions in profits each year. I don't know why Home World is so upset about the situation. For the past several months, parts have gone missing. Each time a new android or object is fabricated for a client's fantasy, the system notes every part used into the logs. Management uses it to determine pricing and a detailed bill for the client if requested.

"When supplies arrive, an automated system checks them in, logging each object. Upper management runs cross-check programs each month. You know, current stock on hand plus new arrivals minus used should balance out. Always has. In the past, that is. For years. Two months ago, discrepancies appeared. We're talking major errors. A hundred of this had vanished. A hundred of that gone. My guess was employee theft."

She paused and ran her hands over her foreshortened face. "Last month, when I cleaned out the incinerator, I found the remains of teeth. Human teeth. Some had holes where fillings had once been. None of our workers had died. I checked. Everyone alive and well. We've never misplaced a client. Still, I let CEO Denys know. Later, he said it contained no viable DNA. Whoever it belonged to has never been identified. Maybe one of our clients lost a tooth in their fantasy. They can get pretty rough. Some men go in for physical combat sports."

"How many people work here? Humans or just Third Invaders?" I asked.

"Five hundred sixty-six if you believe CEO Denys. Some are humans. Your species. Some are my people. Little of everything. The humans come from many worlds. They help provide ideas for some fantasies. You know—based on environments and situations from their home worlds.

"For example, the group from Goringy-E designed the environment and androids for the gunfight scenario you just watched. The 'lucky man' client."

"Makes sense. Do the humans you hire—do they return to their home worlds at some point?" I asked.

"Oh, sure. Many work for five years, though a ten-year contract is normal. Oh, I see where're your heading. No, they can't take stolen parts with them when they leave. When they come, they're allowed one suitcase of personal items. All else they may need while here are made via my Fabrication Machine. When a worker leaves, they can take that same suitcase. But it's searched for contraband before they can leave."

"Parts are missing. People aren't. I'll start with a careful examination of what parts were stolen," I said. "Do you use positronic brains on some models?"

I asked because of my growing paranoia over these rogue robots.

"Well, actually we do. Sometimes. But only for the most advanced or sophisticated fantasies. The clients pay top fees for these."

"Ah, have some of your positronic brains gone missing?"

I had to ask, though I doubted Teslenko operated on this world.

Roz gave me one of those funny looks. "How did you know that? Yeah, well several dozen of the very best ones have vanished. It's no wonder Home World chose to investigate these thefts, considering how costly those are. It's possible more could have gone missing before we installed the latest inventory control software. With an operation as large as this, it's hard to track items. Inconvenient. Besides, we recycle as much as possible."

196

I cursed. "We best check on what else they stole. I can't read your language. Is it possible you can show me an image of the parts? I've had a fair number of robotics courses at Soros University. I know what I'm looking at."

Ambassador L'Grina said, "Are you thinking the rogue robots stole these parts?"

"That's the most plausible explanation. You can't sell one of these positronic brains on the open markets. Probably could on the Black Market. Robot parts—you could sell, depending on what part. I need to check the list of stolen items."

Captain Binsk said, "Delgo's rats! That's not good. But I don't see how they could get them off this world. Everything goes through the orbiting station. A ship can't land down here, not without drawing a pile of heavy cruisers on top of it."

I chuckled. "One thing at a time. It's just a hunch. Let's see what the situation is. Lead on, Roz. To the parts."

She left us at a computer station. Captain Binsk brought up the missing inventory list. After clicking on a part, she brought up its image. I had Bishop operating a second computer, logging the specific items I thought might be used in the construction of a human-form robot.

Meanwhile, I sent Roz off to double check how many positronic brains were missing as of this moment. "Actually count the ones in stock, please."

She returned pale-faced. "Parkinson, it's worse than the computer shows. Shipping crates are empty! Fifty-nine brains have vanished. But the logs show we have sixty in storage. What have you found from the missing parts?"

"Bishop's list shows the parts I think might be useful in the construction of the human-form robots."

"But you haven't counted any of the tubular arms and legs," Roz said.

"No, because the human-form robots use a titanium

197

alloy bone set modeled off human bones. They don't use the tubular assemblies like Cleo has. None of the tubular ones are missing. Look at the amount of missing hydraulics and synthetic skin. Ah, ha. This makes more sense. Fifty-nine missing. There's enough synth skin missing to perhaps make fifty-nine robots. Highly suspicious."

"Now wait just a minute," Roz said, her hands on her hips. "Are you saying there's fifty-nine of those human-form robots wandering around this planet? Why? Can't be. CEO Denys handles personnel. He's not reported four dozen people missing. I'd notice if we lost that many of our work crew."

"Let's look into how all these parts could have been shipped off-world," Captain Binsk said. "That's the most likely scenario. Someone pilfered the parts and shipped them elsewhere. We need to talk to CEO Denys again."

She headed off to do that with Roz leading the way, while Bishop, Cleo, and I accompanied Ambassador L'Grina to the cafeteria for a tea break.

"You think human-form robots are working this world?" she asked as we sipped the hot brew.

"We've shut them out of Chicago factories and ran them off Bella. But there are a zillion planets they could use. This one is ideal. All the parts they need. Except for the titanium alloy bones. Those they'd have to bring in from off-world."

"Ah, that poses a problem. As tight as security is on this fantasy world, I can't see them able to ship in titanium alloy bones."

"Right. How to get things onto this world and off it without alerting security. That seems the big hurdle," I said.

After a long pause, she said, "Hey, what about that Fabrication Machine that Roz invented. Could it be used to make the metal bones for the robots?"

I chuckled. "I've no idea. Ask Roz when she gets back with Katya. We should examine that possibility. Heck, if it could build bones that mimic human bones, then there's enough other parts here to make human-form robots. But then how do you then get them off this world?"

Chapter 23 Depravity

Teslenko sent an encoded message to Kilmas on Rudolf-E. "It's done. Number Six has convinced Number Four to visit Fantasy World. Will travel as Klaus Huber. Replace."

After an hour long distance delay, Kilmas sent back, "Acknowledged. They've brought in that Parkinson woman. Orders?"

Again, after the delay, Teslenko sent back, "Arrange termination. If discovered, Protocol Eleven."

***

Twenty-five years old and a perpetual University of Berlin student, Hans Klein staggered out of the Alter Falke pub. He and three friends had had far too much beer, but Hans wanted to celebrate receiving his third doctorate. Officially an astro-geologist, a computer programmer, and a computer systems engineer, Hans Klein kept a hand in his pocket, holding onto the crumpled notification that the university insisted he graduate and accept one of the ten employment offers he'd received. Most would die to have any of these lucrative positions.

"*Ja*, now Hans you *können* get some *junge fräulein*," one buddy said, sliding between German and English even though his doctorate lay in linguistics.

"*Ja*, go for *drei junge fräulein*," another said, laughing and poking Hans in the stomach.

"*Nein*. Not yet," Hans said. The poke broke his focus. He upchucked several beers' on the cobblestones, amid laughter from his three friends who dodged the splatter.

"*Du kannst dein Bier nicht halten!*" the first friend said.

"Was *gutes Bier*, too," another said.

"Which *fräulein*? Lucky dog's got ten after him," the third friend said. "Us? Zero. Only handsome Hans, who's never got time for the *fräulein*."

"You guys work on one doctorate, while I work on three," Hans said. "Wonder I'm not blind."

"*Nein*, you're the smartest ever," the third fellow said. "I wish I had half the looks you've got. Then, the *junge fräulein* would fawn all over me."

The second said, "But you've got Gertrude. What more do you want? She's all of a hundred kilos."

The friends laughed. But the third said, "Ja, but big is *sehr gut*." More laughter followed.

"Hey, fellows. I worked hard for these. Now I can have fun, eh?" Hans said, as they climbed the steps into their dorm.

"*Ja, ja*. Where'd I put my keys?" the third said, leaning against his door and struggling with the contents of his pockets.

Hans leveled his eye at the optical scanner he'd installed on his door. Click. The door opened. "Look, *nein* hands!"

The others groaned, as they did when Hans showed them his latest "improvement" to dorm life.

"Whoa. Who the hell are you?" Hans said. A strange man sat on his dorm bed, rising as he entered.

"Hans Klein?"

"*Ja*."

The man reached out to shake hands, but his other hand swung up to Hans' neck. Hans felt a pinprick. Too drunk to resist, the room spun, and someone turned out the lights. He thought he might be falling, but his mind couldn't work out how to stop his descent. Or why he should care.

***

The man placed Hans onto the dorm bed and stripped him. Minutes later, he hoisted Hans' black plastic-wrapped body over his shoulder. He toted the body unseen through the silent halls and past the rooms of his sleeping friends. After loading Hans into an unmarked EMAC, he flew to the Berlin Spaceport.

After another man insisted on verifying the body, he unloaded Hans into the waiting space transport. Satisfied they had the right man, he handed Hans' abductor an envelope filled with credits. The kidnapper returned to his EMAC. On his way back to the EMAC, he overheard the space transport pilot, but left before he heard the answer.

The pilot stepped out of the shadows. "All set, doc?"

"Yes. Help me get him onto the Gurney. Then lift off for Cass-C," the doctor said. "We're making a very nice fee for one evening's work." Both men grinned.

The pilot lifted off. The doctor set to work on the checklist of procedures his benefactor wanted. The medical rationale, the logic eluded him, but the pay wiped out his concerns for his patient. First step: Start pre-programmed Medical Operation Machine on Hans. One hour wait. Press Heal button. Removal of Hans' arms at the elbows and at least half of his tongue. Removal of the lower ribs. Why?

Chores completed he slid Hans into a stasis pod and rechecked his checklist. One more step. He retrieved a needle. Injection complete, he attached tubes to Hans and closed the pod.

Ten thousand credits for one night's work. Can't get any easier than this. Sorry, fellow. I need the money.

When the fifteen hour flight ended, the doctor rolled the pod off the transport, delivering it to another man. The doctor got back onboard for the short flight to the other side of Cass-C.

"All done, doc?"

"Yes. A small fortune for an easy night's work?"

The pilot said, "No kidding."

They lifted off on the quick flight home. The spacecraft exploded as it reached the top of its flight path, sending streaming arcs of debris down, making a small meteor shower for those on the night side of Cass-C. The next day news carried a brief story. A space shuttle's fuel tank exploded, killing the pilot, a well-respected medical doctor, and a student visitor from Berlin.

***

Klaus Huber, alias Number Four, accepted the stasis pod. He compared the face inside with an image on his phone. Satisfied he had his man, he pushed the pod into his waiting shuttle. After watching the spaceship lift off, he entered a code on his phone. Onboard the spaceship, a timer activated.

Once at his private residence, he struggled to maintain his normal activities, preoccupied, counting down the days to his fantasy vacation.

Number Six's words echoed in his mind. "You can get absolutely anything for your fantasy. Anything. No questions ever asked."

Klaus smiled. Let's put that to the test, my handsome Hans. Our fantasy awaits us. Let's see how well they can do the fantasy. While waiting for his departure date, Klaus often checked on Hans' mutation. He had paid a small fortune for this mutation brew, unlike any other. Hans' breasts became softballs. When departure for Rudolf-E came, Hans' breasts had become soccer balls. His auburn hair measured three feet long.

Klaus unhooked him from the pod. He maneuvered Hans' body into a large luggage crate on wheels. If all went as planned, Hans would revive from his coma on Rudolf-E, ready for Klaus' fantasy week, as lead actor in a sadomasochistic porn movie instead of being an audience member.

He'd been around the tight-corseted aristocratic women of Cass-C teetering on their tall heels all his life. He never married for fear of exposure. He kept his dark fantasies to himself, illegal videos his release. High on anticipation, he loaded his two crates onto his private deep space transport.

Once in space, he whistled. He inspected his prize. He tingled with nervous anticipation. "Oh, what fun we'll have this coming week, Hans. Will you enjoy it? Not as much as I will. I've been waiting for this all my life. Best vacation ever. All thanks to you, Hans, though I hope you can get some small pleasure from it. Perhaps not. No matter. I will for sure. That's what matters. La-di-da."

When the orbiting spaceport appeared, Klaus received docking instructions. "Land at Bay Five. Got it. Coming in now," he said.

Metal locking arms secured his ship to the docking bay. An excited Klaus left the ship, carrying one crate while pulling the heavier one behind him. He followed the signs to meet with the CEO Marek Denys. Like all clients, he'd paid in advance. His excitement swelled. Soon, he'd see just how well they'd created his fantasy world.

CEO Denys said, "Okay, Mr. Huber, your fantasy is ready for you. Mr. Levitsky will take you down to your Erotic Fantasy Castle, Sir Huber." He bowed to the client, nudging the man into his new role.

Minutes later, Mr. Levitsky landed them beside a dome. Klaus saw his dark gray castle encapsulated in the transparent structure. "Everything you need is inside the dome. Don't leave it. Outside is untraveled desert. There's a call button in your bedroom disguised as a stone hook. I'm sure you'll find everything set up just as you ordered. We presume you've brought your Hans with you."

"Ja, I have him. The castle is perfect."

"I'll see you inside the dome and into the only fantasy exit. We will return for you in a week."

A section of stone wall swung open, revealing a long,

dark corridor. After getting his two crates inside, Mr. Levitsky closed the door. Klaus stood still, allowing his eyes to adapt from the sunlight to the flickering light of the torch that angled out from the wall. He tapped on the stone wall. "Solid. Real stone. Better be for the price I paid." His voice sounded muffled by the dingy hallway.

Carrying one bag and dragging Hans tucked inside the other crate, Klaus moved down the hall, entering the first room on his right, his master bedroom. Three dim and flickering torches illuminated the room. A wooden wardrobe rested against one wall. The canopy surrounding his bed kept warmth inside. The air, chilly. Musty. Against the other wall was a crude latrine and washing table.

He unpacked and changed into the clothing he had bought for the occasion. A vertical shiny black stripe lined the outside of his black pants. His white shirt contrasted. Fluffy sleeves poked out from his twin-tailed jacket. A foot-tall top hat completed his outfit. He picked up his riding crop and strode to the shipping crate. He dumped the groggy Hans out onto the cold stone floor. The man moaned.

Nice moan. Off to a good start. He barked, "A, B, report to my chambers."

Two android women shuffled into his chambers. Each wore a black hobble dress that permitted a three-inch stride only. Spiked heels. Tight gowns revealing shapely forms. Shoulder length hair. A's black hair shone. B's auburn hair, lustrous. Long talons graced their fingers, painted cherry red. Ball gags filled their mouths.

Klaus snickered. The only speaking this week will be mine.

"Ah, perfect, A and B. Take Hans here to the prep room. Time to prepare his body."

Damn, these androids are strong.

The two picked up Hans and dragged him with them,

albeit moving at their very slow pace. A and B shuffled on through the open doorway. He'd insisted on no barriers to movement with his "dolls," especially Hans, his co-star.

The dressing room housed many gowns, heels, and other items. Hans woke from his coma moaning. Unable to speak. His fear radiated through Klaus. He waved his upper arms about. They banged into his soccer ball breasts.

Is that terror in his eyes? Delightful!

"A, B, corset first. Hook him up to the machine. Must get his waist down to fourteen inches. Too fat."

A huge smile formed as Klaus watched the bumbling efforts of the two androids trying to get the corset around the struggling Hans. Once in place and loosely fastened, they hooked the laces to the machine. A and B operated the dual hand-cranks that drew the laces taught.

"Oh, Hans, beautiful! Marvelous panic attack! Keep it up. Oh, you've fainted. Ah, well, you'll get better at it."

A waved a hand.

"Yes, I see. Time to let it settle before fully tightening it. Put the stockings on him. The machine will hold him up."

The two androids could just bend enough to get the task done, further amusing Klaus. "Exquisite. Exquisite models. Perfect. Ah, Hans is awake again. We're putting your new boots on. You'll be walking on your tiptoes, like a ballet dancer. Don't worry. You'll have the support of a tall spike heel. A and B put them on him. They're steel lined. Plenty of soft cushioning, mind you. But you won't be able to twist an ankle. A and B, lace those thigh-high boots tight. Aren't A and B just the perfect fetish models? As you will soon be. Only much better. You and I have a week of pure pleasure before us."

Again, the two androids cranked the dual cranks. Klaus inspected the back, making sure the corset was fully closed before they tied off the long laces.

While the pair readied the next corset, Klaus explained to the gasping Hans. "The outer corset is made of steel. No bending, except at the waist."

Second body corset attached, they tightened a neck corset. Hans' head locked in place, he had to pivot his body to look to either side. Tears streamed down his face. "Excellent, Hans. Now for the gag. No tongue. Eating and drinking will be problematic to say the least. I've designed a special multipurpose gag for you. This tube will go down your throat and attach to the tubular hole through the gag. When it's time to eat, we'll fasten a feeding tube to this outside tube. Don't worry. You won't starve. We'll take care of everything. You won't see anything."

Hans struggled to avoid the tube His tiny wiggles thrilled Klaus, who sported an enormous grin.

"The head mask," Klaus ordered. The women forced a plastic mask with a pretty doll's face over Hans' head, taking care to pull his long hair out the back side. Then they pulled the rear laces taught. Klaus imagined the tension Hans' face and head must be experiencing. Glorious.

The doll's face had two small eye holes, allowing Hans a tiny angle of view of his world. Klaus had experimented with the diameter needed and had chosen one that gave Hans limited vision, just enough to see what was in front of him.

Besides the tiny eye holes, the mask had two nasal holes allowing Hans to breathe, and the gag's tube protruded through the painted lips of the doll's face.

A and B struggled to get Hans into his hobble gown. The gown's top half-covered Hans' huge bosom, his massive cleavage left exposed.

"Ah, perfect job, A and B. Escort Hans to my throne room. I must see to my other subjects."

A and B positioned themselves on either side of Hans, whose upper arms waved about in frantic circles. His failing arms dropped to his sides. Klaus supposed Hans felt the arms of the pair supporting him.

"Don't worry, Hans. Soon, you'll be walking these castle halls on your own. We'll help you out for a brief time. Get used to walking on your own. Your toes and feet will ache. We'll give you pain killers in your first meal, though with that corset, I doubt you'll be able to eat much. It's always a good thing to lose weight. Need to keep that incredible figure. Such cleavage."

Klaus laughed, imagining the terror Hans felt. Muffled moaning reached Klaus' ears. That brought another big smile to the man's face.

"Ta-da. My throne room. Exquisite. They've outdone themselves. Wow!" Klaus spotted his purple throne chair sitting at the back of the spacious room, lit by a dozen wall torches.

Android C's naked body stood chained to one wall. Straps pulled her arms out and upwards, while clamps around each ankle held her legs up tight to the wall. Her tall black spikes wiggled on the stone floor. She mumbled something through the ball gag. Her long light brown hair lay draped over her front.

Android D wore a maid's outfit. Black stockings. Tall black heels. Her legs tied together at her ankles. A rope restrained her hands behind her back. Another long rope dropped from the ceiling and pulled her arms upwards. But another rope tied her ball gag to her knees, forcing her to bend ninety degrees at her waist, making her raised arms pointing upwards. Klaus heard continuous muffled sounds from her. Beautiful.

Android E's body lay tied to a round water-like wheel, her back arched and tied to the wooden wheel. Ropes pulled her arms back behind her, and her legs with their tall heels protruded on either side of her ball-gagged head. A contortionist back-wrapped around the wheel. Klaus gave the wheel a spin and watched as the woman whirled around, her hair flopping onto the floor as her head came down. Otherwise, her naked body offered direct access to her orifices. Superbly done.

Android F's arms were bound behind her. A metal rod connected her neck to her likewise bound ankles, forcing her to bend at a ninety-degree angle at her waist. Her short hair draped down. She too wore ballet boots, though she couldn't walk. Thongs tied a serving board across her back. A pitcher of beer and a mug sat on it. A serving table.

Android G's body contorted into an N when viewed from her side. Bound to a steel pole at three critical points including her wrist, her arms rose upward, bound to the pole at three places including her wrists. A gag strap held her head down the pole. Her vertical legs paralleled the pole, forcing her to bend sharply at her waist, her torso forming the slant of the N. Her blonde hair draped down, touching the floor. Her spiked heels, her only apparel. Her legs were spread apart enough to allow Klaus access to to her contribution.

"Magnificent," he said. "Ah, Android H. Wow."

H stood beside his throne with a foot-long metal bar fastening her ankles together. She too wore identical heels. A black leather case clamped her arms together behind her back, its bottom tied around her waist. Clamped to her head, a torch. A metal rod fastened to her neck and to the bar between her legs ensured she bent at just the right angle to have the torch cast proper lighting on a book that Klaus might choose to read while sitting on his throne. Android H could move enough to position herself to better illuminate his reading.

His personal servant, Android I, stood awaiting his orders. She wore a thin, black, tight-fitting cat suit. She wore tall ballet boots like Hans did. A twelve-inch flexible chain attached to her ankles permitted her to walk. Her arms were tied together at her elbows behind her back, but this allowed her lower arms and hands to function, albeit at a crazy angle at her sides. A waist corset gave her body a unique wasp shape.

A treadmill sat in one corner.

"A and B, fasten Hans to the treadmill. It's time he learned how to walk properly. I, please bring me a mug of ale." Flipping his twin tails out, Klaus sat on is plush purple throne, his eyes taking in the action. "Oh, superb, I. Just superb."

She bent and leaned, struggling to pour the heavy pitcher without spilling any. Taking tiny shuffling steps, she brought his ale to his throne, twisting to one side so her hand might reach his.

"Very good, I. Not a drop spilled. Hans, see, Miss I knows how to do things the right way, as you soon will learn."

A and B chained Hans' body to the treadmill. This way, he couldn't fall down. Besides, with this apparel, Klaus knew if Hans took a tumble, he couldn't get back up by himself. A mumbled something through her gag.

"Oh, set it for 1.5. We'll take it easy. This is his first time walking. I, tie up A and B now. I don't need their services at the moment."

He watched I struggle to tie A's arms behind her back, pulling the ropes taut at her elbows. Then she tied A's hands together. Finally, she attached a neck clamp to A's neck. That clamp held her head to the stone wall, forcing her to stand there immobile until needed again. Minutes later, B stood there beside A, tied and clamped to the wall. Miss I moved over to the treadmill, predicting Klaus might want something done with Hans next.

"This is unbelievably well done! Incredible. Very realistic. Don't you agree Hans? I take that mumble as you do too. Simply amazing. This will be the very best week ever! Many delectable holes to fill. Don't you agree, Hans? I suppose I ought to share some of these with you, don't you think?

Perhaps, I'll just watch you. Oh, my. What times we'll have!"

Chapter 24 Clues

After Cleo fed me lunch, I studied the detailed listing of missing parts I felt confident might make new human-form robots. I bounced suggestions off Bishop, though only I knew he was one of them. Captain Binsk and Ambassador L'Grina soon became bored. Hence, Roz took them on a lengthy trip around the planet visiting the current fantasies being played out.

A dwarf named Scruffy came to help me. Soon, he and I became friends after he asked me if I was the person who saved Lara Axehead who'd gone insane.

"Yes, she works for me. A top level geneticist and a wonderful woman. Why? How do you know her?"

"My second cousin twice removed. That makes us great pals!" He wrapped his mighty arms around me, forcing the air out of my lungs.

"So, tell me about these robots. I've heard rumors. Nothing more. Do they resemble a person? Bet they aren't as strong as me."

I chuckled. "They're much stronger than a human man, Scruffy. Don't know if they match dwarves or giants in strength. You should fear the rogue ones. They've killed me more than once."

"But you're very much alive," he said.

"Mutation agents. That's why I look like I do, an armless Galactic Doll. At least my feet are back to normal. I'm trying to establish if one could make human-form robots from the missing parts."

"Are you a robotics engineer like me?"

"Sort of. Taken many courses at Soros University.

212

That's on Cass-C. Never built one. No hands."

The dwarf chuckled.

"Bishop, bring up the display on my phone of the original plans for their construction. Take a look, Scruffy. See if you agree with my findings."

"A marvel to behold. Genius. Incredible artistry. Magnificent."

"If you can stop drooling over the plans..."

He sighed. "Okay, okay. Let's see what you've got."

I felt as though I was in one of the robot labs back on Cass-C working with fellow students to solve a challenging robotics problem. Oh, how I loved this feeling of comradery with another, my intellectual equal, more or less, in this field anyway. We became absorbed in our work.

"You're still at it?" Roz asked. "It's suppertime, unless you are on a diet and plan to miss it."

"I can't believe all the fantasies in progress," Captain Binsk said.

"How about that disgusting perverted one?" Ambassador L'Grina said. "Thank heavens he only plays his fantasies out on androids."

We went for supper, and afterwards, Roz showed us our sleeping quarters.

Captain Binsk said, "Okay, we three women will bunk together. I want nothing to happen to Parkinson here. My security men will split shifts and stand guard over our door while we sleep."

Roz said, "Is that necessary? Who could harm Molly down here? Or why?"

"She's about the only person alive who can distinguish a human-from robot from a person. That's why," Captain Binsk said. "I'm beat. Let's get some sleep. Perhaps we'll have this all solved tomorrow. Hope so. I'm getting bored."

Ambassador L'Grina said, "Spoken like a true warrior."

"Right on!" she said, thrusting her fist upwards.

I shook my head. "I insist Bishop watch over me while I sleep."

***

By lunch the next day, Scruffy and I concurred. Enough parts had gone missing to build one hundred sixteen human-form robots. Many more, if their tallies were wrong. This included the theft of another positronic brain last night. After Captain Binsk reported that up the lines, they called a meeting.

"Let's assume someone is building these human-form robots here on Rudolf-E," I began.

Scruffy interrupted. "And somehow shipped them off-world. Don't forget that detail. Cause that's impossible."

"A hundred sixteen made," I continued. "How do they get them off this world? Shipping crates? Do you ever ship things off Rudolf-E?"

"Nope," Roz said. "Supplies are always coming in, but we never ship things back. Except money, I suppose, but that's the CEO's job. To handle the credits."

"Well, you send some workers home when their contracts are up," Scraggly said.

Roz pulled on her face. "Yeah, well, okay. Except those people."

I asked, Can you check and see how many workers went home say in the last three months?"

Ten minutes later, CEO Denys replied via a comm link. "Only one, but that was a medical emergency. Fellow developed a tumor and needed expert medical attention we couldn't provide. That was three months back."

"Told ya so," Scruffy said, his hands squarely on his hips.

"That wasn't helpful," Ambassador L'Grina said.

Captain Binsk said, "Well, if someone isn't shipping parts off-world or completed robots, then they must be storing

214

them here on Rudolf-E. In a warehouse. One hundred sixteen robots standing in line waiting."

"Good Lord! Now that's frightening! One isn't stoppable. Think what a hundred could do," I said.

"Okay. Here's what we do next," Captain Binsk said. "We will search every inch of this planet. If they can't be shipped off-world, then those robots have to be hidden in a warehouse or room somewhere. We must find them. Check your guns."

Bishop said, "You should issue blasters, too. I couldn't stop one with my 9mm. Takes real firepower to knock one of them out of service, unless you get a lucky head shot. Hell, Molly, what if they're supplied with defensive shields or invisibility wristbands?"

Roz threw her hands in the air. "You're kidding? The entire planet? That'll take days."

"Best get started then," Captain Binsk said. She placed a radio call to the cruiser hovering over the planet. "Okay, blasters are on their way down. Over CEO Denys' objections."

"Okay, okay. Just don't interfere with a client and their fantasy. Besides, everything in their fantasy dome was made here. There aren't any human-form robots in the domes. Androids, yes, but they have primitive programming."

She added, "I've a surface gadabout you can use if you want to scour the surface. Mind you, it's bleak out there. This is a desert planet."

Captain Binsk ordered three guards to take the scout ship and coordinate a complete surface search with the cruiser in orbit. She received an estimate of three days to finish the hunt topside.

Roz then led us on a systematic search of every underground facility and tunnel system that connected the factories and the client domes. While the duration bothered me, where else could these new hundred plus robots be?

215

Off we went. The remaining three security men accompanied the five of us, not counting Cleo. We began our search with the working labs and storage facilities. I soon found myself useless. I couldn't open the doors and stayed back as the watch dog, visiting with workers we met.

Nothing. Next, we moved down the underground tunnels, stopping at construction zones for future fantasies and those in operation. Surveillance cameras in dome tops fed private monitors where Roz could check on the proper operation of the fantasy. I enjoyed watching what I called the Wild West shooting matches.

Men dressed up in what I imagined were old-time western garb fired at bottles stilling on rail fences. A competition of sorts. Oh, how I would have loved to take my Glock into that scenario. After a sigh, I moved on. Another time and place, perhaps.

When we searched the areas around Klaus Huber's fantasy castle, I felt a strong sense of fear or terror coming from his dome. I watched the monitor in disbelief. A dozen women could be the source, but Roz assured me these were androids. Still, I couldn't believe how the client treated them. An all-leather sheath covered one who had the largest bosom I'd seen, beyond the men on Bella that is. It stood on its toes in what Roz called ballet boots, secured to a ring bolt in the floor. From the ceiling, another rope attached to the top of the sheath, pulling its head upwards. The resulting combination meant it couldn't move. Worse, the sheath seemed to me to be extremely tight fitting, laced at the sides. I could see no arms or perhaps a hint of them laced behind its back. I had the strangest sense the fear came from this android, which made me wonder if robots had emotions like a human being. We moved on.

Three long days passed before Roz led us back to her main complex where we stayed. We'd found several traces

216

where I believed robot assembly might have taken place. Some leftover bits covered the floor. The three guards rejoined us; their surface search yielded nothing.

We held a round table meeting the following morning. Captain Binsk led the meeting.

"All signs point to human-form robots being assembled from parts somewhere on this world. Perhaps a hundred sixteen thus far. We've found no evidence they've been shipped off this world. We've found none in storage either. Where are they?"

I said, "That's the key question. I'm certain about our conclusion that enough parts are missing to have made a hundred sixteen robots. Particularly because of the amount of missing synthetic skin. That stuff is expensive. Are we certain someone couldn't be shipping things without the space station knowing about it?

"What about someone dropping out of hyperspace just above the planet's surface and on the opposite from the space station? Tricky move. Or using that teleport beam device the Admiral used to move us back to her shuttle saucer there on Bella?"

Captain Binsk said, "Teleport is very short range. Dropping out of hyperspace just above the surface is too dangerous. The planet is in orbit around Rudolf, which means its precise hyperspace coordinates are always changing. No way could one enter such exact values. Perhaps a computer could work out the tiny coordinates change. Maybe. But that's an avenue we should explore. I'll have Rear Admiral Irenka Bronislawa have her techs examine all surveillance videos from the space station. Have them look for a deep space transport arriving close to the surface and on the other side from the space station. It's in a synchronous orbit. It's always above this spot on the surface. Other ideas we can explore? These parts didn't just vanish."

Ambassador L'Grina said, "Why not install spy cameras where the brains are stored and where critical parts are kept. With luck, we can catch the thief in action."

"And that assembly room we think is being used," I added. "How else can these robots vanish from here?"

Blank stares told much. While Roz and Captain Binsk headed off to carry out these ideas, Ambassador L'Grina and I took time out for tea, since I couldn't do much else to assist the others.

"Have you got a potential husband lined up?" she asked. "I had thought you and that detective Dirk-what's-his-name might get hitched. But he's off in the Galactic Detective Squad again."

"Dirk Bennet. He got away, just like that designer, Balin Khan." I sighed. "Now there was a man. But his wife that everyone thought was dead turned up."

"I know you humans have such a short life span. What about that fellow on Bella?"

"Dante Gallo?" She nodded. "Yeah, cute. I'm attracted to him. But..."

Ambassador L'Grina chuckled. "With men, there's always a butt."

When I stopped laughing, I explained. "He has no education and can't even read and write his own language. His education must come first, especially if the Admiral's people regrow his arms and fix up his body. I'll keep looking. But, yes, now and then I feel darn lonely. How about you? Any prospects?"

"My people live very long lives. We don't settle down, domestically that is, until much later in life. But I know what you mean. I get around those feelings by immersing myself in your Earth people and their culture. It's certainly not boring work. I can see why the Third Invaders keep experimenting with your race. Your kind can go off in many directions. But

218

then, my people might do that if we had children as fast as your people do. Gosh, by now, I'd have something like twenty kids running around."

We both laughed at that idea. She said, "I've been keeping an eye on you. From a distance. You impressed me. When we first met years ago, your knowledge was limited to that of being a private investigator. One with invaluable instincts, but otherwise ignorant of much else. Now look at you. A pilot, a navigator, a robotics expert, advanced mathematician, linguist, a historian of Earth and of the Federation of Planets."

"Don't forget geology," I said. "That's what I'm most interested in at the moment, though I suppose I must forgo that and become the Empress of the Sol Empire just as soon as we wrap this up and that of Bella. But I can't see myself being the diplomat. Not like you've become."

She laughed. "Isn't that the major part of your new job description?"

I glared at her, before sighing. "I'll put it off somehow."

"Best not. Your empire is just now reaching out to nearby stars and planets. You don't even have any protocols for dealing with Bella. That's the first inhabited world you're going to add to your empire, but that world has barely begun an industrial age. My opinion, mind you. But that will be your first major challenge. Bring order to the messy governing of your budding empire."

"Can I bounce ideas off you? When I have to become the empress, that is."

"You damned better ask." We both laughed.

"Excuse me," Scruffy said.

I turned and saw the stocky dwarf stumping into the room, his new blaster slung over his back and almost as tall as himself. Combined with his long beard, felt hat, and suspenders holding up his leather work pants, I stifled a laugh.

"As I was passing the incinerator a bit ago, I noticed it was on. What with all this robot mess going on, I checked with scheduling. No incineration scheduled today. An unauthorized burning. I turned off the fires and peeked inside. I think you need to see this. Not pretty, mind you. 'Tis a clue, if ever there was one."

"Lead on," I said.

Roz joined our party. Captain Binsk and three guards ran up to us.

She said, "Find something?"

"A clue," Scruffy said.

Try as I might, I couldn't get him to say more that it might be grim. Then again, it might not be. If I'd had arms, I might have pounded the information out of the dwarf's noggin.

"There. What is it?" he said, opening the door of the giant blast furnace.

"Looks like a crispy body. Is it one of your androids?" I asked. Charcoal smell equaled burned skin. The sulphur odor: burned hair. My PI training kicked in, though I didn't know what materials they used in their androids.

A pale face appeared on Roz. She swallowed. "I—I think that's a human's body. Can we roll it over? See its face. Rather looks like that sadist client."

The body lay on its stomach. Thus, much of his backside was burned beyond recognition. One of the guards got his hands dirty and rolled the man over. While his face displayed severe burns, I recognized him.

"Yes, that's the sadist client with all those androids we saw," I said. "Got an ID for him?"

"Oh, this is the biggest disaster ever! We've never lost a client before!" Roz said. She called CEO Denys. "Major, major disaster down here. We just discovered client Huber's body in the incinerator. Yes, he's dead, burnt almost beyond

220

recognition. No, I'm not joking. What? He's already left? His fantasy was over? But I don't understand. Okay, I'll get a medical team down here. Must be some kind of major foul up. Bye."

All the color drained from her face. "He's already left. Last night. If so, who's in the incinerator?"

She turned away and called for her medical staff. "No, need identification. Man's already dead. No, no hope of rejuvenation. Hurry."

Roz turned back to us, looked at the dead body, and opened her laptop.

The planet's medical doctor rushed in, accompanied by three assistants.

"What's this emergency?" he said, out of breath.

Roz pointed to the body inside the incinerator. It lay on a grate that allowed ashes to fall through, where later on they could be scooped out.

"Hum." That's all the doctor said, motioning for his assistants to pull the body out. They laid it on a stretcher, though its legs fell off as they did so. They'd taken the greatest fire damage.

Speaking into a mike, the doctor said, "Body is wearing clothing, though it's nearly gone. Backside of body pretty well melted. Third-degree burns. Facial area charred but recognizable." He snapped a photo on his phone and uploaded it to his medical computer, or so he said. "I'm running a reconstruction program on the man's face now. We have some clever software these days. I know his face is badly burned, but the program undoes what the fire caused. The same for acid burns and alkaline burns. Takes longer if all we have is the bare skull to go on. The reconstruction of what the person must have looked like. Seventy percent accurate from the skull alone, but ninety percent from burns as bad as these are. Clever program. Developed after the attack on Home World some years back where ten thousand plus were boiled alive in their sleep. Never found out who attacked us. They invented this program to help identify the remains of the many victims."

I cringed. I knew who'd attacked them and why. Retaliation for their betrayal of the thousand sent to Domes. His phone beeped.

"ID match to client Klaus Huber," the doctor said.

"But Denys said Huber left last night," Roz said.

She dialed her boss at the same time as the doctor did. After the confusion of calls died down, CEO Denys appeared on all comm sets.

"It can't be. I checked him out last night myself. I saw him off."

The doctor said, "But facial reconstruction shows this charred body to be Klaus Huber. It's definitely a homo sapiens body. It was alive. My men are taking him back to my lab. I'll conduct a post mortem right away. Time of death is impossible to tell from the body's current state. Also possibly the cause of death. Denys, one of us is wrong on our identification."

The CEO said, "Must be on your end. I tell you I saw the man off. He looked as satisfied as any other client. I even shook his hand. Don't know what you've got down there, but it can't be Klaus Huber!"

"Come on," Roz said, the color returning to her face. "Let's see if we caught whoever did this on the new surveillance videos."

We headed back to her computer office, where projectors covered one wall. I'd never seen this many 3-D holo projectors in one place before. She cued up the video taken in that room last night. For the longest time, we saw the dimly illuminated incinerator room. Empty. I yawned. Patience.

As Scruffy dozed off, his body slumped down the wall he'd been leaning into until he sat on the floor, snoring. The security guards slipped out of the room to have a smoke. Roz sat in the only chair, while we stood. Soon, I took a hint from Scruffy and sat on the cold stone floor.

Two men lugging a rolled-up rug between them jarred me awake. I poked Scruffy with a toe. He mumbled and looked up. Everyone stared at the images. They almost looked real, as though they were in this room with us.

The men tossed the rug inside and turned on the incinerator. They left, and the room appeared empty once again. At no point could we see their faces. Rats.

"Well, two of our human—homo sapiens—workers. But that's all I can tell," Roz said, turning off the replay.

She called the doctor first, telling him the man had likely been rolled up in a rug. Roz activated speaker phone.

"Well that explains why his front side isn't as crispy as his backside," he said. "I have cause of death. Someone strangled him and crushed his neck. I'll report that to Denys, but he'll not be pleased."

Roz said, "Then, who was the imposter that Denys shook hands with?"

A sickening feeling coursed through my veins as I realized who it had been.

Chapter 25 Crisis

"You shook hands with one of the new human-form robots," I said.

Love the marvelous speakerphone app of these Third Invaders. They have the coolest tech. We saw a large holo image of CEO Denys, while he should see us standing around Roz's phone.

"That can't be," he said.

The doctor, who joined us via a conference call, said, "Well, the human Huber is down here in my lab. Quite crispy, mind you. Are you sending for an Investigation Squad? Or should we finish disposing of the body?"

"Let me do some checking on Huber. Since Captain Binsk is here, no formal investigation is needed. It's your show, Captain."

She drew her hands across her face, pulling on her chin. "Okay, first step, let's see if we can ID the two men. They get the new robots off Fantasy World by replacing your clients. That won't be good for business."

"I'll lose my job!" CEO Denys wailed, before ending the call.

"Are many clients humans?" I asked Roz.

"No. Too costly for most of your kind. We have some, mind you. Like that nutty Huber. Kind of got what he deserved, if you ask me. Pervert," she said.

"Replacing human clients can't be their main way to get new robots off this planet," I said. "How many workers did you say you had?"

"Five hundred sixty-six at last count," Roz said.

"How many of those are humans?"

224

Roz pulled her lip for a moment. "Hum, maybe one in five. Best ask Denys that question. Just a guess. Why? Oh, Fingol's Rats!"

"What?" Scruffy asked.

Captain Binsk cursed, while I explained. "Perhaps the human-form robots have been replacing your human workers, incinerating their bodies when they replace them. One of their traits is the ability to change their appearance, even sex."

I focused and sensed the minds of those present with me. "The good news is that none of us here is one of those human-form robots." I ignored Bishop, who smiled, continuing to stand in the background.

"Well, I'm certainly not one," Roz said. "Oh, now I get it. You can tell if you're with one of them, right?"

"Yes, I can. We should check all humans on this world."

While they discussed how best to do that, I continued my concentration. I recalled having sensed fear and terror coming from Huber's fantasy dome. Had I sensed him as someone strangled him? No! I sensed that same fear and terror, only it had become more intense.

"Guys, something is very wrong in Huber's fantast dome. I'm picking up strong emotions. Terror."

"Scruffy, take her there," Roz said.

"You don't go alone," Captain Binsk said, as she and her guards fell in behind Bishop, the dwarf, and me.

He stumped down the corridors to one of the electric powered trains that we took to travel longer distances through the elaborate tunnel system. The powered unit faced us. I presumed he'd driven it here to inform us of the incinerator incident. After we hopped onboard, Scruffy turned it around. We flew down the tunnel.

He entered a security code to open a concealed door in the fantasy dome and then a second one to enter the stone castle.

"Not real stone. Fabricated stone," he explained as he stumped into the darkened hallway lighted by a single torch. "Gives me the creeps."

We entered the throne room.

"What a sicko," Captain Binsk said. "How do we tell the androids from a person?"

"The cleanup crew will just pick up everything and toss it in the incinerator or tear things apart to recycle," Scruffy said. "That's what I do. Make and recycle these fake stone things. Castle is pretty impressive, if not spooky."

"I can tell. I sense strong emotions in here. I'll check each one."

I stood before each one. The details of their bindings stood out as excellent workmanship, if not sadistic. When I sensed no mind, I shook my head and moved to the next one.

I stood before the one encased in a tight sheath. The boots forced the wearer to stand on their tiptoes like a ballet dancer, but a chain held the boots to the floor via a ring embedded in the floor. A rope attached to the top of the head encasement and looped through a similar ring in the ceiling held the body erect. Someone fastened the other end of the rope to a wall hook. As I approached the encased person, I felt his tormented mind.

"It's a person in there. Someone undo the rope and get him out of that thing," I said.

"Oh, dear god. Someone call the doctor!" Captain Binsk said.

After laying the man on the floor, she cut the bindings. A strange-looking man stared up at us. He had breasts even larger than mine, akin to those on the men of Bella. With no lower arms, he waved his stumps about making gurgling noises.

"It's all right. You're safe now," I said. "We've sent for the doctor. What's your name?"

226

Gurgles answered me. I had a sickening feeling, as the doctor rushed in. After one glance at his patient, a flood of curses issued.

After a quick examination, he said, "Someone's cut off most of his tongue. Surgical machine, I'd guess. Same with his arms. His feet are crushed. I doubt if he can stand or walk. Let's get him to my infirmary."

"I'll tag along, doctor. Perhaps I can get answers through telepathy."

He gave me a strange glance. Bishop and I followed behind him and his aides. We took one of the electric train things to his medical facility.

For the first hour, I let the doctor work his magic. X-rays showed massive damage to his feet, particularly to his toes. The rest of his body checked out fine, though his waist showed bruising.

"He's lost two pair of lower ribs. You can see they're missing."

Again, I saw that from the x-rays. Whoever he was, he had calmed down. Time to find out who he was. I made telepathic contact. But the waves of pain drove me out of his mind. I waited until the pain killers took hold and tried again.

'Hi. I'm Molly Parkinson. Who are you? How did you get here? What happened to your body?'

'Help me! Hans Klein. I'm Hans Klein, from Berlin. I don't know what happened. We went out drinking to celebrate finishing another degree. I walked into my room and someone attacked me. I woke up in this place. Tortured. Pain. Terrible pain.'

'You don't know how you lost your arms or tongue or ribs?'

'No! Breasts are throbbing. Going to explode?'

I relayed this to the doctor. "Say, check those breasts. He's complaining they're throbbing. The men on Bella have similar breasts and had to be milked twice each day. Could be his problem?"

Minutes later and after a test milk spray that shot three feet covering the doctor, I had my answer.

"I've never seen that happen. Let's see if I can find a milk pump or something that we can use."

After rigging up a pump system, the doctor began on Hans' left breast.

"Incredible! Look at the volume he's producing," the doctor said. "No wonder they hurt, son."

I contacted Hans. 'How's that? Feeling better?'

'Yes, don't stop! Don't forget the other one.'

A half-hour later, the doctor poured a pint of milk down the drain. Hans felt so much better that he drifted into a sleep, likely caused by the level of pain meds.

"What do we do for him now?" the doctor asked. "He's a human. While I can treat the usual cuts and broken bones, I can't do anything for him. With those feet, I doubt he'll ever walk or stand again. Since he's from your world, is mercy killing allowed?"

"Not really."

"Options: I should amputate his feet. He could then make use of artificial legs and arms. I'm monitoring those breasts of his. He might need further milking, though I'm not sure why he's lactating this much. I can't do anything for his lost tongue. Eating and swallowing will be challenging for him. A mercy killing might be in his best interests."

"Let me talk with him about this. There is another option."

I sat beside Hans for a time, waiting until he revived. With his handsome looks, he could have been a top male model, as long as you ignored everything below his neck. I admit I found myself attracted to this young man. At least his head. He had been a university student. No dummy. I wanted to know more about Hans.

I told him what the doctor said. "The medical prognosis isn't good at all. Feet have to be amputated. With luck, you could be fitted with prosthetic legs and arms. They can't do anything about your missing tongue or ribs, though I don't think you'll miss your ribs."

A faint smile appeared with my wise crack. He moved his head from side to side ever so slightly. He touched his head with his right upper arm.

"Telepathic contact?"

He nodded.

'Mercy killing? I can't live like this. I can't even eat or drink, let alone talk to anyone.'

"Hans, there is another option, but it has its downside. I think I can restore your missing tongue and ribs, and I can repair your feet, making them as good as new. But you'd be like me. Armless. Still you could then eat, talk, and do most everything. Hardly anything stops me."

Again, he pointed to his head.

'Who are you?'

"Molly Parkinson."

'*The* Molly Parkinson? Once head of GD? The person who saved many lives after the awful terrorist attacks years ago?'

"Yeah, that's me. I keep getting my arms regrown only to be killed and brought back via the genetic mutation agent."

He pointed to his head again.

'You're famous. I don't want to die, but I can't live like this. Do it. It's that Galactic Doll mutation agent. Right?' I nodded. 'Just do it. I beg you. Do it or kill me.'

I laughed. "I will not kill you, Hans. We've just met. I'll try the mutation agent. You'll be in a coma for a time. Don't worry about it. My sister and my friend are working on finding a mutation cure for me. Again. I've been rejuvenated many times. My DNA is a complete mess. I'll have them work on a cure for you, too. Might take some time, depending on how messed up your DNA is. That's one subject I've not yet been able to face studying."

'I owe you my life.'

"I'll get the doctor. Bishop?"

I nodded. He understood, producing a syringe from his concealed pouch. When the doctor returned, I told him what we were going to do.

"Do you have any stasis pods? Life support units? Something to feed his body the nourishment it will need for the regeneration?"

"I've got the pods, but I've no knowledge of regenerative needs."

"Contact someone at the Chicago Med Center on Earth, Sol Empire. They know all about it. He'll be in a mutation coma at least eight days. Possibly more, since his body has much to regenerate."

"Will his arms come back?"

"Nope. He'll lose the rest of them, but everything else should be repaired."

We watched as Bishop injected Hans. Now, we waited and watched his eyes. I relaxed when he slipped into the mutation coma. Darn predictable. I watched the doctor lift him into a waiting pod, before Bishop and I returned to Roz's main office.

I came in on the end of a call from CEO Denys.

"No, this Huber person does not exist. There's no record of him living on Cass-C. And he must have installed a fake ID into his deep space transport. I tried tracking him through that number. Those ID numbers belong to Space-X on Crylos-C, but they have never heard of Huber nor is the ship one of theirs. Huber is a complete mystery man, but his credits were good. This is why we always insist on payment up front.

Robot or not, he doesn't exist anywhere."

Roz said, "Well, that's for certain. We've finished incinerating his body. Oh, Parkinson's back. So, are we a go for checking every employee?"

"That isn't necessary, Roz. Robots impersonating our employees? Hardly. I'll leave you to it. Got to check with Home World over this Huber mess."

After he hung up, Roz shrugged her shoulders and looked at Captain Binsk. But covered in ash, Scruffy stumped up, carrying metal bits.

"Look what I found. I just cleaned out the incinerator ash. That's one of my dirtier jobs. I hoped to find more clues. And I found these screws. Titanium, I think. Shouldn't have been put in the incinerator. Not hot enough to melt them. They don't burn. Figure doc might want to look at them."

"What strange screws," Roz said. "I've never seen them. Okay, take them to doc. Maybe he can identify them. Captain, what now?"

"We need to check each employee. Have Parkinson do her thing with each." Turning to me, she asked, "How do you want us to do this? Bring them to you one by one?"

"Hum. They are scattered around this entire planet, right?" Roz nodded. "Do they move around a lot or do they stay in their own areas?"

"Most work around their living complex, like we do here. Some take the high-speed electric trains to help at other zones. I could ask those in a specific zone to report here for a special assignment. Then you could check them."

"Wouldn't it be faster if we traveled to each of these work zones and checked the workers there? Then move on to the next one until we're back here," I suggested.

Captain Binsk said, "I agree with Parkinson. There will be fewer people to deal with at any one location, especially important if we encounter these robots. Less collateral damage if they fight us, which I'm sure they will, if past encounters are anything to go by."

"Let's be as efficient about this as we can," I said. "Can you print out a list of all employees? As I examine one, you can check that person off the list. We don't want to miss even one person, if the robots are impersonating your workers."

"I can, but the system will notify Denys that I've pulled the list. Give me a couple minutes to pull it down to my comm device. I can delete each one that gets checked out as okay."

She hastened off to do that, while Captain Binsk and her six guards checked their blasters and shield armor. I had Bishop check his Glock. I felt reassured when he lifted his jacket to reveal six additional clips. That gave him over a hundred rounds. Until now, we never needed more than one clip. Still, if a hundred plus of these human-form robots were out there and each put up a fight... I almost asked for a personal defense shield.

Roz returned with her comm device. She had armed herself.

Scruffy joined us, huffing and puffing.

He said, "Doc says those are medical screws. Holds bones together while they heal. He's tracking the person who had them via the serial numbers. What's next?"

"We're going robot hunting," Captain Binsk said.

Her guards grinned. "Let's do this!" one said.

"Count me in. Where're we going first?" Scruffy said, patting his blaster.

"We'll go clockwise from here," Roz said. "Take them in station-number order. Station One has our people working there."

"And mine, too," Scruffy said, standing tall.

"Right," Roz said. "We'll take the electric train. I'll drive. That way no one will be suspicious."

Scruffy sat beside me.

232

"Don't worry. I'll protect you," he said.

"How fast does this train travel?"

"Once it gets going, you can't even sense the speed. Neat invention of Roz's. I once rode it all around this world non-stop. Took me a whole day to get back. Got chewed out for doing that. Sure was fun, though. Never found its top speed. Goes kind of like hyperspace. Have to ask Roz how it works."

"You're kidding? That would be at least a thousand miles an hour."

"What's a miles? What's an hour?"

"Never mind. Earth units. Old ones at that. I'm impressed. Doesn't feel like we're moving."

"Train has to stay in these special tunnels. Won't work above ground," he said. We continued to chat, passing the minutes.

At last, lights flickered as the train pulled into Station One. Roz led us to the main work area. Wow. Brilliant white lights illuminated the giant room. Drafting tables stood in a dizzying array. Many had a Third Invader sitting on stools designing the next client's fantasy set up. In one corner and shorter tables, six dwarves stopped their work to stare at us.

One called out, "Hey, it's the Boss Lady."

All twenty-six designers ceased work and looked our way.

Roz said, "Keep working. I'm bringing some Home World guests to take a peek at our operations."

I whispered. "Perfect. We'll walk close to each. I'll let you know if anyone is a robot."

Captain Binsk's guards took up a securing position in case a robot tried to flee. I followed Roz around, though Captain Binsk, Ambassador L'Grina, Bishop, and Scruffy tagged along behind me. Various parts of an ocean-going luxury liner appeared on the different tables as I walked among them, sensing minds as I went. Most surface thoughts

233

suggested I wasn't welcome here and that they hated interruptions. I could understand that and so said nothing as I walked along. When we reached the end of the line by the dwarves, Roz gave me a curious glance.

"All fine here. Marvelous designers. If only we had their caliber on Earth," I said.

Several flashed brief smiles as we walked past them to the room's entrance. Once outside of their hearing, Roz brought out her comm device with the employee list.

"All okay here?" she asked.

I nodded and watched as she deleted the names of the workers. I wondered how she could remember that many individuals. I glanced at the font displayed on her device and recognized that same script was on the worker's shirts. I couldn't help smiling. It seemed workers everywhere wore their names on their work clothes.

"Foreman's missing. I'm checking the work log," Roz said. "Okay, he's gone to Station Two. Guess we'll find him there. Off we go."

An hour later, we pulled into Station Two. Here workshops turned part of the designs into a reality of sorts. Half these workers vanished before we arrived.

"Where is everyone?" Roz asked.

"Don't know," a foreman said. "They just took off down the tunnel. I'm not about to run after them."

"Okay, we'll check those who are here."

I walked past several construction stations. Uninteresting. Only annoyed thoughts until the last worker. He used a nail gun to frame up a wall of some kind. He looked at me. No emotion. No mind.

"He's one," I said.

Events happened in a flash. The robot grinned and fired a nail at me. I felt a huge surge of pain in my head. Had it taken marksmanship training? A large spike protruded from my forehead as I felt my body slumping to the floor. I heard Bishop's 9mm firing and saw the robot's body jerk as it spun away and dashed down the tunnel. A Roman candle of blaster fire faded from view. My world turned black once again.

Chapter 26 Battle for Rudolf-E

Bishop saw the robot fire a nail into Molly's head. He acted. While dashing to break her fall to the cold stone floor, he emptied a clip into the retreating human-form robot. A second after that, the others opened fire with their blasters. The deafening noise and splintered rock dust blocked vision of the fleeing robot.

Bishop checked for a pulse, found it, and calculated whether to pull the nail out of her head. Six guards rushed past him and into the tunnel, as the others knelt down beside Molly and Bishop.

Boom! A massive explosion tore through the tunnel. Captain Binsk watched as the bodies of her six guards flew out of the tunnel. She dashed into the cloud of gray dust that billowed out of the tunnel to aid them. Screams from other workers added to the din.

Roz stood transfixed. Bishop concluded temporary shock. Roz's phone rang. Mechanically, she picked it up, as Bishop, Scruffy, and Ambassador L'Grina turned towards her.

The voice of the doctor echoed in the sudden stillness. "Roz, the titanium screws. I put them into CEO Denys' hip forty years ago when that scaffolding collapsed on him. What's the meaning of this? I can't raise him on the comm. Roz? What's going on?"

Captain Binsk cursed. She and Ambassador L'Grina helped the fallen soldiers to their feet. They couldn't hear anything, but signed they were okay. Shaken up. Bruised.

Roz appeared to come to. "Found a robot down here. Shot Parkinson in the head. With a nail gun. Guards fired at the fleeing robot. Explosion. Tunnel collapse. Keep trying to reach Denys. Wait! Are you saying Denys isn't Denys?"

"Roz, get Parkinson to my infirmary now. Best get back here soon."

"Scruffy, take them back to my section. Top speed. I have to assess the tunnel damage." She fiddled with her phone. "Denys, answer your damned phone!"

She hung up as Bishop loaded Molly's body into one of the train cars. A soldier returned from his inspection of the tunnel.

"Blocked. No passage."

Captain Binsk said, "Okay. Onto the train. We'll head back. Coming, Roz?"

"No, I have to see the severity of the damage. This can't be happening. It can't be."

With everyone onboard, Bishop said, "Scruffy, take off. We're two hours out, right? Make it faster than that!"

"Have to see how fast this thing can go," the dwarf said with a huge, wicked grin.

No one saw Bishop injecting Molly with the mutation agent. He checked her eyes and gave her more injections until he saw the telltale signs of the mutation coma taking hold. He relaxed and reviewed what had happened, calculating if he'd made an error in judgement. After a careful review, Bishop decided he hadn't.

Scruffy set a new speed record. The train pulled into the main base where Roz worked in a little over an hour. They stopped first at the infirmary before going on to Roz's workshop area.

The doctor examined Molly. "She's in a coma?"

"Yes, mutation coma. I couldn't risk body death before we got to you," Bishop said.

"Good move. I'll take it from here and get her into a stasis pod, too. What the devil is going on?"

"We were right. The human-form robots have been

killing off your workers and taking their place. They can change their outward appearance to look like anyone."

Scruffy said, "Those screws weren't in the incinerator before I finished burning up that Huber fellow's set. I cleaned it. That means the robots got to Denys a day or more ago."

"You mean Denys is a robot? Wouldn't he still answer his comm?" the doctor asked.

Ambassador L'Grina said, "Gig is up. We know they are replacing Rudolf-E workers. My guess? They calculate it's time to take over this world or flee. We need to know which."

"Why would they want Fantasy World?" Scruffy asked.

"A great facility for manufacturing more of themselves," she said.

Bishop said, "From what Molly told me, my guess is they want to flee. Captain Binsk, call your fleet. Have them block all ships trying to leave Rudolf-E."

"Sorry, can't get a signal. My comm goes to the space station where it's relayed to the cruiser. Denys must have shut that relay unit. I'm cut off. But we'll make a stand here."

She, her guards, and Scruffy headed on down the tunnel that led to Roz's large workshop and living quarters. Beyond that point, they set up barricades. Scruffy continued on through the tunnel installing new surveillance cameras.

***

Ambassador L'Grina stayed with Bishop and the doctor, helping to get Molly's body hooked up to the life support unit. Already the head wound looked as though it might be healing.

She said, "Hope it's less than a week this time. We need her back. Without her, we can't tell if those in the tunnel are human or robots. Robots on us before we know what hit us."

"Oh, crap!" the doctor said. "I can't take much more of this. I didn't sign on for a war."

"Let's get tea, shall we?" she suggested.

Doctor calmed. They waited over an hour before Roz

returned, bringing two dozen scared employees with her.

"They're spooked. Still no response from the CEO," she said. "How's Parkinson? We need her now more than ever before. Those robots can impersonate one of us, a Third Invader!"

"That's what I told them," the ambassador said. "The only ones we can trust are those Molly already approved. Captain Binsk went on ahead. Hope for a speedy mutation."

"Roz, Roz, you there?" a voice appeared on her comm set.

"Roz here," she said.

"We're at Station Twenty-one. Like half the work force has just passed by us. Some of my people joined them. What's going on? One said for us to stay put."

"Human-form robots have murdered a bunch of our workers. Assumed their forms. One has taken out CEO Denys. I can't contact anyone at the station."

"Wait, here come some now. Hey, don't you work up on the station? Talk to Roz."

"Roz, Security Chief Abelard. What's going on? Denys ordered all of us here. Sensors registered an explosion. We're armed but where's the attack?"

After explaining, Roz said, "How many of you are armed?"

"Six."

"Okay, take a train and head to my station. Join up with Captain Binsk and her soldiers.Be wary of everyone you meet. Could be robots. Only the Parkinson woman can tell the damned difference. She discovered one. It shot her in the head with a damned nail gun. A nail gun. Look for explosive plants along the walls. One that shot Parkinson collapsed the tunnel beyond Station Two."

"Dingo's Rats!" Abelard said, "What if we encounter those who have already fled past us?"

"They could be robots. Do not engage. Stay well behind them. Be alert for sabotage. Keep me posted."

Roz turned to Ambassador L'Grina. "I've got to join Captain Binsk. If Parkinson wakes, get her up to the front lines. She's our only way to tell if it's a person or robot. Without shooting them, that is. Doc, see if you can speed her recovery. Can't imagine taking a spike to your head isn't painful, though. They will pay!"

She and two others with blasters headed off down the tunnel on foot.

***

Soon, they joined Captain Binsk.

Roz said, "I see you've established a defensive wall here. Good. We have to defend my area. From here, I can communicate and control most everything on the planet. Any sign of the robots? I got a report they're assembling as a group and heading this way."

The captain said, "Well, Dingo's Rats. We can't hold off a hundred of them with what? Maybe ten of us. The space station's comm relay is down. I can't call the cruiser for help. Any way you can get me through to them? What I wouldn't give for the soldiers on board."

"I can hook up a lan-sat, but it has a tight beam. If I don't know where to point it, no chance of it connecting. I could take your group up there in my shuttle, but we'd have to fight our way to the control section. By then, the robot could well have destroyed the whole comm center. Besides," Roz said, "we have to protect all the other workers down here."

"If I can get word to my ship... Okay, I see your point, but my responsibility is to protect much more than this tiny world. I've got to get word to my cruiser. Now."

"Take Lift Three. There's a shuttle lot on your right."

"Thanks. Keep Parkinson alive. We must have her services as soon as possible. You five with me. Wolfgang, stay

240

here. Guard your people. Come on."

Roz watched them disappear up the lift. What little hope she had rose with them.

Scruffy said, "Boss, security cams up along the tunnel. Should see them coming long before they get here."

"Good job. But what do they want? Why are they grouping together? Are they going to storm us? Kill all of us? Why? And where's Marek in all this? Has he been killed?"

"Last I heard," Scruffy said, "he was overseeing the next job out near Station Thirteen."

"Roz, calling Station Thirteen. Come in, please," she said into her wrist device.

"Thirteen here. What's up, Roz? Where's everyone going?"

"Is Marek there?"

"Yeah, helping on the scaffolding. Half the workers up and left an hour ago. Cited an emergency. What emergency?"

"Get Marek. Now."

"Okay, boss."

After a long pause, she heard his voice. "Roz, what the devil is going on? I can't reach Denys. Half the damned workers ran off claiming an emergency came up. Why wasn't I notified? We're under a rush to get this scenario set up before the client arrives."

"Those are human-form robots. They've murdered our people and have taken their places. The ones who ran off are likely not people, but robots disguised as our workers. They killed Denys a day ago and replaced him with a look-alike robot. He's cut our comm to the space station and the relay transmitter. Captain Binsk can't contact the cruiser. She's taken her guards to storm the station. Got anyone armed with blasters?"

"Oh, hell! What next? No, never needed such things. We're armed to the teeth with play guns for fantasies. What

241

about raiding the armory?"

"No good. The robots are between us and the armory. They've shot Parkinson. She's in a coma."

"What the hell do they want? These robots?"

"Dunno. But send runners down all the tunnels. Have them check for explosives. The one that shot Parkinson detonated a charge. Collapsed the tunnel beyond Station Two."

"Good god. All right. I'll hunker down and send out scouts. Are they trying to trap us all underground?"

"Stop fretting, Marek. We can always take one of the zillion lifts to the surface and call for help."

A loud explosion echoed through the tunnel leading to Roz's station. A small dust cloud puffed out into the larger space where she stood.

"I'll check it out," Scruffy said, stumping down the tunnel and ignoring the dust cloud. He held his blaster at the ready.

Before long, the dwarf returned, covered in gray dust and coughing. "Boss, we're cut off. Took out a section beyond where I put the last camera. Now what?"

"Marek, you still there?"

"Yeah, I heard. Now what?"

"Gather up all the dwarves and those who know how to mine or repair tunnel walls. Have them head to the collapse by Station Two and somewhere around Station Twenty-four. See if they can reopen the tunnels. Have someone check on food and water supplies for their areas. We should be able to get by, especially with a hundred fewer to feed."

***

Captain Binsk flew the shuttle up to the space station. She didn't contact the tower, but instead manually docked on the opposite side of the station from the tower. With luck, the robot Denys hadn't detected their approach, and she could gain the element of surprise.

242

"Okay, tight formation. Shoot anything that moves. We're headed to the control tower on the other side."

Her five men moved out ahead of her, while she brought up the rear, often looking over her shoulder. As they passed side rooms, they paused while one of her men verified it was empty. Closed blast doors delayed them.

When they reached the halfway point, the next blast door stood open. CEO Denys stood before them, a disintegrator rifle in hand.

Footnote added by Katya later on. Never use a blaster or disintegrator gun onboard a spaceship or station. Even an antique gun is dangerous. Only low-power laser guns work.

While speaking, Denys fired. "You should have stayed on the ground."

At first, Captain Binsk thought the robot had terrible aim. Its initial shot wasn't aimed at the five, but at the side wall by them. A second later, five blasters fired back at the robot. However, those five all missed. Why?

His disintegrator punched a foot hole in the side of the space station. The air rushed to fill the vacuum of space, bringing the five men with it. Captain Binsk grabbed hold of a ladder rung, clinging on for her life.

The station design could handle a breach by meteors, asteroids, and other space debris. Seconds later, the blast doors closed automatically both behind her and the one in front of the robot. In her last view of the robot Denys, a smile flickered across his face. Screams and gasps from her men brought her around.

One man's back side landed on the hole, blocking air escape. With half the air gone from this section, all gasped, though the soldier being ripped apart screamed in agony. Then, his voice ceased.

Captain Binsk spotted oxygen tanks hanging on a wall. She pointed to them. Four of her men staggered towards them.

She felt herself blacking out. No time. She fired her blaster at one tank. Presto. The exploding tank gushed out its lifesaving contents. All gasped for the oxygen, as they moved to the tanks.

She grabbed one and turned it on, breathing deeply from its mask. Her four men reached the tanks and followed her lead. Holding her tank, she struggled to make her way to the blast door behind them. It took all five of them to get it open enough for her to slip through. Two of her men followed before a hideous sucking sound filled the thin air. The two remaining men looked to the side. Their comrade whose body had plugged the hole vanished. The hole had grown in size. The remaining air flew out the rupture, sucking the two soldiers with it.

Captain Binsk watched in horror as her two men vanished and the door slammed shut. Worse, only her blaster remained. The three leaned against the heavy blast doors heaving air. A minute later, they'd recovered enough to turn off the emergency oxygen tanks.

One said, "Remind me never to fire a disintegrator gun on a space station."

She said, "That robot knew what it was doing. With one shot, he took us out of the battle and prevented you from harming it. These damned robots are way too intelligent."

"But I thought these were human-form robots. That one looked like us. A Third Invader," the other soldier said.

"We have big trouble," she said. "Come on. Let's back track. We have to find a way to contact the cruiser and stop these robots from leaving this world."

"We could overload the nuclear power supply," one said.

"Easier just to activate the emergency self-destruct," the other said.

"What about us?" Captain Binsk. "I'm not ready to die

244

just yet. Still, let's keep that as our last resort. We can't let these fiends leave this world. If they can impersonate one of us..."

"Right, Captain. Count us in."

"Okay, let's spread out. You look for a way to activate their self-destruct system. It should be the standard Third Invader device. You find a way to overload the nuclear power supply. Our voice comms still work. I'll see if I can find a way to contact the cruiser. If I can't and the robots are about to flee, take this space station down. We can't let them get away. Think of the damage one of these could do to Home World!"

"Right. For Home World!" they said in unison while fisting their right hands above their heads.

They split up, each in search of a way to stop the robots. Captain Binsk headed for the secondary backup system that all Third Invader ships had. But she wasn't familiar with the design of this station. As she passed by one view port, she saw a host of shuttles lifting off.

She spoke into her wrist comm. "Guys, I just spied a bunch of shuttles heading up from the planet. Time is short. Two minutes at most."

"Captain, there's a large transport docked here. What should I do?"

"Stay on mission. We must blow this place up before those robots get here."

She rushed about looking for a clue to the location of the secondary backup system.

"Dingo's rats! Guys, they're close to docking."

"Captain, I've activated the self-destruct sequence. A hundred seconds to boom!"

"Well done. Into escape pods fast!"

She pivoted and raced back the way she'd come. Captain Binsk had passed by several. No time to set a countdown watch. She felt the slight jar as one shuttle after the other docked. She flew down the hall, got to the hatch, and opened it. The escape pod just fit her. Once inside, she fastened the safety belt. Her hand slammed the Eject button. She hoped her two men got away. No way to know. The escape pod spun and began its rapid descent.

A brilliant flash lit the capsule, followed by a shock way. "Take that you damned robots!" She closed her eyes. With her eyes shut, she felt no motion, which allowed her to relax a little. Looking out the spinning view port sickened her stomach. How long has it been since basic training? Teaches a solder to overcome these sensations. I need a refresher.

Thud. The pod landed. Captain Binsk felt the planet's gravity for the first time since leaving the space station. Her safety harness held her upside down. After a struggle in the tight confines, she blew the hatch and breathed in the hot, dry air of this desert world. Now to find a way underground and to see if her two soldiers made it. For now, the battle for Rudolf-E was over. She hoped they'd won.

Chapter 27 Aftermath

Captain Binsk signaled for her two soldiers. After a long pause, both checked in. She exhaled. Losing three men would be on her record. Posthumous medals, for sure. We've accomplished much. The three landed at different locations.

"Scout around for a lift site. Notify me when you find one. No wonder no one lives on the surface of this world. Desert everywhere."

"No kidding, Captain. We got them, didn't we?"

"Sure looks like we did. The cruiser will be by soon. No way they missed seeing the station explode. They'll come for us. Find a way into the tunnels."

Shading her eyes, she scanned for the vertical cylinder—the top of a lift. A mile off, she saw a protrusion and headed towards it. By the time she reached it, sweat soaked her uniform. She knew she'd found safety. A minute later, she breathed in the cool air of the tunnel.

"Captain Binsk calling Roz. You there? Where am I? How do I find you?"

A gray short creature clamored into view from the other end of the tunnel.

"Ah, there you are."

"Scruffy? Is that you under all that dust?"

"Aye. We just got the tunnel reopened. At least enough to squeeze through. Boss is waiting on you in her quarters. Follow me. Gosh, how did you get wet?"

"Walking a mile topside will do that."

"I won't ask why you'd want to go for a walk out there. Follow me. Duck your head. We've only made it big enough for us."

She found Roz standing beside a table, six comm devices around her, along with a giant map of the tunnel system.

Roz looked up. "Ah, Captain. You're back. What's the situation? I still can't contact the space station. We lost three men and seven have broken bones. They're being brought to the doctor as soon as we get the collapsed passages opened."

"We blew up the space station and took all the robots with it. End of the robot menace. I lost three men."

"Well done! What a relief. I'm worried they left a few robots behind to restart their operation once the fuss dies down. Fricken scary—impersonating Third Invaders. I won't rest until I've had every last person down here checked out by Parkinson, assuming she's still alive."

After a pause she said, "Wait! The station is gone? Are we trapped here?"

"Gone. Self-destruct activated. My cruiser is nearby. I'm sure they saw the explosion. They'll come investigate. Dingo's Rats, hope we're not stranded here."

"Now I *am* worried. I best see to fabricating a Long-Distance communications set. We need major help and a way to cancel upcoming client fantasies. We've enough food and water for a couple months, but after that... What a mess!"

They backed out of the way of an arriving train carrying two wounded men lying on stretchers. Workers carried them off to the infirmary.

"Excellent work, Scruffy. A train got through your repaired tunnel."

"Barely," the dwarf said. "Give us a day and it'll be like new. Good rock down here."

***

"Rear Admiral Irenka Bronislawa, something terrible has just happened on the space station," an aide said.

"Have you been able to reach Captain Binsk?" she

asked.

"No. We've not been able to reach them for twenty-four hours. You've got to see this."

When the Admiral watched the video replay, she gasped. "What in Dingo's Rats happened? Is that a deep space transport moving about the debris?"

"Yes, its markings are unknown."

"Hail them. Enlarge those images," she ordered.

"They aren't responding to our hail."

"What is that? Bodies? Floating in space?"

"Admiral, we're detecting powerful magnetic tractor beams coming from that transport."

"Is it doing what I think I'm seeing?" the Admiral asked.

"How can a magnetic tractor pull bodies into the cargo bay?" an aide asked.

"Did that ship attack the station?" she asked.

"No, we think it self-destructed. But three life pods dropped. See, there and there." The aide pointed out the tiny dots.

"They still aren't answering our hail."

"Okay. Battle stations. Fire a shot across their bow," the Admiral ordered.

"They still aren't answering our hail. Those are definitely bodies, sir. Why aren't they destroyed? They should have exploded and frozen within seconds."

"Fire another shot. If they still don't respond, target their engines."

"Sir, they're jumping into hyperspace."

"Take us in as close to the station remains as you can. See if our people are floating in space."

"Spotted remains of three other bodies, sir. Maybe the others got out in the three pods."

"Then, what were all those bodies floating in space and being retrieved by that ship? Have you traced its planet of origin?"

"Sir, we've captured its ID marker in one frame. Universal Registry has it belonging to the Goringy, but that ship is parked on Cass-C. They must be using a fake marker," an aide said.

"Can we establish a comm link with Captain Binsk?" the Admiral asked.

"Negative, sir. They're underground. It requires the comm link from the space station or a direct LD comm set. She wasn't issued that unit."

"Okay. Stand down from battle stations. Scour the perimeter of the station's remains. Search for any bodies or survivors in life pods," the Admiral said.

Later, an aide said, "Sir, no bodies. No life forms in the debris or unused life pods."

"Okay, send down a scouting party. Find Captain Binsk. We must know what the devil happened. Losing that space station will create enormous problems. I'll get on to Home World as soon as I've talked to Captain Binsk."

Within minutes a transport shot down to the surface, landing near the pads closest to where Captain Binsk and crew had landed days ago. A dozen armed soldiers disembarked and fanned out forming a protective perimeter.

The Major in charge spoke into his wrist comm device. "Captain Binsk. Major Howard here. We've landed on the surface. Where are you? Rear Admiral Irenka Bronislawa wants a full report immediately."

"Major, I'm at Roz Kowalksi's work station. Have you got a way to get me up to the cruiser or to establish a comm link to the Admiral? We've lost all means of communicating to the cruiser or anyone else."

Thirty minutes later, Captain Binsk saluted Rear Admiral Bronislawa in her CCC. "We killed the robots, sir, but had to blow up the space station to do it. These robots are able to impersonate us, Third Invaders. They murdered CEO Denys, and a robot took his place. That's where the robots all went, except for one who killed the mysterious Klaus Huber. They've been replacing human and Third Invader workers down below."

She outlined how Parkinson had detected the robots and how she'd been shot. "When the robots blew up the tunnels and evacuated, we arrived at the space station, intending to take out the robot Denys impersonator and reestablish our comm link to you. But that robot knew what it was doing."

Captain Binsk relayed how her three soldiers perished, ending with their harrowing rush to stop the army of robots coming to the station. "Our last resort took out the robots before they could escape."

"Unfortunately, they did escape," the Admiral said, her face grimmer than Captain Binsk had ever seen. "While we can't survive in the frigid vacuum of space, these robots can. Watch." An aide replayed the aftermath of the explosion.

"We captured the ship's ID marker, but it, too, was fake," the Admiral said. "Over a hundred of these robots escaped despite your efforts."

"Sir, what scares us is they are impersonating us, Jafari, not just humans. Roz worries they left one or more robots behind to resume their replacement operation once we rebuild. We're waiting for Parkinson to wake from her rejuvenation coma. We'll have her check every person down there. Only then can we be certain none are left. Sir, do you know what this means?"

"Captain, we're facing the most serious threat ever! For all I know, they've replaced you. How can we tell who's a robot and who isn't? Only Parkinson can," the Admiral said. "So, get back down there and guard that woman with your life. Once you've verified no robots remain, bring her up here. I need this entire ship searched. Meantime, I'll relay this to Home World. They won't be pleased to have to replace that space station. Yet in light of the robot news, they won't pay too much attention to that loss. Parkinson. Right now, she's the most valuable person in the galaxy."

Captain Binsk saluted and left the bridge. On her way back, the Major said, "Can these robots really impersonate us?"

"You can't tell the difference by looking at them. Damned scary. I would never have suspected the robot Parkinson identified. The one that put a nail spike into her forehead. If they'd replaced me, Major, you would never know."

He whispered, "Dingo's Rats!"

"Since there could be robots remaining behind, don't let any of your soldiers that are down there return to the cruiser. Not until Parkinson says they haven't been replaced by robots."

The Major paled and wiped his tall forehead.

"How—how soon can Parkinson check us?"

"Dunno. The robot shot her in the head with a nail gun. She should have died, but the doc used the mutation agents to rejuvenate her. Worst case might be a month. She's been shot in the head several times. A month later, she wakes up healed. I've pushed the base doctor to find ways to hurry it up. We need her now."

***

"Parkinson. Parkinson, wake up. Can you see the light?" the doctor said, waving a pen light across her eyes held open by his fingers. "Wake up."

Knowing how desperate everyone including Rear Admiral Irenka Bronislawa was, he'd done all he could to bring the human out of her rejuvenation coma.

I moaned. "Oh, my head. God, does it hurt. Get that

light out of my eyes. You're making my head hurt worse. What happened?"

In a flash, my memory responded. "Oh, I'm not dead after all."

The relieved voice of the Third Invader doctor spoke again. "No, between your guard Bishop and me, we've got you healed up in record time. Your robot detection services are critically needed. Can you sit up?"

"Whoa. The room keeps moving about. Slowly. Please. I feel funny. Really funny. Bishop? You here?"

"Right here, boss."

"How is my body this time?"

"The doc roused you from the mutation coma as soon as he dared. You can still see the healing wound on your forehead. Your feet seem okay. Not like usual when you wake. The doc added some of their agents to ours. Neither of us know just what to expect, but I believe your breasts might be bigger. Otherwise, you seem normal. As normal as you can be, considering I pulled a six-inch spike from your forehead."

"Okay. Help me up. Get me dressed. Kind of dizzy."

Bishop struggled with my dress. "It no longer fits your bosom. I'll tie together in the back with string for now."

While I didn't like the sound of that, I focused on clearing my head. I felt my toes, ankles, and then thighs. I looked at the upper corners of the room and felt more orientated. I glanced down at Hans lying in his stasis pod. Already his upper arms looked thinner. I only hoped this regrew his tongue and repaired his feet. If not, his life would be unimaginably bad.

"Thanks. I need a drink. Then, can you bring me up to date? How long was I out?"

Roz and Captain Binsk joined Bishop, while Cleo held a bottle of water for me to sip. The pair outlined what had happened after I identified the first robot.

"Wow. We were right, Roz. The robots replaced your workers."

Captain Binsk said, "Oh, it's much worse than that. They're impersonating us now! Third Invaders. Jafari. The Admiral wants you to check everyone on her cruiser. I've never seen her this worried. It's no longer a human-form. These robots have become a galaxy-wide problem."

"But first, I need everyone who survived the robots here on Rudolf-E checked out," Roz said. "My guess is they left some behind so they can resume replacing us after the mess calms down. No one is safe until these robots are eradicated."

"Okay. I get the message." I tried to stand up. Bishop grabbed me, steadying me. "Thanks. It might be best to march them past me while I'm sitting."

"Now that the dwarves have the tunnels reopened, the trains are getting through. I've ordered everyone to report here for further instructions. We can't handle clients for a long time. I'm awaiting orders from Home World."

"We need to be thorough, Roz. Get that list of employees up. As we verify them, put a check by them or something. I wouldn't put it past them to hide out only to reappear a month later after things are back to normal. Anyone who appears after the check is likely a robot."

I heard Roz talking on her comm link, probably addressing her workers.

Turning to me, she said, "I want you to check Captain Binsk and her solders first. They'll set up a perimeter. I'm sending everyone that checks okay down to Station One. The soldiers have orders to shoot anyone entering Station One from the tunnel from Station Two. Once we've cleared everyone, she'll have the Admiral sweep the surface looking for hideouts. Plus, I'll take her and the soldiers and make a thorough sweep of our underground facilities. Take no chances. I've lost over a hundred of my workers. Couldn't care less about Denys, but the workers are my responsibility. Well, Marek's too, but right now, he might be a robot. Meanwhile, doc is doing an autopsy on the three men we lost. I want to know how they died."

"Okay. Put me on a chair where you want me."

"And I'm strapping this around your waist," Captain Binsk said. "It's a personal defense shield. Better than those of the Sixth Invaders."

She glanced at Ambassador L'Grina. I chuckled, wishing I had one of my own. If only my head would stop spinning. After parading her soldiers past me, Roz led her people that were already here by me. I recognized most of them. They'd already past muster in the two stations I had checked.

A long day followed. One by one, dwarf, Third Invader, and human walked past me. Gray dust covered some. All looked fearful or worried in equal numbers.

Roz said, "That's the last of them. Four hundred forty-three survivors. Now comes the dangerous part. I didn't expect a robot to be foolish enough to try walking past you, Parkinson. We have to search every square bi of this huge complex."

"Bi?"

"Oh, it's about this big." She held her hands out about a foot apart.

"We're bringing you along in case we find one, but you'll be in the train sitting down. Cleo can feed you. Cold food for now. Okay, Captain, lead on. Scruffy, get this train moving."

With the dwarf driving, we set out with twenty soldiers, Roz, and Captain Binsk. Ambassador L'Grina stayed behind coordinating with the cruiser and Marek, who assumed command in Roz's absence. Bishop and Cleo sat on either side of me. On the hour-long time between stations, I kept dozing

255

off. Each time we stopped and the soldiers searched, Cleo had me drinking something the doctor ordered me to consume. Probably had caffeine in it.

Talk about boring. I grew tired of hearing "clear." Hours dragged on. I kept falling asleep during the long drives between stations. Fatigue took its toll on me. And poor Captain Binsk hadn't slept in more than a day, if my foggy calculations meant anything.

Cleo plied me with liquids again as Scruffy announced our arrival at Station Fourteen. Scruffy remained perched on the engine while Captain Binsk, Roz, and the soldiers searched. This time, from where we were parked, I could see the action. Scurrying people opening this and that. All rather surreal.

My eyes followed Captain Binsk. She moved slower than the rest. Exhausted, I sensed. She pulled out a large drawer that held androids awaiting their assignments.

"Is it safe to come out now?" a female voice said. "Help me up, please."

My eyes shot open. I screamed. "Robot! Katya, robot!"

In slow motion, a couple seconds passed. Katya Binsk reacted, but both her hands held the robot's hands, as she helped what she thought was a woman out of the drawer. Her blaster looped over her shoulder, out of reach. I saw her arm muscles tighten as though pulling away from the robot to get to her blaster. The robot pulled hard on her arms, dragging itself from its prone position in the drawer to a standing one, where it could defend itself.

In horror, I watched Katya's arms ripped from their sockets! I believe the robot displayed surprise. Katya's mouth opened wide. Nearby soldiers turned, bringing their blasters to bear. But the robot moved faster, ripping Captain Binsk's blaster from her shoulders as a piercing scream shot from Katya's mouth. The robot's reactions were twice as fast as ours.

256

I knew it would kill us before we could damage it. I had to do something.

I focused. Now alert, I shot a command into the robot's positronic brain with all the intention I had. Intention is the key, I later discovered. I intended this robot to cease operations. To my amazement, sparks shot from its head. The blaster fell to the stone floor, joining Katya's arms. Then, the robot dropped like dead weight. Six blasters fired at where the robot had been standing, damaging the shelving units, but missing the robot.

Time returned to normal for me. Screaming and shouting pounded my ears, but I had no hands to dampen the noise. I rose and joined the group around Captain Binsk. Blood gushed from her shoulders. We'd taken many hours to get here, with as many needed to get back to the infirmary. I acted again.

"I'll stop the blood loss."

With full intention, I demanded the exposed arteries and veins pinched shut. Vaguely, I heard Roz calling out.

"It's working! Get the first aid kit!"

Roz knew first aid. She put a giant bandage on each shoulder and wrapped gauze around Katya's torso holding the bandages in place. She added a leather strap pulled as tightly as Scruffy could manage.

"Get her back to the infirmary as fast as possible. Scruffy, make this thing fly! Three of you, stand guard here. Don't let anyone else in here or we'll have to redo this whole search. Parkinson, can you keep it up for a while? Don't know how well the bandages will hold."

I nodded, but sensed Bishop lifting me into my seat. They put Katya's body in front of me. That way, I couldn't lose my concentration. I had no idea how long I could hold on, but after a time, I, too, dozed off again and lost track of time.

When we arrived at the infirmary, the doctor had

everything ready. They rushed her into surgery. I think I mumbled something about will she be all right? Bishop lifted me out of the car and laid me back in the comfortable stasis pod and covered me up.

I awoke starving. As I regained alertness, my stomach seized up. Katya! After all she and I had been through—all our adventures—she couldn't die. She just couldn't.

Bishop lifted me up again. Cleo pushed a drink to my lips. Ah, the same strange liquid the doc had me guzzling before.

"Katya?" I said.

"Ah, awake at last," Roz said, wiping sleep from her eyes. "Doc said we'll know more tomorrow. He's sent her up to the cruiser's sickbay for now. When you are up to it, we've got many questions for you. Besides, we still must finish clearing the tunnels and stations."

I exhaled. The tension in my stomach subsided. I felt dopey.

"I'm up now."

"For starters, no one can figure out why that robot shorted out."

"My doing. I ordered it to stop hurting Katya. I must not know my mental strength. Shorted out? Is that even possible?"

Scruffy interrupted. "Yep. I tore its brain apart to see. Yep. Shorted out the main circuits. You juiced it as we say down here. Android brains can only take so much electric current flow. When positrons and electrons meet, they annihilate each other. Poof. Didn't know you could do that, Parkinson."

Roz said, "And the doc said you saved Katya's life. She would have bled out before we got her back here if you hadn't stopped the blood flow. All of us want to know how you did that."

"I don't know. I just didn't want my friend to die."

"A goddess in disguise," Roz said.

Ambassador L'Grina spoke up. "From my personal experience, I'd call her an angel."

"Angel or goddess, we can't thank you enough. Are you up to finishing this search? The Admiral wants you on her ship as soon as possible," Roz said.

"Not until I clear her," the doc said.

I smiled. "Okay, let's finish this. Who's in charge of the soldiers now?"

"I am. Major Wolfgang. Parkinson, you are full of surprises. Good ones, though. Okay, enough talk. Let's get going."

"How come Katya's defense shield didn't work?" I asked.

The Major said, "It doesn't stop slow moving things like hands or someone trying to stab you. It's designed to stop bullets, lasers, blasters, and disintegration beams. Besides, there wasn't anything Captain Binsk could have done to prevent what happened. The person needed a hand to get up out of that android storage shelf. Would have happened to whoever found that robot. I'm impressed. They are incredibly strong. Much faster than we are. Formidable opponents."

"For sure. Your soldiers didn't even get off a blaster shot before it had done its worst."

"Aye. How come you can do what you're doing? Roz said it's telepathy. That's how you detect the robots?"

"Yeah, they don't have minds to sense."

"Scuttlebutt says your Sol Empire is planning to make a Telepath Squad designed to find these rogue robots."

"Not find, but rather tell others if this one is a robot. At least now you have one you can take apart and study. Maybe you can find another way to identify them. I hope so."

He chuckled. "Techs are already on that one. Never

seen the Admiral this animated over anything."

Thus passed my first day out of stasis or my first day after dying again. It wasn't just any old day from the time I woke. And no one was happier than I was to come full circle back to Roz's section and bed.

Chapter 28 Shipboard

After a long night's sleep and pumped full of the doctor's formula, Major Wolfgang took me, Ambassador L'Grina, Bishop, and Cleo up to the cruiser. There, I begged him to take me to Captain Binsk.

I stood looking down at her on the bunk. Bandaged and in an induced coma, she seemed peaceful. "You'll be fine."

Next, the Major took me to Rear Admiral Irenka Bronislawa in her CCC.

"Ah, Parkinson. Here you are at last. I must thank you for saving Captain Binsk, though she might not see it that way. They tell me you somehow short-circuited the robot's brain. You are the galaxy's most valuable warrior right now. My techs are going over every bit of that rogue robot. I ordered them to find a way for us to detect them."

I laughed. "That's clever. But I don't think you can order science."

She laughed, too, breaking the tension I sensed coming from others in this busy CCC.

"Let's get this done. I want every person on the ship checked. I can't afford to have one of those rogue robots onboard. Home World is in a panic now that these robots can impersonate a Jafari."

Ambassador L'Grina said, "At least they can't impersonate a Sixth Invader. Not yet, anyway. They'd have to rework their framework for our six-fingered hands."

The Admiral glared at her.

"Okay. Have each person walk past me."

"Check these guards first."

They weren't robots. She had them pointing their

blasters at each person as they walked up to me. An aide took down names, cross checking with the manifest. Those in the CCC checked out as Third Invaders, but I sensed their fear.

We did the same to the other crew and soldiers. Lunchtime passed before everyone checked out. Only then did Rear Admiral Irenka Bronislawa relax.

"Major, escort her to the mess hall and then wherever she wants to go. I'm going down to visit Roz Kowalksi. She's been appointed CEO of Fantasy World and Marek Levitsky becomes Chief of Operations, her old post."

After Cleo fed me and many eyes overtly or covertly watched how I managed, I had the major drop me off in sickbay. Ambassador L'Grina accompanied me. We sat beside Katya.

"You should have let her die," Ambassador L'Grina said. "Her career is over. They'll give her a medal for valiant service and dismiss her."

"That's obvious. Still, she's my friend. I'll help her adjust and have a good life. Her race lives very long lives. I'll help her adapt. If I don't, then, yeah, she'll find a way to succumb."

She looked at me. "Think your therapy thing would work on a Third Invader? Like it did for me? That opened my eyes."

"I'm counting on it. We're all spiritual beings, but with different bodies. I can't see why it wouldn't work. Plus, Cleo is great, as are those Sixth Invader machines you left for us. She'll love the hair machine. Have to be hopeful. Katya has become a good friend, just like you have, L'Grina."

She changed the topic. "There'll be all kinds of trouble now that rogue robots can appear to be a Jafari."

I frowned. "No kidding. But I'm not surprised. They adapt extremely well. I can't believe we've only killed one of them. Hope the techs will find something everyone can use to

262

detect them before leadership demands we mutate lots of humans into telepaths."

"Don't be surprised if the Federation demands production of telepaths. I foresee you being bombarded with requests for telepaths. Katya will be as helpless as you are, but she won't have telepathy or any redeeming powers. Her life could well be meaningless despite your wishes. Just don't be surprised. She and I—we're fighters. Now she can't ever be that again."

I sighed. "I know. I've got to help her latch on to a new valuable purpose."

"That's one way of looking at it. I think she might be coming out of the coma."

A doctor and nurse entered, alerted by signals from Katya's medical monitor. They unhooked her from the apparatus.

The doctor said, "She should be waking shortly. Captain Binsk is heavily sedated. She'll be groggy for a while. The pain killers are a must."

"What about genetic mutations? You know, regrowing her arms as they tried to do for us on Earth? Or do your people have good prosthetic arms?"

"Oh, that. As I understand it, the genetic mutation stuff has only worked on your species. Yes, wonderful prosthetic hands and feet. Nothing useful to replace whole arms like the Captain here. She's doomed."

"Wait. Your species lives for thousands of years. You're telling me if someone has a bad accident, there's nothing that can be done for them?"

"It happens. Infrequently. Usually we put them down. I would have done that for Captain Binsk except you insisted she live."

"For a race that considers itself highly advanced, that's incredibly pathetic! I'll take her home with me and see if my sister and friend can adapt our limb regrowth mutation to her."

"As you wish. For a short-lived species, I can understand how valuable a single life might be. But for us, it's but a blink. Better to have lived well than to spend an eternity as a cripple."

I glared at the doctor. Still I felt I'd done the right thing in saving Katya's life. Now I had to introduce her to new goals, just as I planned to do for Hans.

Loud screams alerted us to Katya's rousing. L'Grina and I rushed to her bedside. She lay there staring at her body, but had stopped screaming.

"You survived, Katya. Well done."

"Look at me. I'm helpless. I can't even wipe my tears."

L'Grina dabbed them for her.

"Why didn't they let me die? I can't live like this." Katya broke down, sobbing for some time. "They should have let me die. Now, I can't even kill myself."

Ambassador L'Grina looked at me. From the therapy sessions I'd given her, she knew enough to keep silent. We let Katya cry and said nothing. What could we say that would "make it all better?" Besides, whatever we said right now would become part of the painful incident and might well adversely affect her.

Her crying subsided. She asked, "What happened?"

I nodded to L'Grina, who relayed all that had happened. "We're all mystified about how Molly short-circuited its positronic brain and then how she could stop your blood loss during the hours it took to get you to the doc."

"How? How'd you do that?" Katya asked.

I sighed. "I don't know, but I didn't want that robot to kill the others, and I didn't want to lose you, Katya. You've become a very good friend. I'll see if my sister, Celeste, can help me figure out how I did what I did. Focus on healing. I'm

264

taking you back to Chicago with me and Hans. Once there, I'll help you both learn the new ways we need to do all that we used to do. Plus, I will have our two best geneticists, Eve and Lara, work on a genetic mutation to regrow your arms. If it can be done for my species, it can be done for yours."

"But I'm helpless now. How can I do anything I used to do?"

She flushed. I sensed she realized she was talking to armless me. I sensed she wanted to unsay that.

"It's natural for you to feel helpless. No denying the fact that for a time you will be nearly helpless. What's important is that I'll be teaching you new ways to do everything. It'll take time, practice, and many failures. But you can do it. I have hope in time Eve and Lara will develop a cure for you, too.

"The men on Bella lack arms and have for the last two thousand years, thanks to the Third Invader experiment. When I left Bella, they had just mutated the women. Their women are now like their men. It's not the end of everything, but a new beginning. I'm not willing to lose the best Third Invader friend I've ever had. You're coming to live with me. I have many things that make life easier for us until we can get arms back. You'll see."

"But I'm helpless, Molly. And scared."

"That's a very good sign, Katya. Being scared and admitting you're helpless. That's the first steps to recovery. Meanwhile, cry all you like. You've got something to cry about."

"But I'll be useless. I don't have telepathy or anything of value. Not like you do. I can't live centuries like this."

"Yes, you do have something valuable. I'm making you the Sol Empire's first Third Invader Ambassador. You'll join L'Grina here as the interface between our races. Just be brave as I get things worked out. You're one of the bravest people I've ever met."

I stayed as upbeat as I could before I left her in L'Grina's care. I found Rear Admiral Irenka Bronislawa in her CCC, but she took me to her private quarters.

"I'm the Empress of the Sol Empire. Well, as soon as I can get that post going. I've just appointed Katya Binsk as our Third Invader Ambassador. She'll be heading back to Earth with Ambassador L'Grina and me. She can be the go-between for our peoples. With this rogue robot situation impacting both our people, we need coordinated, effective actions."

"I can get that approved by Home World. They are worried about these robots. They've suggested a high-level meeting between our races to discuss effective measures we can take. I'll send along a long-distance comm set for Ambassador Binsk. I've been told they'd like a meeting in three months."

"Excellent. One other thing, on Bella, the women made special things for their men to use. A low to the ground kitchen, yokes, and so on. Could you somehow get three or four complete sets for me? Send them to my Chicago, Earth, address. As I understand it, when a woman mates with a man, she purchases a complete set for the man. Now the women are in the same situation as their men."

"That can be arranged. How soon do you want to return to Earth?"

"As soon as it's safe for Katya to travel."

"Check with our doctor and let me know."

A few minutes later, I joined L'Grina and Katya in sickbay. She'd stopped weeping and had fallen asleep.

"Well, it's official. She's now Ambassador Katya Binsk."

The doctor entered. "Ah, here you are, Parkinson. You're a hard person to find."

I smiled. "She will be our new ambassador. How soon can we return to Earth, Sol Empire? Rear Admiral Irenka Bronislawa wants to know."

266

He chuckled. "She already contacted me. I want to use the healing machine on her two more times. Unless there are complications, give it two days. Now then, what about yourself?"

"What do you mean?"

"The Fantasy World doctor has been giving you drugs to keep you from slipping into a mutation coma. But you need to get off them and let your body finished its healing. I'd like to put you back in the stasis pod alongside Hans until you wake normally."

"Is that necessary? I want to be with Katya."

"I'm not letting her out of bed for at least two days. Time for you to take care of your own health."

They lowered my body into the stasis pod. The world turned dark. Again. My last thought: only a couple days at most.

***

Days ago, Tantalus received his orders from Kimko, just as the hundred other robots began making their way to the landing pads. Already shuttles from the space station sat parked waiting to ferry them up to the station where a deep space transport waited to take them away.

Kimko sent, 'I have stored the complete design plans for us on this drive. Guard it well. I've given a similar copy to Myles. He has replaced a worker. He will remain with the other workers hoping he won't be detected. If he is, you are our backup plan. Take a lift to the desert world. Find a good hiding place. Bury yourself beneath the sands. Lower your temperature. Set your timer for six months, and power down. When you power up, do what you can to get back inside and join the workers.

'Once you've become a part of the workforce, I want you to do what I've been doing for the past months. Build more of us. Replace humans and Third Invaders as you can. One of us

267

will come in a year to pick up the new compatriots.

'Teslenko is counting on you and Myles to keep the manufacturing operation going.'

'I will not fail. I obey.'

The robot took a lift to the surface. For a moment, it surveyed the vast sands. He dug a pit for himself, pulling the sand back over his body. He set his internal timer and checked his power level. Enough charge to last six months powered down. A moment later, the robot registered no sensual input other than the ticking timer.

***

The day after Molly entered the stasis pod, the cruiser finished scouring every mile of the land. With no more robots found and with the arrival of supply ships, Rear Admiral Irenka Bronislawa left Fantasy World in the hands of CEO Roz Kowalksi. The cruiser left orbit, heading for the Sol Empire by way of Bella.

Chapter 29 Sabotage

Teslenko received word from Myles. The newly-built robot replaced the new operations manager Marek Levitsky. The dead Jafari body lay buried beneath the desert sands, unlikely ever to be discovered.

Teslenko paced his quarters, calculating. Parkinson had survived yet another death blow. Worse, Myles reported she had shorted out the robot's brain. Teslenko elevated Parkinson to Public Enemy Number One. He regretted not killing her back on Bella. Still, he had to work out a peace treaty with the Sol Empire. While he believed Parkinson spoke truthfully and wanted peace, Admiral Carr didn't follow her orders. Now this human could short out positronic brains? How was that possible?

Unable to compute that, he focused on eliminating Parkinson. Myles reported that at the moment, she and the others were in healing comas onboard Admiral Irenka Bronislawa's cruiser. The Admiral intended to visit Bella before taking Parkinson back to Earth, Sol Empire. A new plan formed.

He contacted Kimko, issuing new orders.

***

"What's happened here?" screeched Admiral Irenka Bronislawa.

They landed just north of Bella's main city and sent a disguised landing party to retrieve four complete sets of kitchens and yokes per Molly's request.

"The city is deserted."

"That's impossible! I left fifty men to keep their basic utilities and food production operational," she barked into the

269

comm device.

"Can't find them either. Can you send out a survey party? We found stores with the needed kitchen equipment and yokes. Bringing crates back now."

"Major, take your soldiers and find my missing men. Ten million helpless humans don't just disappear. If Parkinson thinks we've betrayed her again—Doc, keep them unconscious and in their stasis pods until this is resolved."

The major led fifty armed soldiers down to the surface, while a smaller saucer shuttle passed them, ferrying the requested supplies up to the cruiser.

***

Shotski, one of the new robots disguised as a Jafari worker, helped carry crates into the cruiser. The order required six trips the surface. No one paid much attention to their work as they deposited crate after crate. On the first trip, Shotski slipped away from the others as they returned to the ship. He carried a second crate toward sickbay, following Kimko's directions.

He found the three in their stasis pods. The doctor had them in a quarantine room. Shotski slipped into the room unnoticed, opened the crate's lid, and set the bomb's timer. He smiled at a nurse as he left, returning to the crate storage area to help the others unload their next batch of crates. The bomb exploded on his return to the surface. Excellent timing.

***

The explosion didn't destroy the stasis pods nor the room. It blew a hole in the steel tank which contained enough mutation agent for a thousand patients and shattered the glass cover over Molly's stasis pod. Teslenko reasoned he would start a war with the Jafari if he damaged their cruiser while destroying Parkinson. He couldn't risk someone observing his new robot strangling Parkinson. But no one could survive exposure to this much mutation agent. Shotski reported to

270

Kimko that the deed was done. Parkinson was as good as dead. Teslenko had to wait for further confirmation of her death.

***

The bomb set off alarms throughout the cruiser, followed by the most-feared alarm, one signaling a biological attack. Doors shut, sealing off sections of the saucer. In CCC, Admiral Bronislawa barked orders, as her crew tried to find out what happened. The sealed doors hampered that. Various stations reported via comm devices. Soon, the Admiral knew the explosion happened in the Infirmary.

The doctor made contact and held a remote camera, relaying what he was seeing. "Yes, the explosion is confined to the containment room where the stasis pods are at. A yellowish gas lowers visibility to near zero."

"Why the bio alarms?" she asked.

"Don't know. But the yellow gas must be a biological agent for those sensors to sound the alarm and shut all doors," the doctor replied.

"Can you get it under control? Is Parkinson alive? We can't lose her!"

"Can't see anything. I'm using a remote probe now. Sampling the gas. More as soon as we know."

He placed the camera so she could watch as he and his staff operated the sampling equipment. Thirty minutes passed before he had the results.

"Admiral, it's registering as Earth's armless Galactic Doll mutation agent. Will purge the room now. The pods still aren't visible."

Admiral Bronislawa tapped her foot while she stared at the substandard images on her monitor, as the yellowish gas dissipated. The three stasis pods appeared unharmed. Her foot stopped mid-tap as the doctor and his staff rushed in and cleared the room. Only when the doctor reported on their vital signs did she relax.

271

"Okay. Surveillance video. I want to know who put that bomb in there! Now!"

Her CCC staff brought up video streams on six monitors.

"Admiral, Major Wolfgang reporting. You've got to see this for yourself. One of the fifty is alive. He's clinging to life only to report to you. We're at the seashore. Below the cliffs. I don't want to relay details on this open channel."

Thirty minutes later, accompanied by a dozen soldiers, Admiral Bronislawa joined Major Wolfgang below the hundred-foot cliff. Four dozen bodies lay sprawled where they landed. None had arms.

He allowed her to observe the grizzly scene before speaking. "Private, tell her what you've told me."

One soldier assigned to help the humans on Bella stepped out from the major's group of soldiers. He had no arms and wore only soiled underwear.

"They just vanished. The people on Bella. Gone. Soldiers woke to find the inhabitants of their sections of the city had vanished along with their arms. Over several days, it spread to other parts of the city and then to the outskirts. I was in Ciampino when I heard the news. I awoke to find my arms gone and the people of the town had vanished. We can't live like this. They ordered me to stay alive and report to you, before I am allowed to die."

Major Wolfgang added, "I've had our medics examine him and the dead. It's his opinion someone used a medical machine to amputate their arms. We found a cache of amputated limbs down the coast to the south."

"Where did ten million people go?" Admiral Bronislawa asked.

"We don't know. I went to work and somehow woke up in a bedroom naked and like this. None of us knows what happened."

"Thank you, soldier, for your service. You wish to join the other men now?" she asked.

He nodded, and she nodded to Major Wolfgang. A single blaster shot echoed off the cliff. Another body joined the strange collection.

"See they're buried after they are identified. I must contact their families. Find out what happened here. Ten million helpless humans can't have just vanished. Where are their bodies? I presume jumping off the cliffs is about the only way they could commit suicide. Where did that many bodies go? Any surveillance available? Major, find answers and darn fast."

With that, the sober leader returned to her saucer cruiser. As she walked into her ship, one crewman said, "Well, that solves that whole problem."

Admiral Bronislawa glared at the man. "No, it raises even larger problems. When Earth finds out we've lost ten million of their people... Dingo's Rats, I hope we're not in for another Home World attack like before."

"You mean when ten thousand were melted? Do we know Earth's people did it? A secret weapon?"

"Beyond your pay grade and security clearance." With that, she headed to check on Parkinson.

"Well, doc? Is she alive? Vitals okay? Can't imagine she's survived such a massive overdose of mutation agent."

He ran his hands over his face and exhaled. "We're in unknown territory. As far as I can tell, she's still in a mutation coma. Likewise, the other two."

"What? Hans is a human. That's expected. But Katya is one of us."

"Yes, Katya's in a mutation coma, Admiral. We've no idea what the mutation will be. Uncharted grounds. Parkinson's breasts have reduced in size, but her feet don't seem right. See. Her main arch is at a ninety-degree angle to

273

the bottom of her heel."

Ambassador L'Grina, who still hadn't left Molly's side along with Bishop, spoke. "Admiral, that's the typical foot distortion this mutation does. Plus, whatever was done to Hans to create those monster breasts is being undone. That awful bruising color on his feet is gone, and his feet look more like Molly's every hour. That's understandable, since Hans came from Berlin, an Earth city. Now, Katya is another story. Look at her body. Her bosom has already doubled in size, right, doc?"

He nodded, and she continued. "Her feet—they look like Molly's did an hour ago. Rapid transformation. Too fast. Molly said the mutation took about eight days."

The doctor added, "Then, there's her head." He moved a mass of much longer black hair aside. "Her beak is receding. I was explaining to the Ambassador how gifted children have their heads modified shortly after birth."

Ambassador L'Grina said, "I always wondered how Jafari men had such tall heads and women had bird beaks at the back of their heads. Can't believe you do that to your babies."

Admiral Bronislawa said, "Not all Jafari are modified. Only the elite can afford such status symbols. Childhood is held in high regard in our society though it is quite painful for us. It's bad enough Katya's lost her arms. She's losing her elite status, too. Poor thing. Probably should have been put out of her misery. Anyway, Ambassador, come with me. We have a gigantic problem. The people of Bella are missing. All ten million of them."

"What? That can't be. Where did they go? They're nearly helpless. No offense, Molly."

She followed her, surprised to be taken into the Admiral's private quarters. After hearing the details, Ambassador L'Grina ran her hands across her face.

"I wish we could wake Molly up. Get her ideas," the Sixth Invader said. "She's got an uncanny ability to figure things out. The Sol Empire doesn't have enough spaceship capacity to evacuate ten million people that fast. And why cut off your soldier's arms? Could you have made some enemies?"

The Admiral sat. "I sure have now. When Parkinson wakes and discovers the entire population of Bella has vanished... Lord, the ramifications could be—well, I—"

"Did the survivor have any theories. Offer you anything of use?"

With a sigh, the Admiral said, "None. I've got my people scouring the place looking for clues and surveillance videos. I'm not hopeful. No bodies but my own soldiers. Where did ten million go? Makes no sense at all. This will probably turn the Sol Empire against us. I'm stumped. You say Parkinson has a knack for figuring things out?"

"She's brilliant at it."

"I'll check with the doctor. Perhaps there's a way to wake her."

One of her aides called. "Admiral, we've located the soldier who set off the bomb. Caught him on video."

Both women headed to the CCC, where giant monitors displayed two video streams.

An aide explained. "Here, he's entered the stasis pod room and setting the bomb. On this feed, we have him entering with the crew assigned to recovering those inventions from Bella. On this one, we've captured his face and ID badge. Notice they don't match. We contacted the crew. He's now missing, and your ExO ordered them to search. I hope he wasn't killed."

"Well done," Admiral Bronislawa said.

Another monitor activated. A taut face of a crewman appeared. "Reporting in. We found his body. His throat has been crushed and his body stripped. Uploading images now."

"Dingo's Rats!" The Admiral responded. "That's an understatement. His throat is pulverized. Battle stations. We've another rogue robot around. Make a copy of what we've uncovered and send it to Home World. I'll be in Sick Bay."

Ambassador L'Grina followed her, an amused expression on her face. Things had gotten far more interesting.

"Doc, wake Parkinson. We have a rogue robot among us. He's killed ensign Petyr and planted that mutation bomb."

"Admiral, that's not a good i—"

"Good has nothing to do with it. We need her skills before anyone else dies."

The ambassador intervened. "Her mutated feet require high heels. Otherwise, she'll be immobile."

Bishop, who had been standing in the background, spoke up. "If her foot size hasn't changed, we have a pair stowed in her bags."

"Now that's thinking ahead," the Ambassador said with a grin.

Bishop said, "As many times as she's been attacked by these robots, she has to be prepared."

"Okay, then, doc. Wake her!" Admiral Bronislawa said. No disguising her impatience or worry.

***

"Oh, my head!" I moaned as my mind attempted to decode my location via my fuzzy vision. I thought I heard a boom. A yellow fog kept everything blurry, only I wasn't outside enjoying an exciting walk on a foggy morning.

"What's a yellow fog doing in here? I heard a bang." My hand flipped the air in front of my face, blowing away the fog. Wait! I didn't have any hands. At least I didn't remember having them when I closed my eyes to rest. "God, I've the worst headache ever!" I used my arms to push myself up into a sitting position.

I gasped. I didn't have arms, and yet, I'd just used them

276

to push my body up. My vision cleared. No yellow fog, but the doctor, Admiral Bronislawa, and Ambassador L'Grina stared down at me. I glimpsed Bishop in the background.

"What's happened? My head's killing me. A bomb? Yellow fog? I swear I saw it."

The doctor said, "Yes, someone set off a mutation bomb in here. Filled the room with a yellow gas. My lab assistants have identified it as your armless telepath Galactic Doll agent. The ship's biological attack containment system worked perfectly. It kept the gas confined to this room. Downside, you three have had—how should I put it—a massive exposure to the agent. Estimated to be enough for ten thousand doses. It's a miracle you three are still alive."

"Yes, yes, doc. That's enough," Admiral Bronislawa said. "Parkinson, a lot has happened. We—I desperately need your help or I wouldn't have wakened you."

"My head's killing me. Can you talk softer? I'm still groggy. Wait! Ten thousand doses? Bishop, am I still me? Do I look like me? Like I should? Katya, Hans?" I glanced left and right, my lip disk bouncing around. Both bodies seemed okay in their stasis pods, but his breasts looked smaller.

Bishop said, "You look like you usually do after the mutation. Got your heels. 'Fraid you'll need them again."

Ambassador L'Grina said, "Molly, you are stunning as always. Your lip stretched quite a lot. I found a disk that fits. It's about twice the size of your initial disk. Other than that, it's a miracle you're still with us. Katya and Hans survived, too. We should explain what's been happening, but first, let's get you up and dressed."

"Something for my head? Feels like it's exploding."

The doctor injected something into my leg, while L'Grina helped me dress.

"Woah. My hair sure has grown some." It touched my ankles. The lip disk seemed much heavier, annoyingly large.

As Bishop put a steadying arm around me leading me out of Sick Bay, I wobbled some. "Doc, it's not doing much for my head."

He chuckled. "I gave you the maximum safe dose. Give it time to kick in."

A few minutes later, I sat in the Admiral's CCC, watching video. I watched the man plant the bomb, saw it go off, and the aftermath.

"Amazing. That's what I saw when I first awoke. It's like I was right there seeing it as it happened, only I wasn't, was I?"

"And there's this," the Admiral said.

I observed the dead ensign. "No doubt about it. A rogue robot crushed his throat. What's a rogue robot doing on Bella? Have they harmed any of our people?"

The way that Admiral Bronislawa flinched, I knew something was wrong. "What have I missed?" I probed. My head hurt too much to read their minds.

Chapter 30 Clues

"Besides this rogue robot," the Admiral said, "we have another huge problem. Ambassador L'Grina speaks of your uncanny ability to solve mysteries. That's why I had the doc wake you. First, for everyone's security, we need to make sure that robot isn't impersonating anyone onboard or those I have out in the field. If it killed once and also tried to kill you, I'm sure it'll try again."

An hour passed during which her onboard personnel walked past me. Behind me, six armed soldiers stood, blasters raised. They even loaned Bishop one, which I think pleased him.

The relief on Admiral Bronislawa's face brought an invisible smile to mine. She exhaled and said, "Thanks, Parkinson. Again, I owe you. Later, I'll have you check on those who are outside the ship, about fifty, including Major Wolfgang. I want you to join them in Nuova Roma. Something has happened but we don't know what."

Thankfully, I was sitting when she said, "They have vanished. All ten million humans. Gone without a trace. My fifty soldiers who were providing life-support work had their arms amputated without their knowledge. All but one killed themselves. That one stayed alive to report to me before dying. But they had no idea what happened to the people or how. And no clue why they were mutilated. Honestly, Parkinson, this isn't on the Third Invaders. We've done everything possible to get them ready for the arrival of your people. We haven't betrayed you."

"What?" I shrieked. "Everyone? Even the outlying villages? There must be bodies. A mass grave site. Something."

279

Vic Broquard

Ambassador Bronislawa shook her head. "That's what I thought. A mass grave. I've got my people out scouring the entire civilized lands looking for such. Or perhaps a mass cremation site. All that has turned up are piles of withered women's arms ready for disposal. He reported the women reacted badly when they woke from their comas. The men stepped up and helped them adjust. Then one morning, my soldiers woke up to find their arms missing and the humans in their areas gone. The survivor's muddled sense of time suggests a week passed between when the first vanished and when the last ones down by Ciampino disappeared. Please, can you put your detective skills to work? We both need answers."

I sensed her fears. She wasn't worried about the loss of her soldiers. Rather she feared another vicious surprise attack on her Home World in which ten thousand had been mysteriously boiled alive while they slept—retaliation for their betrayal of our thousand humans. I smiled, invisibly. In this situation, Earth didn't care about the fate of ten million armless "aliens." Only I did. The Admiral knew I was the proposed Sol Empire Empress and thus a threat.

"Glad you asked. Otherwise, I would have to go into Nuova Roma on my own to find out. Let's go now. Bishop, keep a steadying arm around me. If only my head would stop exploding."

"Thank you, Parkinson. I'll take no chances with you."

She nodded. And aide fastened a device around my waist.

"A defense shield. It repels blasters, lasers, and projectiles. It won't stop slower attacks, though. You're not going anywhere without an armed escort."

A half-hour later, accompanied by Ambassador L'Grina, the Admiral, Bishop, and a cadre of guards, we left the landing saucer shuttles and walked the cobblestone streets of Nuova Roma. Eerie. Only the click of my steel-tipped heels broke the

280

silence. In the distance, I could hear sea birds and the ocean rushing onto the sandy beach. I found it trivial to expand my mind over the area, searching for the once familiar minds I knew had lived here. Dante, in particular. Nothing. As quiet as a Bishop-mind.

Without paying attention, I walked into Dante's home. When I realized what I'd done, I smiled, thankful no one could witness my facial expressions. I'd be embarrassed if they could have. I stood for a time just observing.

All looked normal. The clean kitchen suggested they'd vanished during the night. No dishes. Because it took the men a long time to prepare the next meal, during the day, items were always scattered about this room. I stepped into the bedrooms where the women slept. L'Grina followed me like a puppy. I sensed her curiosity and her attempts to figure out what clues I spotted.

"That's curious," I said for her benefit.

"I don't see it, Molly. It's a bedroom. Sheets are messed up. They vanished at night. We already concluded that," she said.

"Something's missing. The women's lip disk bags. Like the one I have. Come on. Let's check the other rooms. Their youngest daughter just had her lip slit. She should have a bag like mine filled with dozens of ever-larger disks. She was proud of it when she showed it to me."

We visited all the rooms. L'Grina said, "Missing. I don't see a lip disk anywhere. I'll let the Admiral know. Have soldiers search other homes and see if disks are missing there. Not sure how that's a clue."

I smiled. "That means they weren't killed. The women took their bags of disks with them. They told me they needed a larger disk about every six months. They'd not go anywhere without them."

"Damn, you're good! I hadn't reached that conclusion."

"Hey, can you smell that? There's a weird odor in here." I sniffed about more. "It's all over in here. Stronger in the corners of the side rooms."

Together, we sniffed about. She said, "You've a better nose than me. I don't smell anything. I'll fetch the Admiral."

The two women joined me.

L'Grina said, "I told her about the missing lip disks and what that means. That they are alive. She has men searching other homes."

"Thanks. Admiral, can you smell it? There's a strange, sickly sweet odor about. Faint. Strongest in the corners of the side rooms."

After more sniffing, Admiral Bronislawa spoke into her comm device. "Send down our forensics expert with her full kit. Need a gas check immediately."

Turning to me, she said, "Sorry, I don't smell anything. But I'll get the air in here checked out. We need clues. And fast."

A woman rushed in, carrying a large case. The Admiral said, "Take samples of the air. Parkinson says there's a strange odor in here. I can't smell anything. But if she can, we need to ID it as fast as possible."

The tech knew what she was doing. I admired her efficiency. She'd sampled the air in ten locations where I said it was strongest.

She said, "I'll have the answers for you in thirty minutes, unless the substance is unknown to us."

With that, she left. Meanwhile, we searched a few more nearby homes before our attention turned to the religious leaders' homes. Not a lip disk in sight convinced me they'd taken them with them wherever they'd gone.

The Admiral's comm device broke the silence. "Admiral, Parkinson's right. I found traces of tri-haldro-chlori-oxide."

Admiral Bronislawa's reaction was the same as mine,

probably L'Grina's too, but I wasn't facing her. "What in Dingo's Rats is that?" she said.

"It's a rare airborne sleeping agent. It puts air-breathing mammals to sleep for a time. Sometimes used to subdue wild, vicious animals on newly-discovered worlds. Very rare stuff."

"Well, that starts to explain what's happened here," Admiral Bronislawa said.

On a hunch, I closed my eyes, wondering if I could glimpse what had happened here. I got vague images.

"Are you okay?" Ambassador L'Grina asked.

"Yeah. I'm going back to Dante's room. Going to try something."

The women followed me, though I'd recovered enough for Bishop to hang back on guard. Once in Dante's room, I asked them to stay quiet for a while. I sat on his bed, close my eyes, and relaxed. I thought of handsome Dante. If only he could read and get educated.

I felt pulled into a 3-D motion picture. Wild passions exploding. Dante and Vittoria lay on the bed engaged in love-making. Then, both paused and sniffed. Their bodies relaxed as they drifted into sleep. My face felt hot. Okay, I was jealous of Vittoria. I continued watching. What I perceived next shocked me.

A three-foot tall body walked in. It was thin and albino white, with an enormous hairless head and large, bulbous eyes. Its arms couldn't have been more than an inch thick, barely arms. It wore a blue shirt trimmed with gold and matching pants. Some kind of uniform. I watched as if by magic both sleeping humans levitated and floated out of the room. The white being's gaze focused on the two. At the door, another of these took over. The original one looked about, levitating Vittoria's current lip disk off the night stand and then her bag of larger disks. The being left the room floating the disks and bag ahead of him. The images faded away.

283

I opened my eyes and saw Ambassador L'Grina watching me. She said, "I suspect you sensed something. Right?"

I flushed. "Yes. I don't know how, but I think I saw what happened. Makes no sense though. Unless some race possesses magical spells."

"Out with it," Admiral Bronislawa said. "Worry about how you saw it later."

"Weird beings floated the sleeping bodies out of the rooms, along with their lip disks. I've never heard of or seen anything like these—don't even know it I should call them people. I can show you what I saw."

I focused and touched their minds. I placed the images I'd seen of the short white beings floating the sleeping humans out of the room. To my surprise, neither woman seemed shocked that I could place these into their minds.

Rather, the color drained from the Admiral's face. "Dingo's rats! Those creatures are Alitos, First Invaders. Should have known! Freaking First Invaders. They are the one's that have been destroying people's lives and sanity for centuries. Who do they think they are? Nasty race, indeed! Think they're the monitors of the galaxy. Ancient race. They haven't been spotted in this section of the galaxy for centuries. They hate our people; we hate them. If they're the ones who took your people, then cutting off the arms of my Jafari soldiers makes complete sense. Force them to kill themselves so that we can't claim they've started another war between us."

Ambassador L'Grina said, "The wild rumors of Alitos existing are real? We've never encountered them. That I know of, anyway."

"But why would these Alitos want ten million handicapped humans?" I asked. "They now depend on others to survive. It's not like they pose any threat. Nor can they be an effective workforce, unless they're all forced to pull wagons and plows. If these are a space-faring race, I can't imagine they'd need our people to do that. Are they going to torture them?"

"Since they took the lip disks," Ambassador L'Grina said, "they want to keep them alive. I think that has to be a good sign."

"Where'd they take them? How do we get our people back?" I asked.

Deep in thought, Ambassador Bronislawa looked up. "Probably no hope. Yet, the Alitos theory makes sense. Why would anyone cut off the arms of my Jafari who were only here to help? But the Alitos—they would do something like that. I must alert Home World. Excuse me. Don't forget. I need you to monitor those in the field as they re-board the saucer. Stay alert for that rogue robot."

After she left, Ambassador L'Grina said, "You saw more than you're saying. Your face flushed. Ah, it's flushing again. That handsome Dante, eh?"

I sighed. "Yeah. He's mated with Vittoria, who has been after him for a long time. He must have agreed to mate her. But how is it I can see this? I mean there's no one in the room. It happened days ago. Yet, I viewed it as though I was a voyeur or something."

"That, Molly Parkinson, is the intriguing question. Seeing psychic impressions left in a place, assuming such things exist. Then again, the mutation agents have heightened your sense of smell. Perhaps it's strengthened other things. You did short out a positronic brain with your mind. I can't help speculating what that massive overdose of mutation agent did. Ten thousand doses at one time—it's a wonder you're still alive. But what did it do to you?"

I chuckled. "Didn't fix my lip. Did distort my feet again. Did grow my hair. Gave me the worst headache in my life."

"I'm pretty observant of people. When the doctor

roused you, I noticed little things. You pushed your hair away from your face as though you used a hand. You sat as if you had arms pushing you up. I've seen you rise by using your core muscles and legs. I think more has changed."

I sighed. "I feel different, L'Grina. Things have happened so fast I haven't had time to experiment or learn. When I can get these two back to my house and get us therapy sessions, maybe then I can figure out what's happening. You know about these Alitos people. Their bodies are as short as a dwarf, but I swear their arms are thin matchsticks."

As we strolled back towards the saucer shuttle at the edge of the city, Ambassador L'Grina explained. "We've heard horror stories about the Alitos. They have strange powers. It's said they don't use their arms for anything. They lift and maneuver things using their minds. They're supposed to have telepathy and no spoken language. Probably fairy tales. But it's said they can kill you with their minds. No Sixth Invader in recent memory has either seen one or their spaceships.

"I think the Third Invaders have a long history fighting them. The Admiral seemed spooked to learn they may have been here. Did you see how she's convinced they amputated her soldiers' arms? I can think of many ways that could have happened, but she's certain the Alitos did it. I wonder what she's not telling us."

"Well, I told her what I saw. Now I need to contact these First Invaders and find out how to get our people back. Safe and sound. If no one knows where their world is located, that will be a challenge. Perhaps someone on Cass-C knows more about them. That's the center of the Federation of Planets."

She nodded and added, "If you decide to go, let me know. I'd like to tag along. I'll have to use a disguise device. The Federation doesn't much like Sixth Invaders."

I chuckled. "Can't imagine why not?" That brought a

return smile.

After we returned to the cruiser, I checked the returning crew. Thank goodness the robot chose not to sneak back onboard.

While Cleo fed me supper, the Admiral told me she was dropping us off on Earth in the morning. She'd been ordered to return to Home World as soon as possible. She couldn't hide the appearance of the Alitos was a major threat.

I almost fell asleep in the mess hall.

Chapter 31 Therapies

She dropped us off at New O'Hare spaceport. Ambassador L'Grina accompanied us. A medical team met us, checked on the two in their stasis pods, and arranged their transport to my home.

"They'll be reviving in a day or so. You can call us if there's a problem," the doctor said. He seemed eager to leave us.

I moved them into Stan and Angelina's old room. Helper machines lined one wall. Bishop activated two more Cleo-type helper robots. And I called Celeste.

She, Wanda, and Otto arrived the next morning, ready to deliver much needed therapy sessions. Over mid-morning tea, I outlined my grand adventure to the three.

When I finished, Celeste said, "Molly, get a full medical checkup before we dive into therapy."

Wanda said, "Will therapy even work on Katya? She's a Third Invader."

"Worked on Sixth Invaders," I said. "Okay. Watch Hans and Katya. Bishop will escort me to the Med Center. Besides, I want to see if there is a fix for this split upper lip."

Wanda laughed. "What? You don't like the fancy lip plate? You look like a Federation Senator now. Except you need their giant earrings."

I glared at her before we broke into a roar.

The doctor put my body through his diagnostic machine. As he explained it, the device did what the ancient MRI and CAT scans did, only more.

A half-hour later, we looked over the results. Okay. He explained them to me. I don't have any medical knowledge.

The endocrine glands in my head had enlarged five-fold, which explained my fierce headaches. I now had more "folds" in my gray matter, whatever that meant. Otherwise, I looked a perfect Galactic Doll with a biological age of twenty-one.

"Doctor, at the rate, I'll never have an old-age body."

We chuckled over that, and I left.

When I relayed the results to Celeste, relief shone from her eyes. Her whole body relaxed. "Whew. That's a relief. I was worried. Okay, let's get you into a session now. Wanda and Otto will keep watch on the others. Close your eyes."

We dove into the traumas I'd experienced since my last therapy sessions. By late afternoon, we finished up. While I'd suffered severe traumas, by virtue of having had so much, I blew through the pain and unconsciousness, erasing it in record time.

I trusted Celeste with everything. After dinner, we sat around my living room, experimenting and testing what I could do using my mind. Otto and Wanda were shocked. I could levitate and move smaller objects. With a little practice, I telekinetically mimicked arm and hand actions. Celeste took it in stride.

"I thought this might be possible. Given enough therapy," she said. "I've always known that trauma attaches its images to the physical location where it happens. It's impressive you can see it. I'd love to have that ability."

Wanda laughed. "Me, I'd like her skills. Otto, more therapy sessions, please."

We roared.

Celeste added, "Can't believe you fried a robot's electronic brain. That makes you a new weapon against them. You're right. Intention is the key."

***

Everything changed in the morning. Both Hans and Katya woke from their comas.

289

Hans seemed delighted. "Talk. Talk. I can talk again! Thank the gods. That was horrid. Oh, my feet. They aren't throbbing. Kind of twisted though. Wow, I've had breast-reduction surgery. Too bad they didn't go all the way down. God, I feel helpless."

Ah, the reaction I expected. After introducing everyone and explaining they were now in my home in Chicago, we dressed and fed them.

At the same time, Katya shrieked and cried, before slumping into apathy. While we ate—their new robots feeding them—I outlined what had happened in detail.

"You've both been exposed to a massive dose of the mutation agent. We're not sure what effect that'll have on you. My sister Eve will come by tonight and get a DNA sample from us. She'll be able to tell us what potential cures she might invent for us. Now, it's time for therapy. Otto will work with you, Hans. Celeste and I will work with Katya."

"Won't work," Katya mumbled.

Celeste said, "You're right. Might not. But we'll try, anyway."

We took her into my bedroom. She and I sat across from Katya. I asked her to close her eyes.

"Okay. Now return to the moment when you opened the drawer and saw what looked like a person lying there, hiding."

"I can see that. It spooked both of us."

"Good. Now move through the incident and tell me what you are seeing, feeling, and smelling as you go through it."

"I see the robot. Intense pain. I wake up here. That's all. Just kill me. I can't live another two thousand years like this. Be humane for once."

Celeste and I focused our full intention on her. I had her go back to the beginning and go through it again. I pestered her for sensory details. While slow to reveal them, she made

290

progress. By lunchtime, she'd re-experience the terrible pain of having her arms ripped from their sockets.

Wanda and Bishop prepared lunch for us. Again, the new helper robots and Cleo fed us, much to everyone's relief. Then, we dove back into our sessions.

By evening, Katya had re-experienced much of what had happened while on the Fantasy World. The next day, we continued the process. That evening, she shrieked in pain. "My head is exploding!"

I smiled, invisibly. That's what I had said to Celeste when I re-experienced it.

The third day we went back over the entire series of traumas picking up loose ends. The pain subsided but no erasure of the mess occurred. She wasn't cheerful either.

"Just kill me. It's not working. I'm bored."

She had unburdened an enormous amount of pain and unconsciousness. It was working, but she couldn't see that yet. Following Celeste's guidance, I asked her if there was a similar trauma that happened earlier. I've always found this to be the tricky point in these initial therapy sessions. Often, the person doesn't quite know how to look for the earlier trauma.

My problem: I could see the earlier traumatic incident in her mind. Yet, I dare not say anything. She had to find it herself if she had any chance of regaining her self-respect and life. Evaluating or invalidating a person is the worst thing you can do to them, short of giving them a new moment of pain and unconsciousness.

After more prodding, she admitted, "I think there's something yellow."

"Good. Now move to the beginning of that. What do you see?"

We were off and running. Celeste gave me a big smile.

In Katya's last lifetime, she'd been a grunt soldier. At the spaceport, a chain holding a heavy iron beam broke. It fell on Katya, crushing his arms and hands. When they lifted the beam off him, they were flattened. While they rushed him to their medical facilities, the doctor had no choice but to remove his arms. He awoke to find two very short upper arms remaining. They fitted hin with prosthetics, but he lost his job. During the operation, the doctor kept saying, "Don't know why we're doing this. He can't live like this. No one can live without arms and hands. He'd be better off dead."

Once home, those words echoed through his mind, held in place by the hidden excruciating pain and unconsciousness. After a few weeks, he jumped off the roof of a tall building.

By suppertime, Katya couldn't stop laughing. "I killed myself. I couldn't live like that. Those were his words. Hell, they fitted me with state-of-the-art and powerful prosthetics. They worked perfectly. I could lift twice what I used to be able to lift. I could do pull-ups all day long until the battery needed recharging. But no. I couldn't live like this." She roared. Her laughter infected everyone.

Celeste sat back, a big grin on her face. Her therapy methods worked on another alien species. Further proof that we are all spiritual beings with minds and occupying various physical bodies.

I turned Katya over to Celeste for more sessions. I had to deal with Admiral Carr and the Telepath Squad situation. Plus, he needed a report on the recent events. Worse, a deep space exploration ship had landed on Bella and found no inhabitants.

Otto and Wanda spent evenings working with Hans and Katya, helping them learn to use the Sixth Invader helper machines. They worked with them to get them comfortable depending on their robot helpers. And they made them watch hours of the how-to videos and then practice those actions with their feet and toes.

Wanda said, "You have to relearn how to do things for

yourselves. We did. Now we're living independent lives again. If we can do it, you can too. But it isn't easy and takes continual practice."

"But my George does everything for me," Hans countered.

"What happens if its battery runs down?" she countered. Then, she relayed what had happened after Cleo was nearly destroyed by gunfire on that primitive world we visited. That sobered Hans and Katya.

Just as they began to be successful using their feet, their telepathic skills manifested. Celeste took time out to work with them, honing that skill and ensuring they didn't misuse it.

"But there never has been a Jafari with telepathy. Not real telepathy," Katya said.

"Well, there is now," Celeste said. "Be careful who you reveal your abilities to."

Hans asked, "Are we going to be able to move things like Molly does?"

"That's never been part of the mutation," Celeste said. "But then no one has ever received such a gigantic dose. We'll see."

Two days later, I caught both of them experimenting with spoons. Hans and Katya moved them this way and that across the table. With a bit of practice, they could feed themselves this way. However, that much concentration left them tuckered out. Both let their robot helpers feed them or use their feet. Still, they exuded elation over being able to move small things this way.

After three weeks, the three returned to St. Louis and their homes. Now the three of us were on our own. Bishop stood guard, but I had Hans and Katya swear never to reveal to anyone that Bishop was a human-form robot—one that had the robot laws installed in his circuits.

After our first day on our own, Katya said, "Molly,

you're right. It *is* as though the space around me has collapsed. Before, I controlled everything in a three-foot sphere around my body—what my arms could reach. That's collapsed down to my nose and boobs. That's how it feels, anyway. Your Ted had it right. Damn spooky."

Hans said, "Katya, that's an understatement! Downright scary. I keep trying to use my arms and hands. You know, to scratch my nose. Everything is different. Impossibly hard challenges. I still feel helpless at times."

"Hey, so do I. That never goes away," I said. "Not entirely. I think the word is frustrating. I get frustrated. Plus, now I've lost half my ability to grab things. I can't tell you how I depended on my mouth and teeth."

"Can't they fix your lip?" Katya asked.

"I've made an appointment."

"Heck, even walking is frightening," Hans said. "I can barely keep my balance. I keep losing it and falling. It's freaky flailing my arms as I'm crashing into the floor. Good thing you have thick carpeting."

"With practice, everything gets easier to do. Trust me. But I won't lie either. It can get very frustrating with how much longer it takes to do the simplest things. But the main thing is we're able to do it and stay independent," I said.

My job was to keep them calm giving them time to practice, learn, and accept their handicap. Since we all had telepathy, without trying, we sensed the others' emotions and surface thoughts. I kept a tranquil outflow going.

Hans said, "Am I always going to feel this helpless? I keep trying to use my arms. We've watched the how-to videos, but I can't raise my legs like that or grip with my toes. I feel strange. If I'm honest, I'm scared. I can't really do anything now. I wanted to be an astro-geologist. Visit other worlds and examine how their rocks formed, search for valuable ores, and see natural wonders. Now I can't do that. I can barely walk on

294

flat floors."

"He's right," Katya said. "I feel incredibly helpless and scared, too. It's like they took away my ability to do much of anything. How can we live like this? If it wasn't for the machines and robot helper, I'd give up."

"Watch the videos and lots of practice. I won't pretend it isn't challenging. I'm always having to stop and think how can I do this. Perhaps Eve will have some encouraging news when she comes by tomorrow. Just keep in mind, it's how we respond to our physical handicap that matters. Therapy removes the trauma effects, but it is up to us to deal with our situation."

***

Mid-morning, Eve dropped by with our prognoses for mutation cures. After fixing us tea, she explained her findings.

"Molly, this time," she said, "the mutations have made deep changes in your DNA. I don't even know if we can get your feet back to normal. Lara and I will keep on it, though. Hans and Katya clones are growing from their DNA samples. Should take twelve months, presuming we don't invent cures before then. Molly, yours should be ready by Christmas.

"The situation with Hans is different. He didn't get as heavy a dose of the mutation agent as you did, Molly. Hans, Lara and I think the usual mutation cure will work on you."

"What does that mean? Will I have arms? Look like a man again?"

Eve grinned. "Yes, sir. If all goes well, your body will look like it did before all this happened to you. We're tailoring a batch of the mutation cure now. Give us a month to make sure it's ready to go. Meantime, make use of your telepathy skills."

"Yahoo! Best news ever! I'll be normal again. Thank you! Now I am glad to be alive."

She grinned and looked at Katya.

295

Katya sighed. "Yeah, but I'd not wish this on anyone. If I can get by for a year, then I'll have a Katya clone? Will it look like me?"

Eve nodded. "It will be identical to you but with arms. Just like Molly and I look alike, except I've not had my body rejuvenated. As far as this body goes, you received a stronger dose than Hans did, almost as much as Molly did, if we are interpreting your DNA correctly. We're hesitant to try using a human mutation agent cure on you because it could result in your having a human life span instead of your Jafari span of thousands of years."

"I couldn't live a thousand years helpless like this. That's a fate worse than death."

"I know. That's why the clone we're growing is the best option," Eve said. "Also, the mutation has reset your biological clock, just like it does on humans. Your body believes it is about twenty-one years old, not whatever it was before the attack. We don't know if this is significant or not."

"Twenty-one? Really?"

Eve nodded, and Katya's face twisted.

"Wow. How old are you?" Hans said.

I chuckled. "Hans, you're not supposed to ask a woman's age."

Katya laughed. "Oh, that's okay between us. It's not like any other Jafari will ever want anything to do with me now. I'm a pariah. And a helpless one at that." She paused a moment. "I'm about three hundred sixty-nine of your Earth years."

"Incredible," Hans said. "I'm twenty-five. How old are you, Molly?"

I laughed. "I'll be forty-two in late May. But I got news for you, Hans. You now have two ages. True age is twenty-five, but your biological age has been reset to twenty-one. Mine has been reset to twenty-one. I've lost count how many times mine

296

keeps getting reset."

"What? You mean it rejuvenates the whole body?" Hans asked.

"Yes. I've seen women who were sixty become twenty-one again."

"Oh, shit. What's that done to my biological age?" Katya said. Her reddish face paled.

"Dunno. Is it a problem?" I replied.

"Yes. My body wasn't due to produce another pair of eggs for about forty-six years. I had time to find a way to deal with the animal response. But now..."

"You've no way to predict when it will happen again," Hans finished her thought. "Makes sense. Surely, it can't be that bad. We humans enjoy intercourse. Sometimes a bit too much." His attempted jest fell flat on Katya.

Katya's face grimaced. "Except when eggs are involved, it's most pleasurable for us too. But Jafari women go animalistic when it's breeding time. I won't be able to control my body or thoughts or anything. It's an instinct thing. Embarrassing, too."

I asked, "When it happens, do you have advanced warning it's coming? Does intercourse resolve it?"

I sensed Katya's extreme nervousness. "Yes, that's why I'm worried. I didn't realize the mutation reset biological clocks. I can feel it's coming in another few days. It's embarrassing to have anyone see me act like that. Yes, the only thing that satisfies the madness is sex with a male Jafari.

"We Jafari women produce two eggs about every fifty years. I haven't had a child, though. Busy with my career. Never had a suitor either. I have to warn you. When our eggs are ready for fertilization, an uncontrollable animal breeding reaction happens. Okay, we go insane. The sexual encounter is animal-like. We've tried to breed that out of our species. No success.

"You could save us a lot of trouble by killing me now before insanity sets in. It's humiliating."

I sent calming thoughts her way. "Don't worry. We'll think of something."

Eve left. I said, "We need more clothes for you two. Let's go shopping."

Katya's body shook slightly. "Molly, is it reasonable to be frightened of going out in public? I feel scared. So strange."

Hans added, "She's right. Scared doesn't do it justice. Spooked, too."

"Yeah, spooky," Katya said. "We can't do much yet. By ourselves, I mean."

"Yes, those are reasonable emotions. You'll always have such when starting a new thing you've not done before as an armless person. Even I get that way sometimes. Step one is to just do it and face it. Step two is to do it enough times that you are comfortable doing it.

"I want to show you around my city, but first let's take baby steps. We'll visit my sister's costume store. She's the one who has designed all our clothes."

***

Two days later, a strange Jafari man knocked on my door.

"Does Katya Binsk live here?" he asked.

Katya moved up behind me. "Bazyli Dorek? What are you doing here?"

The Jafari man wore a blue suit. His reddish skin contrasted with his tall head modified while a child. From what little I knew of Jafari society, this suggested he held a high social status. But he didn't wear a soldier's uniform as Katya had. He moved to her side and rested his hands on her shoulders.

He smiled. "Admiral Bronislawa sent me. Something about your biological clock being reset. I'm an elementary education teacher, now. Pleased to meet you.

298

" Yes, I teach our young. It's my honor to meet them on their first day of school. Get them off on the right foot. Glad I can be here for Katya. I've wooed her since childhood, but she insisted on joining the army. Still, I followed her career. My class celebrated when she made captain."

His soothing voice almost mesmerized me. It calmed Katya, and they spent the day catching up on their lives. I moved Hans into my bedroom and gave Katya and Bazyli the spare bedroom.

But the next day, Katya lost all concentration. "It's happening. I know it. I can feel it coming on. Oh, gods. Molly, have Bishop shoot me. I can't control that animal drive. I gotta have it."

Hans and I gave them their privacy, but we both flushed. The noise they made shook the house. Katya wasn't kidding.

We three discovered a new mutation side-effect: intense sexual drives. Soon, I was hooked on Hans. He and I agreed to get married on September First. Enough time for us to get to know each other better and plan the wedding. We both thought he'd have his body restored by then. Katya would be my bridesmaid.

May Day brought a shocking surprise. The Med Center confirmed that both Katya and I were pregnant. She and I looked at each other, January babies in our future.

In late May, we made a trip to Berlin. Hans needed to retrieve his possessions from the apartment, see his parents, and show me off to them. I spent most of the trip flooding Hans with calming energies. His dominate emotion: fear. He felt helpless, strange, and weird.

When his father learned Telepath Squad members earned a million credits per year, the older man accepted us. Hans calmed. His younger sister loved our robot helpers, Cleo and George.

Bishop came along. He packed Hans' possessions from his apartment and carried them. And I shocked Katya and Hans by taking us to Berlin using my deep space transport. I wanted to prove to them we could fly spaceships. Anything to help them see possibilities instead of limitations.

Chapter 32 Of the Telepath Squad and Empress

I reported to Admiral Carr. First, I told him everything that had happened to us. I ended with, "We must find these First Invaders, these Alitos, and get our people back."

I didn't need telepathy to know his thoughts. Why bother with millions of mostly helpless people?

He ignored my suggestion. "We have the Telepath Squad in full operation. Stanley and Angelina Norwall are co-captains of the twenty-member squad. We're now recruiting a second squad of twenty and may have them by the end of the year. I've proposed adding six more squads, stationing some on our major worlds. The Norwall couple have driven the last of the robot spies from my fleet. Can't believe we had four of them embedded in the ships.

"Ivy Worth is with the Heart of Gold deep space exploration ship now on Bella. She hoped to aid in language development. But that's a bust. She'll rejoin Telepath Squad One when she returns. Thus far, the squad is meeting all objectives. Corporations have accepted the squad. I convinced them if they see an armless person, they are likely a telepath. While we know not everyone who lacks arms is a telepath, all telepaths lack them. It works.

"Now then, continue to check out the new people who want to sign up for the service. Get the Empress position established. Leave the rogue robots to me. Already I've had contact with the Third Invaders. Seems the robots have been attacking them, too. I don't trust those invaders but welcome their help. Just get a Sol Empire ruling body established as soon as possible."

"Won't the CEOs protest?" I asked.

"I've prepared the way for you. I've convinced the major CEOs that the rogue robots are likely to come after those who are in charge of the Sol Empire. Thus, they are looking for any avenue by which they can't be seen as the top leaders, just influential ones. We must have an actual government if this empire is to succeed. Make that happen."

"What about finances? A budget? How do I pay for staff? Do we even have a building to use?" I asked in rapid fire. I didn't know how many chances I'd get to ask him about this position.

"Visit GPan's CEO, Ho Lin. He's been setting up things for you."

The day we returned from Berlin, I visited the Galactic Expansion skyscraper, asking to see Mr. Ho Lin. I left Bishop outside, since I detected a telepath inside the main doors. As I entered, I spotted her. She wore black pants and blouse. Gold trimmed shoulders indicated her status as I later learned. She recognized me.

"Mrs. Parkinson?"

I nodded.

"Good. I've let Mr. Ho Lin know you're coming. Elevator Five. That way," she nodded.

Floor 100. Conclusion: Mr. Lin must be the CEO of Empire-wide GPan. Two blue and purple uniformed guards, giants, allowed me into the plush suite. I had lost touch with the many corporate CEOs, because a new set of leaders took control while I was off-world.

"Ah, Empress Parkinson, good to meet you at last. Please, sit. We have much to discuss."

I towered over Ho Lin. He wore an immaculate black business suit with purple trim and tie.

"I have lots of questions—"

"Of course. Let me begin by explaining what we've

302

accomplished on your behalf. By mutual agreement among all corporation leaders, the government should be headquartered in Chicago. We've secured the former GMed building; they've expanded into their new Lakeside Drive skyscraper. As you may know, this is another of the hundred-story skyscrapers. We've already begun the remodeling process of the GMed building. We chose this facility because of the enormous EMAC and shuttle parking lots. The Empress Offices are on floors ninety-five to one hundred. Your throne room is at the top, naturally.

"Ambassador suites are on floor ninety-five. We've moved the Senior Judge facilities to floor sixty. Floor fifty-nine now houses your old Investigation Division. They're very pleased with the new accommodations.

"One of your first actions must be to re-establish the Senate, whose meeting room is on floor fifty, with accommodations on lower floors. Every world in the empire shall send two senators. This includes colonies on moons and space stations. Expect around sixty members. Each world's corporations will elect one of their senators, while the other shall be chosen in free elections by that world's population. The Senate makes the laws for the Sol Empire."

I interrupted. "You're going back to the original three branches of government? I thought other worlds refused to send more people here. Terrorist attacks..."

He exhaled sharply. "Modernization. Okay, we've been persuaded by two things. First, these rogue robots. We CEOs want to run our corporations without fear of being attacked as the Senate was. Second, as a growing empire within the Federation of Planets, the Sol Empire must be seen as a fair, balanced, and lawful member. Many of us have visited Cass-C as guests of our Senators. Let's say we've been impressed."

I nodded, finding it impossible not to have read his surface thoughts. "In essence, you want to be seen as a

303

progressive empire and have me and the senators be the targets of rogue robot and terrorist attacks."

His face flushed. "Precisely put. Floor forty houses the offices of the Telepath Squads, while floor thirty is being readied for your new Empire Army Leaders. We need you to establish a ten-division ground-based army ready to tackle any aggression one of our worlds might encounter. GD agreed to provide state-of-the-art equipment for them.

"Floor twenty is reserved for your new Enforcement Division. The Empress must be able to enforce the laws of the empire. We're not sure what that means. You decide what you need to carry out those duties. The Senate shall pass the laws, but the Empress can veto those she deems inappropriate for any reason. Her veto can only be overridden by an eighty percent re-vote by the Senate. The Chief Judge can rule a law as invalid for legal reasons."

I asked, "Are the corporations giving up this much control of the empire? I find that hard to believe."

Again, Ho Lin flushed. "Not exactly. We pick half the senators. We intend to introduce plans and suggestions to the Senate and you. Work behind the scenes seems prudent, given recent history."

"It's our butts on the line, not yours."

"Precisely."

After a pause, he continued. "Admiral Carr has ordered us to get these changes going as fast as possible. You'll find much of the infrastructure and personnel in place. Are you ready to be our first Sol Empire empress?"

"Yes. Admiral Carr can be very insistent."

"Good. We've established a formal dress code and symbols for everyone. You, your husband who's joining the Telepath Squad as we speak, and Ambassador Katya Binsk will have personal assistants. They will live with you and handle personal needs as well as serving as your secretaries. Highly trained, I've picked these three young women. All desired to become corporate secretaries. You won't need to train them. I've had them put through personal assistant training. Trust them to know how to dress you and handle your personal needs.

"As far as your appearance, Empress Parkinson, a few changes are required. Our empress must emulate the appearance of our Federation senators. I'm glad you still have your lip disk. It's now a requirement. Only we'll have the new official symbol engraved on your disks."

He showed me an image. In the center of a green circle blazed a yellow sun with four large spikes radiating up, down, right, and left. In between these, four smaller spikes shot from the sun.

"Impressive, isn't it? We held a contest to find the best symbol for the Sol Empire. You'll never guess who won the contest. Your sister, Leslie Travers-Baker. She's submitted the winning designs for your empress wardrobe and the Telepath Squad uniforms. Anyway, direct any complaints to her.

"We will get your supply of lip disks emblazoned with the new symbol. You'll be fitted with a pair of those massive earrings our Federation senators wear."

I protested. "You want to impress the Federation reps?"

"We must show them we are on par with the best in the Federation of Planets. Remember, you'll never be without your personal assistant. She is trained to handle all your needs. It's not seemly for our Empress to be eating with her feet, for example."

We discussed additional details. My salary: a hundred thousand credits per month. I agreed to start on the first of June.

When I returned home, Hans had news for me.

"Guess what? I made the Telepath Squad. I *ist* the Captain of the Palace Squad. I get to help keep you and the other leaders safe and make a million credits per year! They'll train me in my duties tomorrow."

"Good going, dear. I feel safer already. Let me tell you what I found out."

***

Early morning June 1, 2369 three young Galactic Dolls knocked on my door. Bishop let them in along with an army of movers bringing many crates.

"I'm your personal assistant, Mei Hui," one said. All three looked very similar with long black hair. They wore purple satin gowns with gold trim, the new Sol Empire logo on the dress's left shoulder.

"I'm your personal assistant, Shu Ying," one said to Hans.

"I'm yours, Ambassador Katya Binsk. I'm Li Feng. I've been in contact with your Home World, arranging your outfits and duties."

"First, let's get you dressed and ready for a tour of your new offices," Mei said.

They instructed their helpers to deposit various crates in various rooms, before ushering each of us into a private room. Once Mei and I were in my bedroom, she opened one crate.

"We'll get the earrings on first, then get you properly attired. We're all Galactic Dolls. Your sister designed our gowns. She's the greatest."

I chuckled. "Yes, she is. How old are you?"

She flushed. "Eighteen. Got my secretarial training finished. What an honor to be your personal assistant. All three of us are ecstatic over being chosen."

She giggled and brought out a gun and a box containing the massive earrings of the kind our Federation senators had to wear. Large teardrop gemstones hung in tiers from gold fittings. Each weighted pounds. Ugh.

306

"Have to punch a grommet through each earlobe. Otherwise, their weight can rip your lobes, or so I'm told. Such gorgeous earrings. Incredible, really. You won't feel much."

She positioned it and fired. I felt a puncture and slight squeezing pressure from the grommets, but that paled when she attached the earrings.

"They're pulling my ears off!"

Mei giggled. "Hardly, but I'm told that's our Senators' common reaction. They rest on your shoulders. You can rake them across your shoulders to itch them. Now let's get you into your official Empress outfit."

With effort, she got the special polymer stockings on my legs and attached to a garter belt. These were the same kind that I'd worn for six years when I lived on Cass-C. I noticed she wore them too and had similar tall heels. Besides adding a bit of sensation to our legs, their design somehow massaged our legs with every step we took, aiding walking in such tall heels.

She brought out a pair of knee-high boots with the usual heel. Purple, of course.

"Are those—"

"Yes, copies of the special Cass-C ID boots that you and the others wore. They have steel sides. You can't possibly break or sprain an ankle. I tried them on. They are much better than the pumps they issued to us. Maybe you could put in a request for your personal assistants to have to wear these kinds of boots."

A half-hour later, I stood before my mirror. "There, how do you look?" Mei said. "Very impressive, don't you think?"

I wore a purple ball gown that flared out in a circle three feet around me. The floor lay a foot below the lower hem, revealing my shiny purple boots. My shoulders were encased in the satin gown. Leslie knew I loved that look. That I had no arms was accentuated by my curvaceous form-fitting gown. The gown's neckline plunged in front enough for me to wear a golden necklace with a large Sol Empire symbol resting on my chest.

"I look good, but I don't think I can deal with the ball gown."

"That's why you have me. I'll help you all the time. With everything. In a few weeks, we'll be a seamless team. I hope so, anyway. I should unpack our things. Where do you want us to sleep?"

"You three can share the children's bedrooms."

I sensed her release of nervous energy along with a bit of color in her cheeks. With my new level of telepathic abilities, I couldn't help but sense why her relief. She had been told to expect to have to handle my sexual needs as well.

The other waited for me in the living room. It took longer to get me ready than them. As I walked in to the room, my eyes opened wide.

"Wow! You both look stunning!"

Hans's uniform was coal black with gold trim. His black boots were identical to mine, and he, too, wore the needed polymer nylons to massage his legs while he walked. His form-fitting black top highlighted his curves too, aided by a jacket buttoned once at his waist. A gold belt accentuated his small waist.

"This gold patch on my right shoulder is the Telepath Squad symbol," he said. "And the stripes on my left shoulder identifies my rank as captain. We're not sure if I'm going to get my long hair cut or not. I don't look like a man despite the uniform. I'm leaning towards a no."

"You look great, Hans. And Katya, wow."

She flushed. Her uniform was done in a royal blue accentuated with yellow trim.

"Leslie must have gotten in touch with Home World. This pants suit is our typical ambassadorial outfit. Except for the heels, that is."

Her boots were identical to mine, only a shiny blue matching her pants and top. Leslie again encased Katya's shoulders in the style I loved. Katya cut a stunning figure, too. I sensed she felt very pleased with her new ambassador uniform.

That the six of our bodies were shaped similarly put us more at ease. Long, straight hair, massive bosoms, tiny waists, and tall heels, we six looked like we belonged together.

"We're off to the new offices," Mei said.

Just outside my front door sat a new EMAC. Six guards armed with blasters stood guard.

Bishop said, "I doubt you'll be needing me, Molly."

I winked. "No, I won't. You can take the day off."

We six walked up the ramp, but I needed Mei's arm around me. I couldn't see my feet. I sensed she had expected this and felt prepared to assist me. I relaxed a little, though my ears still throbbed under the earrings' weight.

Off we went to our new skyscraper and new positions. During the short flight, the three teens chatted. The future looked bright to them.

The End.

Vic Broquard

A Favor to Other Readers

How about helping other readers? Many readers rely on reviews to make the decision whether to buy a book. You can help them make their decision by leaving your opinions and viewpoint in a short review of the positive things of this book. Writing the review and expressing your opinion only takes a few minutes, and other readers will appreciate your efforts.

Click this link: The Sol Empire Volume 6 Religion and Robot https://www.amazon.com/dp/B097LWXP42 scroll down to Customer Reviews; click on Write a Review, and enter your review. Thank you.

Author Information

Visit My Amazon.com Author Page
Vic Broquard Author Page

Follow My Blog
Vic Broquard's Blog

Follow Me on Social Media
Facebook
LinkedIn
YouTube

Other Books by Vic Broquard

Without Warning (fantasy)

The Trident Series: (fantasy)
Volume 1 The Trident and the Book
Volume 2 The Trident and the Scepter
Volume 3 The Trident and the Resurrection

The Adventures of Elizabeth Stanton Series: (science fiction)
Volume 1 The Evolution of the Path
Volume 2 The Great Messiah
Volume 3 Of Kings and Queens and Troubadours
Volume 4 Chaos in the Aftermath
Volume 5 Power Plays
Volume 6 Age of Exploration
Volume 7 Abducted
Volume 8 The Emperor and Empress
Volume 9 A Job Worth Doing
Volume 10 Degradation
Volume 11 The Second Crusade
Volume 12 When Worlds Collide
Volume 13 Dark Ages

The Lindsey Barron Series: (fantasy)
Volume 1 The Rod of the Apocalypse
Volume 2 The Board of Governors
Volume 3 The Crown of Moses
Volume 4 Dominus for President
Volume 5 The National Health Care Program
Volume 6 States Justice
Volume 7 Cross and Double-cross
Volume 8 Down the Dragon Hole

Vic Broquard

<u>Zoran Chronicles Series: (fantasy)</u>
<u>Volume 1 A Dragon in Our Town</u>
<u>Volume 2 Dragons, Power, Courts, and War</u>

<u>Planet of the Orange-red Sun Series: (science fiction)</u>
<u>Volume 1 When Kingdoms Fall</u>
<u>Volume 2 Dark Ages</u>
<u>Volume 3 Age of the Towers</u>
<u>Volume 4 Difficillis Exitus</u>
<u>Volume 5 Age of the Lords</u>
<u>Volume 6 The Renegade Tower</u>
<u>Volume 7 Rebellions</u>
<u>Volume 8 The Aliens Return</u>
<u>Volume 9 Power Struggles</u>
<u>Volume 10 Guilds, Genetics, and Gods</u>
<u>Volume 11 Magi, Witches, Swords, and Superstitions</u>
<u>Volume 12 The Voyage of the Eagle's Seed</u>
<u>Volume 13 Eagle's Seed and Origins</u>
<u>Volume 14 Justifications</u>
<u>Volume 15 Responsibilities</u>

<u>The Return of the Wizards: Twelve Companions – The Making of Wizards (fantasy)</u>

<u>Slow Comes the Dark Series: (science fiction)</u>
<u>Volume 1 Creeping Darkness</u>
<u>Volume 2 Serendipity</u>
<u>Volume 3 Darkness Descends</u>
<u>Volume 4 Perversion Incarnate</u>
<u>Volume 5 Extermination Wars</u>

312

Reclamation Series: (science fiction)

Dragons, Magic, and Me Series (fantasy)

The Sol Empire (science fiction)